Thanksgiving

Thanksgiving

"The key to infinite wealth fluttered like a colorful flag at the finish line, so they raced past the breaking point and into the unfair world of cold-blooded murder."

Gage Irving

Cover art and design—Antoinette Beck
Graphics—Kinga.me

Library of Congress Control Number:		2013919389
ISBN:	Hardcover	978-1-4931-1515-0
	Softcover	978-1-4931-1514-3
	eBook	978-1-4931-1516-7

This book was printed in the United States of America.

Rev. date: 12/11/2013

To order additional copies of this book, contact:
Xlibris LLC
1-888-795-4274
www.Xlibris.com
Orders@Xlibris.com
142560

Prologue

2:30PM Thursday **September 23, 2004** **Interstate 15, Nevada**

Samuel Eveland had to get his hands on some money to save his life, and he'd left a flood of piteous messages on his cousin's answering machine. Richard had ignored those valiant pleas for weeks. Finally relenting, he told the poor sap it would be the last penny he'd ever get out of him for the rest of time . . . and he wasn't going to wire the money. He wouldn't put it in the mail either. Sam had to stare into his eyes if he really needed to get his hands on the moolah. Gushing like a teenage girl, Samuel said he'd pay him back in spades by November and he was more than happy to travel to the coast. Hell, he was looking forward to it.

At 6'2", Samuel Eveland didn't fit into the rental car. He was uncomfortable as he drove through the badlands on Interstate 15. At least the coveted bank check was nestled in his wallet, and he was going home without trepidation. Polishing off an open box of cream donuts on the passenger seat, didn't matter. He remained thin no matter what. Almost sixty, time took its toll in other ways. Rubbing at the puffiness around his brown eyes, he drove into the upcoming rest area. He'd been crunched up inside the small car for hours, and he had no choice. He had to unknot his muscles. If that meant he'd be cooked alive in the process, so be it.

Unfolding himself out of the driver's seat, he stood up, and the desert heat blasted into him like a punch.

The desolate tract was accented by an infrequent cactus plant and the horizon line was liquefied. Samuel's tired eyes looked out at the undulating haze, and his attention fixated on a wavering spot, nothingness in the searing brightness. Alpha waves began to pulse into his head, and he nodded off on his feet. Dragged into a painful daydream, the visions got worse. As if a rattle snake coiled in the sand next to his boot had stuck its fangs deep into his leg the uncomfortable dream turned into a nightmare.

He used to sell real estate, rolling from one property to another and making a lot of money, but those days were gone forever. He tried hard not to think about that part of his life. Asleep while he leaned against the coolest side of the rental, the exorcised memories were marching in again anyway, as sweat poured down his face. He couldn't wake up. The only thing he could to do was change the channel, transporting himself into a cell with no walls in an arid and desolate tract, (similar the one he was actually in) and the only bars were right in front of him. A verdant garden with fragrant flowers, indistinct birds, shade trees and lush grass lay on the other side of the barrier, and he tried to touch the nearest flower. Straining his arm between the illusionary bars, he mimicked that movement in the real world and he almost fell face first on the sand. Waking up at the absolute last instant, he groaned and got back in the car. He'd left the engine on to keep the air conditioning running. Putting the transmission in drive, he hissed up the ramp back to the highway.

He dropped off the rental and stepped out onto the street. He turned left. Only four blocks away from his studio in the Vendome Apartments on 11th street, the distance lengthened like silly putty, and he was afraid he was going to pass out in the heat. He was thankful when he saw the familiar yellow sign, and he dragged himself up the outside stairs to the second floor and unlocked the door. He stumbled into cool relief. The answering machine on the kitchen counter was blinking and he let it keep on blinking. The message had to be from his bookie. Now he could finally pay her off, but hearing the awful threats would still be nerve wracking. Tearing off his clothes, he left them on the floor. He had a shower, and then he passed out in bed. His bladder woke him up five hours later. Done peeing, his body implored him to go back to bed. Instead, he put on clean clothes and burst out into the night.

The taxi dropped him off in front of Caesars Palace, and in his mind things were going to be more than alright; they would be perfect! Walking into the casino, Samuel came alive like a fish thrown back in the water. His exhaustion peeled away as if it had only been a distraction and his eyes got glassy and dilated. Hypnotized, he was pulled along by some inner melody as he passed a legion of slot machines like a leaf in a tidal current. When he saw the card tables on his left and the black and red roulette wheels on the right, his pulse rate rose, and he collided with a cocktail waitress wearing nothing but a tiny strip of white cloth; the casino's idea of a '*toga*'. He enjoyed the pleasant bump. He was on his way to his favorite cocktail lounge, Minerva Cove and when he arrived, the choice bar stool was empty and he sat down. He lit a cigarette and ordered a gin and tonic and he sighed. The impossible mission had been possible after all.

The negativity gnawing at him on his trip to San Diego had only been a chimera. Rick had loaned him $8,000 dollars and he was in heaven. He might as well as be in the Federal Reserve. With a wave of his hand he would transform that paltry amount into $80,000, and from there it would keep on growing! Nodding to the bartender, he ordered another drink and considered which game he should choose to ignite his stalled life. He would court lady luck back into his arms again, and fly out of the fire like a phoenix made from gold.

PART I

You have to stand in the darkness to see the light."

Keith Fischer

"Love the One You're With."

Stephen Stills

8:45AM Friday December 19, 1975 Bridgewater, Massachusetts

The birth of his second son in 1973 had been revolting. Born with pyloric stenosis, the baby's pyloric valve linking his stomach to his small intestine had clamped closed. Food and liquid couldn't reach the intestines. The infant vomited everything out. The newborn would slowly starve to death unless he had the surgery to cut the valve. *Any* operation on a baby that small is dangerous and full anesthesia is tricky, but Robert lived through the operation. However, he picked up a staph infection and it was raging through him. The surgeon told Latham and April their son would probably die, and April was devastated. They spent hours pacing the deserted embankment above the Taunton River, as the distraught parents waited for the final resolution. Their vigil went for over nine days.

A counselor at the hospital informed them that full anesthesia on a newborn could easily diminish Robert's acuity, and his general mental state . . . if he lives. April didn't accept those dire possibilities, but Latham did. An up and coming executive in the Heinem's\ Pharmaceutical Corporation, he was currently tied up in a high speed contract dispute over the company's ability to ship medicine in and out of Canada, and his baby's distress and his wife's unsteadiness was diverting way too much of his time away from the negotiations.

After the gloomy predictions, Robert Donnelly fought the infection off. Latham was worried the next child could be afflicted with the same deformity, and he cut the odds to zero with a vasectomy. He was worried about his wife's reaction to what he'd done, so he decided not to tell her. Two years after the tumultuous birth, April turned 23. She wanted another baby, a female child to balance the scales, even though Latham had been droning on and on that they shouldn't have anymore children. His words hadn't changed her feelings one bit. Cooking a lavish breakfast in their downtown apartment, she'd filled his belly with cajoling flapjacks, bacon, eggs and sausages. She believed it would be easier to change his mind at that point.

Sitting back from his empty plate, Latham opened the newspaper and relaxed as April stood next to the kitchen sink. Sunlight streamed through in the window behind her, highlighting her brown hair with streaks of reddish gold, and she'd turned into a domestic temptress. Her tight fitting exercise clothes accentuated her curves; she would be the exotic dessert after the extravagant meal. Hazel eyes half closed, the center of her attention didn't waver. Latham had the newspaper up like a force field, but it didn't work. He was nothing but a bird with a broken wing.

"Latham, I can't wait any longer for the next child. I'm stopping the pills today. I think we have to agree to begin again."

Putting down the paper, he frowned. Gambling that the last delivery had unsettled her, it was clear he'd lost the bet.

"Oh honey, come on, don't you remember. We made the decision. We're fine as we are now. I mean, what happened to Bertie may happen again, and he almost died, sweetie. I know you don't want to go through that again."

Standing up, he sidestepped towards the door in an attempt to escape. April threw her coffee cup to the floor with force, and a loud crack followed. Hundreds of pieces of shattered crockery flew everywhere.

"I can't wait and I won't listen to you anymore. What happened happened. Robert is fine, and Jay is fine, but I'M NOT FINE! We're going to have a baby girl. It's going to be a healthy baby girl, and you're going to give me what I want!"

Latham had no way out. Caught between her paws, he still wouldn't tell her about the vasectomy. He fervently hoped her frantic urge would sputter out before he had to come up with an excuse when nothing happens, when she does not get pregnant.

"Whoa, honey, hold on. Slow down, I hate yelling in the morning and you're upsetting the great breakfast I just ate." He reached out and held her hand. "Okay . . . alright, you win. We'll make a nice baby girl for you and the boys. Please calm down, everything is going to work out perfectly."

Nine months after their explosive breakfast, any affection or communication left in the marriage collapsed with Holly's birth. Latham would never tell April what he'd done, and the secret lay fallow between them, an un-crossable divide. Of course, he believed his wife had turned him into a cuckold even if his anger towards her was groundless. April had upheld her marriage vows, *sexually loyal* to her husband and she was utterly baffled by his behavior towards her and the new baby. She'd never figure it out. Meanwhile, there was an extraordinary mystery staring up at them from the cradle, but neither one of them realized it.

2:43PM Monday November 9, 1992 Bass River, Massachusetts

In the 70's, a thundering alarm of prosperity woke up the sleepy towns on Cape Cod with the pounding beat of hammers and high-pitched whine of skill saws. There was a mad dash to buy all the shore front property and anything near by. It was quickly gobbled up, and the greedy developers cut most of the enticing pie into quarter and eighth acre parcels.

A hundred years ago, the Donnelly's had put their stake down on Cape Cod. Their homestead was on Bass River and they held on to those 15 acres like a lodestar. Latham Donnelly's father, William, had been a very hard nut. Holding onto his family's future fortune, he watched the ocean tides seesaw in and out of the river. He believed it was a compelling body of water and he was right. The shoreline of Bass River turned into twenty-four karat gold. William Donnelly was in his seventies when the investors approached him with even more offers to buy his land. In 1978, he said no to the first offer of a million dollars, but a couple of years later, he sold ten of the acres for the same price. He held onto the last five acres like a curmudgeon as the land meant security for his son. He hoped it would instill an honorable remembrance of him after his death.

William passed away in 1990. Besides inheriting the money from his father's previous land sale, Latham got something no one else on Bass River had; those five acres. Adding in his salary from Heinem, he became a very rich man. The land grabbers offered him even more money for the land, but he wouldn't budge. He didn't need to.

Driving over the Bass River Bridge and passing a clutch of tall black pines on the left side of the road, the Donnelly's new house glowed like a white beacon on the hill. Latham and April had accepted William's old farmhouse politely enough, but after the funeral, their true feelings emerged. The dwelling was too small. Too countrified. They couldn't invite *anyone* over. At that point, they went into overdrive. They called in an architect, a contractor, a landscaper, and an interior designer. A month later they razed the farmhouse to the ground, and in twelve months, a palace had taken its place.

The driveway swept up to nine thousand square feet of grandiose living space. The main entrance was centered behind three oversized arches adorning the face of the building and the gothic accents sprinkled through-out the architecture somehow interacted well with the overall minimalism.

A tributary broke away from Bass River and that geography defined the Donnelly's property line with natural grace. Eight hundred and seventy-five feet behind the main house, their back yard ended at the water's edge. On the survey, the acreage on the other side of the tributary was stamped 'wet lands', and it would never be developed. The larger 35 foot power boats were tied to the main dock on Bass River during the summer months, but the family had installed a doll-like boathouse and dock on the shore of the small creek as well.

The rivulet remained serene. Only a powerful storm and a full moon behind it could deform its peaceful face. As the occupants of 1900 Bass River Road sip espresso and gaze out of any window facing north, they could meditate on the tranquil scene outside. They might imagine Tom Sawyer sitting on the small dock fishing as the land was laid out like a dream come true. Facing the river, and a gentle brook circling behind, it was an elegant setting for the ultra-white diamond they'd built. Unfortunately, certain pressures inside the family were mounting and the weight of things to come would eventually warp the heavenly dream. The corporate king's castle would soon become a Pandora's Box.

1:45PM Thursday November 11, 2004 Bass River, Massachusetts

Checking on the guest list for a catered cocktail party to impress his well-heeled friends, or flying to Boston for an emergency meeting, Latham Donnelly's family barely intruded into his busy day. He wasn't sure where his children were precisely, and he didn't care.

The oldest, Justin, had reached the age of 32. He'd acquired a law license and Latham knew he was working on a case out of state somewhere. The younger son, Robert, was 31, and he was previously a drug addict and he was in rehab. He'd been in rehab and it seemed he would stay in rehab forever. Holly was working in the local hospital as a nurse. She was 28. That was all the information he believed he needed to know about them.

The Donnellys hadn't a get-to-together for over five years and April was eagerly setting up her picture-perfect Thanksgiving reunion. Justin had finally moved back to Cambridge five weeks ago, and Robert was finally out of the Langhorne Rehabilitation Center. Holly's turbulent problems with her husband, David Russell, were momentarily in remission. Everyone was going to be able to attend. She'd sent out invitations, but April had called them all up anyway. Walking into her husband's office, she wanted to tell him the good news. Of course he was on the phone. He was *always* on the phone.

"Honey . . . Latham! We're having a reunion on Thanksgiving this year, and I've told Vince about it and Mirabelle is going to serve. Whoever you're talking to can wait a minute, this is important. Put the phone down and talk to me. You need to make sure nothing is going to stop you from being here this time . . . and I won't accept any feeble excuses like last minute flights into the city or anything like that!"

Latham turned around in his chair. Facing her for a second, he smiled and nodded. He hadn't heard a single thing she'd said, and he really wished she'd go away. The woman continued tapping her long burgundy nails on his desk top and it became clear she wasn't going to leave until he talked to her.

"Hold on George, I have another call coming in . . . yeah. We've got to wrap this up . . . ah huh, that's right. We'll iron it all out by

Monday . . . alright . . . alright, goodbye." Latham took the the head set off and swirled towards her in his chair again.

"What *are* you prattling about?"

April rolled her eyes, "Thanksgiving dinner, remember? You have to make sure you're going to be there. No last minute crap this time, hmm?"

"Yeah, okay. Everyone's coming, *even Bertie*?"

"I've told you three times. He's out of Langhorne, and he's doing just fine. Robert is looking forwards to it."

Stretching, Latham put the phone set-up back on his head, "Okay, okay, you got me. I'll find the time to be at your reunion with bells on. It'll be like the old days." He picked up a piece of paper off his desk, and his frown of concentration returned. April was frowning too. She wished she could bore holes into the back of his head with her eyes.

"Thank you, Latham . . . oh, by the way, what did you mean by 'like the old days'? That phrase doesn't make any sense to me in the here and now." She knew damned well he wasn't listening to her anymore, but she went on anyway. "The holiday reunion is going to be great! It's about time we reunite as a family again."

She decided she could talk to herself in a more comfortable setting. April wanted to slam the office door so hard it would snap off its hinges and fall on the polished floor with a resonating boom, but instead she closed it softly on her way out.

2:30PM Thursday November 25, 2004 Bass River, Massachusetts

Justin parked the BMW, and took off his sunglasses. He hung them on the visor. The sophisticated cut on his light brown hair flawlessly matched the grey Armani suit he had on his back, as well as the gold Rolex watch and his diamond cufflinks. Genteelly announcing his success to the world, he walked across the auto court to the front door.

He noticed the storm clouds on the western horizon. Justin hoped the upcoming bad weather wasn't a harbinger for personal squalls erupting during the reunion . . .

Pacing back and forth, when she heard the doorbell April raced to the entry hall as fast as her high heels could allow. Coiled sequined snakes were dancing across the fabric of her oriental green silk dress. The color of the dress was her way of expressing her optimism as she believed the overdue reunion was going to be emotional glue for the family. Opening the front door, April rushed towards Justin. Raising his hand, he stopped her affectionate advance.

"Excuse me, excuse me miss, I'm here to see my mother. Who on earth are you?" Grinning, April knocked his hand away and hugged him.

The entry hall was designed to invite guests into their home with a flourish. Behind them, two marble staircases with carved rosewood rails rose to the second floor, blue chip granite tiles glistened under their feet and the ceiling soared thirty feet above their heads.

"It's so great to see you, Jay! You've been gone way too long. Now that you're back in Massachusetts, you've got to stop by once in a while to see us. I hope you're hungry! Latham's in the library and he's starting in on the scrumptious appetizers. You don't have a coat? It's brisk out there. Oh, we've got to catch up on everything! Have you found the right girl yet?" She paused for a millisecond in her monologue to glance at her wristwatch. "Oh dear, I've got to check on dinner, make sure all the place settings are right. Please honey, just go ahead and say hello to your father, okay? I'll meet you in the library in a sec."

"Mom, you've got to calm down and relax. You're worrying about lots of unimportant stuff," and he laughed, "even if the pot is calling the kettle black."

"Of course you're right, but I don't seem to be able to stop myself. Everything has to be perfect for dinner and I've got to check on the last minute details. I'll see you over there in a blink."

April tip-tapped away. Justin's eyes closed in the resulting silence, but it didn't last. A Harley motorcycle rumbled up the driveway and he felt the low-pitched reverberations right through the front door. Outside, Robert heedlessly shut off the engine and put the kick stand down. He'd parked his bike in everyone's way, and without knocking or using the bell, he barreled straight into the house. While he was taking off his leather jacket, he was delighted to see his brother standing there.

"Jay! It's a gas to see you after all these years. Mr. Fantasy is going to play us a tune! I guess you don't know what's happened to me. I'm free, forever free. It won't snow around me anymore. I'm working at Home Depot, and picking up side jobs in the neighborhood. And I want to get a real estate license, so I'm reading up on it. I bet you've been doing the same slimy stuff you learned in school to climb the ladder of success straight into the clouds . . . or wherever it really does go."

Justin looked at Robert with a feeling of dread. In his mind, his brother would never be free from anything and his fraternal sympathy for him had shriveled up years ago. Robert's outfit was brand new, but that did not touch Justin's prejudice. His hair was still too shaggy and *way* too long, yet there was one thing that didn't fit. His eyes. They were clear and bright. And his demeanor was sober. None of that mattered to Justin.

"Good to see you too, bro. I've been working in Connecticut on a trademark case for too long, and thank God it's finally settled and I'm back in Boston." Justin was on his way outside with Robert in tow. "That looks like a mean-looking ride."

"Thanks, thanks a lot. I spent a lot of time cleaning it up. I even fine-tuned the engine yesterday."

"Well, you did a great job. Yeah, it looks brand new. Listen, I think you should re-park it a little bit farther away from the front door."

Robert nodded. He started the bike up, and Justin watched him move it away from the house. Knowing he'd be locked to Robert forever, he sighed and went back inside.

Rol Manona, a world renowned designer, was responsible for most of the interior of the Donnelly's home. Entering the great room, the occasional small interruption of a few feet of blue carpet, didn't disturb the snowy sweep as the marble floor as it poured out to the walls like milk. The room was so large it was intimidating.

In an article in the Architectural Digest about Manona, the author described the designer's penchant for fire and water in some form in all his motifs. It wasn't surprising to find a nine foot wide fish pond shimmering in the center of the great room, and a massive hearth in the north wall; a simmering response. An grand piano huddled in a far corner looking insignificant, and closer to the front door, a set of blue velvet chairs was bunched around a coffee table. Three more chairs hugged the edge of the koi pond and a couch, two stone tables and some wing chairs were arranged in front of the fireplace. The entire back wall was mirrored and Cathedral-sized windows used up most of the west wall.

Hiking through the great room, an intrepid explorer would finally reach a hallway leading to the kitchen, the dining room and the library. Latham had been adamant in his orders to Manona regarding the dining room and the library. He had to have an air of conviviality to surround his business contacts over their shared aperitif, and Rol had graciously bowed to his customer's demands. Dusty green curtains framed the dining room windows and a picture of a gondola in a Venetian canal, painted by Jane Peterson, a famous impressionist was featured in a prominent place. April was responsible the holiday centerpiece. It was a wicker horn of plenty and fresh fruit spilled out of it onto the center of the table with silver candelabras on either side of the cornucopia.

As thunderheads covered more and more of the sky above the estate, natural light was vanishing. Distracted, April flipped the electric chandelier on while she deliberated over the evening's seating arrangements, and one of her long fingernails was repeatedly flicking through the pile of place cards in her hand.

The malpractice suit hanging over his head like a piano on a wire, David Russell had already paid a quarter-of-a-million dollars in legal bills in only six months. His defense attorney wanted more, but he was strapped. Borrowing $500,000 from his father-in-law could allow him to stay afloat. If he does wind up losing his license, what was left of the loan could fuel a new career. Someday, Holly would inherit a third of the estate, but that golden parachute couldn't save him now. Driving over the bridge, he glanced over at his wife. How would she feel about asking Latham for help? Holly hadn't attached his last name, Russell, when they'd gotten married, and he wondered if that was an insinuation that he should always stand up on his own, or something like that. He was going to have to ask for her help either way, and he gulped back his nervousness.

"I'm sure we will all be relaxed right after dinner . . . maybe a little toasted, and I thought it would be a good time to invite Latham to meet me in the library. I'd explain to him about my momentary financial set back and ask him for a small loan. Do you think it's a good idea? Would it work?"

"You're really not that close to Dad, honey. I don't think your idea is the right one. Listen, he's finally accepted me, even respects me these days, so *I'll* ask him. I'll have a better chance. He's come through for me in the past, and I'm sure he'll help us both if I ask him." Holly placed her hand on his thigh with affection. "You've got to let me take care of this for you, okay? *I'll* invite him to the library after dinner. That will have a much sunnier forecast for the outcome of your request."

Holly's true relationship with her father was unstable. Every single thing she had just said was a lie, but David lapped it all up anyway. He wanted it to be true. Only a mile away from the estate, he didn't have a lot of time to reconsider his response to her idea.

"Alright Holly, I'll leave it in your hands. I'm not sure what's going to happen in court, so maybe we should ask for half a million. Do the best you can. The loan means a lot for both of us."

Holly smiled. Rolling over the last thousand feet, David parked near Justin's BMW and Robert's Harley. Getting out of the car, he walked straight to the front door, speeding up with anticipation for the salvation coming towards him later in the evening. The brown corduroy pants, a long sleeved light pink shirt, and a suede vest, made him look like a college professor not a neurosurgeon. At six feet, his extra fifteen pounds of fat wasn't noticeable. Physically and sexually magnetic, he was blessed with a symmetrical face and full lips. Ringing the bell, Mirabelle opened the door. Ridiculously picturesque, he stood on the stoop, holding his jacket over one shoulder with a stray curl of brown hair falling in front of one his large and searingly blue eyes.

"Good evening, Mr. Russell . . . I thought the Mrs. was coming along with you?" The housekeeper took his jacket, and David looked around. Realizing he was alone, he called out his wife's name.

Something in the garden behind the house had beckoned Holly and she'd left her coat in the car. She dashed under the trees towards the hedge maze to get closer to a resonance only she could feel. Looking like a sprite made out of mist, the pearlescent veils of her smoky colored dress fluttered in the air as she ran. Entering the maze, she stayed on the main path until she reached the three tiered fountain in the center clearing.

The water for the fountain had been shut off for the winter and she stood there in silence as she looked up into the branches of a fifty foot tall silver birch swaying at the edge of the circle of grass.

Holly's hair was black as pitch and she had a very light complexion, seeming almost white in comparison. The color of her faintly slanted eyes was unclear. The authorities had printed ***grey*** on her driver's license, the best they could come up with. At 5' 9", her high cheekbones and the body of a dancer had given her an option to be a model instead of a registered nurse. So different physically from the rest of her family, Holly was a mystery; a genetic anomaly to everyone but Latham. He knew the answer, or at least he thought he did and her otherworldly beauty was an irritant to him.

Motionless, Holly looked like an enchanting statue staring up at something far above her head. Soon enough her day to day obligations quickly resurfaced in her mind, realizing they were waiting for her at the house.

The wind picked up and the light was almost gone. Mirabelle waited in the driveway staring out into the distance. David had gone back to the car, thinking Holly might have returned there to check on her makeup or something. Hunching over, he peered into the car windows, and he didn't know that Holly was silently creeping up behind him. She tapped him on the shoulder, and he jumped and gasped with alarm. Instantly jolted with an influx of adrenaline, he twisted around and grabbed her shoulders with way too much pressure.

"Where the hell did you go?"

"I'm sorry. I haven't been here in years and I thought I saw a brown and orange warbler. That bird is supposed to be extinct and I wanted to get closer to it. It was too dark and I couldn't see anything. It was a pointless endeavor."

David kept on clenched her shoulders, and she had to coax him into releasing her. Most people would have sustained bruises from his surprised grip, yet Holly's alabaster skin remained unblemished.

"That is a preposterous story, Holly. You sound like a lunatic running around into the woods for no reason. Can you please come back to earth and think about what we've talked about in the car? Put your mind at work on *that!*"

Holly grinned at him. Regaining his composure, he held her hand and they walked through the front door of the mansion, and Mirabelle closed it behind them.

Nodding politely, the housekeeper disappeared. She took a service corridor hidden behind a brocade curtain in the back corner of the entrance hall, while Holly and David crossed the great room on their way to the library. Far above the clouds that covered the estate, a large and muscular shoulder covered in feathers turned eastward towards the Atlantic Ocean, and Holly got a chill. David didn't notice the goose bumps on her skin or the slight shudder that also ran through her. He put his arm around her waist. Stepping into the library, they were the final link in the familial chain, and the reunion had been joined.

The library was a refuge in the hurly-burly of a global world. The blue wall to wall carpeting muffled the sharp edges of sound and the pinkish-orange filters installed over the recessed lights made everybody look radiant.

The Donnellys hadn't had a reunion in five years, and they were tentative, uneasily feeling things out. When conversation lagged, they'd devour more appetizers. The coffee table was soon cluttered with cocktail glasses and half-eaten canapés. Mirabelle barely had enough time to clean it up intermittently. Every ten minutes, she'd arrive with more hot appetizers on a silver tray.

Latham and April were sitting on the divan, David and Justin, on the couch. Holly and Robert stood at the window to look out at the wind-lashed trees. There was no way they could see the tributary. Seventy-five feet away, a spindly poplar tree had cracked and they enjoyed watching it tumble across the lawn. Then they bowed to each other, honoring the display of the storm's destructive power.

Everyone's apprehension dissolved into alcoholic camaraderie. It began wonderful that they were together again at last! Thirty more minutes went by, until the warm ambience of the library was pierced by cold light from the hallway. Mirabelle had opened the double doors to announce their dinner was served.

The table was big enough for eight people, but only six places were set. The extra chairs were gone. The chandelier was set on 'low', allowing the actual candlelight the upper hand, creating an atmosphere to invite a more gentle life. Straggling in, their place cards were next to the water glasses. Latham and April sat at opposite ends of the table. Justin was on his father's right and Robert on the left, while David and Holly sat next to April. April had known that Latham wanted as much space as he could get between himself and his daughter and she also knew he wanted Justin on his right side.

Mirabelle pushed the cart holding a tureen of lobster bisque through the swinging doors, and she began ladling the steaming soup into April's bowl. After serving the rest of first course, she retreated back to the kitchen.

"This is great! I don't know if I can eat anymore. It's filling me up!" Robert gurgled statements were followed by more slurping noises.

"Thank-you, Bertie. Don't worry about what you can't eat. You can always bring some food home with you . . . tell me, how are you doing at work?" April said.

"It's ultra boring. I'm stocking shelves day after day, but I guess you gotta start somewhere. I'm also going to take a real estate course. It might be fun to sell houses."

April and Robert's simple conversation continued, as Justin turned to his father with a question.

"When is the refinishing of the tennis court going to be done? You know I'm going to beat you next time and that moment of triumph isn't linked with love, sir. Your days of unbroken victory are almost over. I've learned a few more tricks."

Latham laughed. "The court's finished Jay, but I don't think we can play out there tonight. When you find the time, just stop by. I'll play until you get too tired to continue, and I'll throw your so-called tricks right back at you." Tall and trim, his grey green three-piece suit fit him perfectly, and it was same size he was on his senior year in high school. The orange-tinted half-glasses he had on went on to accentuate his youthful aspect.

Removing the empty bowls, Mirabelle returned with the turkey. Latham carved it up. Yams, oyster stuffing, baked potatoes, gravy, fresh homemade cranberry sauce, and creamed spinach were all staying warm in a steam table against the wall.

Everyone got in and filled their plates. David was too busy worrying about Holly's meeting with her father after dinner, and he didn't participate much in the conversation ping-ponged around him. Holding his empty glass up, he got Mirabelle's attention.

"Please, would you mind bringing me another brandy from the library bar?" She took his glass and vanished, reappearing in a flash. Mirabelle had given him a larger glass holding more liquor, responding perfectly to the stress she'd heard in his words.

After dinner, the housekeeper cleared the table, brushing all the crumbs and food particles into a silver 'dustpan'. Latham would ring the bell on the side board next to his seat, the moment they're ready for dessert and coffee. Staring out into space Robert burped, offhandedly excusing himself, and April was talking about vacation spots with David. Latham and Justin had fallen into a convoluted discussion about business law, something to do with a tussle between the Hienem Corporation and a smaller company intent on distributing medicine in Ecuador.

The table had opened up between courses and April's centerpiece was a lot more noticeable. Turquoise ribbons and tiny white satin flowers were woven into the wicker. She'd filled it with blood oranges, plums, red and green grapes, two small pineapples, yellow, green and red apples and furry kiwis. Positioning the colorful fruit in a charming way, she'd changed the decoration into transitory art.

Holly glanced over at Latham and Justin and her peaceful smile flattened into a straight line. She didn't want the social connection between them to keep on growing. While no one at the table was looking at her, she pulled one of the long sleeves of her dress over her elbow. Holly reached out to the pile of fruit, and the very long and sharp nail of her forefinger pierced the soft flesh of a very ripe plum. With her elbow on the table, she lifted the skewered fruit up and plum juice ran into her palm and down the inside of her forearm. Outlandish and silly, the ploy worked. She'd stopped Latham and Justin's conversation in its tracks. In the following silence, the plum fell off her nail and dropped to the table with an audible plop. After that, she held on to her family's interest with a genial dissertation.

"The Horn-of-Plenty is stunning Mom. A phenomenal rendition." April tried to thank her for the compliment, but Holly kept on talking . . .

"Do you know where the Cornucopia, the symbol of a good harvest and endless riches comes from? There are many versions describing Zeus's childhood, but I think the more prevalent one is the best. Rhea, his mother, gave him to Amalthea, a nymph, to take care of him. One day, Amalthea hung the baby's cradle in a tree, believing the placement would connect him to the heavens, the earth and the sea and when he grew up his powers would incorporate all three environments and of course it worked." Holly paused to sip her glass of wine, yet no one interjected. "Giving Zeus goat milk from one particular goat, he grew healthy and strong. Mature, he broke the goat's horn off, and he endowed it with power. Whoever owned it would get anything they wanted and he gave the horn to the loyal nymph in gratitude. The Greeks called it the Horn of Amalthea until the Romans renamed it Cornucopia, The Horn of Plenty. Our remembrance of it on our table today is an optimistic prayer to the old gods, hoping all our endeavors will bear fruit and none of us will starve . . . of course, if we don't stop eating, gluttony will be our ultimate downfall and we'll just pop."

"It's too late, sis. I'm about to explode right now. Everybody . . . duck." Robert started laughing and then he burped again. Holly picked up the fallen plum and bit into it.

"When you're done blowing up, the rest of us will enjoy the unending river of gold flowing out of the Horn," Justin said.

"You wish. You're popping buttons right off your shirt right now. After your last bite of dessert, you'll follow me straight into the beyond," Robert smirked. "Hey! What if I tell a joke I heard at work last week? It's sort of about Thanksgiving."

April looked over at Justin and Latham. She didn't want them to fall back into conversation anymore than Holly did. A smile appeared on her face, and she nodded at Robert, "Oh yes, tell us the joke, Bertie!"

"Okay, Mom. Here we go . . . um, a minister died, finding himself on line to the pearly gates. He asked the man in front of him what he'd done in his life, and he'd said he'd been a taxi driver. The angel at the gate called out 'Next', and the taxi driver stepped up. Saint Peter gave him a golden key and a . . . ah . . . a cornucopia filled to brim with lots of stuff," Robert stopped for a second. He smiled and winked at his mother. "He entered heaven with his prizes and then the minister steps up. All Saint Peter gave him a wooden staff and a crust of bread and the religious man was miffed. He told Peter it was unfair. 'That guy was only a taxi driver and you gave him much better stuff! I spent my entire life worshiping God and spreading his word and all I get is a twig and a dried out piece of bread.'

Looking down at the minister, Peter explained what had happened with patience. 'Up here we only pay out benefits by actual results. Your parishioners slept through your sermons, but everybody riding in the back seat of that man's taxi wailed and prayed that they wanted God's help to save them right away." Everybody chuckled at the punch line.

"Holly, why do you know about where the horn of plenty comes from?" Latham asked.

"Well, I had a minor in folklore in college." She looked straight at Latham. Leaning forwards, she picked up her wine glass. Her hair swung forwards and it was so glossy it reflected the candlelight. To break eye contact with Holly, Latham twisted around his chair to ring the bell. A minute later, Mirabelle came in with a tray holding a carafe and six plates, but Latham's curiosity drew him on. He asked Holly one more question.

"I thought you were there to learn medicine. What would folklore have to do anything?"

"Understanding the mechanics of the human body led me to question our own mortality and the state of the human soul. Folklore encompasses all traditions, customs and beliefs, even religion." With a ghost of a smile, she thought over the rest of her answer. "Historically, our culture is ego-driven, and the power hungry people in charge used religion to mold the population through superstition. The college course was a starting point for me. I wanted to delve into what we don't understand."

Latham's face was a blank. He thought she'd just given him nothing but intellectualizing drivel.

"Well, I can't remember what I learned in school, it was so far back in time. I don't even think the building is standing anymore," and he laughed. "Personally, I have no interest in the invisible workings behind *anything* . . . well, maybe what goes on behind closed doors in some business meeting some place. As far as I'm concerned, superstition is only hot air holding up claptrap and bunk." Why had he started this damned conversation with her in the first place? Holly had been given a raise and a managerial position in St. Luke's Hospital in New Bedford three weeks ago. He respected her diligence, but she would remain an intruder. His current uneasiness around her was increasing.

Mirabelle served coffee and desert. While everyone dug into their pumpkin pie, the housekeeper re-appeared to whisper something in Mrs. Donnelly's ear. April stood up to announce she needed to check on something and she'd be right back. Latham scrutinized her across the table, and then he resumed eating his dessert. Her subsequent disappearance from the ongoing festivities didn't appear to faze him in the least.

Teetering forwards, she moved along as fast as she could. April reached an unobtrusive door in the main hallway across from the dining room that led into the servants' quarters. She cagily looked left and right before she opened the door and walked in. Adapting to her cumbersome footwear, she leaned her body weight on her toes. It was the best she could as she rushed down the thin corridor to get to the common room. She had given the service number to Peter as a way to communicate without Latham noticing it, so it had to be him and she almost leapt towards the phone hanging on the wall across the room. Her hands were shaking as she lifted the receiver.

"Hello, is that you? Why would you call me in the middle of dinner?" April said. She was panicky and breathing hard. Peter had been forced to call her on a public line, as his cell phone had crapped out. It was hard for him to hear her against the blaring PA and the surrounding clamor of an international airport.

"Yes, April, it's me and please calm down. I don't want to be responsible for any new worry lines. Listen, I'm calling you with good news and bad news and there's a lot more good than bad. I'm really sorry to interrupt your dinner, but I'm about to get on a flight to Japan in thirty minutes, and I don't want you to make any decisions until you know exactly what I overheard a few minutes ago."

"Don't worry about . . ."

"I have no time to talk. You've got to hear this right now. Can hear me well enough? You know I *hate* flying so I went to the airport bar to have a martini before the flight, and I overheard a wild conversation. Must have been lawyers or real estate agents or something, but they were discussing *your* estate. They didn't use your name, but you're the only people on Bass River Road who have 5 acres of land and that was the size of the property they were talking about, so I grew big wide ears. Latham's going to sell the house next year! Those gossiping dopes were trying to figure out why he was waiting until next year to do it. I don't care why and neither should you, but it does mean you'll divide the profits from the sale. If I was you I wouldn't do anything, yet. Latham has the mind of a weasel, and he'd want to slice you up in pieces in court so I'd hold back until the sale goes through. You probably won't get any of his stock in Heinem, but I know he can't lock you out of the capital coming out of the sale of the house. Don't you see? We can kick our heels up and relax, if we hold on a little bit longer. We'll be on easy street next year. I don't think it is a coincidence that I overheard that conversation. I think the fates are on our side giving us this wonderful tidbit . . . anyway, I have no more time left. I've got to get on that plane."

"Okay, okay, Peter, I'll hold back. I have to go, too. I told everybody I'd be right back. Call me as soon as you get back home, and we'll have a champagne toast in the cottage." She tried to sound excited, even if the new information was scaring her witless.

"Looking forwards to seeing you soon, sweetheart."

"I love you Peter, and don't worry. It's going to be a fine flight."

It was obvious the secret of her affair wasn't the only skeleton rattling around in the Donnelly's closet. What Peter had told her would help her through the divorce, giving her a better hand no matter what the trickster had up his sleeve. She should really feel better, and she didn't understand why she felt a lot worse.

As soon as Latham knew she was pregnant in 1975, he started to sleep in a different bedroom. He had explained that he might hurt the baby if he was in bed with her; maybe kick her or something while he was sleeping. After Holly's birth, things between them got even worse, and April was living in an emotional wasteland. He had sex with her once or twice a month, but he wasn't making love at all anymore. He rutted like a beast, and he treated her like a whore, and a cheap one at that. Perplexed by his extreme transformation, she also dealt with his constant derision. April should have simply gone to a lawyer or a counselor, but instead she grinned through it without a murmur. He was on a fast track in the company, and he was close to the absolute top. She knew if she left him or even rocked the boat, her luxury and social connections would dry up and blow away. April did not want to stop living in opulence.

Asking him over and over again what was wrong, all she got was silence and an expression of bitter disgust on his face. Unable to fix what she couldn't understand, she finally gave up. Enjoying the fragile warmth coming from the prestige that surrounded him was enough for her a while. He stopped having sex with her completely in 1983. Physically loyal to him throughout the marriage, April finally broke down.

She'd been molding herself with plastic surgery as a psychological release from her farcical marriage and a symptom of her deepening loneliness. Using the same doctor for the ongoing procedures, he'd talk to her in depth about the next operation. He made her feel human again; a woman with sexual magnetism, and it wasn't long until she and Peter became lovers.

Ten minutes had passed since she'd left the table, and everybody else had eaten their dessert. April sat down and stared at her pie, but her appetite had soured. She wouldn't pick up the fork.

"What was the emergency, Mom? Who would drag you away from your Thanksgiving Day feast?" Justin said.

"It really wasn't that important. It was Carmen, a lady I met in the hospital when Bertie was born. We were friends for a while as her baby was sick too. A few years ago, she moved to California and I haven't spoken to her in years. She just called to give us all a holiday greeting, that's all."

She'd come up with a story to tell when she got back, and her forethought had turned out to be life-preserver. Peter's news flash had confounded her. It would have been hard to come up with anything on her short return trip to the dining room. Pushing her dessert plate away, she swallowed the rest of the wine in her glass. Latham was in the middle of asking Robert about his possible real estate adventures. Apparently indifference to his wife's desertion from the table, appearances can be deceiving. Latham had actually listened to every single word she'd said about the phone call, and he cataloged the knowledge in a file in his head.

"Kids, it's almost nine. I don't think I can stay awake much longer. Maybe we should adjourn to the great room to enjoy that fire and drink the cognac I picked out for us," Latham said. Standing up, he walked out of the dining room, and everyone followed him into the hall. David nudged Holly. She sidled up to Latham to whisper in his ear, while David stayed close behind.

"*I've heard something unsettling at work and I think you need to know about it. Please, it would be worth spending just a moment in the library with me. It's too unpleasant for general consumption.*"

Latham reluctantly nodded, and they both reversed course. The rest of the family convened in front of the roaring fire in the great room as Mirabelle arrived with two bottles of cognac on a small tray; Louis XIV and Remy Martin. She filled everyone's snifters, and the perfume wafting up from their pear shaped glasses worked as a delightful distraction. So far, no one had seemed to notice that Holly and Latham weren't there.

The lighting in the library mimicked candlelight, but since their attention was pinned on the upcoming conversation, they didn't think about brightening the room up.

"So what is this all about?" Latham said.

"I'm very sorry to interrupt the festivities, but I can't get it out of my head. Last week in the hospital an overdose rolled into the emergency room and the nurse at the desk told me that the man on the stretcher was using our name in his ranting's. It upset her enough to walk into my office and tell me about it. When the man was wheeled into the main entrance, he was screaming 'Donnelly took off and left me alone'. Everything else he said was incoherent. It could be nothing, nothing at all, but I think you should be aware of it, maybe keep your eyes on Robert a little more diligently, okay? I'm not sure he's that stable, even now."

After living through the long in-house session in Langhorne, Robert was finally drug free, and no one had said anything about the Donnellys in the emergency room. Brazenly lying to Latham, Holly wasn't intentionally hurting Robert per se. Her feelings towards her older brother were on the same par as the love she had towards the rest of her family. Bertie had turned into a pawn in a game she didn't quite understand, and if her actions had cruel consequences, her motives were instinctual, not predatory.

Relaxing on the couch, Holly's laissez-faire demeanor appeared to lift her even farther away from the up-comings repercussions of her latest deceit. Her eyes appeared to be violet in the soft light. Fashion models on the cover of Vogue or Harper's Bazaar never looked real, yet Holly exuded the same unnatural mystique in the material world. Her grey dress hugged her lithe body like a glove, and its flimsy layers whispered to the beholder, "gaze deeper if you dare." Everybody in the family had gotten used to it but Latham and her irritating life as his so-called daughter would go on picking at him forever. Looking over at her, he frowned. He looked out the window to stare at the windswept backyard as a momentary escape.

"I thought the treatment had worked this time. During dinner, he was loopy as usual, but he seemed optimistic, a trait I haven't seen in him in years. I'm really surprised you've gone out of your way to help your brother. Your lives are so completely different. I didn't think you cared that much." Latham looked back at her, waiting for her response. Her head was bowed and her black bangs covered her brow. Under the veil of hair, her eyes seemed to be glowing with a gentle blue light and he shook his head and looked back at her again. The radiance was gone and Latham thought it had been a trick of the light . . . or his eyesight was failing.

"Actually, I'm more concerned about our reputation and the public standing of the family as a whole. If you don't corral Bertie, he might run off the rails so extravagantly it could tarnish us all. His inheritance might be another stumbling block. He'll probably squander all your money for no good reason besides hurting himself."

"Don't you worry about what your brother may or may not do anymore. I'll think it over and consider what should be done, and thank you. You've done the right thing." Latham stood up. "I think we've been away from the others long enough. We don't want them to start worrying about us."

Walking back to the great room, Holly and Latham had a respectable separation of space between them.

"I think you'll enjoy the cognac Holly, it'll take the chill right out of your bones," Latham said. He poured Remy Martin into one of the two glasses the housekeeper had left for them on the marble table. Justin was prodding at the fire with the poker. Replacing the instrument in the iron stand on the hearth, he slapped the fly-away ash off his clothes.

"About to send out a search party to find you two," Justin said, smiling.

"Forgive the disappearance, but Holly wanted to ask me a question dealing with hospital politics, and we didn't want to bore you with it," Latham said. He sat down on the couch, and leaned back, crossing his legs and sipping his cognac. "This reunion has turned out to be a lot of fun. I can't remember the last time we've all been here together. Has it really been more than five years since our last powwow?"

The event was winding down. On the surface, they all seemed emotionally replete, as if their disorganized social connections from the past had somehow been re-forged. Hypnotized by the crackling flames and lulled by the warmth, they basked in this pleasant mirage. Propped up against a corner of the couch, Robert had fallen asleep.

"I think we need another Thanksgiving get-together next year . . . another reunion," Holly said.

"I wholeheartedly concur," Justin replied. "We should underline it on our calendars to avoid any last minute jaunts that would drag us away," directing those words at his father.

"Son, you've been out of state for years, so I don't think you're in a position to preach to anyone on this subject. Be that as it may, you're both right. We *should* do it again. I assure you, my business responsibilities won't interfere with our dinner plans next year, and I'll even give you a toast to cement our resolve!"

Crowding around in a circle they held up their glasses. Robert had woke up to participate. Latham rang out the challenge.

"To next year's Thanksgiving Reunion!" And everyone echoed him in a resounding chorus.

"To next year's Thanksgiving Reunion!"

Their glasses clinked together finalizing the toast. Robert staggered backwards and April grabbed his shoulder to guide him back to the couch. Everyone else laughed.

Justin chimed in, "I have an idea for the meal. You guys know I couldn't eat that wonderful bisque because of my allergic reaction to shell fish, and the oysters in the turkey stuffing always make me avoid most of the turkey meat. Since I really love ham, I know a great distributor in Boston and I could ship you an excellent one for next year. We could have turkey *and* ham. What do you think?"

"Sounds great, Jay. I'll tell Vince about it and he'll prepare it along with the turkey," April said.

Robert got up off the couch to find his jacket and his motorcycle keys. April went over to him and touched him on the back of his hand, "Bertie, I think you should probably spend the night in your old room."

"I agree with her. You don't need to go to work tomorrow and you're too sloshed to ride through the storm," Holly said.

Shrugging, Robert sat back down. "Alright, you have me then. Going back to my old waterbed is going to feel great. You guys didn't throw it out did you?" He smiled sheepishly, "I already put my bike into one of the empty garages. I even wiped it down, hoping you'd invite me."

The family straggled into the entry hall to congregate at the front door. Going through the obligatory hugs and kisses, David winked at Latham as he shook his hand. Amiably enough, Latham winked back at him, clueless.

Justin opened the front door and the north wind swept across the granite tiles. Holly, David and Justin ran out into the storm. April peered through one of the decorative windows outlining the massive door for a moment as they raced across the auto court. Latham was long gone. He'd returned to the library to watch a football game on TV, and Robert was staring at the wall like there was something to see.

"Bertie, you must be exhausted. Don't you feel like going upstairs to rest? There are pajamas in the lower left drawer of the bureau, and if you're still hungry I could bring you something to nibble on later on." April was talking to him as if he was a child. Robert was 31, but some things never change.

Robert's interaction with the blank wall ended. "It's okay, I'm fine Mom. I'll just go upstairs to bed." He hugged her, and kissed her on the cheek. Clutching the banister, he swayed up the steps to the second floor landing. From there, he ambled down one of the corridors. Passing an exercise room on his left, the rest of the doors were lined up on his right. The third door opened onto his old room and he saw that his waterbed was gone. A king sized bed had replaced it and he sat on the cushioned seat under the garden window overlooking the river. He was dejected. Clumsily raising his legs up on the bench, he almost fell on the floor. Pressing his forehead on the cool glass, he couldn't see much. The red tail lights of Holly and David's Mercedes disappeared around the first curve on Bass River Road. Wind-driven rain ticked softly against the window pane, a spontaneous lullaby, and it quickly transformed Robert's quiet breathing into paint-peeling snores. His head slid slowly down to the sill.

In the mad sprint for the car, Holly had deftly pickpocketed her husband's car keys. Getting to the car four seconds before he did, and she opened the driver's door and got in. She locked it. David squatted and rapped at the window. Holding his jacket over his head to block the rain was his only defense against the downpour.

"Get out right now! I'll drive us home just fine. I'm OK, really. I drank lots of coffee after dinner and I only had two cognacs. With my weight and the elapsed time, my blood alcohol level should be fine. I'm getting wet, damn it!"

Holly looked past her husband as if he was invisible, as if she couldn't hear the tapping on the glass or anything he'd said.

"You drank a lot more than I did, so I should drive, damn it!" The rain was relentless, pounding hard on him. He had no choice. He ran around the car to get in on the passenger side.

David Russell knew damned well his wife had an inhuman tolerance to alcohol. If a three hundred pound defensive line backer tried to match her, he'd pass out and fall on the floor long before she felt a thing. During the last cocktail party they'd gone to a month ago, Holly drank eight or nine martinis. Some of them doubles. At the end of the evening, her makeup was flawless, her clothes unspoiled and her diction was faultless. She was acting as sober as a judge. With a medical degree, he had to find a way to explain her ability somehow and he chalked it up to her metabolism. A feasible excuse for the nonsensical. In his mind Holly's body burns up the alcohol when it hits her blood stream too fast to get her drunk, and the silly justification was enough to control his astonishment and most of his fear.

He closed the passenger door, gratefully out of the rain. Holly glanced over at him and giggled.

"Right now, you should shake your head like dogs do to allow yourself to see. Your thick eyelashes are way too wet and they're drooping into your line of sight."

It was true, but the teasing was irksome to David. He wiped his palm across his eyes, and glowered at her. She eased the Mercedes across the wet tiles and down the long slope of the driveway.

"What happened? How did it go? Dad winked back at me right before we left. Does that mean I'm going to get the money? I told you, Wilson is biting at the bit and he's not going to defend me anymore until I give him a lot more money." He didn't sound very stable.

"How much celebrating did you do tonight, sweetheart?" Holly's voice caressed him, as soft as velvet. "Have you forgotten? Two days ago, you told me your malpractice insurance isn't going to run out for another four months so you're not going to be destroyed quite yet. You said you wanted five hundred thousand dollars to hold the fort, but . . ." and her attention shifted to the wet road, leaving David hanging.

He cried out, "What happened? For God's sake just tell me!"

"Couldn't you consider going to Las Vegas to solve all your financial troubles by using your winnings at the tables?" Holly was smirking.

David straightened up as much he could inside the car. He pivoted towards her with his fists clenched.

"Gee, that's the best idea yet! Why didn't I think of it first? Going to Vegas and gambling . . . for God's sake, Holly, you've got to stop this and answer me. I'm serious. I need to know what happened between you and Latham, right now!"

"Alright, alright, I can tell your knickers are in a twist. He's got a CD ready to mature in four more months, and you can borrow *that* money, okay?"

In the darkened interior of the car, David's tension escalated, and he started rocking back and forth in the seat. Instead of screaming, his voice hissed out in a sibilant whisper.

"And how much money is there in the CD, honey? Would you please consider telling me that? Is it twenty-five cents or maybe twenty-five thousand dollars or is it the correct amount I've asked for? "

Holly sighed. She couldn't poke at him anymore. "Its five hundred thousand dollars alright, so calm down and have a nap or something. I'll safely drive us the rest of the way home."

David reached over and kissed her and yawned, melting into the seat.

"Thank you. It's darkest right before the dawn and all of that. You did come through for me today." Settling farther into the bucket seat, he followed her advice and passed out.

11:58PM Thursday November, 25th 2004 Bass River, Massachusetts

Robert had fallen asleep in a terrible position, and he woke up in the garden window with a crick in his neck. He got up and left the bedroom to take the elevator to the kitchen. There might be left over pumpkin pie in the cooler and that could take his mind off the pain. After he gets done with his midnight prowling, he grudgingly decided he'd lie down on the damned bed instead of returning to the uncomfortable window cushion. Walking down the corridor to the lift, he pushed the call button. He hadn't been in the house for years, and he'd completely forgotten about the seamless technology his father had installed throughout the house. Hearing nothing at all, he thought the elevator was broken, and he was startled when the doors whisked open in front of him to reveal the bright steel car. Riding to the first floor, he took the service corridor to the back entrance of the kitchen. He opened the door and put on the main lights and he blinked in the symphony of twinkle screaming at him in response. He wished he had on sunglasses. Copper pots and pans gleamed on a track above two commercial ovens and the center island glittered with tiny mirror pieces dusted into its bronze surface. The unrelenting sparkle danced over to the counter tops and splash guards made from the same man-made granite used in the center island, and the floor tiles looked like they were wet. Moving around the island, he disappeared inside the cooler to prod at some of the containers stacked on the shelves. He couldn't find the pie and he was getting cold. The refrigerator door closed behind him with a whoosh as he walked back into the kitchen. Noticing a plate of pastries under the closed serving window across the room, he went over there to grab a croissant. Then he heard voices. Quietly opening the mirrored shutters on the serving window, he could make out the conversation a little bit better. It was his parents talking in the library, and curiosity pulled him into the dining room. The pastry in his hand was utterly forgotten.

Latham had dropped the flat-screen TV out of its hiding place in the ceiling and he was relaxing on the divan to watch the game. A remote in his hand, he could adjust volume, angle, color and brightness on the screen without getting off the cushions he was laying on. The game was exciting and the score was close, but his interest was flagging. What Robert might do in the future had become a real problem in his mind. While he lifted a glass of sherry to his lips, April appeared out of nowhere and kissed him on the cheek. His drink sloshed onto his chin and upper chest.

"Is it a good game? I guess it's running late. It's almost 12:30."

"Was it necessary for you to have me drool on myself, woman? Watch yourself in the future . . . yes, it's a good game, but I'm thinking over what I should do about that idiot passed out upstairs. I haven't paid a lot of attention to football."

"Why do you talk about him that way? Bertie looked great tonight. After years of rehabilitation, he's starting a new life. Did you know he's thinking about real estate? I haven't seen him looking so . . ." she thought for a moment, "*happy* in a long time."

"And did you see what he drank tonight? It was excessive." Latham stood up and stepped over to the bar, unsteadily re-filling his own glass.

"It was a party, for God's sake and a reunion on top of that! If he was tipsier than Jay or Holly or even you, it's probably because he doesn't have the same tolerance anymore. He hasn't been out in the world for a very long time." April was very upset with Latham's unfair reaction to her son. Refreshing her own glass of white wine, she perched on the arm of the couch.

"Alright, alright, you have a point," Latham said, and he shrugged. "But you don't know the scuttlebutt Holly told me after dinner. There's a rumor at the hospital linking Robert to drugs again and *she* was worried. It was important enough for her to pull me aside and talk to me about it." Leaning against the cushioned edge of the bar, his smile seemed to mock the entire world.

"My God! I don't believe it. It's nothing but hearsay. You don't even know if it's true. It could be nothing . . . a misunderstanding. Perhaps . . ."

Latham interrupted her, "I've had it with his non-stop screw ups and I'm not going to support any more hospices, rehabilitation centers *or* his goddamned rent. If he makes it, he makes it. If he doesn't, well that's the way the cookie crumbles. He can't be left alone with large amounts of money at his disposal in the future. What on earth would he do with it anyway? Probably buy more drugs and alcohol. It's for his own good and the family's reputation, and I'm going to put a stop on things."

"Wait, Latham wait a minute!" Raising her voice, April stood up and lifted her hands in a gesture of appeal. "You have to check on the source of the story before you do *anything*."

"I'm going back to Boston day after tomorrow and I don't have any time to corroborate something like this. Robert's a lost cause, and I don't want his filthy habits to besmirch our reputation and through association, our colleagues as well. I don't care what you think, April. I'm calling Attison tomorrow to revise the will. I'm going to leave Bertie's money in a trust, and I'll put Justin in control of it and if Justin dies, then Attison will take over. There always has to be someone with discretionary control over his money after we're gone."

April didn't think the hospital story was true and Latham's reaction was preposterous, but there was nothing she could do to support Robert . . . after all, her *own* economic future takes precedence. In her paranoia, she thought Latham was probably checking on everything she did financially, and maybe he was paying someone to follow her around. Thank God she was blessed with a daughter like Holly! Perhaps she should call her up and ask her about what she'd actually heard at work about Robert.

Living under the same roof with Latham was getting tougher every day as his behavior was becoming more impossible. April's joie de vivre earlier in the afternoon, imagining her marriage coming back to life during the reunion had been squashed by an onslaught of dingy truths thrown at her during the evening, like the gravy stain on the shoulder of her beautiful dress. She'd never get that spot out.

Robert moved closer to the far wall of the dining room. What they were saying about him was awful, and Latham's judgments were devastating.

"April, I've had it with his non-stop screw ups . . ."

Obviously, he was going to lose his inheritance, and Justin would dole out dribs and drabs if he felt like it. This was a very bitter pill for Robert to swallow. He dropped the croissant, and ran across the room.

He opened the hallway door with a bang, but April and Latham thought it was part of a commercial on TV.

Racing across the great room to the fireplace, he was fortunate Mirabelle had left the cognac on the table. While the dying embers of the fire hissed at him, he remembered the piercing disdain in his father's words and that sudden perception burrowed into his marrow like a poisonous seed. Reaching towards the liquor bottles, he froze. A very important structure inside his personality snapped, and the fragile ropes he'd woven over the past few weeks to anchor him to the real world were quickly unraveling. Casting off into his own unforgiving shadow, he started moving again. He picked up the cognac bottles and sprinted up the stairs to his old room.

10:55PM Thursday November 25, 2004 New Bedford, Massachusetts

It was on Merchant Drive, a one-story bungalow on an acre of land with a line of mature blue pines marching along the edge of their land. There was dark purple wall to wall carpeting in the office, three bedrooms, and the large main room that included the living room and the dining room, plus two full bathrooms and an expansive kitchen that David and Holly barely used.

The remote for the garage door had broken a week ago. Holly had to park outside in the pouring rain and they had to run for the front porch. Getting inside, they shook out their jackets and hung them up.

"Do you want anything?" David said, on his way to the fridge to grab a beer.

"Some water, thanks."

Returning to the living room, he tossed the bottle of water over to Holly, and then he sat down in the armchair in the corner. He turned on the TV, half-heartedly flicking through the channels, while Holly began to read a magazine article. She was quickly engrossed in the piece.

The author, Keith Fischer, was a world-renowned marine technician. A shipping magnate wanted him to do the electrical work in his custom yacht, and so from there, *American Yachting* had asked Fischer for a detailed article to describe the project. He'd just invented a breakthrough in shipboard communication. It was a new way to direct the integration of the components onboard by wiring the different systems into a main frame to mimic the human nervous system. The vessel under construction would have an intelligence of its own, and only one person needed to monitor and update the different systems in real time. It was easier to control the huge craft. Besides, the new invention would also limit the size of the crew.

Interested in his innovation, Holly wasn't sleepy. Drawn to the man himself, she was lost in the complex article, while her husband hadn't found squat on the tube. He was bored. Going back to the kitchen for another beer, he couldn't avoid the engaging picture of what was pressing against the inner layer of Holly's dress, knowing she wasn't wearing a bra or any panties. Maybe the help she'd given him earlier with his father-in-law had been a sign, she was warming up to him again and she'd keep on helping him until the sun comes up.

David should have ended it where it started in the supply closet on the third floor of the hospital. When Holly found out about his affair with the intern last year, the imbroglio ripped his marriage to shreds. Not wanting to divorce him, she didn't want him in bed, either and time passed. In the beginning, he hoped she'd relent, but after a couple more months, he began to pray for her forgiveness until he ached. He was a very good-looking man with a healthy sex drive, yet he couldn't touch anyone unless he was cutting into their brains with a scalpel. The illicit orgasms David had enjoyed with the young ingénue hadn't been worth the painful results and the building pressure was making him crazy. It was late, and he was tired and foggy with drink. No longer thinking logically, he decided to seduce his wife.

Talking to her about it would have been a much safer choice.

Holly was curled up on the couch in front of the picture window. Five feet behind the couch was a love seat, facing the fireplace. David emerged from his lonely TV corner and stepped behind the couch to massage Holly's shoulders.

"I'll take all the tension you have out, honey. I'll smooth out any of your painful knots," he said.

Turning another page in the magazine, Holly wiggled her shoulders away from his kneading fingers, but David leaned over and put his hands on her breasts.

"I'm busy, David. Go away."

Since her response had been a quiet one, he crouched behind the sofa and nibbled on her ear. What she'd actually said didn't matter to him. The softness in her voice had tricked him and a green light turned on in his loins. Standing up, he went over to the stereo to pick out what he thought would be a turn on for her; an old instrumental track from Pink Floyd. The music drifted out of the house speakers, and he lowered the lights in the room, while Holly switched on a lamp on the coffee table in front of her. David shrugged. He wasn't ready to give up the fight quite yet. Moving back behind the couch, he reached out and turned off the light she'd just put on. Crouching down again, he whispered in her ear.

"Remember those magnificent nights we used to have? You were my savior tonight with Dad, and I think we should start up a new chapter in our relationship."

He paused to slurp at his bottle of beer. Forming the next enchanting line in his mind to allow him to unlock her fleshy doors into her delightful and heaving heaven, he slid his hand along the curve of her neck. Without enough light to read, Holly's concentration was finally redirected to David. That was what he wanted after all. Squatting behind the couch, he didn't see the faint blue light rising up in her eyes.

He was planning his next move. He would jump over the back of the couch and snuggle up to her and describe a Tantric position they'd used in the past. Holly remained stationary and silent and David thought she was mesmerized. Rising up from his squat, the back of her left hand connected with the side of his face. His bottle of beer sailed through the air with the greatest of ease to shatter against the front door. The profound force in her backhanded slap transported him over the top of the love seat five feet behind him and he kept on going. This unforeseen flight ended when his head met the bricks surrounding the fireplace in the far wall.

Looking over her shoulder, Holly saw him unconscious on the floor. Able to assess the damage her action had caused by simply looking at him, she knew the injury to his neck wasn't permanent. He'd be out for another three hours, and his hangover would be a little bit worse as the day wears on. She sighed. With a tinge of regret, Holly flicked the table-light back on. Having struck him a bit too hard, she would have to fine tune her abilities. In the future she would respond perfectly in any upcoming situation. Whistling along with the obscure melody floating through the air, she resumed reading the article.

6:25AM Friday November 26, 2004 Bass River, Massachusetts

The Donnellys paid her well. Mirabelle's overall disinterest in the secrets of the people who employed her was highlighted in her resume and it landed her the job. During the four years she'd been there, a wintry bleakness in the atmosphere of the mansion always surrounded her, but she hadn't seen many secrets hidden in the closets she'd cleaned.

Years ago a man had been bludgeoned to death and his body had been found on the kitchen floor in his multi-million dollar house in Easthampton. The electrician hired to install the security system of the estate was suspect, as he was having sex with the murdered man's wife. The investigation revealed that the adulterer had implored her lover to slaughter her better-half. Two years later, the homicidal wife died from cancer and her electrician rotted in jail. Mirabelle had read about the tragedy in the news and the moral was clear to her. Maintain a discreet distance from whoever she was working for.

She knew Mrs. Donnelly was having an affair, but she didn't really consider that a secret. In Mirabelle's head everyone cheated when they got married. Adultery was an integral part of the drama of marriage as it infused the contract with even more excitement. Nevertheless, she would not talk about April's transgressions to anyone.

There was a soft breeze in the crisp air and it was certainly a beautiful day. Her car left an impressionistic wake of swirling leaves in the draft behind it as she drove up the curved road to work. It was 6:30AM when Mirabelle drove in and parked in the lot set aside for the help. Besides Tuesday, she went through the exact same thing every morning. Hurrying to the side door, she used her key to get in. Once in a while, the Donnellys would hold lavish charitable events on the estate. That would necessitate bringing in a lot more workers, so Mirabelle walked past a utilitarian looking dining room near the kitchen where the expanded staff would have their meals. Farther along the same corridor, she opened the heavy door of a walk-in closet. She took out the cleaning cart. Since Vince had cleaned up the kitchen the night before, she pushed cart into the dining room. Pausing, she closed the serving window. Pieces of pastry were crumbled on the carpet in the corner of the dining room. That did not slow her down at all as she used the central-vacuum to suck it up in a flash, and the faint purring from the motor in the basement hadn't intruded on her ability to hear Robert's motorcycle engine rev up outside. She was surprised. Why would he zoom away so early in the morning? Taking off the attachment she'd used to clean up the crumbs, the roar of the Harley faded away. She kicked a button near the floor and the long vacuum hose was sucked back into the wall.

April was resting in her personalized suite of rooms on the second floor of the mansion. A sauna, steam room, dining alcove, kitchenette, and a sitting room as well as the main bedroom comprised her small apartment and Latham had the same thing farther down the hall. Robert's early departure hadn't awakened either of them. The suites were far enough away from the auto court to prevent that possibility.

Sometimes Heinem's bio-chemists come up with remedies that work too well, and they would never reach the mass market. However, some of these miraculous inventions do find their way to Latham's bathroom cabinet. Waking up a few minutes after ten, he staggered straight into the bathroom and he opened the large mirrored door above the sink. The oddly marked pill bottles standing at attention on the shelves in front of him would allow him to mask or relieve almost anything that was bothering him. He picked one out, and opened it, popping two pills down his throat even before he urinated. In fifteen minutes, his hangover would be gone and a jolt of healthy energy would replace it. Showering and dressing, he ordered coffee from the kitchen on the intercom. In six minutes, Mirabelle knocked on his suite door with a large carafe. Sipping the fresh java, he dialed the family lawyer to tell him about the revisions he wanted to his will and Attison told him the changes could be inserted in only a week and all he needed was his signature. Hanging up, Latham was relieved. Robert wasn't going to throw the family money around willy-nilly when he was gone. The non-existent bugbear that Holly had inserted into his head the night before was gone, and he went back to mulling over his possible relocation to Russia.

His feelings towards his family were shifting like the sand dunes in the Sahara. If he had ever loved his wife, that fleeting affection had turned to disgust with April's third pregnancy. For the sake of his reputation he'd endured her, even if that sanctioned her adultery, but those days were over. If the up-coming divorce plasters the whole family's dirty laundry across the front pages of all the tabloids and the news shows on TV, it wouldn't bother him. He'd become untouchable in the corporate world, and only his crazy schedule and years of familiarity that had stayed his hand thus far.

When Attison had met him two months ago at the main headquarters to tell him about the company's possible encroachment into Russia, and that he'd be in charge of the commercial invasion, the lawyer had painted an adventure for him in his head. It had goaded him into calling a realtor to talk about selling the estate on Bass River Road, and he secretly began divorce proceedings against April. With some malicious timing, he could fly off to a different country and leave his wife behind, dumbstruck and broke. Latham stepped over to a window overlooking his property. As cumulus clouds raced over his manicured backyard, they'd magically transformed the green grass into a tapestry of light and dark, but he was blind to the natural beauty as he busily calculating his next move.

April walked into the dining room, hoping to have breakfast with Bertie. The room was empty. Entering the kitchen, Mirabelle was arranging fruits and pastries on a platter.

"Have you seen Bertie?" April said, picking up a spray of cherries in the pile of fruit.

"Good morning, Mrs. Donnelly. Would you like something to eat? Vince is out shopping, so I could rustle something up for you. Oh, I'm sorry. Robert left around seven this morning, I believe. I assumed it was his motorbike I'd heard."

"Did you talk to him before he left?" April instantly dropped the cherries on the counter.

"I didn't see him at all. I just heard the engine outside."

"Okay. Alright, I'm going to check on that . . ." and as April left the room, her walk changed into a run.

When she reached Robert's old room, she was breathing hard. No one responded to her knock and she tried the door. It was unlocked and she walked right in. The bed hadn't been slept in and one of the crystal bottles they'd used the night before holding the cognac was shattered on the floor. Inhaling the powerful smell of the liquor puddled under the broken glass, she saw the matching decanter teetering on the window sill across the room. Small pieces of glass grinding under her feet, she stepped farther into the room, and her body weight ended the debate as the other bottle fell off the sill. Splintering into hundreds of shards as it fell to the floor, April's hands covered her cheeks in distress. She moaned. What Holly had told Latham must have been the truth; otherwise Bertie wouldn't have ridden away like that. Trembling, she worried if he'd even made it home and she felt worse. It was clear that Robert didn't care how *she* was going to feel, leaving her alone and forgotten and no one really cares about her at all. The silly feeling of '*oh woe is me*' went on for a minute or two until the concept of her lover intruded into her head. Remembering the romantic tryst they'd talked about on the phone the night before, got rid of her anxiety about her son's selfishness. She lifted her head and gazed through the window. It was a beautiful day out there. She should go out to the garden and see if there was any wind damage from the storm the night before as Mirabelle would get rid of mess in the guest room in short order.

Latham watched April walk into the garden maze, and whatever patience he had left for her was gone. That phone call from Carmen in the middle of dinner last night was unconscionable. He knew exactly where her personal phone book was, and it seemed he had a good opportunity to check things out. Leaving the suite, he strolled along the corridor to April's complement of rooms, opening the door and walked through the sitting room and into the main apartment. He slipped into her bedroom. The palm-sized pink phone book sat on the nightstand next to her bed.

He winced. Digging through her stuff behind her back made him feel like a louse, yet he couldn't stop himself. He needed to know how virulent the truth was behind the bullshit April had slung at him last night. Looking up Carmen's phone number, he entered it into his own cell phone as he glanced out a window to make sure April wasn't on her way back to the house. He put the phone book on the table where he'd found it, and he slithered away like a snake in the grass.

Back in his own suite, he refilled his coffee cup and lay back in a massage chair. He had no idea what Carmen's schedule was. It was possible she could pick up his call in the middle of the day, and he had to come up with an excuse to mask his real motivation for calling her. He punched in the numbers.

"Hello."

"Hello, is this Carmen?"

"Yes it is, and who am I speaking to?" There was ferocity in her voice.

"Forgive me. I'm Mr. Donnelly, I'm April's husband. You called April last night and since she's tied up today, she asked me to call you to give you the information she forgot to give you last night."

"I was at a benefit last night. I didn't call anyone."

"Oh dear. Well, I guess everyone at the dinner table last night must have been a bit too happy. I am so sorry to bother you. We have had a communication breakdown," and he chuckled. "I guess I heard the name wrong. Again, forgive my interruption as I give you a belated Happy Thanksgiving and say goodbye."

"Yeah, okay, I guess. It all sounds pretty weird. Maybe I should call up April later on. I haven't talk to her for years. Anyway, I have to get off the phone too." Carmen sounded squeezed and she was talking faster by the second.

"Alright my dear, no worries. Have yourself a great day."

Latham could care less about how the woman felt or even if she was going to call up April. Softly replacing the wireless receiver back in its cradle, he broke the connection with a tap. So April was having another affair . . . maybe it's the same guy she had sex with twenty-nine years ago.

The duplicitous call interrupting his Thanksgiving dinner the night before had galvanized Latham Donnelly. The impending cruelty he'd planned for April had ratcheted up another notch, and pulling the financial rug right out from under her feet was no longer good enough. Now he was going to take the floor under the rug out as well, so she'd fall into the basement and break her neck.

10:15PM Monday November 29, 2004 Las Vegas, Nevada

A mile from the pyramid crowning the Luxor casino and hotel, the pulsing neon lights on the main strip didn't make it to the darkness on Lamb Boulevard. On that dingy thoroughfare, the garbage-ridden alley between Fred's Fast Draw Bar and the pawn shop next door was even drearier. Earlier, a scofflaw had tossed the last of their lunch through the window of their car and the crumpled paper bag was haphazardly kicked down the same filthy alleyway by a passerby. More time went by. Something must have gotten in to gnaw at the decaying hamburger meat, as the bag was moving around way too much for the wind to be responsible.

The owner of Fred's Fast Draw Bar continued to ignore the garbage piling up in the alley next to his establishment. Every couple of months, the city would write out a citation and fine him for the unsanitary conditions in the alley. Fat and happy on Fred's negligence, the creature inside the paper bag had suddenly stopped gorging. Something was going on only three yards away, and it peered through the crumpled opening to blurrily watch an appalling drama unfold. Tantalizingly close, it sniffed at the warm rivulet of blood breaking away from the growing pool. Its tiny heart rate sped up with nervousness and excitement. The scavenger didn't understand the conversation the men were having way above its head, but it grasped the threat in their voices; a signal more food would soon arrive.

"Didn't Cindy tell you about this? The date was the twenty-eighth, Jake. *I spelled it out for you last month,*" as Lazzo accentuated his words with an upper cut into the man's thorax. "Found you yesterday in Washington's strip club on Randall Avenue, and that was after you told us you were going to meet us at seven-thirty at the coffee shop on Third. Nope . . . you did not make that meeting! You were . . . not **. . .** there!" Two more punches emphasized the latest admonishment. He let Jake go, and the man collapsed. Edgar, Lazzo's partner, stepped over and kicked him in the head.

"Laz, are you sure Sinderella told us to write this guy off?" A huge smile was plastered on Edgar's face.

"You know you're not supposed to use her old name, Eddie," Lazzo said. He hoisted poor old Jake off the ground again with one hand under his collar. He leaned him back against the wall. "Cindy don't wanna remember her dancing days. If she ever hears you talking like that, you'll be sorry. "Then Lazzo's voice got louder, "As to your other question, yeah, she did tell us to shut this relationship down." His next two words were directed to Jake, "Sorry dude."

Badly injured, and barely conscious, the man was trying to beg for his life. "Ple . . . plea . . . aagh . . . magh."

Lazzo let go of him again, and he slowly slid into a pile of brown plastic bags stuffed with garbage. Edgar looked up and down the alley. He even checked the two grimy windows set high in the east wall. *No one was watching*. Reaching under his jacket, he took the hand gun out of his shoulder holster. Lazzo had left his boot on the man's throat, even though the recalcitrant gambler wasn't going anywhere on his own at that point, but when Edgar screwed a silencer onto the muzzle of his gun, Lazzo moved away. Bending down slow and easy, he pressed the gun to the prostrate man's forehead and pulled the trigger. An extremely brief sibilant hum followed the bullet into Jake's brain.

Ms. Cindy Grayson had arrived in Las Vegas in 1990. At the age of twenty-one, her long strawberry blonde hair, big green eyes and oversized breasts turned out to be the perfect tools she needed to climb the ladder in the world of an exotic dancer. Unlike most of her competition, she held the unusual card of double-jointed fluidity up her sleeve. Cindy could wind around those poles and wriggle across the stage like a sexually hungry sidewinder. Contorting her serpentine body into rarely seen and never forgotten poses, her audiences found her breathtaking. She displayed her intimate flowers for a growing fan base, enjoying their appreciative whistles and claps. Her stage name had been Sinderella.

The wealthiest and most powerful bookmaker in town fell for her hook, line and sinker. He lived with her for two years and then he decided to marry her. Three weeks after the ceremony, an aneurism bulging out of the side of an artery coming out of his heart let go and the following internal flood stopped his heart.

Cindy's intellect had been cleverly hidden behind her mesmerizing emerald eyes, but she knew it was time to peel off the baby doll disguise. Just like a seasoned wrangler tying up a calf in a rodeo, she scooped up all the legal and illegal reigns of her departed husband's businesses. She took full control faster than a snake bite, and the scavengers were left hungry at the gravesite.

Retiring from stripping, her new business offices were located behind a private dinner club on Freemont Road. Ms. Grayson's inherited enterprise was extremely well-run, even thriving under her dominion. At the age of 35, Cindy appeared civilized and gracious with a wink in her eye. She'd use her sultry voice to invite customers in to close the deal, and the interest on her loans was the lowest in town. No one thought about what could happen to them if they were late on their payments to her. They didn't want to think about men like Lazzo or Edgar.

A noxious version of existentialism flowered in their minds as the paid assassins strolled nonchalantly back to the street without a second thought over their actions. Jake sank deeper into the pile of garbage bags on the side of the alley like a forgotten pile of wet laundry, and to Lazzo and Edgar, the body could have been there since the beginning of time.

"Should we go to Ventura or Caesars?" Edgar said.

"Did you see that?"

"See what?"

"It was the size of a small dog!" Lazzo was pointing into the darkness. "I watched it run right out of a paper bag . . . right . . . over . . . there. I almost tripped on it."

"Sorry, I wasn't looking. Come on, where should we go?"

Blown away by the size of the rat, Lazzo wanted to see it again and he was scrutinizing the rubbish against both walls. He didn't know their heinous act had turned the already dark shadows in the alley, pitch black. There was no way he was going to see *anything* in that iniquitous ink. Giving up his pointless search, he off-handedly answered Edgar's question.

"Wherever . . . I don't care. You pick it. We'll just go and relax."

Samuel paid off his debt to Cindy as fast as he could. Letting go of the tiny flat on 11th street, the Ventura was Samuel Eveland's favorite casino. He was staying in the presidential suite on the thirty-third floor. The borrowed money had been all he needed. Whether an angel was on his side or he was gifted with the luck of the damned, the eight thousand dollars had expanded exponentially. Defying the odds, the house was not winning. The associates comprising the consortium controlling the casinos on the strip were watching him like hawks. He hadn't done anything out of the ordinary, so they pampered him a little bit longer. They were confident his streak of good luck would run out soon.

Samuel was sitting on the overstuffed chair in his luxurious rooms, and he had a glass of champagne in one hand and a young woman named Willow McCabe in the other. Her sequined dress wrapped around her body like a python, and most of her creamy skin was exposed. Besides the mint the maids placed on the satin pillows of his king sized bed every day, Willow was another perk the Casino gave him to enjoy.

"Isn't it time for dessert? My guess is you're probably hungry. We go out for a stroll and see what we can stuff down our gullets, hmm?" Samuel spoke with a contented drawl. Putting the champagne glass down and letting go of the girl, he stepped into the walk-in closet to pick out a suit to wear.

Under a palm tree near a man-made waterfall on the main floor of the Ventura, Edgar and Lazzo sipped on their Long Island Iced Teas. Remaining uninspired by the normal ebb and flow of customers milling around them, they perked up when they saw Samuel Eveland and Willow.

At 6'4", Lazzo was a rock. He diligently goes to the gym every day to maintain that physique. Edgar was a lot shorter than Laz. He was only 5'10", but his innate speed and sadism held the peculiar balance between them in place. Two legs of the tall stool Lazzo was sitting on were off the floor. His shoulders were pressed against the wall behind him to hold the position, and smoke rising from the thin cigar in his mouth lazily drifted away. The big man was wearing a tan cotton suit and a snake skin belt. Three golden chains, each one weighted down by a cross, disappeared into his chest hair.

Sockless, Edgar wiggled his toes inside his loafers. It made him feel free. Hours ago he'd neatly tucked a long-sleeved black silk shirt into the waist band of some khaki pants held up by a gold belt. The dried spots of Jake's blood staining the right cuff of his pants were barely noticeable.

Parading passed the deadly duo, Samuel felt like royalty in his well-tailored charcoal silk suit with a high-priced escort under his arm. He looked straight at them and nodded. He had no idea who they were . . . at least for now.

Shaking a menthol cigarette out of a platinum case, Edgar lit it up and made an impressive line of smoke rings out of his first exhale.

"So there goes Sammy the winner," he said. A sardonic smile appeared on his face, while his eyes turned to steel. "I still can't believe he hasn't come back for more money yet." Willow was affectionately leaning closer to Samuel as they sashayed through the main doors and onto the strip. Edgar had been enjoying at least part of the couple's departure as he was riveted to the hypnotizing swing of Willow's sequined derriere.

"No one knows how he's doing it, but I hope he makes it through 'cuz he's an older guy and things get tougher when you're older," Lazzo said. Edgar looked across the table at his partner and sniggered.

"You'd like a fairytale ending for him wouldn't you? He can't stop gambling, you numbnuts. Sooner or later he'll start losing and we'll see him back at Cindy's door." Whistling up a cocktail waitress, he ordered another brace of drinks.

The Long Island Iced Tea was one of their favorite drinks, and they'd gotten used to it. For the uninitiated, it's a wolf in sheep's clothing. Sweetly spiced in a flavorful disguise, it rolls over the taste buds as a 16 ounce, non-alcoholic sugar sweetened iced tea and the tender taste invites you in for a swim. Margarita mix and Coca-Cola were collaborators, holding hands to support its placid surface while a gang of sharp toothed spirits circled beneath. A shot of vodka, a shot of gin, a shot of rum, and a shot of tequila are blended in the tall glass with a soupçon of triple sec. Still sober enough to order another one, the posse is already inside your castle walls, silently and speedily robbing you blind. After drinking the second one, the larger crew can burn down what was left of your house to the ground.

8:00PM Friday December 3, 2004 Finalhaven, Maine

A corporate lawyer, a trustee, *and* the Chairman of the Board of the Hienem Pharmaceutical Corporation, he has as many heads as a hydra. No one really knew what Attison Korybante's true age was. With his own intervention, the DMV in Delaware printed 12\21\55 on his driver's license, indicating that his current length of time on this planet was 49 years. His un-dyed dark hair fell across his brow and curled over his shirt collar without a single strand of grey. His ancestry was another mystery, and he would never answer any questions in that regard. Attison's name and swarthy complexion harkened back to a bloodline from Greece or Italy, however there's no proof to support the connection.

Attison owned about seventy-five percent of Finalhaven, a small island off the coast of Maine, equaling 44 acres. The northeast coastline of the island was rock ridden, besides a thousand feet of uncluttered sandy beach. Two tiny picturesque islets, dotted with their own small portion of fir trees were right off to this seamless beach. You skip a stone across the water and hit one. Attison owned the sandy beach, the islets and the rest of the northeast coast of the island.

Thousands of years ago, receding glaciers had thoughtfully gouged out a cove on the west side of island. Erecting a dock in the natural harbor, Attison's yachts were moored there during the short summers.

He'd built his manor on a pre-existing elevation and it over lorded the Atlantic Ocean. Made out of concrete dyed soft beige, the reddish brown shingles melted around the complex edges of the roof like warm brown butter. Heavily reinforced, the structure had weathered through the storm ridden winters pristine.

The interior was graced with every nuance. The first floor boasted a great room, living quarters, two kitchens, an oversized pantry and a health spa with an Olympic size swimming pool, as well as a hot tub, steam room, sauna, and an exercise room. Covering 14,000 square feet of living space, the extravagance seemed redundant for one individual, but Attison's wants and needs were inscrutable. He owned another place in Belize, and one more in England, but the island property, remote and frozen for a major part of the year, was his favorite. The echoing bastion reminded him of the fictional Fortress of Solitude.

Floating in his whirlpool, jets of water pounded on his back. A mobile phone and an antique goblet filled with absinthe perched at the edge of the pool. Absinthe was banned in America in 1915 by an unsupported superstition, and the restriction wouldn't be lifted for another year. It didn't matter. Attison lived his life outside normal parameters. Not above the law, he was sideways to it.

Latham disliked his family, and that feeling was growing every day. Spearheading the venture in Russia looked like a final and ultimate escape from them and that infused him with excitement. Attison hadn't been completely sure if the project was going to happen or not after their phone call a week ago, and that uncertainty was niggling at Latham. He wanted to shore up his hopes, so he punched in a two number sequence on his office phone. A instant connection to Attison's personal line.

"Hello."

"Hello, Attison. Hope I haven't interrupted you?"

"Hello, Latham. None of your calls are interruptions. What can I do for you this evening?"

"Well, I've been thinking over Heinem's future in Russia. Last week you weren't positive if it was going to happen and I was wondering if things had gotten any closer to a final decision. It seemed to be a great opportunity for me at this point in my life."

Attison got out of the water and sat dripping on the edge of the whirlpool.

"Its good news, sir. During a conference call yesterday afternoon, the primary movers are all in agreement, and it's a go, Latham, it's a go. Sounds like you've already been bitten. If exploration is your cup of tea, then we'd be grateful for you to lead the operation."

"That's very good news! Thank-you. I've left my plans in neutral until I knew for sure, but now you've given me a direction, a good direction."

"I think we should have another meeting to hash out our strategy," Attison said. He grabbed a towel off a hook above his head and he dropped it over his muscular shoulders.

"I agree. Lets set it up, right now."

"My Jaguar has been re-painted and it's catching dust in one of my garages in Boston. I haven't had the time to even see what the new paint job looks like, and this is a wonderful excuse to put that car through its paces and answer my own curiosity. I'll drive over to the estate and we'll fine tune our tactics. Sound okay?"

"Perfect. Let's set a date," Latham said.

"How about the day after tomorrow, that would be the fifth?"

"Hmm . . . I'm supposed to be in the city tonight, but I'll be done with the licensing problems by tomorrow afternoon. There shouldn't be any problem for me to get back and meet you at Bass River on Sunday."

"Fine Latham, I'll see you there."

1:30PM Sunday December 5, 2004 Finalhaven, Maine

As he ran across the roof of his manor to jump into the waiting aircraft, Attison's long coat was blown sideways by the wind generated by the rotating blades of the helicopter. The pilot dropped him off an hour later at Logan International Airport, and a limousine was waiting for him there. Dropping him off at the garage downtown, he walked up the ramp to the second level as his footfalls echoed in the cavernous building. The Jag was parked in the back corner. When he got there, he eagerly rolled back the dust cover. Aquamarine. They'd used a lot of fine silver, gold and bronze flake in the mix, developing a heavy metallic sheen and the extraordinary color was deep, so deep it was haunting. Attison was pleased. He opened the driver's side door and tossed his briefcase on the passenger seat. Getting in, he started up the engine, and then he got out and took off his coat. He tossed that inside the car on top of the briefcase. Waiting for the engine to warm up, he intertwined his fingers and raised his hands over his head and stretched. He was looking forwards to the drive.

Attison took Exit 11 off the interstate onto Route 3, following the coast all the way to Cape Cod. Passing other cars with a seasoned touch, he was frustrated. There was too much traffic. He couldn't let the Jaguar breathe. Daylight was waning when he left Route 3 outside of Plymouth to hunt through a maze of smaller roads in his search. He ended up in the middle of St. Andish State Forest. He'd found what he was looking for: a well paved long straight-away with nothing around it but woods. His speed increased over 110 MPH. He was smiling.

A bloated moon was stuck on the horizon, and across the sky, the searing lip of the sun was slowly sinking out of sight. The last degree of lumens left of twilight intertwined with the curious fingers of our cold satellite and they both latched onto the glistening skin of the Jaguar. Whistling through the radiant cling of the celestial tag team, the car was unencumbered. Nothing would slow it down. As if the wheels were suspended a millimeter over the surface of the road, Attison Korybante pushed the Jag to 135.

After dealing with a long day to maintain the peace, he'd stopped at Carla's Coffee Bean to buy some donuts and a large regular coffee, so Officer Sellman could spend the last hour of his shift in the rest area on the straightaway through St. Andish State Forest. Local kids sometimes used that part of the road through the park to race. Sellman angled the radar and flicked it on and then he leaned back to enjoy his coffee. One more ticket would raise his weekly count to the crazy level the main office was insisted they all come up this. Parking there was a feasible excuse to ease him out of the rest of the day. He tossed his sunglasses on the dashboard, allowing himself to vigorously rub his temples and then he took a cinnamon bear claw out of the bag.

A gentle thump shook the patrol car and a half a second later a high-pitched whine needled into his ear. After a long breath of tomb-like silence, the birds started singing again, but the display on his radar gun was blinking. 137 . . . ***137***. He dropped the pastry like it was on fire, and he put the old cruiser in drive. Speeding out of the rest area as fast as he could, the bear claw jittered off the passenger side of the seat and onto the floor.

Negotiating a wide curve, Attison dropped to 95. The road straightened out again, and he returned the car to triple digits. Hearing a siren, Attison looked into his rear view mirror. A police car was attempting to overtake him, and he gently shifted the transmission down. He rolled the sports car to the side of the road and parked and then he turned off the engine. Watching the officer get out of his overheated car to walk aggressively towards him, Attison powered the car window down. He looked up politely as he greeted the uniformed man.

"Good evening, officer. What can I do to relieve your worried mind?"

Any local teenager couldn't have passed him like that. Sellman had been forced to push the old cruiser hard enough to make the frame creak and he'd heard the engine scream. He began to hear some awful loud metal pops; very disturbing noises, but he had a job to do and he could not . . . . slow . . . . down! Unable to outrun the Jaguar, he was relieved when he saw brake lights come on in front of him. In his short walk towards the vehicle, it appeared to be glowing, as if it had a ghostly light of its own and Officer Sellman got a funny feeling that something wasn't quite right.

"May I see your license and registration sir?"

While Attison reached into his jacket for his wallet, he looked up into the officer's eyes. Normally, Sellman would gage the dilation in the driver's pupils as a response to that stare, but this time sweat beaded up on his own forehead and his toes and fingers tingled. He felt extremely uneasy. An ancient knowledge he didn't even know he had awakened inside of him, while those shadowy eyes tenderly drew him in . . . *and he started to drift away*. Rapidly shaking his head, he snapped himself out of whatever it was, instinctively looking away from the face of man in the sports car. He didn't want to fall back in.

"I guess you know why I stopped you. You broke the speed limit and you broke it so badly a judge will probably put your license under suspension," Sellman said. Attison gave him his license and registration and Sellman walked back to his cruiser. The farther away he got from the parked car, the better he felt.

"Wait. Hold on, Officer. Would you mind coming back here for a moment," Attison's voice caressed him, yet the words were burrowing into Christopher Sellman's head like a swarm of tiny worms with razor sharp teeth. Returning to the Jaguar, Sellman was sure he was about to listen to the same mewling protestation of innocence he'd listened to a thousand times before; *I really wasn't driving that fast . . .*

"I really wasn't driving that fast. I can understand it may have seemed that way, as this is a fast looking car . . ."

Officer Sellman interrupted him. Already exhausted, he'd been forced to drive at breakneck speed against his own wishes and those two factors were responsible for the nasty edge in his voice.

"The legal limit on this road is forty-five. I clocked you at one-hundred and thirty-seven miles per hour, *sir*. It was digitally recorded on the radar," and he turned away again.

"I'd like to see the number on the gun."

"You don't need to see anything. It'll work out fine for you in court."

"You should know I'm a lawyer and I know what my rights in this situation are. I have the right to see the instrument, before you write anything down. What's your name, by the way?"

Sellman wasn't positive about the state law, so the blood sucker might be right. What difference would it make? If he wanted to look at the number, he could look at the number.

"Fine. I'll bring the gun over, and my name is Officer Sellman."

Inside the patrol car, he punched Attison's driver's license number and the vehicle plates into the on-board computer and then he took the radar out of its brackets. Waiting for the interesting history attached to . . . he checked the license, *Mr. Attison Korybante* to appear on the screen, he held the radar gun in one hand and tapped his free fingers on the dashboard. His interaction with Korybante had made him queasy, and when absolutely zilch came up on the screen, he felt even worse. How could *anyone* drive around in a car like that with nothing on their record? Well, whether he was an alien or an angel, his days of anonymity and blessedness were over. *And*, according to Officer Sellman, *it's about time the angel was finally caught in the cookie jar.* He got out of the cruiser with a smirk on his face, and the incriminating radar gun in his hand. Slamming the door hard enough to make the cruiser rock, he stamped back to the Jaguar. Officer Sellman held the radar at his waist so Mr. Perfect could clearly see the consequences of his evil ways.

"It's forty-five on the screen. You just told me that's the legal speed limit on this road. Maybe you're over-tired and seeing things that aren't there," and Attison had a tinge of disdain in his voice, as if he was talking to his truant son.

"You're the one that can't see!" Sellman said, and he turned the gun around to look at the display himself. Shocked by what he saw, he violently slapped the side of the gun with his hand, hoping that would fix the problem. It didn't work. *Damn it, how could the blasted thing be broken? It had to malfunction at the worst possible moment? This nerve-wracking pursuit was utterly pointless?!*

Sagging into the side of the Jaguar, his belt holding handcuffs and a gun could be scratching the paint job, but Attison wasn't worried about it.

"It seems there won't be problem for me in court after all. You're going to have to accept this disappointing number on your little screen with aplomb. Officer Sellman?" Attison then began to sound sympathetic. "I know you're at the end of your shift. You need to return to your car and close your eyes and have a catnap. I've got a meeting to get to and I think it's time we go our respective ways. Don't you agree?"

Sellman rallied, exasperated. He got out of his unprofessional slouch on Attison's sports car, straightening up and standing tall.

"You *were* speeding. I know it and you know it, but something went wrong with the radar. You're very lucky. Racing around like a madman will wreck your life and sooner or later you'll crash and burn and I pray to God you won't take anyone else with you!"

Hard-driven and badly over-heated just like his cruiser, he stomped away with his shoulders badly hunched up.

"You need to wind down and enjoy the rest of the evening, Christopher," Attison said. Officer Sellman faltered in his final retreat. He didn't know why Korybante would know his first name, but he kept on walking. He wasn't going to turn back and ask him. This disquieting mystery would remain unsolved and that was fine. He wanted to forget the entire incident and it would be peachy keen if he never saw Attison Korybante ever again. In the future he'd park someplace else to relax and drink his coffee.

Back in his car, he looked down at the number on the radar gun. *It was supposed to be 137, damn it!* He looked down at the pieces of pastry on the floor mat and that made him groggy. After only sixty more seconds, a profound sleep overwhelmed him.

Looking in his side view mirror, Attison saw Sellman stumble as he walked back to the police car. He started the engine and checked his watch. Patiently waiting for three more minutes, he then dropped the transmission into first gear. He pushed the gas pedal down, and he left two streaks of rubber on the asphalt. A flippant adios.

"Ah, it's always nice to let the wild things run with nothing to hold them back," Attison thought. The Jaguar reached 60 mph in less than four seconds as the natural beauty of the state owned forest on the other side of the car windows melted into an abstract blur.

Looking at the clock in the dashboard, Sellman realized he'd been out for at least half an hour. He got out of the car. He heard nothing but rustling leaves. Walking over to the spot where the sports car had been parked, he could make out two dark streaks on the pavement in the moonlight. Korybante had burned them there in defiance of his presence and he'd slept right through it. Returning to the cruiser, he straightened things up and checked in with central dispatch. Putting the radar gun back into its cradle on the dashboard, he paused. The screen wasn't registering 45 anymore, and he held it in his lap for a long time. It read 137, as if nothing had ever gone wrong.

He never told anyone about that day but his wife. The other guys would have ribbed him for years, or worse, hinting he'd flipped out and made the whole thing up. He'd put in a requisition to replace the defective radar gun, having come up with an explanation that had nothing to do with the truth. Waiting for the replacement, the 'broken one' worked perfectly. Not a glitch.

While the chronological distance from a painful memory increases, the emotional irritation decreases, but Officer Christopher Sellman would never be completely free. Like a poisonous flower blooming in his mind's eye, Attison kept driving that ghostly Jaguar into his dreams with the regularity of a full moon.

6:15PM Sunday December 5, 2004 Bass River, Massachusetts

Latham glanced over at the grandfather clock. There was no way he could cement his role in the company's expansion until he talks to the Chairman of the Board to iron out all the kinks, and Attison was supposed to have arrived at 6:00 PM. Twenty years ago, he'd guided the growing company to greatness, however he'd turned into a bored shepherd to the hulking goliath. He needed a time-machine to land himself back when Heinem was just starting out, and working on the project in Russia would allow him to become the conniving shark he used to be. It was also the ideal bolt hole. He could shed the family he no longer needed or cared for, like dry skin.

It was 6:25. He started to pace until he looked over at the clock again. 6:35.

April had disappeared and Latham didn't care where she was. Probably having sex with her back door man. He hoped her lover boy didn't have a nickel to his name, as he was about to yank the silver spoon right out of her mouth.

6:40, and a resonating hum vibrated through the front window glass He polished off his martini and checked his appearance in the mirrored wall behind him. Turning away, he briskly walked to the the front door.

"Good evening, Latham, and please forgive my tardiness. I'm looking forwards to our evening of collaboration." Attison gave Latham a firm handshake, and then he put his arm across his companion's shoulders as they entered the great room.

"No problem, sir. I was running late myself. I knew you were going to get here sooner or later, whatever transpires on what you consider your personal race course." Latham was excited. "Well, was it a fire or flood this time?"

"A small disagreement about how fast I was driving."

"I will never understand how you get out of all those tickets, but I personally won't let you drive me anywhere again. The last and only ride I had with you after the meeting in Long Island City a few years ago was unforgettable, and that's a nice way to describe it," Latham said, laughing.

"You made your flight didn't you?"

"By the skin of my teeth, and it was miraculous that the heart-stopping ride didn't actually stop my heart. You must be a cat with nine lives. I really thought that getting older was going to slow you down, but I guess I was wrong! Want something to take the edge off the road trip?"

"I'd like an Irish coffee, thanks. Where is your wife? I'm guessing April must be excited and wired about the move."

Attison had wandered over to the koi pond and he was looking into the water as if he was reading the future in those shallow depths. He had on a black silk suit with an open white shirt, and he was physically stunning. The common stereotype of a middle-aged corporate lawyer doesn't usual evoke a vision of a Mediterranean lothario.

"April had a previous commitment, and right now she doesn't know anything about it," Latham said. Hitting the button on the intercom with a punch, he asked Mirabelle to bring out two Irish coffees, relieved he hadn't broken the device.

"I see." Attison was amused by Latham's brutality on the intercom.

Mirabelle sailed almost instantly, and she left the steaming drinks on the table next to the couch. There was a short silence. While they raised the coffee cups to their lips, Attison was fine-tuning what he was about to impart to Latham Donnelly. To him, the meeting didn't have much to do Heinem's expansion into Russia. Latham needed to understand what was at stake; taking this road would transform his life forever.

"True intelligence is a hidden attribute, yet the acumen behind all your decisions for Heinem over the years have panned out exceptionally well for the company and you are not hiding behind the curtains anymore. Your business perspicacity stands in the spotlight. You consider all the repercussions of any move you make, by surveying the game board twice. You've given us a solid financial base and spot-on forecasting."

"I'm honored by your praises. Thank-you, Attison." Suddenly infused with merriment, (an emotion scarcely seen in the Donnelly's home), he tilted his head back and mimed a bow.

"I've been looking up the economic trends in Russia during the millennium, and there's a shift towards . . ." but he stopped in the middle of the sentence, and the host overruled the industrialist. "Listen, Vince has left some dinner for us. If you're hungry, I'll have the dinner brought out for us right now, or perhaps you'd rather have more Irish coffee?"

"I'm fine for the moment, thank you, Latham. I think a drop of that cognac on the side board shall suffice. Tide me over for a few more minutes." Attison stood and poured the golden liquid into a large snifter he'd taken out of a rack on the table. "Heinem doesn't want to lose you during the new expansion, but it's extremely important that you re-consider your decision. Moving to Russia will take you away from your family for a very long time. Its possible April can meet you over there after the start up, but you won't be able to see any of your children for months and you'll be up to your neck with work. I know, I know, you put work in front of your personal needs, but I urgently advise you to weigh your options. It might be a long time before you slow down and enjoy the simple pleasures again. Maybe you should really consider having a heavenly vacation on one of your yachts or take a flight to some Polynesian island and play tennis with your family for a few months? You could watch a Broadway show if you wanted. Look, you've won. It's impossible to get any higher on the ladder. We don't have a lot of time on this planet. It's actually miniscule in the scheme of things. Since you can do *anything* you want, I advise you to enjoy yourself. The life force inhabits us, surrounds us and displays an endless list of miracles and mysteries right in front of our eyes, and I implore you to ignore day-to-day minutiae and dive into the magnificence. You could infuse yourself with the timelessness of the natural world. Of course, there are endless alternatives . . . you could buy a fast car so we could race."

Latham looked away and frowned. He got up and grabbed a poker to stir the embers of the fire. Flames crackled up and he returned the implement to its stand. Then he wrestled a log out of the nearby stack, tossing it on the burning pile.

"Look Attison, there have been a lot of things going wrong in my family for years. We don't need to discuss the details of my own dirty laundry right now, but I have a divisive problem in my marriage and Russia is the best option. A perfect escape, a brand new equation for me to solve. Heinem as always been and always will be the most powerful force in my life and my commitment to the company is my own reward. This separation from my family is a blessing, not a curse."

Latham's simplistic answer raised one of Attison's eyebrows in silent rebuke, contradicted by a faint smile.

"It seems you really do want to go through the metamorphosis, and I give you congratulations. You certainly have what we need to sink foundations into the bedrock of one of the biggest countries on planet earth."

Attison solemnly toasted his CEO's resolve with gravity in his words, and Latham didn't hear the soft sigh that followed.

Pressing the button with a much gently touch, Latham called the kitchen to order their dinner. Mirabelle arrived with a platter of rarebit, and she lit a Sterno flame under the dish, before she disappeared. The philosophical slant in their conversation devolved. Attison told Latham it would probably take at least a year to entrench themselves into Russia's monetary structure, and they were kicking the nuts and bolts around on how they were going to do it.

Latham knew it was time. It was time to pull Attison in and use his help to betray his entire family and his wife. He wanted to use the

Heinem Pharmaceutical Corporation as a foil, and he hoped that Attison would accept this duplicitous and vicious double-dealing plan with aplomb.

"I'm not sure what April is going to do and I don't care. I want to separate my holdings from any possible divorce decrees by creating an open-ended agreement with the company to buy this property and put my capital gains into an escrow account. We could insert a hidden clause in which the funds would revert back into my name in thirty-six months. Of course, nothing could happen without my notarized signature. Without it, the funds would rollover and stay in the company's holdings for another cycle. Another thirty-six months. If I die, the contract dissolves, and Hienem gets everything. You told me the command center is going to be in St. Petersburg. Is it possible the company might buy or build a new estate for me in Russia and camouflage my ownership in a bundle of LLC accounts somewhere in a back file in Heinem's assets?"

Attison laughed. "You've thought this whole thing out, haven't you? You absolutely don't want April or anyone else to live on your laurels, do you?"

"Well . . . yeah. I considered pulling Justin in, but he hasn't settled down, and he's not giving me any grandchildren. I'm starting to think there's something wrong with him. Anyway, what I do to about him is besides the point. Will you help me? I don't know if you're up to this kind of chicanery or not."

"Certainly, Latham, I'm more than happy to oblige. I'll slide it under the eyes of the board so fast they won't even read what they'd just signed. I'll follow your plan it to the letter, maybe refining it a little bit," Attison said, with a shrug. "You've done so much for us over the years. I think Heinem can shoulder this unusual transition without a burp. What's going on with the rest of your liquid assets?"

"I've already siphoned a chunk of it to some off-shore accounts in the Cayman Islands and Belize."

"I can accelerate the process for you. The remaining wire transfers will come out right as rain, perfectly legal. Would you like Hienem to absorb even more of your money temporarily? All sorts of things can happen in a complex international move like this," Attison said.

"I appreciate any support you feel like giving me. We could go through my business files tomorrow and you could wave your bureaucratic wand and send most of them into the next dimension. With your help Attison, my churlish family will at last understand the concept of independence." Latham pressed the intercom button and asked the housekeeper to bring out their espresso. "I hope the legal shuffling won't use up too much time?"

The clattering of the serving cart interrupted their conversation. Mirabelle cleared the dinner dishes off the table, and replaced them with a coffee service. Latham complimented her and Vince for the rarebit. She nodded politely and vanished. Attison served himself a cup of coffee and Latham lit a cigar.

"The whole thing should be done in sixty days; no worries," Attison said. His voice was calm and reassuring, but his eyes had darkened. Tiny black snakes could have coiled up and found a home his pupils, and the expression on his face was unreadable in the firelight.

12:25PM Friday February 11, 2005 North Dartmouth, Massachusetts

Parked across the street from the state offices in North Dartmouth, Robert Donnelly was huddled in his pickup truck. His eyes were closed, and he didn't want to go anywhere. Since he'd failed it miserably only a month ago, he didn't understand why he'd just taken the real estate examination again. The same envelope with the latest results would arrive in his mailbox, and he knew he'd screwed it up again. Opening his eyes, he watched thin lines of snow snake across road, pushed along by the same northern wind rattling the cab of his truck. Robert closed his eyes again, imagining his motorcycle throb between his legs while shrubbery and trees rushed past him on his dream road.

He hadn't felt well after the reunion in Bass River. Whittling his work load at Home Depot down to 20 hours a week, it was unfortunate he had to work a half day that afternoon. Exhausted every day from his nightly high wire acts on coke, he was spending more and more time hiding in the sprawling warehouse instead of working. So far, the floor manager hadn't noticed his disappearances, and Robert didn't care if he did. Five more minutes went by. He looked out at the colorless world and groaned. He started the truck engine.

Living through the afternoon at work, time dragged until it crawled to a stop, while fluorescent lights were buzzing like insects over his head. Mind-numbing minutes piled up against him like a wall of lead. Lining up the last gallon of latex paint on a shelf in aisle 12, he tossed the empty cardboard carton on the pallet behind him, almost screaming out in frustration.

An acquaintance had set up a birthday celebration that night at Heavy Turns, a biker bar in Dartmouth. He was looking forwards to making money at the party, and when he finally clocked out, he broke into a run. Getting inside the cab, he inserted his hand behind the rotting fabric on the ceiling to grab the small vial he'd hidden there. It used to give him a lift, but these days it meant a lot more. He had to use some to feel normal on his drive back to his rental in Fall River.

Heavy Turns was packed. Squeezing up to the bar, Robert ordered a shot and a glass of beer. Across the room, a young woman was waving at him, energetically weaving through the crowd to reach him.

"Where have you been?" she yelled.

"Great to see you, Jennie!" And Robert gave her a hug, "have you seen Mark?"

"I'm pretty sure he's sitting next to the dance floor very close to the stage."

Normal conversation was replaced with shouting matches as the Almost Brothers, a tribute band, pounded out music loud enough to make the floor was shake. Robert gulped his shot of whiskey at the bar, and then he carefully inched his way towards the dance floor. He was trying to make the beer stay in the glass. Seeing his collaborator at a table next to a group of gyrating girls on the dance floor, he made it over to him and sat down.

"How are things, Mark? Pick up any new orders?" Robert bellowed out.

"Hey, Robert, it's about time you got here! They're going nuts. You have it with you, don't you?"

"You're an idiot."

Swallowing the last of the beer in his glass, Robert wiped the foam off his lips with the back of his hand. They got up and wriggled through the crowd to a locked door in the back wall and Robert had the key. Stepping inside the storage room, they had the necessary privacy plus the walls held the decibels back enough for conversation. Robert divvied out the drug, and their talk was over in minutes. Leaving the momentary hideaway, they both went to work to get as many people as they could ridiculously high. And after that even higher.

Robert had contacts in the crowd, diverting more eager clients straight to him. After a profitable exchange outside in the parking lot, he'd come back inside to hang out at the bar and drink. Once in a while, he'd go to the bathroom and snort up a few more lines. The wad of greenbacks in his wallet was growing and he should have been happy. He should have been a lot of things, but the high levels of alcohol and cocaine in his blood stream was mucking him up. His neurons were endlessly injured in the skittering crossfire in a self-inflicted biochemical battlefield in his brain, and Robert's psyche was losing cohesion, emotional equilibrium almost gone.

The band stopped at 2:00AM. Most of the party-goers were gone, and Mark and Robert were in the back corner of the bar playing pool. Ears ringing from the excessiveness of the live band's exuberant output, the music coming from the in-house speakers seemed tinny and distant. During the evening, the snow storm of benzoyl methyl ecgonine had numbed them to the bouquet of spilled beer and half-eaten chicken wings overflowing out of one of the nearby garbage pails, numbed them to the fog of human sweat molecules suspended in the air, and yet this multilayered olfactory symphony was enough to make a hound dog howl.

To hold onto the infamous tickets to ferry over to the lonely paradise on the island called escape, they had to dampen or distort their own reality as fast as they could. Eventually arriving on those exotic shores, they would find ecstasy in their momentary dance while the land beneath their feet slowly sank beneath the waves.

"Damn it, Mark, you did not call that shot! It's my turn! We can't play this game by your rules."

"I *did* call it, you just didn't hear me, too busy staring at Sallie's ass when she walked into the kitchen. Don't you remember whistling at her when she picked up some crap in the corner? Nope, you didn't hear a fucking thing I said."

Sallie was one of the three cocktail waitresses called in to work that night, and she'd been moving like the wind during the entire party. The crowd was gone, so she could move even faster while she cleaned up her station. She wanted to go home. The double doors leading into the kitchen slammed open again and she raced past them in what was close to a sprint.

Robert looked at her. Then he looked at Mark.

"Alright, damn it, *go.* I know you're gonna screw up the bank shot you're about to shoot anyway," and he shook his head with frustration.

Mark won the first game. Robert knew he was going to win the next one; he just knew it. As the second game progressed, Mark missed a shot and Robert went on attack mode. He sank his three remaining balls, and the cue ball was lined up in front of the eight ball in a perfect straight shot into a corner pocket for the win.

"Wow, Rob, I'm impressed. Looks like you're gonna to get your fifty dollars back."

Robert Donnelly grinned. Rubbing blue chalk on the tip of his pool stick, he felt like it was about time he won something! He could tap the cue ball with the right amount of force at the right angle to end his busy day in triumph. The song coming out of the jukebox abruptly ended, and he was distracted. He didn't want to screw up his shot, so he waited for the next selection to come run for a minute or so. "Eleanor Rigby". He found his center and he bent down and shot the eight ball straight into the pocket. That was good, however the cue ball followed it down and that was bad, very bad. He'd lost the second game with a scratch shot, a very dumb mistake and a seasoned player like himself shouldn't have done it. Robert slapped the pool stick on the table with a loud bang. Mark cringed backwards.

"That's it. I've had it. I'm going to the bar to have one more drink. If you want to come along, *you're* buying." It was a thorny invitation.

"Sounds fine to me," Mark said quietly.

On his way to the main bar, Robert sang along with the melancholy lyrics of the song . . . *"Father Mackenzie writing the words for a sermon that no one will hear, no one comes neeaaar. Aaall the lonely people, where do they all come from . . . Aaall the lonely people where do they all belong . . . I look at all the lonely people . . .*

Most of the bar stools were empty, and Nick, one of Robert's best customers, was able to come straight over to them.

"What can I rustle up for you gents?" Working in high gear for over six hours, he was exhausted. Slightly rotund, he had pale skin and flaming red hair, and Nicholas was also the best bartender the management of Heavy Turns had ever seen.

"I'm bored of beer. I'd like to end the night with something different, but I don't know what I want," Robert said.

"I'd like to try something else too," Mark said.

Nick went over the many drink options stored inside his head, and he quickly came up with a great option for them.

"Wanna try a concoction I invented last week? I call it "Broken Glass". It'll give you a tinge of summer, and I'll only tell you that there's vodka in it. The rest of it will remain a mystery."

A memory of warm weather was more than enough to have them order the new drink. Waiting for Nick to mix and pour, Mark told Robert about his latest family soap opera.

"I gotta tell you what my sister did to me last week! The bitch told Glenda that I went to John's apartment in Boston, and since I didn't invite her to come along, she won't talk to me now. What kind of a loving sister would stab you in the back like that?"

The tidbit lit a long fuse inside Robert's soul and it began to smolder towards something as dangerous as cordite.

"What your sister did to you was tiddlywinks. Your whole family could hang out with the Brady Bunch, next to the pit of rattlesnakes I'm stuck with," Robert snarled, "and I know something I shouldn't know about what my father is going to do to me. He's going to take away all the money I was supposed to inherit."

Nick served their electric blue cocktails on the bar in front of them, and Mark instantly sipped at his. Robert just stared at the bubbles rising to the top of the glass.

"Hey, this tastes great. It's even the same color as swimming pools," Mark said. Nick couldn't acknowledge the compliment, as Robert kept on bellyaching.

"I'm nothing but crap according to Dad. Nothing but a piece of crap. He's gonna give all my money to my older brother. Finally straight for once in my life, he didn't even acknowledge it. Shit, I should have stayed high for the rest of my godforsaken life . . . maybe they'd treat me better." Robert was talking to his own reflection in the mirror above the bar, and Mark and Nick might as well have been potted plants.

"You gotta calm down, Rob, get a handle on things," Nick said. He placed his hands on the bar and straightened his arms, a posture to underline his upcoming advice. "It's never as bad as you think it is. Really, it isn't. Hey, maybe he'll change his mind." Picking up a work towel, he started cleaning the top of the bar with a worried expression on his face. He repeatedly glanced over at Robert.

"He'll never change his mind and he's about to change the will or he's about to and it's over. I'm over. He'll give it all to Justin or the damned lawyer. I'm nothing but a sack of shit . . . maybe I should stop him, stop him in his tracks. Hit him on his head or push him off a cliff, or something and even the score. Change his mind alright, wouldn't it! Yeah, I might . . ." Nick interrupted him.

"Rob, you can't talk like that. You have a lot of good things in your life." Attempting to make one of his customers feel better, in this case he was up against an unmovable force. "You're doing great now, aren't you? I'm guessing you made a bundle tonight. Why don't you just fly away? Vacation somewhere south of here, where it's warm, think about it, okay?"

"You're right, you're completely right. I've been dreaming about escaping and a vacation is the best ticket to ride, Nick . . . thanks. I just need a send-off and I think a funeral would be a perfect choice, a most satisfying get-away party I can think of. After that, I won't worry anymore . . . yup. I'm looking forwards it."

Sitting back on his barstool, Robert stopped talking and drank his glowingly blue cocktail and he was smiling like the Cheshire cat.

The real estate license examination results arrived in his mailbox four days later. Ripping it open, he read it and threw the piece of paper and the envelope into the fire burning in his wood stove. He went back to the kitchen and grabbed another beer out of the fridge.

3:30PM Friday February 11, 2005 Boston, Massachusetts

Thick clouds squatted on Boston's jagged high rises with irritation. The weather report predicted snow, and the barometer had plunged. The low pressure was responsible for increasing the pain in David Russell's neck and he was fuming. For the upcoming date with Holly at the Boston Park Plaza Hotel at five, he'd picked out a dark blue three-piece suit, a silk shirt in a lighter shade and a sapphire tie. The outfit would accentuate his eyes, and he absolutely positively didn't want a glaringly white brace around his neck. It would screw everything up, but he'd didn't have a lot of options. Without that ugly support, his bedroom eyes would squeeze closed in pain the entire time and he would look even worse.

His lawyer wasn't going to work for him anymore unless he gave him more money. The frantic messages he'd left on Latham's service had been utterly ignored. He was running out of options. He called Holly three days ago, howling to her that he was in dire straits. He was about to borrow half a million dollars from her father in thirty days, so why couldn't he drop a few bread crumbs for him right now? Holly had listened to David for a moment or two. She chimed in and told him she'd take the next weekend off and meet him at The Swan's Nest, a comfortable cocktail lounge on the first floor of the Plaza. She had a surprise for him!

Two and half years ago, using her own money, Holly had purchased a cottage on Nantucket, an island thirty miles south of Cape Cod. In January, she'd taken out a loan on the equity of the property for $100,000 dollars, knowing she'd pay some of her husband's legal bills in the near future. After David wailed at her on the phone, she went to the bank the next day and wrote out a check to be paid to the Parker Foundation; the law firm involved in his defense. She could have easily wired the money, but she wanted to go to Boston and play with David instead. He was amusing on occasion.

Parking in the hotel garage, Holly closed the door of the Mercedes and strolled towards the elevators as if she had on sneakers, not the five inch heeled purple boots from Prada. Without looking back, she lifted the keys over her shoulder and locked the car behind her.

The idea of spending a night or two in a motel would incite most women to bring along more than they really need, but Holly was not like most women. Intrinsically different from anyone else on earth, she'd brought almost nothing with her. A small bag with a long strap hung over her shoulder and it held makeup, lingerie, a small PC, a sequined clutch and a paperback on marine electronics written by Keith Fischer. She breezed through the access door and onto the streets of Boston and the minimal weight of her shoulder bag didn't slow her down. It was 4:45 PM.

The Park Plaza Hotel was situated at the intersection of Arlington Road and Stuart Street, and its understated entrance was on Arlington

Road. David was staying with an old college chum on Blackstone Street, and the apartment was only five blocks away from the Plaza. An easy walk. He was waiting for a break to cross the street, and the nip in the air had hunched David over. The afternoon light was almost gone, when he entered the Plaza. The lobby dripped in royal elegance; walls and ceiling papered in light gold and the granite tiles on the floor were pink and gray. A three tiered fountain sprouted in the middle of the concourse, adorned with marble nymphs and trickling water, while a crystal chandelier sparkled in the distance at forty-five feet above his head. For a second, he thought he'd passed through a time portal. A courtier with a white wig on his head in emerald studded robes might just walk around the corner.

The Swan's Nest's neon sign snapped his mind back to the modern world. Opening the glass door under the sign, he stepped inside the lounge. Drawn to a line of tables and chairs set up along an elongated window at street level, he sat down and ordered a martini . . . no, a double. He hadn't seen Holly in over three weeks, and any kind of buffer would soften the memories he had regarding the unwanted reminder of her unusual abilities clamped around his neck. He couldn't take out of the money pit he was in, and his license was on the edge of revocation. His blood pressure was rising by the second. The waitress put his martini on the table in front of him, and he guzzled it like water. She didn't have enough time to walk away before David ordered another double. It was 4:45, according to the clock above the bar.

And it was snowing. David saw it start to cover the grass in the park on the other side of Arlington Road until his eyes widened. He was struck by the vision of his wife striding down the sidewalk towards the hotel entrance, and the wind was coyly tugging her black cape away from her body exposing her purple mini dress. Her long legs were revealed clad in black stockings with purple cashmere legwarmers riding halfway up her thighs. Holly had on fingerless gloves made from the same material, and a meaningless thought popped into David's head; at least her palms and knuckles were warm. For a few seconds, she was inches away from him on the other side of the glass and he could see snowflakes melting on her glossy black hair. It all looked staged. She had to be a model on some fashion shoot, not a run-of-the-mill hospital bureaucrat, and he didn't understand why he'd never gotten used to the sight of her. Watching her effortlessly sail along the sidewalk, he was still stunned even after all those years. Then his curiosity kicked in, driving him into calculating how much money she'd put on her back that day. The outfit had to be Yves St. Laurent, or maybe Ralph Lauren, so it was around three to five thousand dollars. She'd probably picked out cheaper stuff to assuage his pennilessness, and he quickly ordered another drink.

The long mirror above the bar had etchings of swans crooning or nesting or flying, and the other walls in the room were adorned with more mirrors decorated in the same way. Cushy sofas and armchairs sat in conversational groupings, and recessed spotlights illuminated different areas of the room. Holly stood in the brightly lit landing in front of the coat check, waiting for the girl to give her a receipt. Everyone in the lounge, including the bartender and the waitresses, were gawking at her. Restrained by the neck-brace, David had to twist painfully around in his chair to see what was attracting so much attention. Since she'd just flashed by him on the street outside, he really should have known and he winced at his own idiocy. His dark angel had fluttered to earth.

Gliding over to him, Holly stopped behind the back of his chair, and he felt a feathery kiss on his cheek. He stood up and embraced her, not knowing if she'd mimicked his botched attempt at seducing her months ago.

"Holly! You're right on time, it had to have been an easy drive. Can I order you a drink?"

"Hello, dear. Oh course, thank-you, I'd like a Cosmo," and Holly frowned, "I really thought you'd be done with that brace by now and yet there it is."

Tossing her bag over the back of the chair, she dropped into the seat. David motioned to the waitress to come over, and he ordered their drinks. Sitting on the other side of the small table, he leaned closer to her. He was about to ooze out mountains of obsequiousness, and he'd use every weapon in his personal arsenal to coax her into getting him out of the hole he was in. Somehow, someway. Maybe she could get to Latham again.

"I'm sorry about the brace honey, but the snow storm pulled the barometer down and my neck pain is a consequence. If it was a clear spring day, I'd be a suave and well-dressed neurosurgeon on the prowl for you . . . without this awful thing around my neck. If it weren't for the weather, you'd already be in my net. The current situation has transformed me into a woebegone hack, and I can't even visualize women like you in my dreams." To David's relief, Holly began to laugh.

"What you've said is ridiculous, and you look fine. I just thought you'd be healed by now. Hold on a sec, I have a possible answer for your problem. Last week I met a physical therapist at the hospital and she told me all about a new kind of massage they're using in the rehabilitation of all cervical sprains. She even explained the entire thing to me in precise details. Mind if I try it on you? It might free you from this pain once and for all. With any luck you'll never have to put that irritating thing back on your neck again."

Whether she'd done it intentionally or not, she'd crept up behind him again and bent over his shoulder to plant another kiss on his cheek. His paranoia bloomed. He heard something in her soothing words that hadn't been there . . . *rid him of his pain once and for all, and how* ***exactly*** *would she get that done?*

"Okay, I guess," David said. He bowed his head and removed the brace. She started massaging the tendons and muscles in his neck. The young women who'd taken their order was still nearby cleaning off table tops, and Holly didn't want anyone to see what she was about to do. She patiently waited until the waitress went back to the bar.

"Your touch is amazing, sweetheart. I think its really working," So far, Holly's miraculous massage wasn't fixing anything, and David was lying between his teeth. That was about to change. The waitress had gone and there weren't any customers close enough to matter.

What happened next had absolutely nothing to do with the non-existent therapist Holly had not talked to at the hospital. A light grew in her eyes and at the end of her fingertips, and it quickly flared up in intensity, suddenly conspicuous in the dimly lit lounge. No one saw it. An uncommon kind of heat radiated out of Holly's fingers straight into the injured part of her husband's neck. This supernatural warmth swirled around his cervix for at least five seconds and David's face went slack. Whatever was wrong inside *let go*, and the damage and the pain resulting from it was gone. A bit regretfully for her earlier overuse of her power, Holly had completely cured him.

"No, Holly, *I'm serious*. The new massage thing you heard about really worked. Nothing hurts. I can feel it, it's vanished!" The emotion in David's words squashed the acting job he'd done two minutes ago.

The radiance in her eyes faded, and Holly smiled. The ongoing pain resulting from her misjudgment that day in the past had been resolved and she was content.

David looked at the brace on the table. He didn't need it anymore and that was wonderful, but he certainly wasn't free. The consequences of the days he'd done surgery drunk were circling him like bureaucratic sharks, and they were coming in for the kill. Gulping with childlike impatience, a question blurted out of him like intestinal gas.

"I can't stand it, Holly. You've got to tell me what the surprise is!"

"They do have a good bartender here . . . this is a great mix." Taking the sequined clutch out of the larger shoulder bag, she opened its glittering hasp. With a trace of 'come-hither' in her gaze, she looked into David's eyes. She removed a bank envelope out of the clutch and put it on the low black table between them.

"Is that the surprise? Can I open it?" He was shaking.

"Go ahead."

He picked it up. Ripping the envelope open, a check slipped out and seesawed towards the candle burning on the table below, but David snatched it out of the air with the speed of a conjurer.

"A hundred thousand dollars! But it's out of your *own* bank. You don't have that kind of money lying around. What did you do? How did you do it? Why didn't you just ask Latham to help us out a little earlier?"

"Whoa, David, slow down. I thought you'd be happy. I know, I know, it's not enough, but it should hold the fort until Dad's CD matures in March. Getting the money wasn't very hard. You forgot about the cottage on Nantucket. I just borrowed on the equity. I know you'll reimburse me as soon as you have the money from the loan so it's not that big of a deal, it's not . . . calm down!"

His face was flushed as he reached across the table for a heartfelt hug.

"You're a God's send. Thank you, thank you and thank you again! What a terrific surprise. I didn't know what I was going to do," as he snuffled the words into the side of her neck. He didn't want to let her go, yet a muscle in his back was sending him a nasty retort, and he reluctantly returned to his chair. Using the palm of his hand to wipe a tear off his face, he was revved up. He energetically explained the twists and turns of the case to her, prattling along with renewed hope. He believed he was going to hold on to his license after all. He was even confident that Holly would invite him to spend the night with her. She looked demure and attentive. In reality, she wasn't listening to him at all. In her mind, she was back to mulling over her overzealous response to his attempt to make love to her, and she thought about recalibrating her internal governor. After posting a mental note to find the time for the necessary mental homework in that regard, she finally turned her real attention to David by interrupting him.

"David . . . David, please, wait a minute . . . shush. The rooms in the lower floors in the Plaza are too small, so I reserved a larger suite on the twentieth floor. Would you like to spend a night here with me?"

"I'm not sure, honey. I've gotten used to living on cold soup out of a can in Steve's drafty apartment. I know it sounds bad, but the taste of the can in the food has turned into a delicacy. Whether I should wrap myself up in an old blanket in a gloomy brownstone tonight or stay here in a penthouse suite with you is a difficult decision."

The beatific expression on the face of a child about to unwrap his gifts on Christmas morning was flawlessly reproduced on David's. An answer wasn't really necessary. The couple adjourned to the main restaurant to have a languorous dinner, topping it off with a dessert of Tiramisu and a shot of Frangelica in their coffee.

It was after midnight, and behind the door of suite 228 on the highest floor of the Boston Park Plaza Hotel, David lay back accepting the only bond he would ever have with his wife. Holly stretched him beyond any ordinary thresholds of pleasure; it had always been her way. Hungrily consenting to her heavenly domination, his fingers felt her muscles contract under her skin as he held onto her torso as if he was drowning. He could feel tendons slip across her rib cage like they were moving through hot oil, as she swiveled and arched above him like a double-jointed acrobat from Cirque du Soleil. Holly writhed in ferocious concentration, but the public would never see this carnal dance. Finally, her rapture thrust David over the cliff into a heart stopping *petite mort.* Experiencing this small ecstatic death in their union, his orgasm snapped the connection in their euphoric tug of war, and David fell asleep. Holly got out of bed and stepped over to one of the windows. The city was covered in sparkling white with thousands of lights twinkling like jewels scattered across miles of cold satin.

He looked peaceful six feet away, but he'd actually fell fathoms below her, lost in a dangerous place. Moving down a dream corridor in a hotel ten times the size of the Plaza, he was already uncomfortable. A couple of the doors on the endless hallway were partially open and he tried not to think about what could be happening in all those vacant rooms. Going passed the open doors, it was too dark to see inside those rooms . . . and he couldn't hear anything at all. The pervading silence bothered him, and he started to walk a lot faster. The hotel was empty . . . it had to be empty. At the end of the interminable hallway, he turned the corner to stare down another one. He could barely make out the end point of it in the distance, and his uneasiness turned to fear. He started to run. The place reminded him of the Overlook, a fictional hotel in a book called The Shining. They'd made a movie out of it and it had given him the heebie-jeebies when he saw it in the theatre. Was it possible? Could he be inside that dreadful building? No . . . NO! That can't be! There's nothing in any of those rooms and there's nothing for him to be worried about . . . *he just needs to get the hell out of there.* Running however wasn't fast enough and he broke into a heart pounding tear until he raced around the next corner only to stop in his tracks. Twenty-five feet in front of him was an expansive staircase, leading down to a lobby big enough to be called vast. A roaring fire burned bright in a huge fireplace in the far wall about a half a mile away. The staircase and the lobby were just like the ones in the movie. His uncertainty was gone; he knew he was in the Overlook, but at least the power of his scream hauled him out of the dream. Sitting up ramrod straight, the bed sheets around him were wet with sweat, and he was shaking badly. Eyes wide open, he was still only partially awake. Tendrils of the nightmare clung to him like Velcro. The armoire in the corner of the room had turned into a troll and the lounge chair near the window was a prehistoric reptile, but these terrible overlays were slowly diminished. He realized he was in the Park Plaza, not the Overlook and he wasn't alone. Holly was across the room, staring out the window. Her naked body appeared phosphorescent, and that didn't calm him down in the least. Fumbling around in the dark, he tried to find the switch for the light next to the bed.

"*Holly . . .* ***HOLLY!*** *Please get over here,*" David cried out. She went on looking through the window as if she hadn't heard him. Getting the lamp on, the electric light smoothed off the prickly corners and the odd creatures nibbling at him in the dark were banished. But it wasn't sufficient. It wasn't quite enough. He still had not made it hundred percent back to day to day reality yet. Of course, Holly wasn't glowing anymore and she looked normal at first, but when she turned her head towards him, the enigmatic smile crawling onto her lips was not.

12:35PM Sunday March 27, 2005 Cambridge, Massachusetts

It was off the beaten path. Trattoria Decapua on Huron Avenue in Western Cambridge had a phenomenal chef, so it was the perfect choice. Stuffing the necessary files in his briefcase, Justin glimpsed at his watch. He snatched his coat and left the office, on his way to a business lunch. He was meeting Arthur Baxter, the vice-president of a new cable channel with call letters spelling out 'PYNCH'. Cute.

He'd reserved a table in the corner and he always arrived early at all his business meetings to check things out. The restaurant's interior was done in a natural wood, and furnished with rustic looking tables and chairs. It was reminiscent of a café in the countryside of Italy. Justin sat down, and slid his briefcase under the chair. He ordered a glass of merlot. Far from the front door and the busy entrance to the kitchen, it was a quiet place for the meeting. The restaurant had been spotlighted in one of the local rags, and he hoped the unavoidable boredom he'd deal with in the meeting would be offset by some very good food. Opening the menu, he was instantly absorbed. Someone quietly sat down on other side of the table, but he hadn't noticed it. Putting the menu down, he was astonished to see his lover, Alan Popolizio smiling at him.

"Hello, Jay! It's great to see you here. How on earth could you have possibly known I was critiquing this place today?" At 39, Alan was working for one of the city papers as a food critic. A lot younger looking than he should be, Justin had decided the buttery resiliency in his skin came from his Italian and Indonesian heritage. Whether the family tree was responsible for it or not, Alan's sultry beauty was powerful enough to fan anyone's envy into rage.

"So, we're having lunch together! Ah, it's kismet drawing us together again," Alan said.

Justin was very grateful he'd arrived early. With any luck, Baxter would run late, but he still felt flummoxed. Smiling back at Alan with painful regret, worry lines dug deeper into his forehead.

"It's great to see you, it really is, but . . . but I'm waiting for a client, damn it. I'd love to have lunch with you, but the meeting is business and the guy is about to arrive."

"Alright, alright . . ." One of Alan's shoulders went up an inch, acknowledging the problem. "It seems coincidence is telling us something today. Haven't been able to see you in public for a long time, and you should balance the weight of the long list of places we aren't supposed to be seen together as a couple and our crazy schedules against our love. Now we've been pulled apart yet again. It's time. You've got to figure out your priorities, honey, because I'm not going to be a prisoner in this gulag your family has erected around us much longer." Justin's eyes were glued to the front door, but he flinched. The truth hurts.

"He just walked in, Alan. Look, we'll iron this whole thing out on the phone tonight. I'll call you by eight, I promise. Don't worry. I'm going to come up with a new strategy by then. I'll figure out a way to get us free and open some doors." The words had tumbled out of him in reckless abandon to break a speed limit that even a seasoned auctioneer would have been impressed by. He was trying to save his relationship and the meeting at the same time.

"Dear, dear, your colors are showing. Uh-oh! Now, they're dripping. We can't have that happen, can we?" Alan stood up and turned on his heel, intentionally bumping into the mousey looking man heading towards the chair he'd just vacated. Sashaying across the room, he picked a table in the sun, as far away from Justin as he could get.

Done with the entrée and right before dessert, Justin put the briefcase on the table. He and Baxter looked over the changes in the contract, and the conference went well, even if the talk with Alan had turned his belly, torpedoing his gustatory palliative. Paying the check, he watched a busboy clear off Alan's table. The love of his life was long gone and he was afraid there was a dreadful ring to the idea '*long gone*'. Stepping onto Huron Avenue, Justin said goodbye to Mr. Baxter and he whistled up a cab. Fifteen minutes later he stood in front of his building, forsaken. Trudging inside, he rode the elevator up to his floor and he felt even worse. Unlocking the office door, Justin tossed his briefcase in the general direction of the couch. Wanting to throw himself on the carpeted floor and pound his fists up and down, he restrained himself. He slumped behind his desk, and rested his head on his forearms. He began to weep, realizing that hiding in full sight wasn't going to work anymore.

It was obvious his father wanted him to pass the Olympic flame onwards, but he was trapped between a rock and hard place. His younger brother was out of the running and Holly had never been considered in the royal line, while the rainbow flag was wrapped around his crotch tight enough to end the Donnelly's line of succession like dry ice. He got up and went over to a tall cabinet near the door and he pressed a panel. The cabinet swiveled into the wall and a wet bar took its place. Pouring out a shot of Chivas Regal, he swallowed it down, numb to the burning at the back of his throat. He couldn't find a way to get out of the situation he was in. No way out. How could he give Alan what he wanted in the upcoming call? Pacing like a tiger in the confines of his office, when the phone rang, he let the answering machine pick it up.

"Hello . . . Justin, I know you're there. I have something you need to hear. Jay, damn it, pick up . . ." Hearing that voice, he decided to be the honorable brother despite her awful timing, and he picked up the call.

"Hello, Holly. What's got you so fired up to make you call me in the middle of a busy workday? I've got a full calendar." He thought he was masking his emotional pain seamlessly.

"You're upset and you shouldn't be. Listen to me, I know Dad's hard to pin down, but I got my hands on him last week, right before he was about to fly off to another one of those endless meetings. We sat down and drank espresso in that solarium of his, next to the pool." She paused. She was going to tell him a whopper. Inserting a believable emotion and resonance in her latest invention, Holly took a very deep breath and concentrated. It had to ring true as it would have been easier to get him to believe the moon was formed from blue cheese. Her half-brother could still easily dismiss the whole thing as hokum.

"A lot of time has passed Jay. I decided to test the water. We're in the new millennium after all, and western society has accepted homosexuality, hell, we idolize it . . ." Justin interrupted her.

"Holly, you are spinning like a top. I have absolutely no interest in what you think the world thinks about sexuality. Our father is a relic from the middle-ages. We should knock him out and drop him off at a taxidermist. Then we could display him in a museum for over priced antiques. I guess you've completely forgotten that he rejects you from the get-go and he's on a warpath against Bertie? In his mind, I'm the only one to continue the family line, and his interest in me has increased since I got back to Massachusetts. It's getting me nervous. He wants to play tennis with me in about two weeks, and I'm antsy about that too. How do you think he'd react if he found out I was gay? Blow a gasket, is what! Disinheriting me would only be the first act in a painful litany of things he'd do to torture me! Do you really think you have an answer that would get me out of the squeeze play I'm in right now, *sis*?" Justin had given up any pretense. No longer trying to sound fine, the timbre in his voice dove off a building into despair.

Over the years, Holly had insinuated herself inside everyone's heart but Latham's. Anyone in the family needing emotional rescue, Holly was a female rock of Gibraltar in their minds; a life-preserver if everything else failed. If her support does not resolve the problem, at least she calmed their nerves.

Justin's nimble excuses, double talk and flirtation weren't going to hold back Alan's exasperation anymore. He was afraid a tsunami of righteous indignation was about to wash their relationship out to sea. While the innate prejudice he had that Holly was a miracle worker intertwined with his intense helplessness, his emotions overwhelmed his logic. Her sweet deceit found root in what should have been barren ground.

"Stop talking like a martyr tied to the cross, Jay. I'm trying to tell you something important. I raised the subject of homosexuality to Dad, so now you have to listen to me, *bro*."

"Oh, alright . . ." Justin grumbled. "I just had a terrible afternoon, and I'm looking for an answer to an unanswerable question, but for you grasshopper, I will meditate on whatever you are about to impart." He poured another shot in the glass in his hand, and he tossed it down his throat, while a tear dripped off his edge of his chin as he returned to his desk.

"Good. You sound much better. I was asking Dad about some of the current TV shows and movies dealing with the gay lifestyle, and he told me that some of them were funny." Justin started to laugh at this farfetched portrayal of their father.

"No, *I swear to you.* He actually watches them and he told me his limo driver is gay and that guy told him he saw you and Alan in Worcester, in that little bistro. You know, the hideout where you guys '*hide out*'. Obviously, the driver was a blabbermouth and an idiot, assuming Dad already knew about your personal life."

"Oh my God! He'll kill me, I think . . ." Holly spoke right over Justin's instant hysteria.

"He told me he'd told the driver that he'd suspected you were gay, since you never show up with girlfriends and remained unmarried, stuff like that. Dad sounded reasonable. He was hoping it was just hard work that was impairing your love life, but he's not stupid. Hearing the unwanted news left him resigned, but there were no royal decrees of banishment. Nothing like that."

"What did he say exactly? I mean what? Can I show up at the estate wearing garlands with Alan by my side and we'd skip through the tulips together or *what?*" He was too upset to talk normally. Louder and more strident with every word, Justin's frantic questions rose into what sounded suspiciously like a flat out scream.

"Shush . . . relax, damn it and no. I don't think he's up to meeting Alan quite yet, but you guys certainly don't have to hide in the closet anymore. You can go where ever you want."

"He said that? 'I accept Justin's homosexuality,' he really said that?"

"Yes he did, he really did."

After talking to her for another twenty minutes, he reluctantly took Holly's assurances as truth. Saying goodbye, he hung up the phone, but he didn't start pacing again. The dreaded phone call to Alan no longer hung over his head like a grand-piano on a thread. He could call him and invite him to that hot dance club downtown. He'd love that and it wouldn't matter if the whole world sees them together. Apparently, Dad has finally seen the light, yet Justin was still dumbfounded by it. Holly couldn't have created a convoluted story like that and besides, she'd always been on his side. She had no reason to make the whole thing up. Dad had just changed with the times, is all. Of course, Justin wasn't going to call him up about it. That was too weird. He'd gingerly broach the subject to him after the tennis game.

11:45AM Sunday April 17, 2005 Miles above Plymouth, Massachusetts

Slethim rode a thermal, effortlessly climbing higher on the updrafts. Two miles above the earth, the weak rays of a spring sun warmed its feathered shoulders as it scanned the countryside below. Pupils encircled with golden irises, it watched people walk out of their churches and drive home. The entity was amused. They moved like insects through treacle and it was just a dash of the misanthrope in its breast that spurred Slethim into coming up with a joke in which their intelligence was as microscopic as their tiny doll heads. Raising its left wing five inches, it dropped five hundred feet and veered southeast. Flying at 45 miles an hour, it would be circling over Bass River in half an hour.

11:55AM Sunday April 17, 2005 Bass River, Massachusetts

Parking in front of the mansion, Justin was afraid the north wind would ruin his game. He had on tan chinos, a white T-shirt and a white sweater, and he'd picked out the perfect sneakers. They weren't the most comfortable pair he owned, but they would give him the extra traction he was looking for. It was more than worth the trade. Reaching over the front seat, he grabbed the racket. Over the past five years, he had really become a better player and the passage of time should have slowed Dad down. It should give him the advantage; the final tipping point. He'd topple the king. Jogging around the house to meet Latham on the patio, he imagined walking through his parents' garden holding Alan's hand, Mom and Dad waiting for them at the gazebo. In this tilted apple pie future cast, he envisioned April and Latham laughing out loud in delight when they see the star crossed lovers emerge from behind the hedge wall.

"Justin, it's great to see you! We're going to have a lot of fun breaking the new court in," Latham said, and he shook his son's hand enthusiastically, even if his true feelings towards Justin were less charitable these days. He went on by giving him a short manly hug, played the part to the hilt anyway. The ugly darts of green in his son's brown eyes reminded him April's hazel ones and that could have been the coup de grâce. No longer sure he wanted Jay to be part of the Russian adventure, severing all his connections to his disloyal family was gaining hold. Cutting away the last tiny bit of this cancerous growth, he'd be cured when he landed in Russia. In his mind, the idea of flying solo after his happy-go-lucky divorce was the right answer.

"Hello Dad. I know *I'm* going to have a terrific time, since you're going to lose. You can go ahead and do your damnedest, but I'm about to bump you right out of the winning circle." Justin was grinning ear to ear.

"I'm very sorry you believe that, and are you going to tell me that water runs uphill too? I'm not worried. Nothing will save you from my backhand. By the way, Mom's set up lunch next to the pool after the game. I know it's windy, but we can put down the plastic barriers if we need them."

"Sounds good. I know we'll be hungry that's for sure. Are we going to play three sets, like usual, two out of three wins?"

"Yup."

Latham stepped onto the court. He went over to one of benches and re-tied his sneakers and after that, he trotted out onto the poured clay with way too much of a bounce in his step. There was a lot more speed and agility than most men his age would have. Justin spent more time adjusting the tension in his laces, as Latham impatiently bounced a ball on his racket.

The game began, and Justin worked as hard as he ever had in the past. His confidence faltered and the triumph he'd anticipated drifted away in the wind. Latham's long legs easily transported him to almost every single one of Justin's far-flung balls. Through out the exhausting volleys, Latham's endurance resolutely held on. Justin's five year absence hadn't impaired the older man in the least, and he returned his aggressive fire with equal vengeance.

Latham won six games; Justin, five. At a pivotal juncture in the contest, Latham could win the game, the set, and the match with only one more point. If Justin got the point, they'd have to play another game to break the ensuing tie. In the middle of this possibly final interchange, Latham had expertly aimed the ball to the back corner of Justin's side of the court, and it landed half-an-inch inside the painted line. It had been a dangerous maneuver. Latham thought the game was over, positive his son couldn't get there in time. He was wrong. Justin's aching desire to win had twisted him to the outer-limit as he raced to the edge of the court like a human bolt of lightning. He returned the ball! Justin watched it sail over the net with a split-second of exultation before it landed out of bounds.

Cutlery, crystal goblets, and a pitcher filled with homemade iced tea had weighted the linen table cloth down, so far defying the wind's impudence. The day before, April had told Vince what she wanted for the luncheon: chicken salad, ham and spinach quiche, corn chowder, and a bowl of fruit salad. The picnic would begin at the Gazebo at 12:30 PM on Sunday afternoon. That morning, she stopped at the kitchen to make sure her menu plans were being followed. Of course, it was a cursory visit. Everything was as it should be, and she went on to her suite on the second floor to freshen up.

A wealthy man's wife can create a sumptuous lunch for her family effortlessly. One of the many reasons she continued living the onerous role of the devoted spouse for a smidgeon longer. It was partially to pry more money out of him in the divorce proceedings, after the real estate venture goes down. Relaxing in her rooms, she decided not to call Peter up after all. Her loneliness would soon be gone with Justin's arrival. Fixing her hair and makeup, she went out to the pool to stretch out on one of the lounge chairs out of the wind. Lying there, April pictured her new life with Peter on some tropical island next winter, but the fantasy blinked out as soon as she heard Latham and Justin walking up the path. She stood up and waved, glancing over at the table for a second . . . *ah, everything was perfect.*

"Hello, Jay! How did the game go? I hope you won! I hope you trounced him," April said. She hugged her son and pecked his cheek.

"Hi Mom. Yeah, not so much. I was going to get the gold, but at the last minute I felt sorry for him, and I let him win one more time. I just couldn't let his world crumble, and watch him cry like a baby."

Latham chuckled, "It's your world I crushed. I didn't even breaking into a sweat. You need a few more lessons, maybe more than a few."

Father and son sat down together at the table, grabbing at the ice tea pitcher at the same time. Justin demurred to Dad. April walked over and Latham pulled a chair out for her. During the meal, their conversation touched on Justin's law business and gossip about the people they knew. Justin was nervous. He wasn't happy about bringing up the subject of his own social life, but it had to be done. Drumming up enough courage to swim into the dangerous and uncharted waters, he started off tentatively. *Perhaps he'd win something after all . . .*

"A bird whispered to me that you heard about my hideaway in Worcester, the place my lover and I go once in a while."

April froze. The shrimp on her fork didn't make it into her mouth. Eyes wide, she squealed with excitement, "Well, it's about time, dear! What's her name and why haven't you brought her along with you today? How long have you been seeing her? We were so afraid you were homosexual! Thank God that confusion is finally over."

"You didn't tell Mom about this, did you Dad?" Justin stared at his father.

"I didn't have anything to tell her, Jay, but who cares! This is great news. I'd like to know about your hideaway too. It's taken you too long to let us know about your secret love life."

April jumped back in, "After you got your degree, you never brought any of your dates over to the house. Three weeks ago, we were absolutely terrified that something could be wrong. I was crying, Jay, I really was afraid. I wouldn't be able to see you anymore and Dad would change the will and everything. *What a relief it's over!* I don't know why you've been so mysterious about her. Is there something odd about her? Go ahead, tell us more!"

Justin's face was the color of paste. Sweat erupted on his forehead and between his shoulders, and it was painfully clear he wasn't going to win anything. Winning? Hah! Forget about winning. He might lose the entire enchilada, if he goes out of bounds again. To repair his terrible jack-in-the-box faux pa, he needed to change tracks faster than a speeding bullet and he was momentarily confounded. His dream of redemption was shattered and he had almost talked himself off an emotional cliff. To reinforce the façade of his heterosexuality, he had to dive through a verbal ring-of-fire with the finesse of a seasoned acrobatic. The sudden free fall was slowing his reaction time down, so he drank a lot of ice tea. He needed a few more seconds to collect his thoughts.

"Slow down both of you, and hold on a minute," Justin patted the air in front of him like a school guard at a cross walk. "Her name is Vera, okay, and I broke up with her last week. I was afraid you might have heard about our explosive tiff. Right now, I'm heartbroken about the whole thing and I'd rather not go through the painful details with you. Please excuse me. My left calf muscle has cramped badly and I have to, um . . . walk it out. I'll be right back." He remembered to fake a limp as he hobbled away from the table.

"I'll put some fruit salad in your bowl. You can have it when you get back. We'll talk about brand new beginnings." April's comments were directed to Justin's back as he disappeared into the hedge maze. Latham's interest in his son's love life was gone, vanishing like invisible ink and the information he'd just been given was flushed out of his head like yesterday's weather. He went back to thinking over the project in Russia and he put more chicken salad on his plate.

Hitching out of sight, Justin's limp disappeared. As he walked deeper into the garden, his upper body had doubled over in a spasm of fury.

Holly had made the whole thing up! The heavenly freedom to go anywhere with Alan was gone. Nevertheless, that painful irritation dwindled against his feelings about the erasure of a dream of himself and his lover hanging out on the estate in the near future. Mother and father's continuing malicious prejudice became a catalyst for things to come, and his profound disappointment savaged his conscience to a stump. The resulting aberration in his personality latched itself to his core like a tapeworm, and he started to sing . . .

"*Living a lie, until they die, oh my, oh my, bye bye bye,*" and he ended this dreadful ditty with a laugh. Humming along as he walked, his hands were clenched into fists. When he reached the center of the maze, the muscle spasm curling him over let go, and Justin straightened up and looked over at the fountain in the middle of the clearing as a shadow passed over his head. It must have been a hawk. Squinting up, he shielded his eyes from the glare with his hand, but all he saw was blue sky. Whatever it was had flown out of sight.

PART II

"If you can hear a melody in dissonance, you are in danger; dance to that tune, you are doomed."

Keith Fischer

Born in 1875, Carl Jung is responsible for a lot of concepts in modern psychiatry. Using patterns in mythology, alchemy, and the supernatural to support his theories, his rationality and internal logic reinforced their final acceptance. As constraining as the Achilles' tendon and his heel, one of Jung's main concepts was the collective subconscious mind. Our dreams are configured by iconical archetypes, imbedded in our minds at conception. His communal subconscious mind is populated with a pantheon of prototypes apparently inherited or culturally implanted, but it's possible it could be an interactive one as well, telepathically linked in this intangible dimension. The collective unconscious may be the source behind our unexplained and untapped psychic powers and someday we could become *one* made from *many* . . . just like an ant hill.

If this conceivable adaptation of his premise *is* real, billions of minds are coalescing planet-wide, connecting the multitude in their dreams. There's a chance for a collective obsessive on one apparition, or one archetype, for an undisclosed period of time. Like pinpointing the power of sunlight through a magnifying glass, the gargantuan power of billions fused into one, could thrust that emotionally driven image outwards; perhaps transmuting the dream model into *material form*.

Perhaps there weren't enough people on planet earth until now. The global population has grown exponentially from 3 billion to 5 billion, but that number wasn't quite enough, possibly holding us back. A larger number of people asleep at the same time in our current overblown level of 7 billion human beings could have tipped the balance. If the collective power of all those minds blended into a single ferocious beam with godlike results, we'd be blind to the outcome . . . at least when we're awake.

We should have grown wings instead of opposable thumbs, and our craving to fly discharges in flocks of angels fluttering through our stories, religious tracts and Hollywood movies in an attempt to satisfy the need. The Wright Brothers found part of the answer in 1903. Their invention evolved into a swarm of lumbering behemoths, but that certainly wasn't the end of our problem. Sitting in a 250 ton commercial jet on our way from Rio de Janeiro to Copenhagen, we feel nervous as it lifts up into the air like a dandelion. Flying in the porous metal tube 6 miles above the earth does not release our inner wants. Unable to unfurl our heavenly wings, we continue to grow them. A hang glider and similar inventions do let us feel a bit more birdlike, and it's the best we've come up with. Some of us trust the premise, even though these playthings do break once in a while. A rogue puff of wind sometimes flips the faithful unfairly into forever.

Would that yearning galvanize us into transforming our wish into a living form . . . *perhaps an embryo inside a chrysalis hanging off a tree limb in a rainforest in Southern Belize. After seven months of gestation, it grew too big for its womblike prison. A full moon pulsing in its blood, it lunged at the walls of its lucent cell. Ripping free from the fragile golden chamber, it flew off into the jungle to enjoy its first day of life by eagerly hunting for food.*

If our collective wish did come true, what would its motivations be? Are we a gentle, intelligent, and peaceful species? And if you extracted the essence of everyone alive on the planet and mixed it into one fragrance, what do you think it would smell like?

Jung's propositions are more likely nothing but vacuous extrapolation. Intelligent and creative, he'd cleverly tricked people into believing in a head game. The ultimate explanation for the inexplicable probably has nothing to do with our humanity. Extraterrestrials could have already inserted themselves into the mysteries we think we have unraveled, and we may be oblivious to the insidious possession. Either way, it's probably too late.

Lonely and isolated, we can't find a mirror in this galaxy. Pointing our technologically advanced eyes and ears out to the universe, so far hasn't netted us a reward. It's more likely those ingenious cameras, telescopes, and radio receivers are only awkward contraptions, and we may be blind and deaf to an ominous approach.

Hurtling through empty space, we remain forlorn. The endless solitude encourages a self-serving recklessness. The polar opposite of a teenaged wallflower at the masked ball, we're infused with drunken bravado; the life of the party in outer space. Sooner or later, our endless invitations will finally be answered and on that day we will dance with a mystery hiding behind a mask. To end the long term pain of disconnection and confusion, we'd clumsily grope around in the dark to hold the creature's hand. Embracing the unknown in our arms, we'd carelessly untie the veil to behold our partner's real face and there would be no time to recall our impulsiveness.

11:30AM Monday May 2, 2005 New Bedford, Massachusetts

David got out of bed and stumbled towards the kitchen, half-asleep. The belt of his terry cloth robe hooked over the door knob on the hallway closet, pulling it sideways. The garment slipped off his shoulders and he left it on the floor in his unsteady trip to the kitchen counter.

Things were in a holding pattern in court, and he'd left Boston and come back home. His wife barely acknowledged his presence in the house, and he felt lonely and directionless. Liquor his only solace. In his mind, the loan his father-in-law was going to give him would be his redemption; the miraculous saving grace on the horizon. Even though he knew he would have the money very soon, soon was turning into an eternity and Holly had tried to console him the day before.

"Dad's wiring 200,000 to your lawyer's account next week and with Wilson's assurances, you should be back to work pretty soon," but her enthusiasm hadn't worked. His daily input of alcohol ratcheted up another notch.

Taking coffee and filters out of the cabinet, he set up the machine. He sat down and he leaned back, putting his feet up on the counter while it percolated. Gazing at the abstract silver rivers running along the side of the coffee machine, he was quickly lulled back to sleep. Slowly falling off the edge of the chair, he was saved by the ringing of the phone. He picked up the handset, and he tried to respond with as much clarity as he could muster.

"Hello David, its Wilson. Listen, something came up and the judge is impatient. He got a cancellation and he wants your case on and off his desk like a summer storm. The hearing that was supposed to take place on June 10th, was re-scheduled to May 10th and the hundred thousand dollars you were supposed to send to us next week has to be sent *now*. By the end of the working day today, OK?"

"Well, good morning, Wilson," David said.

"I know, I know. It's not what anyone would want to start the day hearing, but I can't sugar coat this, I'm sorry."

"Yeah . . . and there's no way I can get it to you until Wednesday. That has to be good enough." David had woken up fast, and he was frightened. The upcoming call to his father-in-law wasn't going to be easy.

Hi 'Lath', old buddy. Just go ahead and wire the money to my law firm, ***now*** *instead of next week, okay . . .* Oh God. If he does get Latham on the phone, the man would probably gnaw his head off and swallow it.

"I guess it'll work, but you have to add another twenty-five thousand on top as we're going to have to work overtime to get the whole thing ready for the hearing. Listen David, the firm won't let me put anymore extra time on your bill. If we go in unprepared, you'll probably lose your license, so it's very important that you get the funds in the account by Wednesday morning, and don't forget about the bump for overtime. If its there in time, you have a good chance for dismissal."

"Alright, alright. I have to get off the phone and put it into motion."

"I understand. The judge has put you in a squeeze play, so I'll sign off and let you get to it," Wilson said. He sounded amused. "Life is like a chess game. Sometimes we can move out of danger fast enough to avoid checkmate. Call me when your knight is ready to hop over the evil queen's approach." Laughing at his own metaphor, he hung up.

. David attempted to will himself into a positive mind set for the up-coming desperate call for salvation. He imagined Latham relaxing at home in a great mood, more than ready to wire the money straight over to him. Taking a deep breath, he poured another jolt of coffee into his cup, and brought it with him as he returned to the bedroom to change. Putting on presentable clothes for the call would be a small offering to the gods, another superstitious prop. There was a good chance he would fail, and to David the failure seemed tantamount to being hauled out in front of a bureaucratic firing squad.

It was 1:00 PM, when Latham tossed his suitcase on his *own* bed. He'd just gotten home after traveling to New York, Connecticut, New Jersey, and Washington to rustle up the team he wanted to bring with him to Russia. An exhausting fourteen day stint, he was looking forwards to this short hiatus at the estate with relish. The house phone rang, and he ignored it, picturing himself floating in his pool. Mirabelle's voice came up on the intercom to inform him his son-in-law wanted to talk to him. Normally, he'd tell her to tell David he was out of town or something, but the fact that he was actually calling him tweaked his curiosity, and he picked up the receiver.

"Hello David. Is your house on fire? What's up?"

"Hello Latham. I didn't want to bother you about wiring the money over early, I mean, we've already set it up for next week, but Wilson told me the court calendar had changed. I need to pay the firm right away, so I'd really appreciate your help with this. Would it be too much of an imposition to wire the money over to them today or tomorrow?"

"Please, go ahead and explain exactly what it is I've set up for you." Latham's weary smile had him look like the cat that ate the canary.

David gulped. His answer hadn't sounded right. Nope, it hadn't sounded right at all, but he didn't want to believe he'd heard the beginning of the end.

"Well, ah . . . Holly told me you're planning to wire five hundred thousand dollars to my account next week. I'm sorry to bother you sir, but Wilson just told me the hearing has been rescheduled. It's moved up on the calendar. The firm needs the money right away so they can iron out the last details of my case in a shorter length of time."

"Sorry to burst your bubble, son, but I haven't talked to Holly about anything like that. You're married to the woman, for God's sake. You must know by now she does not always tell you the truth."

"You don't remember the conservation you had with her in the library at the reunion? You were going to break open one of your CDs and loan me the money for my defense team. I'm sure she explained it all to you. I mean, of course I'll reimburse you as soon as I go back to work." David had raced through his words to avoid gagging.

"I talked to Holly at the reunion, yes, but she didn't mention anything about your financial problems or your court case. Sounds to me like you're in a pickle."

"Ah . . . well, yeah, I guess you're right. Look, I know this is last minute, but maybe I could still borrow one hundred and twenty-five thousand dollars for a couple of weeks? You know I'm good for it." All he could hear was laughter, and then that hilarity ballooned into a wail of guffaws.

"This isn't funny, Latham. I'm about to lose my license and I really . . ."

Donnelly hung up on his son-in-law with rock-solid indifference. Still giggling with merriment, he stepped into his walk-in closet to find his swimming shorts.

Soldiers loaded their Winchester rifles in the sudden silence of a dead line, and David could even imagine the sound of metallic snaps as the men used the lever near the trigger to cock them. Latham's ending laugh heralded the end of his career. He dropped the phone. It bounced across on the carpet to land three feet away as he sank down against the wall. He would have ended up on the floor if he hadn't accidentally encountered the seat of a chair. His shock was turning into a full blown freak-out. David had to rescind what was barreling towards him and replace it with anything, anything at all. He'd like it if a burglar was hovering over him with a raised sap to knock him out, maybe even killing him, or a rabid pit bull could be charging down the hall to sink its teeth into his leg. Yup, those were fine options.

A full-blown panic attack got him off the floor and into the bathroom as his heart pounded like a sledge hammer. Grabbing a pill bottle with the name **Lexotan** printed on the label out of the medicine cabinet, the chemical name for the stuff was Bromazepam. He snapped the top off the plastic vial with shaking fingers, and he popped two pills.

He tried to speed things up by chewing them instead of swallowing them down with water, but either way, it would still use up about twenty minutes before he enjoyed the effects. Checking his wristwatch, he knew those minutes would crawl and he tossed the bottle in the sink. He raced outside into the afternoon sunlight, leaving the front door wide open and he started jogging down the sidewalk. The jog became a full tilt run. All he could think about was his own disintegration. When he reached the intersection, he sprinted around the corner to find himself on Cowlip Lane and he kept on running. He was running away from nothing to get nowhere as quickly as he could, pointlessly arriving at Route 22.

More powerful than Ativan or Valium, the tranquillizers began to quell the apocalyptic alarm and his frantic pace diminished. After four more minutes, he stopped dead in his tracks. What had propelled him two miles away from the house was tied up and muzzled, but going back was slow going. Almost like a slap-stick joke in reverse, it seemed he was walking through molasses and the syrup was getting deeper by the second. When he got to Merchant Drive, he was staggering. Walking inside the house, he didn't care that he'd left the front door wide open, yet even under the thick blanket of drugs, his fury towards his wife was building and he found enough strength to close the door with a petulant slam.

Holly had strung him along for months, and he wanted to do more than slap her backstabbing face. The stain of his own blood on the bricks around the fireplace restrained him, and he wouldn't or couldn't confront her. Down the road . . . way down the road, he'd turn the tables on her in a definitive and irrefutable way. Meanwhile, he'd be a defrocked drunken ex-neurosurgeon living on his wife's money, and his new career would be 'house husband'. It was a hellish forecast, but he would accept the awful changes with a smile, outwardly unruffled.

At that point he was zombified, and he poured into the pillowy chair in the corner of the living room, resting his hands on the arms like white stones. The feeling that his skull had been replaced with a shrunken head wasn't irritating him much anymore, and the shine off the gold cufflink on his shirt sleeve hypnotized him into a state of delight. In half-hour he was snoring in a drug induced stupor.

The breeze had dropped away in the gloaming. Majestic blue pines on the edge of Holly and David's property were responsible for the indigo shadows elongating across their lawn like paint, while incandescence leaking out of the windows of the houses on the rest of the Merchant Drive gently smothered the last note of natural color. The sound of car doors clunking closed was intermixed with the muted clatter of pots and pans and with the touch of a button, outlandish visitors, carefully locked away behind those flickering screens, popped into existence in almost all the homes.

Looking down at the drive in the dark, it glittered like a string of rhinestones, yet there was a small break in the chain. David hadn't turned on the outside lights as he was passed out in the same chair in the living room. It was as if he'd flown straight into window glass, a song bird unable to realize the invisible barrier in his way. Everything he had strived for had vanished in the moonless night.

Breaking the speed limit all the way home, Holly wheeled into the driveway at 8:15. The garage doors went up and the outside lights flickered on from the remote she had in her hand. She entered the house through the garage door, pausing at the main panel in the hallway, and she used her forearm to switch all the lights in the house on. Sailing into the living room, she tossed her satchel on the couch, and then she hung her spring jacket in the closet near the front door.

"Hello David. Seems you've been napping this afternoon," and she patted his leg as she passed. "I'm going to microwave one of those gourmet Italian dinners from Scotto's and toss a salad together. Would you like some?"

Taking her computer out of the bag, she put it on the dinner table. She bent over to plug it into the nearest outlet. Tight around her torso, her dress flowed freely from the hip line down with a glimmer of gold in the dark green fabric, and her day-to-day appearance remained so remarkable it negated its regularity. Standing up, Holly stretched. She linked her hands together, pushing her palms towards the ceiling and then she pulled out the chopsticks that were holding her hair in a knot on her head. The glossy black river cascaded down her back as she walked towards the kitchen. David's voice stopped her.

"I'll need an allowance and you'll revive my membership in the Bourdon Club. I'd like to brush up on my golf game this summer."

Resuming her trip to the kitchen, Holly raised her voice so he could hear her in the living room. "Okay, just tell me how much you'd like per month. Oh . . . I already called Bourdon yesterday. We're both signed up for the summer. I don't know how much time I'll have to play with you, but at least we're set up. Are you sure you don't want one of the eggplant rollatini dinners?"

He didn't answer her. Unconscious in the same position for hours, he stood up and his body cracked and popped as if he was an old man. Limping over to the bar, he poured himself a brandy. Holly had brightened the living room lights and he dimmed them. In the kitchen, Holly opened a premixed bag of greens, and she tossed them on a plate. Unfazed by his ongoing silence, she inserted the frozen dinner into the microwave. She went back out to the dining room and sat at the table and turned on her PC. The microwave would beep when the dinner was done in a few minutes.

The first floor of their bungalow was an open and breezy affair, and the living room and the dining room were adjoined with nothing but a hint of an arch to suggest the variation. David was motionless in the darkened part of the large room, staring at Holly with something absolutely appalling in his eyes. After over ten minutes, she looked over at him and gave him an off-handed smile, apparently immune to his dangerous attention, and it didn't matter whether he was there or not.

1:17PM Wednesday June 15, 2005 New Bedford, Massachusetts

The Bourdon Golf Club's dining room and outside café opens every morning at 6:30AM, and it closes thirty minutes before the entire club shuts down at seven. David was picking at a plate of congealed Eggs Florentine under an umbrella on the outside terrace overlooking the course. Mr. Duncan Hartley, a congressman, sat across the table from him, pontificating about everything and the endless drone didn't bother David. He'd nod and agree, as if he was actually listening. The humidity was low and there was a slight wind. It was a picturesque day. David had just gone through 18 holes with the congressman, ending up seven strokes above par. Not good at all, and he also lost the game. After the dreary hearing in May, his medical license had been revoked, so losing had become his middle name.

Duncan stood up and shook his hand as he was leaving. Agreeably mumbling that they'd meet at the same place at the same time next week, Holly dashed up to the table wearing tennis whites and holding a racket.

"What a day!" She said, and she shook the older man's hand. "It's great to be outside . . . it feels *so good.* I don't care if I win or lose, just breathing this air in and smelling the sweet smell of lilacs with a clear blue sky over my head is more than enough."

Surprised by her sudden arrival, Duncan looked her up and down appreciatively. She was radiant in a very short white tennis skirt and a sleeveless tank top.

"My, my Holly, you become more delightful to look every time I see you. Listen, I'd like to stay and chat, but I have a meeting with my cousin at three. I'm afraid I'll be late if I don't run right now." Holly thanked the man for his compliment and then he walked away, tossing a royal wave over his shoulder.

"You didn't eat all your eggs, dear. I thought you liked the cooking here," she said, looking down at David's plate.

"Hello, Holly. When did tennis become part of your work week over there?"

"Well, it's not a scheduled event, mind you, but it *is* necessary once in a while," and Holly grinned at him. "I was wheedling a donation out of Raytheon. One of the board members told me he loves tennis, and I let him know I felt the same way."

"Since you don't really like tennis, it must be a very large donation indeed to go out there and jump around like a maniac." David looked up at her.

"It was a great game and I loved it. He's meeting me in the office in a little while to draw up the paperwork. The company is donating three million dollars to the hospital so I've got to run."

"What does Raytheon make anyway?"

"Marine electronics for water craft. Government and civilian, and they're huge. The main factory is in Braintree. I heard they were interested in some of our research projects, so I decided to shake that tree. It worked out wonderfully. See you later on, dear."

Watching her heavenly ass sway towards the parking lot, he went back to mulling over an escape plan with as much clarity as he could. David felt like a helpless and hapless drunk shriveling away in Holly's shadow. Too young to be mold on the side of a rotten log in the woods, there had to be a way out. Reaching inside his jacket pocket, he got out his cell phone. He had to do *something.* Justin lived in Cambridge and he decided to set up a meeting with his brother-in-law. He didn't know if it was worth the effort to try to get his license back in an appeal, and Justin would be able to tell him about his chances. Besides, a week ago, Holly mentioned something about her brother's irritation with Latham so they could commiserate. Justin's number was stored in his phone's memory and he hit speed dial. In a second he heard it ringing.

"Hi Justin, it's David . . . yeah . . . no, I'm hanging on. Listen, I've got an appointment on Friday morning in the city and I was hoping you could squeeze in a few minutes to meet me for a drink." There was no appointment. He wanted to sound composed, not desperate. "I wanted to ask you a few questions . . . sure . . . late afternoon is fine . . . what about six o'clock at the Swan's Nest in the Boston Plaza Hotel? Great, I'll see you there."

Holly had lured him to the Swan's Nest to give him a band aid and an empty promise, but maybe a second meeting there would give him better results. It had been a nice place, anyway.

5:45PM Friday June 17, 2005 Boston, Massachusetts

David arrived early and he sat down at the bar. In the long mirror behind all the liquor bottles, he saw deep furrows between his eyes and he tried to flatten them out. He had a feeling that the chances of reinstating his license were bleak and it was very difficult to erase the scowl on his face. No more juicy sweetness left in his life, he'd become a puckered up raisin.

Justin's last appointment ended at six. Already wearing the uniform of the upwardly mobile professional, spiritual instability was professionally stitched into the seams of his suit. He didn't have to go back to his condo to change, and the taxi dropped him off in front of the Plaza. Hugging his raincoat tight to his body, he ran twenty feet to the canvas pavilion. The BMW was in Cambridge. He didn't want any problems driving home if he was going to have a couple of drinks. Pausing at the entrance to the lounge, he looked over at David at the bar. He looked forlorn, with the air of an overgrown child and a terrific sense of fashion. Nut brown corduroy pants and a sports jacket were fused into flawless elegance, and Justin shook his head. Women would want to take him home and give him cookies and milk and then offer themselves up as the last morsel on the plate. Checking his raincoat, Justin could see that the rest of the room wasn't very crowded, and he liked the swans etched into the mirrors. Right above the bar, the birds looked black, black swans.

Getting off his stool, David shook Justin's hand. "I'm surprised the secret order of solicitors has given you a pass to kick your heels up with a civilian."

"Hello David. Oh, come on, I couldn't miss a meeting with you, considering what our family has been up to lately. We need humor to ride through this nasty keelhauling," and Justin slapped him on the shoulder. He sat down on the nearest stool. "How's your case going? Last I heard it wrapped up a few weeks ago."

"Oh, it ended alright. It imploded and sank. I can't practice medicine anymore," David said, and he gestured to the bartender. "Your sister told me she'd arranged a loan for me from Latham to take care of all my legal bills, and I made a mistake. I believed her. Isn't pyrite just as good as the real thing?"

The bartender came over and Justin ordered a White Russian while David asked for another martini.

"I'm not surprised you got duped. Holly really should have gone into law instead of medicine. She was born with such a powerful knack to make anyone believe anything. I've seen her turn fairytales into ironclad truths. Have you noticed her increased interest in the family? She even found the time to tell *me* a doozy. My head started to spin so fast I thought I was in the *Exorcist*."

Using a squeaky falsetto, Justin tried to sound female. It didn't come out very well.

"*You should know that Dad knows your gay and it's just peachy keen with him!*" Then he dropped his voice into his normal range, "That nugget of horse manure in my head, I went to the estate to play tennis with Dad, and I almost cut my own throat by saying the wrong thing. Every single thing she told me was crap and I should have known better. You're not alone. Falling for something we both should have known was bullshit, we fell head first into the lake of stupid. We threw the penny into the wishing well as if we both believed it was going to come true. That woman can make fool's gold glitter like it was formed in paradise."

"Whoa! She threw you into boiling oil, too? Wait until I tell you what she did to me! Remember when she disappeared with Dad after Thanksgiving dinner last year?" Pausing, he nodded a 'thanks' to the bartender as he left their drinks on the bar in front of them.

"On our way home that night, she told me Latham was going to give me a loan to pay my legal bills. I was blindfolded for months. What she'd actually been talking to Latham about had nothing to do with a loan, and I never got the money I needed. I was skinned alive in court. I'm not sure I want to know what the subject of their real conversation had been."

"Personally, I don't care what went on last Thanksgiving. I'd bow out of the next one, if I could. Dad acts like a preacher from the eighteen hundreds, not the power hungry corporate madman *he is,*" Justin snarled, and he gulped down half of his drink. Staring up at the large TV screen bracketed to the ceiling, it was tuned to a sports channel and the announcer's voice was muted. They were listening to a soft rock radio station and "Message in a Bottle" had just ended and "Sultans of Swing" began.

"When my court case was jumped a week earlier, I was stuck with calling up my father-in-law and the friendly chat I had with your father on the phone, asking him to wire the money over to me, last minute, didn't come out very well. He laughed at me so hard he almost blew a gasket. Yeah, oh yeah, I'm not looking forward to go to the reunion either!"

Drinking fast, within an hour they were both toasted.

"What if I poison the ham I'm gonna send over there and then stay home? Pushing that delicious stuff down their gullets, my difficult situation could disappear." Justin said, and then he laughed raucously.

"If you decide to go ahead and do this Jay, I'd appreciate a heads-up so I'd know to stay with the turkey."

"Aaah . . . it's just a day dream." He sounded wistful. "I'm gonna deal with the entire thing carefully and politely and I'll control myself. The perfect son, living the righteous life. Right now, I have no choices and no options and when Dad picks up that electric carving knife to slice up the damned bird, you should know I'll be wanting to use that blade to carve up something else."

Their conversation got louder with their tipsiness and three stools away, two middle-aged ladies drinking sherry had clearly heard Justin's pronouncement. They were flustered. Make-up precisely applied, their faces were constricted with distaste, and Justin stared back at them with an evil grin slashed across his mouth like a scythe. The old girls nervously looked away, and they started to whisper back and forth behind their lifted hands.

"Who are you torturing with that awful expression?" David said.

"Nobody . . . a couple of strangers behind you at the bar. My plans offended them."

David reflexively looked over his shoulder, but he really wasn't worried about anyone getting upset with their puerile gags. He was too fixated on his next question.

"Uh-huh, I see them. Listen, I'd appreciate your advice about my revocation. Is there any possibility of an appeal? Maybe I could find a way to get back to work."

"You know I'm in commercial law, don't you? I don't know a lot about malpractice cases. I do know appeals are expensive and generally pointless, but I've heard that once in a why somebody makes it through."

"That doesn't sound good at all."

"Look, I've got an acquaintance in the field. I can go to the back corner over there, where it's a bit quieter and I'll ring him up. He can answer your question absolutely." Justin got off his stool and walked away, casually gesturing to David, "Who knows, maybe there *is* something we can do."

"Thank you. I wouldn't mind a miracle at this point."

David began to talk to Arden, the bartender, about whether the Steelers would keep on winning the Super Bowl forever and a day. Soon enough, Justin returned and sat down next to him.

"I can let you know that he'll be more than happy to take your case. However, most of the time appeals leave him richer and the unlicensed doctor poorer and still locked out. This guy is good, David, so I'd take his advice. I'd pick up your marbles and go home. Sorry, I know this isn't the best news you were looking for right now."

"I'm not surprised. I really appreciate your help, on checking it out for me, Jay, but even if your friend had given me better odds, it probably wouldn't have mattered. I'm tapped, drained, and busted, and the only thing I have left is an allowance from Mistress Holly."

His defeat was apparently sealed, and he drank the rest of his martini with gusto. They kept on grousing and grumbling to each other for another hour with real satisfaction and then Justin asked for the bar menu. They ordered sirloin burgers with potato skins on the side, and they wolfed the food down. Both of them were well-oiled, and it was time to go. They paid the exorbitant bar bill without a peep, leaving a generous tip for Arden.

"It won't stop dripping out there," Justin said, as he buttoned up his coat. "Are you still staying with your friend nearby? I'm taking a cab home, and I could drop you off on the way."

"Thanks, that's generous of you . . . ah, Justin, you haven't changed your mind about the dinner have you? You aren't really going to send a deadly ham in your stead. I seriously need to know." David followed his brother-in-law out to the street, and Justin was chuckling while he waved down a cab.

"As much as I want to send in the poisoned cavalry to save our respective hides, I can't. I just can't, it's not right. It's morally reprehensible."

Locking up its brakes, a taxi went into a long slide to end up stopping only fifteen feet away. They got in. After David closed the passenger door, the driver carried them off on the slippery streets of Boston.

Dropping David off, they drove over Longfellow Bridge across the Charles River to Cambridge. Justin got out in front of his building, the Regatta Riverview Residences on Museum Way. The sirloin burger had only stabilized his belly, and he was unsteady as he entered the lobby. Getting in the elevator, he leaned against the metal wall of the car while it hurtled to the twenty-first floor. His silly joke about the poisoned ham was stuck in his head like a needle skipping on an old vinyl record. It kept on repeated itself over and over and over again. He got out of the elevator and swayed up the corridor to his door. Letting himself in, he left it dark. The ambient light coming in from the large picture window in the living room guided him to the fridge at the bar. He took out a bottle of water, and he flopped into the chair in front of the window. It gave him panoramic views of the city lights and the bridges crossing the river and usually it zoned him out. After a long and stressful day, he'd stare out there and unwind, making himself into a sea gull flying above it all. Gazing out at the twinkling cityscape, the only thing he could think about at that point was the tainted ham. He couldn't get the needle out of the scratch. He couldn't stop imagining a life in which his whole family was blinked out . . . *and what if he brought that vicious prank to fruition?* Sipping at the water bottle, he thought it over. It had seemed crazily absurd an hour ago, but certain angles became more plausible by the second.

> *In Justin's future world, Alan was sitting in the hot tub wearing that white bikini bathing suit he loved so much. His buttery skin was golden brown, and it had to be late spring. The sweet aroma of flowering lilacs surrounded them and he held his lover's hand. They pushed the intercom button together, and Mirabelle answered. "Yes sir, what do you require of me?"*
>
> *"Bring out black caviar, truffles, and two hurricanes to the pool. Don't forget the multi-colored umbrellas on those drinks and after that you can call Maurice and schedule our massages at five under the gazebo.*

11:13AM Sunday June 19, 2005 New Bedford, Massachusetts

Holly was long gone. According to the clock on the bedside table it was 11:15. She always disappears on Sunday mornings and he didn't know where she went. He didn't care. Sitting up in bed, David reached for his robe. Badly drained from his futile jaunt to Boston, he'd driven home the day before with a heavy heart. He got out of bed, and put on his bathrobe. The belt on the robe was way too loose as he slogged towards the kitchen. It hooked on the closet doorknob in the hall and he kept on going. The robe slipped off his shoulders and he left it behind, crumpled on the floor. Setting up the coffee machine, he remembered that his bathrobe had come off exactly the same way a few months ago, and it felt like a kind of Déjà-vu. He could be locked in a loop on a high channel in someone else's cable subscription living through a boring docudrama, or even worse, a nightmarish sequel to *Groundhog Day*.

The answer he got from Justin in Boston had been depressing. No miraculous cures for his condition, and he couldn't bring the dead back to life. Sipping at his coffee, he slouched over the kitchen table like an exhausted troll. At least Holly had left the local paper there for him. He flipped through the pages until he saw an article about a memorial for Arthur Mercer. For some unknown reason it captivated him. Mercer and his family had built the largest shipyard in New Bedford and he'd been a cornerstone of the community. David looked down at the picture of Mercer's friends and relatives gathered around a mausoleum for a long time. Putting the paper down, he closed his eyes and the recollection of the dream he'd had the night before flooded in.

Foggy and dank, a graveyard reminiscent of the 1800's, and he was the only mourner at the internment of five coffins. No one was around, but the priest. In the distance he saw a female silhouette flittering between the tombs, but that ghostlike outline quickly disappeared. The white robed clergyman stood over the open graves, delivering an obscure religious passage from the Bible. Closing the good book, he walked over to him with a message.

"You've been blessed, son! You are free now," and the holy man gave him a glowing key, radiating more light than anything else in the cemetery. Then he raised up heavy chains and manacles he'd hidden in his robes over his head, throwing them into one of the graves.

David opened his eyes. Was the drunken repartee' he'd had with Justin yesterday responsible for that dream? He'd asked Justin if he was going to bring a poisoned ham to the next Thanksgiving dinner so he'd know not to eat it or something, and Justin had sloughed the whole thing off, saying it was only a joke. He wasn't doing anything like that. Yeah, the joke about poisoning everyone could have ignited this prophetic dream; a clear signpost on his new path for the ultimate resolution.

11:25AM Sunday June 19, 2005 Cambridge, Massachusetts

Drinking was undermining his health. Justin was on his way to the exercise room on the third floor to attempt to even the scales. Power walking out of the elevator, he opened the glass door of the fitness center and he crossed the room to the treadmills. He got on one next to the window. He set up his vitamin-enriched water and the Sunday paper in the holding tray. He believed he could sweat out all the deleterious garbage he'd put in his body the night before.

Forty-five minutes later, the screen blinked. He'd reached four miles, but he wasn't done yet. Hair plastered to his forehead, he kept on jogging. To pass the time, he read the leisure section of the paper. There was a section about oyster stuffing and that made him think about the stuffing his parent's chef always made on Thanksgiving. *Oysters, what was it about the oysters in the stuffing?* After the meeting with David two days ago, a nefarious plan grew like a pearl in his subconscious mind, and it was growing layers like a real one. The recipes in the newspaper dragged it out into the light.

Four years ago, he had a case involving the poisoning of a patron in a Japanese restaurant in Connecticut. The customer insisted the poison of a puffer fish he'd eaten there was responsible for his sickness. He was suing the establishment. The owner maintained they didn't even have that fish on the menu. The puffer fish secretes a neurotoxin called tetrodotoxin, and Justin had to research the deadly poison. The fish used to be imported into the States from Asia, until it was banned a year ago. Still served in Japan, a customer at one of the Fugu palaces (restaurants catering to people who enjoy gambling with this hazardous dinner) would occasionally die. All of the poison was supposedly removed before the fish was cooked and eaten, but the cleaning process was never foolproof. Once in a while, a few of those dastardly molecules were missed.

Other fish and reptiles used the exact same chemical. A rough skinned newt had enough tetrodotoxin in its tiny body to eradicate thirty people and Justin also knew about a certain festive looking octopus, just as deadly. Fifty times more lethal as cyanide, it was one of the fastest and deadliest concoctions in the natural world.

The prosecution had used a lot of contradictory evidence and they didn't have a chance. Anyone ingesting tetrodotoxin and surviving to talk about it was infinitesimal. Paralytic shell fish toxin's side effects were identical to tetrodotoxin *in the beginning,* but the effects diverge dramatically after ten minutes, and that poison wasn't fatal. The fact that the so-called victim in the case had more than enough time to eat something else from a different source ended the debate, but Justin's memories of the case had nothing to do with whether he'd won or lost. The old research he'd gone through gave him the answer he was looking for. Switching the treadmill off, he drank the rest of his water, put his towel around his neck and the paper under his arm and he strode to the elevators as if he had to be someplace in a hurry.

Injecting tetrodotoxin into the oyster stuffing, the investigators would at first suspect they'd died from paralytic shellfish toxin. After the lab results, the poison in the stuffing wouldn't match anything an oyster could ever produce and they'd turn to his father's commercial competitors as possible suspects. Justin was allergic to shellfish, so he'd be the only survivor by happenstance, and after sending the gourmet ham, he could innocently enjoy eating a lot of it. He might even get away with nibbling on some breast meat from the turkey with piles of that great homemade cranberry sauce on the side. Getting out of the elevator, he trotted to his door. After an invigorating shower, he began to figure out a way to get his hands on the compound.

1:22PM Tuesday June 21, 2005 New Bedford, Massachusetts

Wearing loose-fitting white chinos and a cotton T-shirt, David perched on the edge of a lounge chair in the shade of the covered porch facing the backyard of his home. He gazed down at a sand garden on a table in front of him, and the end of neon green straw coming out of a large plastic tumbler disappeared between his lips. He was sucking ice tea and vodka down his throat, absentmindedly pushed a tiny rake through the ultra-fine sand in the garden.

A week ago, Holly had left a giftwrapped box near the front door with a note saying her secretary had left the present in her office. She thought he might like it. David ignored it, and the package sat in the hallway until Sunday afternoon. When he got home after a late lunch at the club, curiosity finally drove him into snatching it up and un-wrapping it, and then he left it on kitchen counter. It rained hard and endlessly the next day, and David wandered through the house like an oversized child. He was trying to plan the 'perfect crime' and he couldn't figure out what the golden key in his dream meant. Coming up blank, the incessant rain pounding on the roof was driving him nuts.

The next morning was brisk and dry, but the static in his head was still there. Going through the breakfast ritual like a dead thing, his logic circuits had been tangled up by emotion and the answer he needed was out of reach.

It came to him that perhaps he should try to meditate by moving the sand around in that silly garden Holly had left for him. Maybe it would help him think outside the box. At that juncture, simply *thinking* might be helpful.

The slurping noise at the bottom of his plastic cup caused him to drop the little rake. He got up and walked over to the outside bar, and he opened the small fridge. Lifting the flap of the freezer, he grabbed the bitterly cold neck of a bottle of vodka he'd left inside. The icy glass startled the nerves of his hand, and the puzzle piece he was searching for clicked into place. A cocktail party he'd gone to with his wife a year ago, lit up in the darkness of his mind as clear as a bell. He was holding a martini, while he conversed with another neurosurgeon called John Armata. They'd been standing near a swimming pool, and music was coming from outside speakers and the smell of chlorine wafted up to them from the water.

He needed to edit the recollection like a film clip, but the blood at the end of his fingers was getting way too cold. Honing in on the pertinent part of that long gone conversation was letting him lose too much of his circulation. Carefully holding onto the precious memory as if it was gold, he got the bottle out of the freezer. He poured some vodka in the cup, and he topped it off with more ice-tea from the carton, putting the bottle back in the freezer. Returning to his lounge chair, he relived the necessary part of the discussion he'd had with Dr. Armata over a year ago.

> *"You didn't see the insert in last week's local Sunday paper, did you? How could you have avoided the front page! "Four Found Killed by Yew". The bodies were found next to a cooking fire near Dunstable on route 113. Now, I live on Rockville Road, so I'm the only neighbor the Lyman family has, and they're the ones who own those hundred acres of land the kids got lost in." Doctor Armata tilted his head and sipped on his daiquiri.*

"I was locked up in a clinical study, John. It's a new treatment for long term non-responsive coma patients. I've been locked up in a laboratory. If Holly hadn't dragged me here, I'd still be in the lab, so no, I didn't see the paper. It sounds like a strange story." David was leaning against a pillar supporting a trellis thick with vines. "If you're the only neighbor, you must know more about the story than anyone else."

"You're right about that. Last year, Melissa and Phillip were relieved when I bought the adjoining property as they'd felt desolate out there. Anyway, they called me as soon as it happened. Their daughter was home for the summer and she'd gone out riding on the back trails following the creek, and she saw the bodies in a clearing near the river. Three of them were law students and one was learning archeology. They'd all watched the Blair Witch Project, a movie that came out a few years ago, and it had turned into a cult classic. I think the enigmatic ending of that movie was what sent them into the woods. The budding archeologist had heard about the so-called "lost" farmhouse built in the eighteen hundreds on the Lyman's land and in 1965, a group of young people tramped off into the same woods to find the farmhouse because they wanted to live in it. No one saw any of them again. The locals have no idea where the farmhouse is, not even sure if there really is one. Flying over the land hasn't helped. It's way too overgrown. Anyway, the students were on spring break and they wanted to find the building too, but they got lost. The only thing they found was the stream, and they thought it could lead them out. Logical enough, but they ran out of food. Stopping to pick wine berries, they saw a yew tree and they thought it was a holly bush. Over a small fire, they boiled up a fruit stew out of all

the berries they'd found in the metal pot they'd brought along. If only it had been a holly bush! They could have just thrown up and lived, but the digestive acid in their bellies had opened the shells of the seeds of the non-toxic yew berries. The concentration of poison inside the seeds themselves killed them. Did you know a handful of yew seeds could kill an adult in only twenty minutes?" Dr. Armata looked astonished, even if he'd known that fact for days.

"Good God, that's awful. This happened a week ago? I'm going to have to look it up. I bet TV and newspapers are bombarding us about the new assortment of hazards in our own backyards, busily telling us the end of the world as we know it is only three feet away."

"It's over the top, David. Even the magazines are grinding out lots of articles about it. I still can't believe you haven't heard a thing about it until now!"

"Well, you've certainly got me curious. I'll read up on it. It's a horrible story, with a horrible ending. It doesn't even sound real. A wild plant growing in an eastern forest is responsible for the devastation of four young lives." David shook his head. "Have you ever asked your neighbors about the lost farmhouse? Is it possible they could have a hint on where it actually might be?"

David broke away the memory, and he picked up the tiny rake again. He gently pulled it straight across the length of the garden. The dead end meeting with Justin had turned into a stepping stone. Dredging up what had been buried in his mind, the triviality hidden in a conversation he'd had twelve months ago had given him the key to Fort Knox.

He'd brazenly lied to John at the party. He never read a single word about the case. Now, he was about to rescind that lie with the religious fervor of a convert. He'd dig up anything he could find about that treacherous yew.

9:35PM Friday August 26, 2005 Las Vegas, Nevada

Samuel drove his Ferrari into a rest area on Interstate 15, sixty miles away from Sin City. He'd closed his account in San Diego, and he'd wired the $50,000 dollars to his bank in Las Vegas. It was the last of his money, and he was on his way home.

The long streak of good luck that had cloaked him for almost a year had vanished. The week before he drove to San Diego had been dreadful. Pile after pile of his chips had been whisked away from him. He kept on losing. Imperceptibly woven in the possessed jabber and jangle of the slot machines, and laced in the babble coming out of the milling crowds, he'd heard the melody of his own funeral dirge.

Getting out of the car, it was a comfortable 75 degrees, and he rested his palms on the cooling guard rail. He stared out at the throbbing city, a neon pulse on the horizon. The last time he'd been on his way home, he'd had his cousin's money burning a hole in his pocket and the air conditioner in the rental was barely holding on. This time, he'd had the savvy to cross the desert after the sun had set, yet the arrival of some nuts and bolts practicality hadn't rid him of possession. The caustic part of his spirit had stayed the same. If he'd been on the deck of the wounded Titanic, he would not have gotten into a lifeboat. He would have swayed back and forth like a faulty metronome to enjoy the last songs the doomed men in the band were playing before they all tragically slid into the frozen water to drown. Nevertheless, there was momentary crack in his armor. Alone in the darkened rest area, an undercurrent of painful clarity slammed into him like a punch, hard enough to awaken a flicker of self-preservation.

He'd gone a long way on Rick's loan. Did he really believe this road would go on forever? In the murky world of a full-blown addict, he was returning to his own quicksand and annihilation waited for him in Las Vegas, yet that appalling consequence wasn't bad enough for him to hit the brakes. Late on his payments to Cindy and the sports car, he had been parking himself and the Ferrari in different spots every night, hoping to avoid repo in all forms.

If he suddenly decided to drive north over the Canadian border, he could wire the last of his money out of Vegas and squirrel it away in some small town on the coast of Hudson Bay. He could live a different life and forget about gambling . . . forget about the tantalizing seconds in which he feels immortal, free from the ropes that hold down the rest of us. He must forget the unforgettable. Samuel got back in the car and started the engine.

Luck runs in waves doesn't it? Isn't it possible he could do well on his first night back from California? Poised on the exit ramp, he felt the powerful vibration of the eight cylinders rumbling through the seat cushions. North or east? His eyes were partially closed, and he wasn't looking at the bright green highway signs over his head. Samuel was drawn toward the deep shadows under the shrubbery at the edge of the paved road, and he imagined a treasure chest of gold twinkling in that lightless gloom . . . *he was under too much pressure and the compression from the deep water he was in should rise the bounty to the surface . . . shouldn't it?* He dropped the clutch, and shifted the transmission into first gear. He burned rubber on the ramp to celebrate his decision.

Samuel walked into the Purple Tumble Weed, a casino on the outskirts of Las Vegas. Planting himself at the bar, he wanted to test the water before he dove in. The place wasn't up to the standards on the strip, but the air was fresh enough. The polished wood of the bar was hard-used and gouged, and the wide orange and purple stripes painted on the walls were fading. A strip of purple paint near the back exit was actually peeling off the wall.

A young female, presumably the barkeep, whirled up to him on the other side of the bar.

"Hey, hey, ho, ho! What can I bring ya?" She was wearing a pink leather jacket and sprayed on jeans, and her hair was light pink. She looked 14, and her name was Megan. Conservative with her makeup, the rose eye shadow and plum colored lip gloss had her innocence outwardly intact.

Samuel ordered a gin and tonic. He looked down at the poker machine installed into the wood of the bar in front of him. *Only a dollar a game.* He inserted a bill and he broke even on the first game. Megan returned with his drink, and he kept on playing until the computer spit out a very good hand for him. One more card, the right card, would give him a straight flush. He could fold or bet on the second deal if he throws out the two of diamonds. Samuel had been waiting, more like praying, for the uncommon luck he used to have, so he bet the limit. His digital opponent would have to replace the two with a six of spades or a Jack of spades, and he did get the Jack. He won $1,500 dollars; a portent for him. It was a sign of good things to come. It seemed that Lady Luck had daintily perched herself on the barstool next to him again, even if the heavily-veiled creature whose pulse he lived by might not be a lady at all.

6:57PM Saturday August 27, 2005 Las Vegas, Nevada

The entire west side of the eight-ton sculpture of a lion in front of the MGM Grand Arena at the intersection of Las Vegas Boulevard and Tropicana Avenue had turned fiery orange by the light of the setting sun. Later on that day, Bernard Hopkins, aka "The Executioner" would defend his middle weight crown against Jermaine Taylor at 9:00 PM inside the arena.

The heat in Nevada is usually dry and tolerable in the late afternoon, but on that day the air was sluggish, and the streets, torrid. Traffic around the complex had snarled to a stop, and the running engines of the gridlocked cars radiated a lot more heat of their own. Fumes coming out of the exhaust pipes of all those vehicles hung only three feet over the sizzling pavement. A band of poisonous fog, and it was getting thicker. Anyone who'd parked a few blocks away to watch the exhibition fights before the main event wasn't enjoying their stroll to the arena. The air-conditioned environment waiting for them inside the main building had become a life preserver, and they were all straining to get there as fast as they could.

Inside the MGM, Lazzo and Edgar read racing forms and stared up at the wall-sized screen of changing information about the ongoing horse races.

"It's getting late. Mike and Cindy gave us really good tickets and I think we gotta go." Lazzo lifted himself off the plastic bench, and he nervously waved his wristwatch in front of his partner's face. Staring up at Lazzo with a scowl, Edgar put down the form he had in his hands.

"It's only a few minutes after seven, numb nuts," but he got up too.

Imperious in her orders, Cindy had instructed her henchmen to meet her in her private box suite that overlooked the ring after the match, and Edgar and Lazzo were agitated. They were nervous she was going to reprimand them, afraid they'd done something wrong.

The lights went out and a booming voice echoed its pronouncements through the entire darkened stadium. 'The Executioner' was on his way to tangle with 'Bad Intention'. Suddenly, Hopkins was pinned by three powerful spotlights, and the lights followed him all the way to the ring like glue. After that, more blazing beams of radiance zeroed in on Taylor, highlighting him to center stage as well. 17,000 fans clapped, whistled, and screamed at the top of their lungs, forming a wave of thunder powerful enough to shake the cushioned floor of the ring. The heavily-muscled prizefighters touched gloves in a remembrance of civility and the crowd quieted down. The bell rang. The dance began, and besides the short rest breaks, they'd go at it until one of them fell down. If they were evenly matched, they could make it all the way through all twelve rounds. At that point, the judges would use a point system to decide the winner.

Cindy needed to be as close to the action as she could get. It was like a drug for her. Sitting in the front row, she could actually smell the sweat running down the fighter's bodies, and she was sexually turned on by the aggressive power discharging off the fighters. Careening against the ropes above her seat, Hopkins landed a punch to the side of his opponent's head. A small drop of Taylor's blood escaped from his mouth and it landed on the inside of Cindy's thigh. The silk stockings she had on were held up by black garters, and while the red stain spread through the thin fabric, she crooned with pleasure. The boxers shuffled away from the ropes and across the ring, and then the bell rang again and they stumbled to their respective corners.

Tall and extremely pale, Michael Rickert sat right next to Cindy. He watched her green eyes go glassy, and her breathing getting faster and harder. He knew about her excitement. When Bernard and Jermaine retired for their short time out, Rickert instantly started to whisper twisted seductions in her ear.

"I know you have a business meeting after the match, but you can't forget the appointment you have with me later on. I won't let you forget it." Sliding his hand along the inside of her upper thigh, it disappeared under the laced edge of her leather dress . . . and it kept on sneaking towards a tease.

Cindy tossed her head violently to the left and her auburn hair swept out in a beautiful arc. Rickert continued to murmur nasty things in her ear and then she moaned.

"My warehouse is set up for my own diversions, including the complete and painful domination of you. I've checked the handcuffs. They're still anchored in the cement to hold you down. I've also decided to use nipple clamps on you this evening," and she felt his fingers forcefully snake deep inside of her. Rickert continued to coo to her.

"You know I really need them, hmmm. Aaah . . . I need all my other tools. Do not arrive at my door without them, or there will be hell to pay." Removing his hand from under her skirt, he leaned back in his seat and adjusted his sunglasses. Cindy smiled and nodded, mouthing the word "yes" at him. Crossing his arms, he looked away from her. Anyone noticing their unusual display of affection had studiously overlooked it; what happens in Vegas stays in Vegas, after all.

Lazzo and Edgar waited patiently for her after the end of the fight. The current king had lost his crown. They reclined in the comfortable lounge chairs in front of the glass, and they watched thousands of fans bleed away like water through a drain. The suite had a small kitchen, a wet bar, and a bathroom, but her previous guests were long gone. By the time Edgar and Lazzo showed up, Edgar had to use his key to get in. Bottles of alcohol were carelessly left open on the bar and mauled-over appetizers were in disarray on the serving table. Lazzo reached over his shoulder, picking out a wilted cracker topped with crab salad, while Edgar got up and made himself a Bloody Mary. He sat down next to his partner again, and he explained to Lazzo that his intestines would knot up bad if he ate anymore of that crap. Lazzo grinned at Edgar between bites. When the cracker was gone, he snatched another one loaded with more of the so-called crap. He wolfed it down with happy abandon.

They heard a loud bang, and the door behind them slammed open. Standing up and turning around at the same time, they turned into a very clumsy chorus line. Cindy was in the doorway, breathless and flushed, the living proof that the homily "you can't judge a book by its cover" was true. The fine scarlet lace at the hem of her dress and the velvety timbre in her voice defied and distorted the fact that she was a cutthroat bookmaker and a seasoned murderer by proxy. "Hey guys, did you enjoy the fight? Did you think the Executioner was going to lose? I did not see it coming." She frowned. "Why do you both look like I'm your worst nightmare? Come on, sit down and relax. I've got more work for you, a little more moolah in your bank accounts."

Lazzo and Edgar moved over to the bar, and Cindy nestled on the couch across the small room.

"Hey Boss, you look great," Lazzo said.

"Hello Cindy. I didn't think he was going to lose either . . . ah well, nobody really knows how things are going to go for sure." Edgar waved at the bar behind him, "How 'bout a drink . . . what'd you like?"

"Same thing you're having, Eddie. A Bloody Mary will top off the evening's entertainment nicely." Nodding at Lazzo, she said, "Thank-you sir, I love compliments."

The second Edgar handed her the drink, she got up and put it back on the bar. She wanted to get straight to business, and her underlings were about to hear the frustration in her voice.

"I've had it with Samuel Eveland. I'm not playing anymore games with that idiot. He owes me over a quarter of a million dollars, so you can go ahead and find him and tell him he owes me double. Tell him he can pay it off up-front, or you can shake as much as can out of him. I'd rather have the money, and I'll double your normal fee if you can actually get your hands on some of it. If not, well, you know what to do."

"Are you in a hurry?" Edgar asked.

"Not really. Just go ahead and look under all those sleazy rocks in an easy pace. I've got a lot of things going on and it's a big old world out there. I don't care if you pick him up tomorrow or in six months, but it's important that you eventually do pick him up. Eveland has finally reached his limit and its time to close down his account."

She flowed back to the couch like warm oil, and her former life as a double-jointed exotic dancer bubbled into view for a second. After that unconscious demonstration, she relaxed on the leather cushions, content that the important part of her meeting with the boys was over. Eyes half-closed and a languorous grin on her lips, Cindy was reminiscent of a venomous spider half asleep in its web.

5:56PM Tuesday August 16, 2005 New Orleans, Louisiana

Saplings twenty years ago, the living barricade of maple trees rustled in the afternoon zephyr as they shadowed the elegant townhouses on Dalton Avenue. It was a main thoroughfare and cars whizzed by on the outside lanes and a trolley car, connected to an overhead electric line, clattered down the center.

Justin was on his way to the last conference, and he liked the trolley ride. The position he was in on the bench allowed a patch of sunlight warm the side of his face while lines of slanted shadows traveled sedately across the floor of the car. The whole thing was relaxing him. Stumped for weeks, he hadn't been able to figure out how to get his hands on tetrodotoxin without leaving any clues behind until he got part of the answer on the tread-mill in Massachusetts.

Partying the Fourth of July weekend away in the Hamptons, a connection to an old case against a restaurant in Connecticut lit up in his mind. He was dipping a jumbo shrimp into a bowl of cocktail sauce at one of the constant parties at his friend's house in Westhampton, when the new idea hit him. The plaintiff, Barry Rand, had set the whole thing up and Justin had eaten him up alive in court. After that drubbing, Barry wasn't going to talk to him about anything . . . but his older brother might. Morgan Rand could have the information he was trawling for. If his brother had really used paralytic shellfish toxin to poison himself, he must have found those chemicals somewhere. Returning to Cambridge on Tuesday, he went straight to his office to find Morgan Rand's telephone number in one of the old files. Building a contrivance before he called the man up, he needed a sugary sweet ploy to wheedle what he wanted out of Morgan. According to the file, he lived in North Grosvenor Dale, near the Connecticut-Massachusetts border. If things went well on the phone, he could take 395 out of Boston and arrive at his doorstep in only two hours.

"Hello, Mr. Rand? My name is Travis Stutz, and a couple of years ago I was doing research on your brother's case in Connecticut. Right now there's a similar case on the docket, and I was hoping you could put some light on one of the mysteries that's confusing us. I'd be able to compensate you for any information you may be able to give us surrounding one of the ambiguities in the old case. A profitable trade I think, Mr. Rand . . . Hello?"

"Well, it's about time somebody called about that jackass. I haven't been hanging around with him lately, not since last New Years. We went out together and he got tanked and he told me *everything*. What are you interested in Travis? As if I don't already know."

To Justin, things sounded great. *No love lost between those two.*

"We're worried that the same poison involved in your brother's case is also being used in the latest situation. We're on their side of course, but we don't want to be stuck holding the bag, so to speak. If evidence surfaces to disprove our premise, we'll be in bad shape. Do you know how your brother found the poisons? Did he buy them?"

"My uncle died last month and the cause of his death was undetermined. They couldn't figure it out, but I know exactly what happened, since Barry got a good chunk of change from the will. The greedy bastard killed him, so I'll tell you the real story about what he tried to do to that restaurant in Connecticut. The shit-heel told me everything in his drunken black out on New Years night. Yup, I'll tell you everything, but you're right. You're gonna have to pay for the down and dirty. How 'bout I meet you at the Woodbridge. It's only a mile out of town. You can't miss the sign on Route 131. What about 4:30, tomorrow afternoon? I'll just put on my white and blue checked jacket, so you'll know it's me, and we'll hash out the reward you're gonna give me when we get there."

Morgan didn't think his brother had the brains to come up the story he'd told him, and that's why he was sure it was true. Over the second cup of very good coffee, Justin wrote what he'd told him in a small notebook.

> *'Travel to New Orleans and buy the daily rag, it's the Times-Picayune. Look through the classified section until you see an ad for "Organic Herbal Tonics at Veronica's Plantation". There's an address and a phone number on the bottom of the ad. The address is bogus, and the phone number is real. Call the number and tell whoever picks up that you're friends with "Blue Beard", a code name that lets you in the back door.'*

And that was it. Justin had what he wanted. 'Travis' gave Morgan $3,000 in cash and then he drove out of Grosvenor Dale. The young lawyer had been juiced up on self-confidence and caffeine.

Returning home that night in July, he'd sat down in front of the window and considered his options. The directions were in his briefcase, and he better come up with an excuse of some kind to *get* to New Orleans. Ah, the final hurdle. A week went by, and Justin's new frustration swelled until blind coincidence knocked on his door, in the form of a phone call from Scott Weaver, one of his old business acquaintances. Weaver wanted his help in closing down a textile factory, and he wanted Justin to set up building permits so his client could refurbish it into condominiums for retirees. *The work was in New Orleans*. Justin accepted his offer with so much eagerness, Weaver thought he had to be strapped for work. He didn't realize he'd just given Justin the proverbial cherry on top of his virulent cake.

The muted rattle rising up from the rails shook him out of his reveries, and Justin checked out the numbers on the avenue. 1225 was near enough, and he pulled the stop cable. Walking into Weaver's home, they went through the documents he'd brought along in his briefcase and his acquaintance congratulated him and the job was done. They decided to have a celebratory dinner in the French Quarter, driving there in Weaver's car. Having a wonderful dinner in a topnotch restaurant, they ended the meal with fig and pecan pie. Over the pie and coffee, Justin told Weaver he was flying back to Boston the very next day and that was a flagrant lie.

9:30AM Wednesday August 17, 2005 New Orleans, Louisiana

The Ambassador Hotel had been built in the 1800's with blocks of granite and it had been renovated in 2004. The stained glass skylights and the stone columns anchored in the marble lobby sustained its timeless elegance, but Justin had picked it because its location, not the way it looked. The French Quarter was two blocks away.

Waking up the next morning, he called room service. He ordered coffee, eggs, and a copy of the Times-Picayune paper. His room was the seventh floor, so when he rolled out of bed and stepped over to the window, he could make out the older part of the city revealing itself by a drop in the height of the roof lines five hundred feet to the south.

A service worker dropped off his breakfast order, and Justin opened the newspaper even before the door shut behind him. He didn't need the notebook holding the name of the business he was looking for. It was already burned into his head. Gulping coffee and nervously nibbling at the eggs, he turned one page after another as fast as he could as he hunted for the advertisement . . . and there it was! He reached for the hotel phone, dropping his fork on the carpet. He punched in the number at the bottom of the add and the ring was echoing as if it was in a warehouse a thousand miles away.

"Bonjour, ma cher."

"Ah . . . hello, I hope you can understand me. I can't speak French, but I'm a friend of 'Blue Beard' and I need your help."

In a heavily accented voice, she began the prescribed oration she'd probably gone through it a hundred times before: "Queen Tallu Boca will meet you tonight at 10:45 in her shop, the Magic Eye. It's at the intersection of Royal and Dumaine streets in the Vieux Carre. You must bring along eight donations to the cause and then she will honor your request. Ciao," and she abruptly hung up. Justin was momentary puzzled by the so-called *donations,* assuming she was asking for $8,000 in cash.

Justin wanted to walk to the Magic Eye. At 10:00PM he went to the front desk and he got directions and then he started out on Baronne Street. It was a warm night, and he took off his jacket and hung it over his shoulder. New Orleans was unique. She mixed the old with the new without polluting either one. In five minutes, he stepped into the famous French Quarter, and it looked like a Hollywood sound stage set up for a romantic motion picture. The neighborhood was so vibrant and alive, it didn't seem real. Not clinging to the past, it swirled its history around you like a velvet cloak, and the faithless currents of the modern age floated away from you like smoke in the wind.

Most of the buildings were made from wood or brick, and a lot of them were painted in a pastel color; light blue, light green, coral, pink, yellow or even lilac. It reminded him of the tropics. Almost all the second and third stories had balconies (or galleries) decorated with elaborate iron filigree in their rails and shutters, and the adornment was a reflection of the cultural repercussions of the Spanish invasion of Louisiana in the 1700's.

The iron streetlights were twenty feet above the ground, and curved black arms jutted out to end in ornamental glass boxes. Justin thought the lights reminded him of what London could have looked like hundred years ago and when he stepped onto Dumaine Street, the appearance of cobblestones under his feet intensified the effect. Most of the businesses had closed for the night, and the antique looking the lampposts only gave him isolated spots of light. That reticence allowed the darker shadows to sweep farther out, like dark eddies pulling at his legs.

When he got to Royal and Dumaine, the described intersection, one of the streetlights was out and the bar on the adjoining corner was closed, and he couldn't see anything in the gloom. He didn't feel like he was in a city anymore, and there was nothing to direct him towards the shop. A faint blue glow coming from a narrow alley on his right, enticed him into moving down the thin passage and there was the sign. The word magic was painted on wood, with a neon eye hanging below. Justin wasn't impressed by the directions he'd been given, as he opened the small door and entered the shop. Incense burned on the counter at the far end of a long and narrow room, and the smell of patchouli and curried lamb changed his irritation into curiosity. Jars and bottles stuffed with herbs, bones, and undecipherable curiosities were stuffed on all the shelves that lined the walls of the Magic Eye. Candles of every possible size, shape and color were also jammed around the containers and ancient looking books filled the lower two shelves just off the floor, but it was too dark for him to make out any of the titles.

The information Morgan had given him *was* over five years old. Things might have changed. He was apprehensive as he walked up to the counter. Behind the register, even more shelves rose all the way up to the ceiling, and he was staring at a large urn stuffed with rough skinned newts at eye level. He didn't know he was staring at the poison he was trying to find, as those particular newts were also loaded with Tetrodotoxin.

He rang the bell on the counter and nothing happened. Was he alone in the shop? A door in the wall behind him quietly opened and an enormous mahogany-skinned woman sailed closer to him. She had on a floor length purple dress, a turban and a scarf embroidered with shiny glass beads encircled her shoulders. When he heard the fabric rustling behind him, he turned around to see hot red lips beaming out at him in the dim light.

"Oh . . . hello," Justin said. "You must be Queen Tallu Boca. Do you know why I'm here? Can you help me?"

"*Je sais qui vous etes, ma cher, et vous etes dans un endroit dangereux, et Pa Pa Legba n'est pas entendu votre message.* Spirit Vudu cannot help anyone tonight. We must change our course. We are here only for the ultimate celebration of the renewed spirit . . ."

Justin interrupted her, "You have to be interested in my donation, Queen," and he gestured towards the satchel over his shoulder.

"I cannot be enticed into doing the things the Bokor who was here in this place before was doing." She waved her bejeweled fingers and manicured nails in the air. "He must a' been cooking up a zombie brew with Datura to sell those dirty potions. No, no . . . you must go. Forget your quest. You must leave my shop." Pointing her taloned finger towards the front door, diaphanous strips of lavender fabric hung theatrically out of the long seam of the sleeve of her dress.

"Alright, okay . . . but then why would you set this whole thing up, only to shoot it down? I mean, you're paying for the ad that got me and you answered the damned phone for God's sake. There's no logic behind any of this and I'd like to have an explanation. Come on, go ahead. Give it a try, go on!" He was getting madder by the second. "I don't think there really is a reason for this Hoodoo Voodoo crap, Queenie pie. It seems my entire trip as turned out to be nothing but a dead end and a joke."

"*Pourqoi je devraite*? You are snarling like a *bete*. I know nothing about code names," yet while she spoke, she pressed a folded note into the palm of his hand, and that was followed by a conspiratorial whisper, "*You really must go*."

"Right . . . ah huh . . . as you command," Justin was already reading the note.

> *The Magic Eye has been bugged we will bribe the Officials again and it will be safe here in two weeks then you can return and we can go ahead with the sale*

He dropped the scrap of paper and marched to the exit, slamming the door with an intentional bang. Storming down the alleyway, he was bubbling with exasperation. When he reached Royal Street, Justin no longer cared where he was going, and he randomly stamped onto Bienville Street . . . from there, Bourbon Street. A jazz band was playing live in a nearby bar and he looked at his wristwatch. 11:08. He was about to walk into that establishment to order a double shot of anything with a kick, when a black limousine stopped in the street right next to him. The front passenger window slid down and the driver leaned over to talk to him.

"Aren't you a friend of Blue Beard, sir? I think you should relax and get in and I'll drive you over so you can meet him. He'll take care of your problem. Doesn't that sound like a great idea . . . sir? Hello, can you hear me?" The driver was wearing a chauffeur's uniform including a traditional cap and white silk gloves, and he was alone in the limousine.

"Yes, I can hear you perfectly and I'm a great friend of that nasty pirate. If you can get me where I need to be, then I guess your invitation can't be ignored," and Justin threw caution to the winds. He got in the back seat of the car, and they rolled back out into traffic. Justin watched Bourbon Street rush past. They turned onto Tulane Avenue and his exasperation faded and a hint of hopefulness crept in.

"How long before we get there?" He sounded like a child and he flinched.

"Five, maybe ten minutes, according to the traffic and the lights, sir."

Only three miles away from the center of the French Quarter, it seemed they'd transported themselves to a different city as the limousine sailed into the parking lot of 413 Rocheblave Road. Justin read a metal plaque set into the concrete wall next to the main entrance, engraved with the name 'Hudson Biomedical Research Institute'. The building had eight floors, and it was flanked by two windowless rust colored columns.

"Stay on the sidewalk that followed the edge of the building. You can get in through the back entrance. It's unlocked. Finding yourself in a long hallway, the person you want to talk to is behind the fourth door on your left. Have a nice evening, sir."

Justin thanked him, and got out of the car. He looked up at the structure. Every single window was black. What he'd just gone through in the Magic Eye had left him highly skeptical. Meeting another stranger in an empty office building in the middle of the night, could be a continuation of an episode of the *Twilight Zone*. Or maybe he was in a modern version of the Phantom of the Opera. A white-coated biomedical researcher from the institute was playing a pipe organ in the basement, and he'd left the back exit unlocked to allow his audience of one to hear his performance.

Following the sidewalk with apprehension in his heart, the backdoor was open and he entered the hallway. The red glow coming from the exit signs and the panel of glass installed above the metal door let in enough outside light to describe the corridor. Brightness leaked out under the bottom of the fourth door down the hall and that light let Justin know it was the right place. Knocking, he heard a muffled invitation and so he walked in . . . and ducked. A paper plane zoomed by right where his head had been a second ago.

Fifteen-by-twenty, the office was utilitarian and cabinets fronted with glass lined the walls. Behind the plastic tiles covering the ceiling, florescent lights buzzed over his head and the grey industrial carpet clashed with the beige walls and tightly closed pea-green window blinds.

A white man in his thirties was sitting behind an ugly metal desk. He was folding another airplane. The combination of his big nose, the oversized brown Afro and his polyester brown suit came up with a reflection of a young Howard Stern, but the visual similarity vanished as soon as Justin heard his voice.

"Forgive me. I'm remorseful for the obfuscation I've put you through, but we're both naughty boys and it's clear that one of us is a practical joker. Don't concern yourself with the Magic Eye. I was having fun at your expense." He grinned. "My title is Professor and my name is Byron Adkins, but you may call me Ronnie." He stood up, and reached across the desk to shake Justin's hand. "Please, relax. Go ahead and sit down." He waved to the chair on the other side of his desk.

"Hello, sir. I'm Travis Stutz. I don't appreciate screwing around with my head like this, and the finale' of your joke was cruel, professor . . . ah, Ronnie, but I guess you have a point. Buying dangerous things should give me fair warning to expect the unacceptable and the subsequent bruising." Justin shrugged. "The woman on the phone hadn't been clear about payment. Mind giving me the price?"

Folding the last crease in his latest creation, Professor Adkins slid the plane to the side of his desk top, and then he leaned back in his chair.

"Eight thousand dollars, Travis and all my donations go to a wonderful charity. The paper trail won't lead anyone anywhere but towards more charitable thoughts. You can write the check out to PAVE, the Prism Alliance for Veterans Education."

"I had no idea you had a cover that deep. I didn't bring a check, just cash. I hope that's alright?"

The professor grinned. "Of course, I can pick up the weight of hundred dollar bills with aplomb." He got up again and went over to one of the cabinets. Opening the door, Adkins removed a bottle and placed it on the desk in front of Justin. Unable to read the microscopic lettering on the label, Justin didn't need a magnifying glass to make out the word *TETRODOTOXIN* printed in large and bold letters at the top.

"How did you know that this was the chemical I want? I mean, maybe I wanted cyanide or salmonella . . . or maybe paralytic shellfish toxin." Justin took off his satchel and parked it on the floor.

"My donations come from fairly intelligent people. Most of you want the fastest and most extreme poison I can provide. Of course, there are a couple of snake venoms that are even worse, but tetrodotoxin is really a universal soldier. Ergo, my prediction has a wonderful track record. Would you like a syringe to go with it?"

To Justin, the Professor sounded like a waiter in a diner in hell, and he imagined a continuing spiel coming out of him to inform a hungry customer during the luncheon rush. *"And there's a special today, sir! A pitcher of human blood for only $3.99. Would you like to enjoy that on the side?"* But Professor Adkins wasn't in the underworld, he was in New Orleans, and even if the hand of the devil himself was used in their manufacture, he was actually advising Justin about real implements he might want.

"Since the top of the bottle can be easily pricked by the needle, you could fill the syringe without opening the small flask. I can also give you a traveling case to hold the bottle and the syringe. Less chance for an accident . . . oh, you really shouldn't fly home. You'd be better off driving back."

"I know, you're right. Airport security would certainly sink me," and Justin chuckled. He took out packets of hundred dollar bills out of the bag, lining them up in orderly piles on top of the desk. "The syringe and the case sound indispensable, and I'm looking forwards to using them. Thank you, Ronnie."

The professor opened the top drawer of the desk, and he took out the needle and the black traveling case. Nestling the bottle and the large syringe in the pre-cut holes in the grey foam padding inside the box, he closed the cover with a snap. Justin watched him press a small catch hidden on the side of the container allowing him to open the box again. A simple trick to avoid stupid mistakes. No one could open it without knowing where the catch was. Justin nodded. He closed loaded case and put it in the interior compartment of his satchel. Zipping that pocket closed, he was going to be careful, careful to hold on to the prize. He was holding a golden key to open a door to heaven here on earth by sending all his problems to the grave.

2:30PM Monday August 22, 2005 New Bedford, Massachusetts

A bristlecone pine tree grew on the top of a mountain in California, and it's supposed to be 4,845 years old. It may be the oldest tree on Earth. In South America, a Patagonia cypress grows taller everyday at the venerable age of 3,622, and the baobab trees in Africa easily reach 2,000.

The bald cypress, the oldest tree in the state of South Carolina, has been chronicled at 1,622 years. A giant sequoia in the Pacific Northwest is the oldest one recorded in its species, and its next birthday cake would have to be big enough to hold 3,267 candles.

There's an ongoing dispute over the age of the yew tree. Everybody knows it's the oldest living tree in Europe, but there aren't any rings in its trunk to count. They can't pin the exact number down. The largest ones are conservatively assessed at 2,000 years old, but there's a very good chance they're much older. Following historical clues, some experts believe certain trees are well over 5,000 years of age, *but David Russell knew that.*

By the fifth century, Christians had assimilated the older pagan religions that had been flourishing in Europe. One of the ways they integrated the living culture surrounding them was to erect their new churches on sites the indigenous population had already found divine or magnetic. The apparently immortal and occasionally deadly yew tree had become compelling to the villagers, so many of the older churches had those trees on the property or in the adjoining cemeteries.

In the infancy of the contrivance, the clergy told their flock that they'd been the ones who planted the yew trees near the churches to ward off herds of cattle and sheep. If their animals nibble on the yew they'd sicken and sometimes die, so the townsfolk attempted to stop their flocks from tramping irreverently on sacred ground. Using concrete instead of clay to prop up their lies, the ancient plants had actually been rooted there long before God even winked at Mary. As the new generation of innocent celebrants took their place at the altar, they fell head over heels for their own hoopla and the decades piled up around the holy buildings while they venerated their version of the truth. *David knew that, too.*

Facts get rubbery with the distortion of time. That pressure warps every bump in the topography of human history, and the slow hand of erosion cleans up what's left. As the Great Sphinx in Giza baked in the blazing sun and pummeled with rain and dust storms for centuries, the beginning and final straw for its eternal communication came from a king's order for a partial defacement of the statue. A monumental piece of limestone became an exhibition of the staying power of physical evidence.

Short-term memory transcribed in some way could trap continuity pretty well, and it's too bad we weren't there with a video camera right after the sculptors had put down their hammers the day the sphinx had been completed.

Not only do we have the problem of physical disintegration, the farther away we travel from any moment on the time line drags us closer to someone else's opinion. Attempting to understand the past, we are unknowingly inhaling an invisible cloud of ego.

In the old parlor game called Telephone, someone would write out a sentence and whisper the exact same thing into the ear of the next player. The phrase circles the room confidentially and after that, the original note is read out loud, followed by whatever the last player had just heard. Badly twisted from its printed form, everyone breaks out laughing at the ridiculous deformity.

The same dynamic in the telephone game runs rampant and unheeded through out everything we do. We unknowingly insert our personalized adaption to any action to pull it a millimeter out of true. It's possible there's a global telephone game responsible for defacing, destroying, or deforming any positive influence in human evolution, and we may be lost forever in a house of mirrors.

The first settlers had come from Ireland and they'd built a village on the outskirts of New Bedford in 1810. They called it Fairhaven, and they'd brought along a yew tree from their homeland. Planting it behind their newly erected church, it was a way to psychologically root them to the strange new world, and it helped them to alleviate their bewilderment and loss.

One hundred ninety-five years went by, and the alien sapling became a flowering tree. Branches heavy with fruit, the entire plant is contaminated with poison, and only the flesh and the skin of the red berries were free from taxane. The wild birds feasted on them without peril. The highest level of the toxin is concentrated in the seeds inside the berries, (also called arils) but the bird's digestive juices couldn't dissolve the shell. Bellies full, the winged emissaries seeded the European yew hither and yon simply by evacuating their bowels.

The arils on the tree in the cemetery in Fairhaven weren't ripe yet . . . *and of course David absorbed that knowledge as well.*

Holly took his Mercedes to work, and David was using the Triumph in its place. He'd driven over to the New Bedford Library that morning, and he was sitting in front of one of their computers on the second floor. Reading a page from the Wikipedia, two library books, The History of the Yew Tree and The Rose and The Yew Tree, (a murder mystery by Agatha Christie) were momentary forgotten on the seat of a chair next to him. He never check-out any book like that, only reading them when he was at the library. He was afraid that taking them home might leave a record. It could incriminate him.

After leaving medical school, he hadn't had the time to use a PC, but things had changed. The internet had turned into a garden of unlimited knowledge. He could have easily bought himself a new computer, but he kept on using the one in the library. It was a prudent choice. Holly could have easily seen what he was up to. Besides, it was great excuse to go somewhere else besides the golf club. Diving deeper into the world of the yew, he was currently reading a tidbit he'd put on the screen.

> **The names of their kings, such as Ambiorox and Catuvolcus are undoubtedly Celtic, which would seem to suggest that at least the upper echelons were Celtic or had adopted a Celtic language and culture.*
>
> **The tribal name has also been explained as being Celtic.*
>
> **eburo-meaning 'yew (-tree),' which is also attested in personal names and place-names such as Eburacium (York) and Eburobrittium. [5]*
>
> *This etymological derivation would give Caesar's story in which King Catuvolcus committed suicide by taking the poisonous juice from the yew-tree an extra meaning.*
>
> *The etymology is rendered somewhat less certain by the existence of Germanic* ebura 'boar,' although this element is not as well represented in the contemporary onomastic record . . .*

Hunched over, he crawled the digital web and the summer day outside did not call to him. Hours evaporated like minutes, until David's concentration began to flag. It was getting late, and his mouth had become dry. His manicured hands were shaking. Ah, the addiction tugged for attention, and he must obey. Logging off, he replaced the books back on the shelves, *correctly*, not wanting anyone at the library to know what he was doing either. Jogging down the main stairs to the front door, his concentration funneled into a one-note symphony. He wanted to race to his car. He wanted to sprint, but he restrained himself to a speed walk instead. Getting inside the Triumph, his entire body was trembling, and after he started the engine, he had to wait for the car to warm up. Feeling uncomfortable, he wiggled there for a minute or two. Most people in his condition wouldn't do that, but then they also wouldn't have a watering hole of their own just five minutes away.

3:00AM Tuesday October 4, 2005 New Bedford, Massachusetts

David quietly closed the door of the bedroom. He didn't want to wake her up. He'd change his clothes somewhere else and corduroy pants, a shirt and a jacket waited for him in a bucket in the corner of the garage. When he was done dressing, he got in the Mercedes. It was quieter than the Triumph, so he'd use it on his trip to Fairhaven. He made sure all the things he'd need were in the shoulder bag: surgical gloves, dishwashing gloves, and thicker commercial gloves, plus a heavy duty flashlight. A small stone bowl and pestle rested under the pile of gloves on the bottom of the bag. Good. It was all there.

When his wife had come back from work the night before, she'd gone straight to the bathroom to have a shower. David used that brief stretch of time without fear of discovery, as he put a garden shovel in the trunk of the car and a face shield and a rain slicker on the back seat. Plastic bags, the last thing on the list in his head, were stuffed in his jacket pocket. Hitting the remote control, the garage doors went up and he drove out onto the empty streets.

Holly sleepily listened to David's covert departure, and she didn't care. Turning over, she went back to sleep. In her last unconnected thought, she wondered if David's long eye lashes would impair his sight . . . it was dark outside. It would be dark in the cemetery.

He drove carefully and legally into Fairhaven. David avoided the main parking lot in front of the church on Brewers Lane, and he turned onto Harding Road instead. He wanted to park in the smaller parking field *behind* the church. Watching the street numbers go by, he slowed down and shut off the headlights when he saw 400 on a mailbox in front of a white ranch. The number of the rear entrance to the church was 464, and when he saw it, he drove in and nuzzled the car between two high hedges near the office. It was impossible to see the Mercedes from the main road, it was also barely noticeable from the secondary street behind the church. Shutting off the engine, he turned the leather bag next to him upside down. The contents rained down onto the passenger seat, and he picked up the heaviest gloves, putting them in his jacket pocket with the plastic bags. He grabbed the flashlight, and he left the rest of it on the passenger seat.

Jogging to the northwest corner of the parking lot, a wooden arch decorated the start of a path that led into the cemetery. David knew exactly where he was going. He'd Googled the satellite image of Saint Mary's Church and the surrounding property on the library computer a thousand times. Walking along the footpath, the smell of freshly cut grass rose up from under his feet. An energizing perfume. The darker silhouette appearing above the next corner was the tree, and he got one of the larger plastic bags out of his pocket. He put it between his teeth while he used both hands to get the heavy gloves on.

Uneasy for a moment, he looked around, but everything was copacetic. Things were alright. He was still alone. Turning the flashlight on, he stared straight up. So many berries. The branches were drooping with the weight of them. With a nervous giggle, he perched the flashlight in the top of a nearby hedge, pointing it at the tree. He feverishly tossed handfuls of the berries into the open plastic bag, and it only took him three minutes to get more than enough. It felt like he was holding over four pounds, and he zip-locked the bag. He snatched the flashlight and trotted back to the car. Leaving the berries and the flashlight on the hood of the car, he took off the gloves. He tossed them and the flashlight on the back seat. Getting surgical gloves out of his pocket, he put them on, as he gingerly inserting the bag with the berries inside two more. Then he zipped his prize in a pouch inside the leather shoulder bag. David left the surgical gloves on when he got back in the car.

Behind the wheel of the gracious silver ghost, he quietly traveled along Harding Road with the headlights off. Passing the first intersection, he turned the lights on and sped up. He drove onto Manchester Lane, following a route already mapped out in his head. Half a mile down the lane, he passed the city dump, and turned onto Gooseneck Road. It was nothing but a dirt track following the perimeter of a parcel of land New Bedford City designated as land fill, and he stayed on Gooseneck until it petered out on a rocky plateau a mile and half behind the dump. He put the Mercedes in park, and he left the engine running and the headlights on. Having studied the satellite images of the town for months, he'd picked this spot out for a reason. There was nothing but miles of undeveloped and barren land surrounding him. It was a neutral zone. He could do what he wanted without the interference of an audience.

He replaced everything scattered on passenger seat back in the bag. Pulling a knob on the dashboard, he unlocked the trunk. He twisted around, and grabbed the rain slicker and the face shield off the back seat, and then he opening the driver's door with his other hand. Getting out, David walked around the car and got the shovel out of the trunk. With the leather bag hanging off his shoulder, the headlights guided him to a patch of soft dirt in the generally stony tract of land. He knelt down in the crab grass to remove the bowl, the pestle, the gloves, and the plastic bag of yew berries out of the bag. Putting on the rain slicker and the face shield, he finalized his precautions by putting the dishwashing gloves on under the commercial ones. Manipulating his fingers at that point was difficult, but it didn't matter. He wasn't doing brain surgery. He poured the berries out of the plastic bag into the marble bowl, crushing them into paste with the stone pestle. Making his mush as similar to the homemade cranberry sauce as he could, he left some lumps in it. Nobody would notice the dark specks from the smashed seeds.

Peeling off the heavy gloves, he went back to the car. He returned with the flashlight and a soup spoon he'd left in the console. He needed another light source for the next stage, as the headlights alone made too much contrast between light and dark. Visually confusing, David tamed it, by putting the flashlight on a nearby rock and angling the beam towards the same grassy area he was working in. It worked perfectly. He kneeled down and spooned the mashed berries into a smaller plastic bag, *very carefully*. He made sure none of it had smeared on the side of the bag. Inserting the smaller bag into the two larger ones again, he put the hard-fought reward back into the interior compartment of the shoulder bag. He took off the raincoat, the face shield, and the dish-gloves. Picking up the shovel, he dug a hole in the ground, and he used the curved edge of the shovel to nudge the stuff into the hole he'd made . . . even the spoon. He shoveled the dirt he'd taken out, back in, and he stamped it down to flatten it. He was exhausted. Picking up the shoulder bag, the flashlight, and the shovel, he trudged back to the car.

The garage doors closed behind him. He looked at the clock in the dashboard. 5:23 AM. He had more than enough time for his last chores before Holly wakes up. The sand garden was catching dust on a high shelf in the garage, and he set up the ladder to get to it. Climbing only a couple of rungs, the box slid into his arms. The Zen garden had helped him unearth the key, and it seemed appropriate to use it again to hide it. There'd be no heat in the garage until December, and he could already see his breath while he walked around in there. The berries would remain fresh. No fermentation in his bag of tricks. The cranberry sauce at the Thanksgiving dinner had to taste great, like it always does. Setting the box on the work table, he took the garden out. David could have pushed the sand to the side of the container with his hand, but he used the rake instead. In his mind, a moment of meditation would solidify his visions. Taking the crushed berries out of the shoulder bag, he raked a furrow in the center of the garden, gently placing the dangerous slop into the depression he'd made. He was careful he didn't tear the plastic with one of the tines as he covered it over with the fine sand. Replacing the garden back in its carton, he put it back on the upper shelf. He changed back into his pajamas, and he felt relieved. The plucking, crushing and shoveling was over and the result of his devilry was out of sight. He whispered, *"That's all folks!"* to himself, and he opened the side door into the house. It was ten to six. Her alarm wouldn't ring for another thirty minutes.

Back in bed, David's anxiety about harvesting the yew berries drained away, and as he drifted into a peaceful slumber, he truly looked angelic. As soon as he was completely asleep, Holly opened her luminous eyes and she looked over at her husband with calculation.

3:35PM Monday November 21, 2005 Bass River, Massachusetts

April returned to the estate late on Sunday evening, after a romantic weekend with Peter. She didn't think that Latham cares where she goes anymore, and if he does, he'd only imagine her tied to some railroad tracks on a busy line. At least he had told her he was going to Chicago for a week and from there, a convention in Las Vegas. Yet she hadn't gotten a single word out of him about the house, their relationship or anything relevant about Hienem. The utter dearth was a good assessment of their marriage, and she knew that questioning him would be pointless. He always turned a cold shoulder to her . . . more like a frozen one, and he hadn't asked *her* anything for a very long time. 'Living together' was oxymoronical. If the mental and emotional distance between them could be measured, she'd have enough rope to orbit Mars.

With Peter's support, she was trying to extricate herself out of the marriage in one piece financially. Flummoxed by Latham's bizarre behavior over the past year, she'd instructed her lawyer to draft up a divorce decree without a date stamped on it. Waiting for the hammer to fall, waiting for the madman to put the estate on the market, she held her breath. She was enduring a cold year with him in the house. *He's got to let the cat out of the bag in the upcoming Thanksgiving dinner. He just has to!* He'd be flying home from Las Vegas on Wednesday (or early Thursday morning), and he was supposed to go to California the very next day. Assuming he was going to sell the house and dump her, she had the perfect ammunition to return that salvo with Olympic speed . . . *but what if he doesn't.* If he doesn't do anything, she had no recourse and she had no legal power to put the estate up for sale on her own. If she doesn't duck from his first legal punch, her standing in divorce court would be a weak one. He had to end this fiasco before he goes out of state again. After Thanksgiving dinner, after the rest of the family goes home, she needed Latham to give her a divorce decree and the card of a realtor, yet her prediction isn't carved in stone. April was riddled with apprehension, and her optimism weakened every day. Whatever affection Latham had ever had for her was beyond gone. Her husband was intelligent, devious and powerful, and she understood that something ominous had curled up inside his heart. She doesn't want to find out what it was.

Shadows on the white marble floor lengthened, while April slumped in a chair next to the koi pond. Gazing into the water with a far away expression on her finely sculpted face, she wasn't positive that Latham would even show up at the reunion this year. Nothing would work if he doesn't get home for the holidays. Fanning her resolution into courage, she got up and strode to the library. She'd call him and cajole him into a solid commitment, yet that nerve-wracking enterprise might be a bit easier if she looked out the library window to absorb the peaceful scene outside; a solace against his piercing words. Entering the room, she poured herself a glass of Chablis at the bar, and then she curled up on the couch with the house phone in her hand. Staring at the little boat house on the small tributary with nothing but wild woods on the other side, she took a very deep breath and punched in the number.

With Latham's help, the board members of the Hienem Corporation had organized the metropolitan district in Chicago before his departure. The well dressed group of business men concluded their bureaucratic maneuverings only an hour ago. Latham's flight to Las Vegas wouldn't depart for another six hours, and he was rested in his motel room. Everything had been taken care of. The estate had been absorbed by Heinem, just as Attison had told him it would be, and a company jet was fueled and ready for his flight to Russia on Friday. He thought over the devastating call he was going to place to his wife when he landed, and he smiled. When he disappears on Friday morning, a divorce decree would take his place. Assuming April doesn't hang herself, she'd be holding those legal papers in her hands while he croons out the rest of the news to her on the phone. There would be nothing for her or the children to fight for, whether it was in divorce or probate court, and the orchestrated viciousness of the end of their marriage would leave April close to destitute. That fact was partially responsible for his newfound equanimity. During the last hours left for him on American soil, he'd overact his vacuous role as the devoted family man with real delight, and he'd be standing on irony thicker than quick-sand. The phone on the table next to the bad began to ring and he picked it up.

"Hello."

"Hello, dear," April said. "The dinner plans are in motion and everyone is committed, and I need to know what time of day you're going to get here. Mirabelle has some personal responsibilities with her own family that day, so she and Vince are going to set up the whole dinner for us even though they'll both be gone by late afternoon. It'll be simple enough to serve ourselves . . . cozier too."

"Sounds fine. I can't believe the reunion is holding on for another year. Last year had to have been pretty damned good, besides the ugly surprise. Thinking about that sour note, I'm a little worried about Robert. Are you sure he's actually going to make it? Does he really want to attend?"

She had never heard serenity come out of his mouth in thirty years, but Latham's voice was dripping with honey. Like he suddenly cared, and that was even more unnerving. The rocky road she was on was becoming more unstable. April stood up and stepped closer to the window. Acres of velvety green grass rolled out to the tranquil brook, but it wasn't helping.

"Hmm, you might be right. I'll call and check on it. So, when are *you* going to arrive?" Swallowing the rest of the wine in her glass, she went back to the bar and re-filled it.

"I'm flying back on Wednesday, I told you that. I should be home very late that night or possibly early Thursday morning. I'm guessing the latest I'll get there would be around two or three in the morning. Don't worry dear, I'll be there! Remember, I have to get to California on Friday. I haven't told you that there's a good chance I'll find a break in the west coast madness and hop a jet to get back to you and say hello at some point in the next couple of months."

"Latham, you sound so weird, like you're suddenly ultra cheerful and you're freaking me out." The smarmy affection in his voice had turned her apprehension into dread, and the real distress in her words delighted Latham. Be that as it may, he had to explain his ebullience to her somehow, but not with the dangerous truth.

"Sorry . . . I'm . . . ah . . . I'm excited about the California project, that's all. You know I was getting frustrated. It's not challenging for me here anymore, just hum drum and boring. This is a real turning point for me."

"Oh . . . I didn't think the west coast was such a big deal for you. I had no idea you were so fired up about it . . . anyway, I'll be looking forwards to seeing you for sure on Thursday and I hope your conference in Las Vegas goes well." All those injections and nips and tucks made it hard for her to scowl, and her grimace was only a flinch. April's eyebrows were stuck in one position, quivering to get closer together.

"It'll be fine. No problems and no worries. Hey, what would you like for a Thanksgiving day present? Las Vegas is nothing but a huge shopping mall, and I thought you'd enjoy something. Maybe a pendant? Earrings and a matching ring or a paper weight . . . what?"

April's gorge rose. She held it down with everything she had, not wanting him to know he'd got to her that badly.

"Huh . . . ah . . . oh," she mumbled. Swallowing back the rising tide, she hoped it sounded like she was trying to make up her mind. "I don't know, perhaps . . . a new watch. I've always loved the d . . . d . . . dia . . . diamond encrusted ones, okay?" The stuttering another symptom of her valiant fight against vomiting on the carpet.

"Well, that's an easy order to fill," he said. "I'll pick out the best one in Vegas and I'll give it to you with bells on. April, my dear, you are younger and more beautiful every time I see you."

After slathering this supercilious compliment on and into her ear, he hung up. Then he lay across the bed and stretched like a satisfied cat.

Her husband had inserted an insult inside a parody and then he was gone. Looking down at the beige handset in her hand, it looked like a cancerous lump. Buzzing like a bee, April threw it into the far corner of the couch and the receiver landed upright, jammed between two leather cushions. She glanced at it with annoyance on her back to the bar to fill her glass.

Things were unraveling, and the conversation had left her bleeding. She needed more than alcohol to stabilize herself. Her purse was on the coffee table and she sat down on the couch and dove into the bottomless pit of it. Eventually finding the bottle, she popped three Ativans in her mouth, swallowing them down with wine. The drug wasn't going to help her right away, so she sat there motionless trying to muffle the racket of doubt on her own. The ridiculous anxiety shall be gone soon enough . . . yet the minutes were dragging and Latham's voice resonated in her head. Shying away from it, she wished he would shut up forever. All of it had to go! Her fingernails dug deeper into the couch cushions. She had to think about something else . . .

> *Bertie, that's right, Bertie. I'll call him and confirm. He told me last week he was intent on coming, but his moods change like the weather.*

4:03PM Monday November 21, 2005 North Dartmouth, Massachusetts

By now the ground should be white and the roads slick, but the dusting a week ago was gone, swept away by the wind. It seemed the winter queen was holding her breath.

Robert's motorcycle sparkled in the brittle air next to the yellow cottage he was renting on Bryant Street, and the grey truck was sagging low on its frame nearby. Dead weeds sprouted from his window boxes, and long brown grass graced the front yard without shame. He'd closed the blinds tight as he huddled over a glass table in the unlit living room. The only illumination he had came from the bathroom in the hallway. He'd left the light on and the door wide open.

The interior of the cottage was immaculate, and the Harley outside might have been sitting on a show room floor, but for some unknown reason the frenzied cleaning sprites flying around inside of Robert's head were oblivious to everything else. A rock ballad called a Bridge of Sighs quavered in the air around him, but he was temporarily blind and deaf to the real world. He couldn't hear the song, nor see the lines of coke on the table in front of him.

He'd started out okay after his long stint in rehab. He diligently avoided what had overwhelmed him a thousand times before, and he was healing. However, the timing of his late night foray in the kitchen at the family reunion and his sister's meddling had sent him over an emotional landmine. It exploded under his feet, derailing him. These days, he was in a downward spiral, simmering in self-loathing. No longer working at Home Depot, his only earnings came in from dealing cocaine and the business was thriving. He was getting thinner, and the bankroll fatter, while fragments of his intellect would crack off and vanish in the ether. Addicted to the product, he'd fallen head over heels into the looking glass. He was living in Wonderland, and the Red Queen was on her head, ordering his capture and execution, but Robert didn't care about the danger he was in. Any of his positive memories were sucked into a black hole his father's pronouncements about him had opened. Latham's razor-sharp words had been an great excuse to let him cut his conscience from his core. He was beyond redemption, hypnotized by the tolling of an imaginary iron bell welded on a watchtower overlooking the abyss.

Robert's body was on the brink as well, and his youth couldn't sustain him much longer. His autonomic nervous system would occasionally stop for a moment and he'd teeter on self-termination. He didn't want to accept the real world anymore. Because he was responsible for the deadly situation he was in, his superego was grasping for straws; building an island in his head, a fantasy island. It was a short escape. Sometimes he'd go there and play a directionless game with indistinct and non-threatening human forms. They'd toss colored balls back and forth on a glowingly green grassy field.

A dying orchid drooping in his expensive leather chair, he was on his island of nothingness when the phone rang. It was sitting on the glass table right in front of him, and the loud ringing pierced the veil.

"Hello, Bertie. It's Mom. I'm . . . I'm just confirming, huh . . . um . . . I needed to know if you're going to be here on Thursday. I hope so. You know we love you Bertie, you know that." Between the tranquilizers and the wine, Mom was three sheets to the wind.

"Hi, Mom . . ."

"Bertie, are you there? Can you hear me? Can you hear me? *Bertie!*"

"Hello, Mom . . . yeah, I'm here, I can hear you and I'll be there. When would you like, I mean what, I mean, when do you want me to . . ."

"Robert? Can you hear me?"

"Yeah, Mom, I hear you. Everything's okay. You want me to come to the party, right?"

"You could arrive on Wednesday. A day early, if you want . . . or Thursday, that's okay . . . okay. Bertie are you still there?" April had stumbled over to the library window again, but it had gotten dark outside. All she could see was her own reflection in the glass.

"Yeah, ah . . . alright, I'll show up on Wednesday then. Wednesday's going to be alright."

Robert's feelings were turbulent about the family reunion. He was certainly going and he had no plans to attack anyone . . . he had no plans at all, but it remained extremely important that he get there. Leaning over the glass table, he snorted up a line of coke, and he flew through the ceiling and the shingled roof. Boosted into the cold air above the cottage, it was a lot harder for him to make out his mother's voice. Nevertheless, he found a way to remember the upcoming information his mother was about to tell him about his father's travel plans.

"The day after the reunion, Dad's going to have to go to California for at least six months. We won't be able to see him for a very, very . . . . very long time. He's driving to the airport on Friday morning, so it would be great to bring, to bring the whole family together for Thanksgiving, don't you think so? So you'll be there? You're going to make it, right?"

"Of course, I'll be there!" And he said it with conviction.

If he'd heard the terrible desperation in her voice, he might have been able to help her, but the only thing Robert could discern these days was the tolling of that fiendish bell.

PART III

"Technology has lured us into our divinity and the forgotten gods seethe on the other side of worship. Creating heaven or hell with the push of a button, are we facing the pantheon in the mirror or will the dismissed break the looking glass?"

Keith Fischer

2:00 PM Wednesday November 23, 2005 Ventura Casino, Las Vegas

Samuel Eveland wouldn't take his sunglasses off. He was hunkering over a glass of gin and tonic in Minerva Cove Lounge, and he was furtively looking around to make sure no one he should be worried about was nearby. After hearing a story on the grapevine that Cindy's goons were out hunting for bigger fish over the holiday week, he thought it was safe enough for him to enjoy the main strip for a few days. Dangerously late on his last payment, it's possible the scuttlebutt was actually directed at him, but Samuel hadn't thought of that. With a target on his back, and hunters tracking him down, he remained naive about the degree of danger he was in. In his tilted mind, a whirl of the wheel would pay off his debt and he'd be back on top, but hanging out in the Ventura Casino was not a healthy thing to do.

Mirrored sunglasses on his nose, a Panama hat, a shaggy red wig and the garish Hawaiian shirt with flamingos flying over a tropical lagoon, Samuel believed his flamboyant disguise would make him less noticeable. At least he hoped so. Swallowing his drink, his personalized mantra stated, "*Nothing bad will happen to me, nothing at all*" and it kept on repeating itself in his head. Right across the aisle, he watched a tall, skinny man insert money into one of the dollar slot machines. About 6'

2", he had on an expensive linen suit with an open shirt and no tie, and the man looked familiar. As if he knew him personally, or something. He squinted at him and he sat up straighter so he could see the strangers face a bit more clearly. *Whoa! He really looked a lot like . . .*

And Samuel picked up the newspaper somebody had left on the bar. He opened it up and raised it in front of his face, but he was captivated by what was going on only fifteen feet away from him. He tried to make it look like he was reading it, as he peeked over the top.

"Hello there, Samuel. It seems you've won big, with a suit like that on your back. Even a Rolex watch! I guess the winnings have gone straight to your head. What da'ya think, you schmuck? That we weren't looking for you anymore, shit, I can't believe you're that dumb." Lazzo was holding the CEO of the Heinem Pharmaceutical Corporation by his collar as he scolded him. Edgar was leaning against the nearest slot machine and he was cleaning his fingernails.

"My name isn't Samuel, damn it. You've got the wrong man! Let me go or I'll put you both in jail for assault," Latham was angry and full of himself.

Edgar chuckled, "You sound ridiculous. Pay up now *with interest*, or we'll close you down completely."

Latham couldn't free himself from Lazzo's grip. Then Lazzo started to shake him like a bottle of salad dressing, and Donnelly's eyes rolled straight up. The beaded chain around his neck holding his key card snapped and fell to the floor. Edgar grabbed one of Latham's elbows and Lazzo took the other, and they raised the man half an inch off the floor. They moved him rapidly towards the elevators. Latham was dizzy. He didn't get his bearings until they were almost inside the car. He saw one of his employees, and he thought he could stop this travesty in its tracks if he could get his attention . . . *but he had to remember his name!* Was it Bella? Bender? It clicked. It was Benson.

"Mr. Benson . . . hey, BENSON! Tell these maniacs who I am?" Latham yelled. Cindy's thugs had dragged him inside the elevator car with machinelike resolve. Leland Benson looked at his CEO with an expression of concern, but it didn't really reflect how he felt. For once, his hoity-toity boss wasn't in control of the world and he was gratified the tables had been turned . . . more than turned. They'd fallen on Donnelly's head.

"He's Latham Donnelly, the CEO of Heinem Corporation. Listen you guys, you've got to let him go or I'll call security right now!" Leland said. He was a chubby man, generally untidy, and his belly protruded over his belt. The thin comb-over on top of his head didn't help the situation, but his appearance was moot. The kidnappers would ignore *anyone* at that point in the game.

"Listen," Latham screamed at him, "call Mr. Korybante. Tell him what's wrong, just don't call security! Korybante will take care of this whole thing and . . ." The elevator doors closed.

Latham didn't want any police involvement. When Benson calls Attison, he knew the lawyer's intervention would be more than enough to get him out of the fire, and he didn't want the world to know about a bump in the road like this one. It would muddy up his departure to Russia day after tomorrow. He couldn't let bullshit like this slow him down.

Benson was pissed at Latham Donnelly. The CEO was leaving and his friend and co-worker, Harrison Griffin was supposed to replace Latham, but nooo . . . someone else had been in his boss's pocket from the beginning. *Yeah, yeah . . . he'd call Korybante in a minute. The guy's phone number was in his cell phone in a drawer in his room, and he was already in the main lobby. It wouldn't hurt anything if he played just one game before he went back to his room to get the number.*

Samuel watched Lazzo and Edgar drag Latham away, and his heart pounded hard against his ribs. Dropping the newspaper on the bar, he left a fiver under his glass. He trotted across the aisle to the machine Latham had been playing as he'd seen the plastic card around his neck snap off in the scuffle. It didn't take him long to find it on the patterned carpeting, and he picked it up and slipped it into his pocket. Walking fast to the nearest public bathroom, he ducked into one of the privacy stalls. He locked the door and took the card out of his pocket, turning it around in his hands. It was a key card, and he thought that over. There were no markings on it, so he had no idea what room it was connected to, but he might dig out that important nugget . . . *with a little luck.*

Samuel unlocked the stall and stepped over to the counter. He stuffed the sunglasses and the wig into the garbage can next to the entrance, and he looked at himself in the mirror. Was his hair the same length? He aggressively ran his fingers across his scalp to fluff up what the ridiculous wig had flattened. Getting a comb out of in his back pocket, he civilized himself the best he could. He needs to get rid of the Hawaiian shirt. He left the bathroom and walked along the main promenade until he saw a sports store. Almost broke, the best he could do was an olive green polo shirt. Thirty-five dollars was about as low as you could go to buy any piece of clothing in the casino, yet his thrifty purchase put him on the bottom of the barrel, and he wondered if the flimsy t-shirt would be enough to fade the lines between burlap and gold?

He went back to the same lavatory. Tossing the flamingos on top of the rest of his disguise, he took the T-shirt of the bag. He shook out the fold wrinkles and ripped the tags off. Samuel put it on and stood in front of the mirror, praying this simple outfit would let him pass . . . *as himself?* He shrugged and left the lavatory. Walking nonchalantly to the reservation desk, his hands were hidden in his pockets and they stayed there. He had crossed his fingers for luck, and he was going to ride that superstition as long as he could.

The main desk wasn't too busy, and they were working at a comfortable pace. Samuel hung out a little bit away from the main action, hoping someone would notice him before he said anything and he watched the credit card receipts slide back and forth across the polished granite countertop. The tips of his fingers were turning white, but he left them crossed. He needed to. He had to use everything he could come up with to save his own neck.

"Good afternoon, Mr. Donnelly. Is there something I can do for you?" An Asian woman with perfect make-up stepped over to him and a smell of wild flowers and vanilla followed her.

"Hello . . . Kara," Samuel said, reading her name tag. "Did anyone leave a message for me? I haven't made it back to my room yet and since I left my cell phone there, I was hoping you could check that out for me." The mojo was working and he uncrossed his fingers and took his hands out of his pockets. Circulation returned.

"We'll know in a second, sir," and she swirled around to push a couple of buttons on the keyboard behind her. "Sorry. There's nothing on the screen right now. Is there anything else I can do for you?"

"Yes, I think there is. I'm expecting a small package this afternoon and I'd like you to send it up to my room . . . 358, no 385, or is it 853? I'm sorry. I'm having a brain freeze here."

Laughing in commiseration, she gave him exactly what he needed. "You're in room 1453, Mr. Donnelly. Hey, at least you remembered two of the numbers. You're on the fourteenth floor. I'll send the package straight to your suite as soon as it arrives." Glancing back at the screen for a second, she went on, "I've noticed you're checking out later on today, and I'm hoping you'll change your mind and extend your stay with us!"

The subtle dusting of glitter on her lovely cheekbones magnified her smile, and Samuel was about to tell her it would be wonderful to stay there in the Ventura Casino for another night, but his ongoing problem with his own mortality quickly broke the charming hold she had on him.

"Kara, I'd love to stay here forever if I could, but I've got commitments I can't break. I must painfully decline your offer." The next step in his malleable plan rolled into his consciousness.

"Alright, sir. We'll look forwards to your next visit with us, and I'll send the package when I see it."

Walking over to the elevators, he took the key card with the broken chain out of his pocket, and he caressed it until the doors opened. He got in and pushed the button for the fourteenth floor, and he moved towards the back of the car. Other guests got in and out on the lower floors, and the elevator was empty by the time it stopped on the highest floor. Trying to look regal, he walked down the corridor to his presidential suite, and he inserted the key-card into its slot on the door. He stepped into a concentration of luxuriousness as the place invited his own memories of the good life; as tenuous as it had turned out to be.

Looking at his wrist-watch it was 3:45. He had no idea if the kidnappers were going to believe Donnelly's statements, but if they did, it wouldn't take them long to get here. He didn't have much time. Not a lot of time to steal someone else's life and get out of the town, and he shifted into high gear. The first thing he had to do was to find the luggage. He went into the bedroom. There were two bags on a high shelf in the closet, and he grabbed at one of the handles. Both bags slid off the shelf and fell on the floor, missing his head by an inch. He began to pack Latham's things in his luggage as fast as he could, *and he absolutely positively wasn't going to leave anything behind.* The frantic pace escalated, even while he attempted to be more methodical. Stuffing files and papers he saw on the hotel desk into the computer bag, he saw the plane ticket and he stopped for a nanosecond to read the information printed on the back. He put the ticket in an outside pocket of the computer bag so he could get to it easily later on. He smiled. It was a free ride out of Dodge, and then he frowned. Donnelly's PC had been inside one of the bags he'd heedlessly crashed on the floor, and he prayed the cushioning in the expensive bag had averted any damage.

There was a suit in the closet in a dry cleaning bag. It had to be the one Donnelly was going to wear on his flight home, and Samuel turned into a snake molting on methamphetamines. Peeling off his old skin, he started out naked. He went through the drawers to find new briefs, new socks, and a soft Egyptian cotton undershirt. Taking the suit out of the bag, he wriggled into it as if he'd grown a brand new layer of scales. Everything fit him to a tee; custom tailored to his body. Leaving his old clothes on the floor, with one sock and his underpants hanging off the side of the bed, he'd deliberately left his old identity behind in plain sight.

Combing his hair, he knotted a beautiful ivory silk tie around his neck. He looked in the mirror and the reflection stopped him cold . . . as if he was in petite-mal seizure, *but he also knew he was running out of time!* The fear of death by violence wrenched him back to reality and he instantly went back to unceremoniously packing everything else Donnelly had in the wheeled traveling case and the computer bag. Zipping them both closed, he realized he was almost ready to run. He'd left his wallet, still stuffed with most of the money he had left, in the back pocket of his old pants. That should help cloud the water for Cindy's retrievers if they do get to Latham's suite. How uncomfortable the poor man would feel as he adamantly insists the wallet isn't his. The vision made Sam giggle. Latham had left his cell phone on the desk and he slid it inside the breast pocket of the suit, snuggling it up to the man's wallet. Latham had left everything behind in the suite, a life-saving stroke of good luck for him, and he didn't care why. Lady Luck was giving him a ticket out of town. Putting the key card on the top of the end table near the bed, he positioned the computer bag strap on his shoulder and the handle of the suitcase in his hand. He looked at himself in the long mirror next to the front door one last time. He straightened his shoulders and raised his chin. Inhaling, he opened the door to sail away from his own downfall; a phoenix, emerging from the fire *one more time.*

Getting out of the elevator on the first floor, Samuel was going to walk straight out of the casino and whistle up a taxi for the airport. Donnelly's flight was not supposed to board until 8:00PM and that was just fine. He needed the extra time for his own edification. He'd use a Wi-Fi connection in a coffee shop in the airport, the safest place for him to be while he punched up as much information about Latham as he could on his computer. Breezing through the main concourse, a disheveled and badly intoxicated middle-aged man waved at him. Samuel didn't want to stop at all, but the man jogged over to him and he couldn't get away.

"Do you still want me to call Mr. Korybante, Mr. Donnelly? You're looking much . . . in bet . . . better shape than you were before, with with . . . those men, those awful looking men. Didn't you know who . . . who they were?" Leland hadn't called Attison. That was bad, very bad, but at this point in the game, he was too drunk to care. Samuel understood that Latham had to have asked this guy for help while he was being hauled away, and he quickly came up with an adequate response.

"No, no. I'm fine. It was just a disagreement and it's all straightened out now. You don't need to call anyone, as things have worked out. I think it would be prudent if we all forgot about that confusing moment of dissention, okay?" Samuel spoke with power in his voice.

"Sure, no problem, sir," Leland said, and he stepped closer and whispered, "it's our secret." With a finger up to his lips, he kept on muttering, "You can tell me the secret . . . what was really going on, 'cause you ss . . . sure, sure looked . . . screwed up."

"Look, I have a plane to catch and I can't talk to you anymore. You go ahead and keep on, keeping on and take good care of yourself." Samuel turned away and briskly strode over to the nearest exit, finally escaping the casino.

3:30PM Wednesday November 23, 2005 Las Vegas, Nevada

They'd locked Latham in a storage room in one of the basement levels under the main floor of the casino. With despicable pronouncements about the things they were going to do to him when they came back, Lazzo and Edgar had tied him to a chair, blindfolded, and gagged. They went back to the main floor of the casino to have a drink in Rose's Petals, a cocktail lounge with live music. A tribute band was playing Rod Stewart's music, and Lazzo *loved* Rod Stewart.

"The vocalist isn't bad Edgar, he really isn't. He sounds a lot like him, don't you think?" Lazzo had another Long Island iced-tea in his hand, and this time he was drinking it through a straw.

"Maybe it wasn't such a good idea leaving him down there so long . . . I mean, when we get the job done, Cindy will be happy. It shouldn't take a lot of time for that dope to spill the beans . . . oh, you're right, Lazzo, his singing isn't bad. Come on, let's go, we have more work to do."

Edgar dropped a fifty dollar bill on the bar and Lazzo sucked up what was left in his tall glass to follow his partner out of the lounge. They passed the elevators, and ducked into a service door. From there, they clattered down some steel stairs to a lower floor, and then they got into a commercial delivery elevator. Edgar hit a button, sending them one more level down. Getting out, they walked the entire length of a long concrete passageway, finally stopping at some double doors. A padlocked chain was looped between the two metal handles, and Edgar dug into his pants pocket and produced the key.

Latham heard the big doors open, and their footsteps moving towards him. His heart beat sped up, and he was damp with sweat. His shirt collar was drenched. Tied to the arms of the chair way too tight, his fingertips had turned white, and he pressed himself against the back of the chair. Scrabbling at the leather padding on the arms with numb fingers, his pale face got pastier. Those were the reactions Lasso and Edgar were trying to achieve in their prisoner.

"So, Sam, have you decided to live another day by relieving yourself from the heavy debt you owe to Cindy?" Edgar asked. He untied Latham's blindfold and gag. "Its important you know we've run out of patience. Come on . . . tell us where the money is right now. If you *don't* tell us, something bad may happen to your body. You may lose certain parts of it," and he sniggered. The captive only croaked out hacking noises, unable to get enough saliva in his mouth to talk.

"We have to give him something to drink, Ed," Lazzo said. He winked at his partner. "If he drinks some water, I think he'll be able to tell us what we want to hear. It could speed things up."

"Yeah, I guess you're right."

Lazzo went over to the utility sink in the corner of the room and he filled a paper cup he'd found under the sink. Holding the cup to Latham's mouth, he gulped down a few ounces of water. Then he started to cough.

"I've, agh . . . told you, aagh . . . I'm not who you think I am and . . . . I can prove it. I can prove . . ." He started coughed again. Lazzo brought the cup back to his mouth and he swallowed more water. At last clearing his throat, Latham started to talk as fast as he could. "I'm staying in the presidential suite on the fourteenth floor, room 1453." He looked at his chest, and the chain was gone. "I *had* a key card, but you probably took it. Just call the desk. They'll tell you who I am. *Latham Donnelly, staying at 1453.* Just get me there and I'll give you any amount of money that guy owes you. Hell, I'll even give you more and everyone will be happy. Please, you've got listen to me! We can go to my suite on the fourteenth floor and then you'll know the truth!" Latham was becoming hysterical. His desperation should have in ended in reverberating screech from a wonderful crescendo; however the last words struggled out of him in a pathetic whisper. Shock interfered with his breathing, and Lazzo and Edgar were staring down at him as he gasped for air.

"Whadaya think? It'll only use a couple of minutes to check his story out. I mean maybe he's living two lives and we've finally roped him up so tight he's been found out. You know that happens a lot in this town. People change their names while they're in Las Vegas. Gambling is like going to a Halloween party." There was a questioning expression on his face.

"Good point, buddy." Edgar bent down. He looked deep into Latham's eyes. "On a *dead issue,"* and then he straightened up. "Of course you're right. Nothing to lose. If he can even out the score, we'll give him a chance to do it. Yeah . . . okay. I'll get the master key from Tommy, and I'll meet you up there. Give me a five minute head start," and he faded into the shadows like a ghost.

Sunlight twinkled on the acres of glass adorning the towering hotels and casinos on the main drag, yet the corridor on the fourteenth floor of the Ventura had no windows. The designers replaced heavenly light with an oversized crystal chandelier in the foyer in front of the elevators and every thirty feet, royal blue curtains framed digital displays of mountains or country fields. The tiny small trees bent in a computerized breeze and even the birds flew around. As Lazzo herded Latham to the corner suite, neither one of them was interested in the décor. When they got to the door, they waited uncomfortably for Edgar and the key. Latham knew salvation was waiting for him on the other side of that door, and in only a few more minutes, he'd be out of Samuel Eveland's shadow. Edgar finally came around the corner and trotted up to them.

"Here you go Sam." He gave Latham the key. "We're looking forwards to seeing all the piles of money you say is there for the taking."

Latham inserted the card into the slot above the knob and he pushed the door open, and he heard the sound of the bottom of the door rush over the thick carpeting.

"You should have just taken me up here in the first place. We could have avoided all of this confusion . . ." But his exuberant statement died when he opened the drawer under the counter where he'd left his wallet, and it wasn't there. Nothing was there. No cufflinks, no receipts. Even his favorite golden ballpoint pen was gone, and a chill raced down his spine. He raced into the bedroom. Somebody had tossed filthy clothes across the floor and on the bed and he was shaken. Checking the bathroom, even the medicine cabinet was empty, and that didn't help his crumbing disposition.

"This can't be . . . it can't be! It isn't right. Someone stole all of my stuff, damn it."

Lazzo shoved Latham into a chair in the corner of the room.

"Nooo," Latham howled, looking up at his abductor, "let me go! This whole thing is wrong. Give me the phone and I'll . . ." Lazzo slapped him with the back of his hand. The powerful blow stunned him, and it silenced him for the moment. Edgar entered the bedroom and picked up the street pants off the floor. Reaching into the back pocket, he removed a wallet and he found fifty-five dollars in the billfold. He looked carefully at the driver's license, and tossed the wallet on Latham's lap.

Horrified by the picture of Samuel on the license, what was left of Latham's blush of anticipation was gone. That piece of identification stuck behind a clear plastic window in the billfold changed his complexion into a living corpse.

"You don't look very good, Sam. What's wrong with getting your wallet back?" Edgar reveled over Samuel's reaction. "Where's the foot locker brimming with gold? Is it under the bed? Should we check for it there, hmm?"

"Look, I'll just call my bank in Massachusetts. They could wire whatever amount you want, instantly. You've got to believe me. I *can* give you a lot of money. My name really *is* Latham Donnelly and I am the CEO of the Heinem Corporation. If you've ever used a pain pill, my company probably made it . . . and anything else your doctor prescribed to you. This guy," Latham waved the open wallet in the air, "has stolen all my stuff . . . *for God's sake!* Wouldn't you rather have a million dollars instead of a dead body? Just let me call! I told you, I'll give you more than what you've asked for!" He sounded like an auctioneer under the gun, speaking in breakneck speed. Short breathy huffs came out of him, a precursor of a panic attack.

"You're badly are out of touch with the world Sammy, my boy," Edgar said. "Tomorrow is Thanksgiving. Right now the banks all are closed and they're going to stay that way until Friday." He was talking to him very slowly, a counter point to Latham's previous rapid-fire delivery.

"*Shit*, you're right, blast it. Listen, listen to me . . . I know! Just get me to my estate in Bass River. I have over a million dollars in cash in my safe, un-marked, and un-dyed and I won't miss it. *Seriously*. This is an offer you guys should not ignore. You'll win big and I won't do anything at all to get it back . . . please! *Oh, please!*"

He'd painted a pretty picture, and it grew tendrils in their minds. Besides Latham's ragged breathing, silence reigned in the suite of elegant rooms.

"What happens if we do haul his ass to Massachusetts? No problem. If the whole thing is a con and there's nothing there but a big empty field, we could just dig a hole and close the account. She might even go for it, since the problem leaves Nevada completely with a chance we could get a lot of cash for the effort," Lazzo said.

"It does have a pretty good wind up. I'll call and see what she thinks. I know she'd love more moolah if it works out."

Cindy picked up instantly and Edgar explained what was going on. Latham was cowering on the chair during the interchange on the phone and he heard nothing but one-syllable grunts coming out of Edgar's mouth. He had no idea what the end result was going to be. At least it was a short call. Putting the phone back in his pocket, Edgar frowned. He stood in front of his captive, basking in the dread he saw in Latham's eyes . . . until Lazzo interrupted his fun.

"What did she say, Edgar? I need to know."

"Alright, alright. We're gonna take a red eye to Massachusetts tonight, or maybe early morning tomorrow on standby, so we better get moving." Edgar manhandled Latham out of the chair. "You better make sure Sammy here has his wallet with him, otherwise we aren't going to be able to get him on a plane."

Latham was slowly returning to the land of the living, at least for the time being. He might get out of this mess in one piece, possibly making it to Russia on Friday after all.

3:00AM Thursday November 24, 2005 Over the East Coast

Soaring over the Canadian border and into the United States, the biting cold five miles up, didn't bother Slethim. The entity effortlessly coasted on a south-bound jet stream. The ceremony and the re-birth was about to take place in Bass River and it had been summoned to the event. Another hour went by. Moonlight reflected on the glossy black feathers covering the massive muscles that powered its overlarge wings. The creature had navigated itself high above Gloucester, when it raised one wing a millimeter. The slight angle was responsible for Slethim's ongoing drop in altitude during the last miles left in its southern voyage.

7:30PM Wednesday November 23, 2005 Las Vegas, Nevada

Samuel had used all the extra time before the flight to dig out information about Latham. It would be nice if he could act with decorum when he gets to Donnelly's house, and he had to learn as much as he could in only a few hours. Stumbling around through the personal files in Latham's laptop, he tripped over a confidential document labeled "landscaping notes". The first entry was a year old, and the latest had been inserted a week ago. Samuel read the man's cheerful plan to double-cross his wife and family, and the culmination was linked to his final transfer to Russia on the 25th. No one knew about it, but Attison . . . whoever that was. The family believed he was going to California, and the wife had no idea that a divorce decree was about to arrive in her hands on Friday afternoon. He surmised the wrapped box he'd packed into the luggage in the presidential suite was part of the ruse as Latham Donnelly would slather more simulated honey on April in the last hours he had left in America. Speed reading through the digital trove of material in the computer, a dark portrait of his double emerged. He was a cruel and mischievous man.

The ending to Latham Donnelly's abduction would probably be fatal, and that would certainly simplify things for him. He'd drain money out of one of Latham's bank accounts and wire it to a different account *somewhere*. When his proverbial pockets were filled to the brim with more gold, he'd disappear off everybody's radar forever on Friday afternoon. Samuel was ecstatic. He'd been given a fortuitous shot at redemption.

Flying out of Vegas dropped him in Boston at 2:15AM in Eastern Time. He left Logan Airport holding the parking stub he'd found in Latham's wallet in his hand. "D45" was scrawled on its back, indicating which parking field Latham had left his car. Gazing across a lumpy sea of fiberglass, plastic, and steel, he squeezed through the tightly packed cars until he reached section D. He hit the button on the car keys, and a coffee-colored Mercedes answered with a beep and a flash. Stowing the luggage safely in the trunk, he started the engine, and a GPS system lit up in the dashboard to guide him to his new home.

It was 3:53 in the morning when he drove over Bass River Bridge. Looking to the right, he saw the river running straight out to the sea and the setting moon silhouetted the trees along the shore. The map on the screen was blinking, urgently telling him he was almost there. Samuel felt anxious and out of sorts. It was difficult to accept the surreal role he must now perform and act the part with aplomb. During the short time he'd on the computer, he quickly made out the disconnect between Latham and his family and that should shuffle his stage fright right out the door. He could put on a cowboy hat and dance an Irish jig across the dining room in the middle of dinner, and that would likely make the dinner guests feel a lot better. Hell, they'd probably start clapping and join in with him. Envisioning that odd scene, he smiled and he drove the last twisty mile up the slope, a little bit calmer.

Blazing white arches in front of the house declared he had arrived. Staring at the adjoining four-car garage, he had no idea how to open the doors and he didn't have any more energy to figure it out. He inched the Mercedes closer to the building, right next to a Harley-Davidson motorcycle and he put it in park and shut off the engine. Taking the bags out of the trunk, he walked up to the front door. He used the keys he'd found in Vegas to open the door and he stepped into the entry hall.

Samuel looked up at the grand staircases on the other side of the room, but he instinctually went over to the large arch on his right. It opened into a dark cavern of a room. There was a light panel on the wall and he randomly pushed one of the switches. A chandelier in the middle of the great room lit up. There was a couch in the distance in front of a very large fireplace, and he trudged over to it. He dropped the handle of the suitcase, and he placed the computer bag on the nearby marble table. Samuel yawned, and lay down on the couch. He stuffed a throw pillow under his head, and exhaustion knocked him out in the space of a sigh.

10:00AM Thursday November 24, 2005 Bass River, Massachusetts

"AH!" The chef was delighted to see his employer, "Good morning Mrs. Donnelly."

"Good morning, Vince."

"There are no worries for the evening repast. I've set up all the sides; wild rice, fresh yams in syrup, fresh petite peas, chestnuts, homemade cranberry sauce and of course, the oyster stuffing." Tapping his finger tip on his palm to emphasize the items on his list, ended with an operatic bow, palms facing up in a gesture of surrender. Straightening up, he beamed at April, and she smiled back as the tantalizing aromas wafting around her justified the exorbitant stipend they paid him.

"The turkey is roasting in a slow oven. Mirabelle will baste it before she leaves at two, but someone has to baste it every hour after that. Please, put it on your schedule and get back to the kitchen and do it again at three, okay? The ham is baking in the other oven. I glazed it with orange brandy, triple sec, and garnishments of extra fresh pineapple rings from Belize arranged on its back. Please relay my kudos to Justin. I have no idea where he found this superior ham as I've never heard of the company before, but the seasonings they used in the brine were exceptional."

"I'll let him know," April said. "It does smell good. Every time we have a Thanksgiving dinner with you, we say it can't get any better, but somehow you out-do yourself every year!" Picking up a spoon on the counter, she stirred the broth simmering on the stove. "We're having dinner at six. As you know, Mirabelle can't serve us this evening, but I'm sure you've figured out a simple presentation for us. I know we'll be able to handle things after you both leave."

"Right now, Mirabelle is stacking the side dishes in the cooler. She'll put them in the steam table in the dining room before she leaves, so everything in the trays will be up to the correct temperature by six," Vince said. The housekeeper came out of the walk-in cooler and nodded hello to April on her way to cut up carrots for the appetizer tray.

"The temperatures in both ovens are set to coincide with your dinner hour. The ham and turkey will be ready to serve. Of course, you need to take the turkey out at five thirty. It needs to rest for half-an-hour before you carve it up. Besides that, all you have to do is baste the turkey once an hour, there's really not anything else to deal with. Always use gloves when you take anything out of either of the ovens. A work-towel isn't foolproof and I don't want anybody to burn their hands."

Vince had his overcoat on, and he was patting one of the side pockets until his car keys jingled. "I'm so sorry I can't stay with you for the entire day, but I told you my in-laws are coming in early this year. I've got to follow my wife's orders."

Mirabelle's voice piped in from the far corner of the room, "I hope you'll be alright. My sister got sick, and I have to drive everyone everywhere tonight. I'll be back in the morning to clean up before anyone wakes up."

"Both of you stop worrying! Everything is fine. It'll work out perfectly. We'll have a more intimate family get together, and you've both done a wonderful job setting the whole thing up. Thank you, Vince.

You've got to run, so go ahead and run," April said, and she nodded magnanimously towards the door.

"Have a good Thanksgiving, Mrs. Donnelly, and give my good wishes to the rest of the family. Mirabelle, I pray you and yours have a wonderful holiday too!"

"Happy Thanksgiving, Vince!" Mirabelle called out.

"Happy Thanksgiving," April said, and Vince waved goodbye as the service entrance door closed behind him.

Her faultless make-up and expensive clothes hadn't masked it. Mirabelle saw the pain in Mrs. Donnelly's eyes while she was explaining what she wanted on the appetizer cart. The housekeeper nodded, already working on her orders, but she stopped for a second and looked over her shoulder as she walked out of the kitchen. She was moving erratically, as if something invisible was hunting her down.

Leaving the kitchen, April looked through one of the large windows in the west wall of the great room. Latham's Mercedes was parked outside. Her head tilted with curiosity. Why didn't he put in the garage last night? Then she saw his suitcase next to the fireplace, her belly lurched. Gingerly tip-toeing closer, she found him unconscious on the couch. *And why wasn't he in his own bed?* Turning on her heel, she was on her way back to ask Mirabelle about it, when Samuel's voice stopped her in her tracks.

"Hello, April. How are you?" His voice was raspy and he was having problems ungluing his upper eyelids from the lower ones.

"Hello, Latham. I'm fine, but you look horrible. Why didn't you go upstairs when you got home last night? Wouldn't you feel much better in your own bed?" She was trembling as she spoke.

"My, my, you're just full of curiosity aren't you? Alright, I'll tell you. I was wrecked when I got here, and I was too tired to make it up to my own bed, but I agree with you. I'm going upstairs right now. I need to sleep for a couple more hours. When is dinner?" Sitting up, he reached for Latham's suitcase and un-zipped it.

"About six . . . what . . . what are you doing?"

Digging into the bag, he brought out the present. "Here honey. I picked this up for you in Las Vegas. I know we don't have a lot of time, and I thought you'd rather enjoy opening it before everyone else gets here."

Taking the box out of Samuel's hand, April felt queasy.

"Thank you, Latham."

She tore off the wrapping paper to reveal an olive green box with '*Monaco's*' printed in gold on the lid. Lifting the top, she stared down at a ladies wrist-watch. The delicate band was encrusted with diamond chips, and a fairly large bluish diamond, almost a karat and a half, was embedded in the center of its face. In eye popping brilliance, quarter karat diamonds circled the central stone embellishing the twelve hours. Her initial reaction to it wasn't the true barometer of her feelings and just one single tear dribbled out. This expensive bauble was a clear symbol of the beginning of the end, and it may be the only thing she'd have left when her marriage to this madman disintegrates.

"I can see by your face you really do like it!" Samuel stood up and gave April a peck on her cheek. Needing more sack time, he started the mysterious trek to the second floor.

April's spoke softly, "It's quite . . ." and then she went silent. Samuel was already ten feet away, and he hadn't heard her; searching for Latham's bed a priority. Like a deer frozen in place in the woods, she stood alone in the cavernous room for almost ten minutes until she fell spinelessly onto the couch. Lying there, she looked straight up at the ceiling and said "lovely."

In Chapter 19 of Genesis in the Bible, the reader could intuit that Idis, Lot's wife, had allowed too much sentimentality in her actions. An angel had been sent to warn her and her family not to turn back to watch the destruction of Sodom, their lifelong home. Idis looked over her shoulder anyway, and for this rebellious transgression, God transformed her into a pillar of salt. In the past, sodium chloride was the economic equivalent of gold, however gold couldn't blow away in the desert wind. Changing her mortal body into a very unstable sculpture was a cautionary act, underlining how deleterious her attachments to the material world were. In our archeological findings, Sodom and Gomorrah seemed to have been destroyed with a volcanic event, not the hell born brimstone and fire described in the good book, and describing the transformation of Idis into salt was probably another metaphor too. *Probably*.

And if angels were really flying around in the sky hundreds of years ago, most of them would have been scorched right out of our atmosphere by now. Between heavy jet traffic and our global disinterest in their messages, April's internal devil was free to goad her with no winged intervention to ignore.

Sam climbed the staircase to the second floor, and he was breathless when he reached the landing. There were two hallways diving into the bowels of the house, and he found a coin in his pocket, he flipped it. Heads, he'll go to the right; tails, to the left, and tails it was. He considered the general layout of the building, and he decided to start his search from the other end of the corridor. Walking all the way to the end, he was standing in the center of a small sitting area, with the addition of colored light streaming in from a stained glass window installed high in the back wall. He turned around and faced the front of the house again. All the doors were on his right. Knocking on the first one, silence invited him into a large suite. The décor was blue and light pink with a smell of perfume in the air. He went back into the hall. No one would ever know what other people hide behind closed doors, but he was fairly sure those rooms weren't Latham's. The next one opened into a storage room filled with cleaning supplies. Samuel was badly burnt out and he really needed more rest, and he was relieved when the next door was the right one. He put the suitcase down, and he rested the computer bag on the top of a bureau in the main room. He closed the drapes against the morning light, and he took off the suit. His long, lean, and aching fifty-nine year old body curled up on Latham Donnelly's California king bed. Moaning with satisfaction, he pulled the covers up to his chin as the memory foam on the mattress formed around his body as if he'd been sleeping on that bed for years.

3:00PM Thursday November 24, 2005 Boston, Massachusetts

Lazzo and Edgar and their well-behaved prisoner spent hours in McCarran Airport until three seats opened up for them on a flight leaving at 6:00AM on Thanksgiving Day. Edgar and Lazzo had all the necessary permits they needed to transport their handguns out-of-state and Edgar checked the bag holding the tools of their trade as luggage without a problem. It was 12:00PM when they landed in Boston, but they'd changed time zones. It was three in the afternoon in Eastern Time when the three men stepped off the plane into Logan Airport.

Cindy had been renting the executive series from Apache in Las Vegas for years, and the company was nationwide so while they cooled their heels in Vegas, Edgar called the office in Boston. A black Lincoln Town Car was already gassed up and waiting for them. Taking the escalator to the ground floor, Edgar picked up their bag at the carousel and then they walked over to the line of rental companies near the outside exits. The kidnappers weren't watching Latham quite as diligently as they had before. It was possible while they crossed the terminal, their prisoner might have been able to escape, but it wasn't going to happen. About twenty years older than his kidnappers, Latham was too washed-out to try. He just wanted to get home, and he thought his only way out would be to pay these low brow lackeys off.

Standing in front of the counter for Apache Rentals, Edgar took out his wallet.

"Hi. We talked on the phone about arranging some transportation for the Phalanx Group, a business from Las Vegas." He raised his eyebrows. The man behind the counter gave him a polite hello, and he punched the company name into the computer.

"Yes sir, it's all ready," and he slid a rental contract over to him. "I'll have someone drive it around for you, right now." Signing on the dotted line, Edgar handed over his credit card. In five minutes they stood outside the terminal while a Town Car wheeled around the corner of the building to stop right in front of them. The driver got out, and trotted over and dropped the keys in Edgar's hand and Lazzo gave him a generous tip.

As soon as they left the airport, holiday traffic congealed around them. Edgar was driving, and Lazzo was riding shot-gun. Latham was stretched out on the very comfortable back seat and the soft leather upholstery under his head was singing a lullaby to him, yet he couldn't relax enough for sleep. The two violent men in the front seat wired him out too much and he wasn't looking forward to the hours on the road. Since the cat-nap was out of the question, Latham wracked his brains to come up with something to calm his nerves . . . *what about a conversation about something that had nothing to do with this atrocious journey?*

"Hey Lazzo, we've got some time to kill. I was wondering if I could ask you a personal question. Would that be okay?"

Edgar and Lazzo twisted around in their seats, startled he'd piped up at all. Lazzo had been playing a game on his phone, but his oversized fingers had made it hard for him to control the action. He was bored to tears, more than happy to answer a question. He put the phone back in his pocket.

"Sure, Sam. What is it you want to know?"

"Well, you don't seem very religious, so I was wondering why you have three gold crosses around your neck? What's the reason for it?" Latham had leaned forwards to ask the question. After that, he sank back into the seat and clasped his hands behind his head.

Lazzo laughed, "I like to hedge my bets."

Staring up at the upholstered ceiling inches away from his nose, Latham responded. "So it's a joke? I hate to say it, but it seems lame."

"No, no, its not. My family is Greek Orthodox and when I was a kid I learned a lot about God. I went to church once a week with my family."

"And you believe God sits on a throne in heaven?"

"Yeah . . . of course," Lazzo said.

One of Latham's eyebrows rose while he exhaled a noisy puff.

"Alright, but I can't come up with any western religion that could accept what you do as righteous. I don't think any of our deities would let you get into heaven. Do you really believe that a cross or even a collection of them, would give you a key to the golden gates?"

"You think you know what I do for a living, but you don't have it right, Sammy, not at all. First of all, I just do what I'm told, and I get rid of bad people . . . people who run out on their financial responsibilities, like *you*. Lazy, greedy, dumdums. I'm cleaning the world up." Having come up with an illogical and ludicrous rationalization, Lazzo smiled. He thought it was a clever explanation. Edgar was smiling too, for a different reason.

"What about the ten commandants? Do you remember the law that said, '*Thou shalt not kill*'? It was a biggie, and I'm pretty sure you've broken it once or twice," Latham said.

"'An eye for an eye' is another truth from the bible too . . . and . . . ah, hmm . . . there's the other commandant that says you can't steal. God works in mysterious ways, and I think he put me here to stop people like you, who break the other law. How's that! Oh, if you're still curious about it, I can explain why I have them on. It's because of the Trinity . . . the Father, the Son and the Holy Ghost. I think each one should have its own cross."

In a different situation, Lazzo's answer might have got Latham laughing, but he restrained himself. He was worried any condescension like that could spur the ungentle giant into a hurtful action in his direction.

"And all these years, I never knew why you had on so many crosses. I never asked you, 'cause I didn't wanna get you mad," Edgar said. His long-term curiosity suddenly appeased, he looked back over his shoulder again, and said, "Thanks, Samuel!" with real gratitude in his voice.

"You're welcome," but Latham said it dead-pan. Unlocking his hands from behind his head, he placed them on his knees and stared out at the passing scenery. He really hadn't gotten any kind of release in the conversation he'd provoked. Two lunatics still had him in their power, and he considered the awful possibility that the pile of cash he was going to give them might not save his life.

3:06PM Thursday November 24, 2005 Bass River, Massachusetts

Mirabelle drove over the Bass River Bridge towards town, while David piloted the Mercedes in the other lane. Honking and waving, they squeezed past each other on the thin bridge with only inches to spare.

David was magnificent in his custom-tailored winter coat, a polished squire to present his lady to the court. The lady was a breathtaking treasure herself, and under her velvet cape, Holly's electric blue dress, rucked along the side seams, embraced her body like butter on bread. Her long hair, elaborately knotted on top of her head, had blue satin ribbons braided into it and ringlets were let free to swirl gracefully to her shoulders. The square neckline of the dress was cut low. On a platinum chain between her collarbones hung a hexagonal sapphire with the depth and power of a pool of blue fire.

Yet the couple's physical seamlessness did not reflect any symmetry within. Holly and David hadn't had a friendly conversation with each other in quite a while. Driving from New Bedford to the reunion on Cape Cod, they'd been serenaded by *The Twelve Dreams of Dr. Sardonicus*, a concept album from a band called Spirit. As the miles flew by, hypnotic harmonies and innovative polyrhythms recorded thirty years ago reigned supreme.

An hour before they were going to leave for Bass River, David Russell had gone back to the upper shelves in the garage to grab the plastic bag hidden in the Sand Garden and he secreted it in his suit jacket. A poisonous retribution against his duplicitous wife, it would also drag the whole family down with her. The end result would reward him with the financial and professional freedom he yearned for . . . at least that was what he thought would happen.

In the on-going silence between them, Holly considered her own future plans. It began important to speak to David one more time before they got to the house and she turned the stereo down. A catalyst for some of the irritations now seething in the family, she had a powerful feeling that the consequences of the Donnellys' communication breakdown were probably going to be tragic.

"Ever wanted a boat, David?" Holly purred to him.

"Well, a few years ago I dreamed of a comfortable thirty-five foot yacht docked in some marina off Pope's Island. I imagined going on a long vacation on it with you, but things have changed. These days, I try not to think at all." David was very careful. He didn't know how far he could go with her.

"We should get one, right now! You're blowing in the wind and I've been tied to the cross at work endlessly banging the drum to rustle up donations for the hospital. I've been running straight into a wall, since the new definition of 'politics' is schizophrenia and its running rampant through a power structure that's sabotages what's left of the health care system. I'm stuck in a boring and pointless struggle and I haven't had time to even tie my shoes. Getting that promotion hadn't been worth the headaches it came with, and I think we both need a break from everything. I pray you feel the same way, sweetheart. We should sail away for a while on a new dream."

Holly dug into her evening bag to get her lipstick. The bends in the road not withstanding, she applied it perfectly. David looked over at her as long as he could without driving off the road. His wife had just turned into a different person, and he was confounded. In the past year, he'd sunk into a financial swamp with no way out, and between Holly's lies and his father-in-law's scorn, he'd felt like the child in Charles Dickens' novel 'Oliver Twist'. He'd politely asked them for a crust of bread, only to be denied. What on earth could she be offering him now? He'd even heard romantic overtones in this strange invitation, and it sounded like she wanted to renew their relationship. The idea of living in sexual utopia with his exquisite and powerful wife re-bloomed in his heart, yet that alien flower wilted quickly. His paranoia blew her appeasement out the window, and the woman he was afraid of and loathed returned. In his mind, all she wanted to do was to bring him into her web and get rid of him. Why use time and money in a divorce court? They'd just go out on a joy ride into the Atlantic and as soon as they got far enough off shore, she'd push him off the deck, leaving him behind as shark bait.

"Don't you have a fleet of yachts in some cove off the coast of Rhode Island, honey?" David said. He had a wry smile on his face.

"Didn't think you knew about them. I guess you also know about the small cruise ship, Aspersion's Foil anchored in the Mediterranean right now," and Holly grinned right back at him. "Why won't you answer the question, David? Doesn't this invitation ring a bell for you? Should I put out some feelers for the boat and write out a resignation to the hospital?" She put the the gloss back in her bag, and she leaned back against the seat.

"My answer is yes, honey. It sounds great. I'm just surprised. You'd have to break your addiction to work and that sounds difficult. I guess the situation has really become untenable for you, and that's actually a good thing. A fairytale for the two of us to glide off into a valentine heart painted around a sunset on the horizon. It seems it's going to come true after all." David wasn't worried anymore, and he wasn't going to be thrown off the new boat. What was in his interior pocket would snip that problem in the bud.

"I'm trying to tell you I need a break . . . we both need a break. If you mean what you say, I'll start looking out for a good deal on something," Holly said. She wasn't really going to do anything. Hearing the insincerity in his voice, she knew her offer had been rejected.

David parked next to Robert's Harley, surprised that Latham's brown Mercedes wasn't in the garage. They got out of the car, and Holly hooked her arm around his, and they walked to the front door and rang the bell.

"In only a few months, we'll sail away . . . or motor away, anyway," she said.

April held onto her flimsy predictions, even if her husband's smarmy attitude had shaken her to the core. The bad wolf was about to announce his evil intentions, and she'd use her foil to deflect and parry. Arranging a curl of hair on her forehead, she didn't know a tear was running down the side of her face. She had buried the truth down deep in her head, and the unwanted kernels were germinating into bad-tempered ghosts. Unlike the make-believe monsters we thought were hiding under our beds when we were children, these chaos born gremlins could easily extinguish her life in madness.

The sparkling new watch on her wrist let her know it was three o'clock. Ah, yes. The turkey needed to be basted. Tying a yellow silk scarf around her neck, she left the suite and took the elevator to the kitchen. There was an apron on a hook near the sink, and she dropped it over her head, and then she put on the oven mitts. She opened the oven-door. Straining, she lifted the twenty-eight pound of turkey onto the center island without mishap. After spooning pan drippings over the roast, she put it back into the oven, arm muscles shaking, and April was going to give the rest of the basting responsibilities to Justin or David. Leaving the gloves on the counter, and the apron on the hook, she walked back to the great room. She stopped in front of the mirrored wall and scrutinized her appearance. A long sleeved white satin shirt was tucked into a flowing white skirt that ended at her calf. The skirt was printed with spots of green, orange, yellow and blue, like paint spatter over black lines in geometric patterns. She was wearing a gold belt and matching high-heeled shoes and the yellow scarf topped it off.

The doorbell rang and she walked away from the mirror smiling. More of her children were arriving! Since April's make-up was waterproof, the occasional tear wasn't going to mar her glossy coat. She opened the front door, and embraced Holly with enthusiasm.

"Happy Thanksgiving! It's wonderful to see you."

"Happy Thanksgiving, Mom." April's hug was so tight, Holly's response was a bit breathless.

"Happy Thanksgiving, April," David said, and he leaned over and gave his mother-in-law a kiss on the cheek.

"Don't you take your coats off yet! You have to see the new topiary in the garden." April skipped over to the closet like a child to grab her jacket. Holly and David looked at each other. "I know, I know. You're expecting a jockey on a horse, or a chess piece, but this one is different. It should really surprise you." She led them to the back door in the library, and they all walked out to the garden maze.

Arriving the day before, Robert had woken up late that morning. He'd taken the elevator to the kitchen to fill a large coffee cup with espresso. Neither Vince nor Mirabelle saw him, and he snagged a pastry off the center island and returned to his old bedroom on the second floor. The coffee hadn't been quite enough. He fell asleep again. Something wicked prowled through his dreams until it bit him, and he woke up shaking and wet. Rolling out of bed, he opened his backpack and he removed a tiny case with a glass tube taped to the side. Ripples of anxiety left behind by the nightmare had him set up lines of coke on the mirrored top of the table next to bed. After snorting them up, nothing bothered him anymore as a human-god and he could momentarily live forever. Perched on the padded seat in the garden window, Robert stared out at the front of the property. A silver Mercedes drifted up the driveway and parked on the other side of his Harley, and he watched his sister and brother-in-law get out of the car. A muscle began to twitch under his left eye and he rubbed at it. He took the flask of brandy out of the back pocket of his jeans, and he twisted off the cap. Swigging some down, the irritating twitch kept on twitching nonetheless. He had to calm it down somehow, and it came to him. *Hashish*. He'd left a block of it behind on the bike. Shit. That stuff would soften the edges. His lower eyelid continued to be tugged down by the tiny muscles in his face, and they were locking and unlocking uncontrollably. It was time to go outside and get the hash.

April, Holly, and David entered the hedge maze. Around the first turn, April stopped and pointed up. Gusts of wind, almost twenty miles an hour, intensified the illusion that a pod of green dolphins made from fluttering leaves leapt and swam, barely anchored in the Donnellys' garden.

"That's delightful! I've never seen anything like it before. How on earth did you come up with the idea?" Holly said, holding her cape around her body. The leafy pod rocked forwards and backwards, capricious in the gusts of wind.

David chimed in, "Holly's right. It is surprising! Where did you come up with the idea of fish?"

(Naked in bed with her plastic surgeon was where), but she didn't want to tell them that. Oohing and aahing over a stunning photograph of dolphins leaping out of the Gulf of Mexico, they were talking about living there after the divorce and the picture was stuck in her head. The sculpture in the hedge garden was a symbol for her, marking her final escape. In the meantime, April came up with a different story to explain it.

"You've heard of Charlene's in Boston, haven't you?"

"Of course, I know the place. They won't give me the time of day and they're worth the money if you can get in." Holly answered the beginning of her mother's lie with one of her own. In reality, the owners pampered her like a star. To them, she was a living billboard. They thought she could bring in more business, the right business and they were right.

"Well, I was sitting there waiting . . . oh, they have great organic fruit drinks by the way, and I was flipping through a magazine with photographs of wildlife. I fell in love with a picture of dolphins and I couldn't get it of my head. When I got home, I called up Gregory and Paul. Remember the arches they made near the large fountain and the little Q-tips around the boat dock we installed a few years ago? I told them what I wanted and presto, here they are!" Another tear leaked out of April's eye. The wind was tossing her hair around and no one saw it.

Robert popped his head into the hall. The mansion was silent. Mom had probably taken everybody out to see the garden fish. He'd been dragged out there to see the silly things the day before. He left the bedroom door ajar and he put on his leather jacket. Silently moving down the hall, he glided down the stairs. He crossed the entry hall, and opened and closed the front door softly. He unlocked the seat of the motorcycle and he lifted it up, to get to the tool kit. The hash was wrapped in silver foil inside the small plastic container, and he wiggled the tool kit out of the metal holder and opened it. The silver lump was squished into the corner and he picked it out and stuffed it into his front pocket. But that was not enough. He selected a pair of pliers that were in the tool kit too. They were there for cutting electrical wire, and they were razor sharp.

His mom had said his father was going to drive to the airport the very next day, and that knowledge had tunneled into his mind like a worm. He stepped closer to his father's car, and he looked around. Dropping to his knees next to the front right tire of Latham's Mercedes, he flipped over on his back and shimmied under the car. He knew what a brake line was, and he cut the front line leading to the wheel on the passenger side with the pliers he'd brought along. Then he wriggled out and trotted over to the other side of the car. Back on his knees again, he was about to repeat what he'd just done, when he heard the sound of a car driving up and he froze. Justin's BMW. He didn't have time to get up and get to his Harley and stand there nonchalantly. He was afraid his brother would figure out exactly what he was doing. He flattened out and rolled father underneath his father's car and stayed there. Justin parked next to David's Mercedes and his driver's door opened and closed, punctuating his short trip to the front door. Getting no answer, Jay disappeared around the corner of the house. Since Robert was already under the car, he just moved a smidgeon nearer to the wheel well under the driver seat . . . **Snip**. *That was it, easy as pie.*

Cutting *all* the brake lines wouldn't have worked. It would have bled the system out way too fast, and his father would notice something was wrong before he got out of the driveway. With only two lines out of commission, the brakes would be sluggish. By the time he loses complete control, it would be way too late. A mile away from the house, Latham would be driving downhill on a twisty road. He sniggered. Patricide was a culmination for him, and he'd come up a practical plan, but it wasn't ingenious. Logic hadn't found a toe-hold in his twisted head. Leaving behind a lot dangerous clues, Robert was more concerned about someone else's tomorrow than his own.

3:32PM Thursday November 24, 2005 Bass River, Massachusetts

Shutting off the engine, Justin saw two Mercedes sandwiching Robert's Harley. Opening the glove compartment, he removed the black case from New Orleans, and he slipped it inside the inner pocket of his satin lined camel coat. Tree branches were flailing in the wind, and he flipped up his coat collar and got out of the car. No answer at the front door. They had to be out back and Justin passed the Olympic pool on his way to the gardens.

"HELLO! Can anybody hear me . . . HELLO!" Justin stuffed two fingers in his mouth to create a whistle with ear splitting volume.

"Jay . . . Hello! Come down the path, we're right here," David yelled through the hedge. Walking into the maze, Justin found the group around the first corner and he gave his Mom more compliments about the dolphins. He asked her why Robert and his father weren't there.

"Dad got home very late last night, so he's sleeping a little longer before he meets you all for dinner. Bertie was badly overtired when he got here yesterday, so I guess he's resting too." During her explanation, April's expression began to disintegrate and she looked up to see clouds racing north. The trees and bushes were whipping around more wildly by the moment. "It's getting way too windy and cold out here. We should go inside and start in on the appetizers that Vince and Mirabelle have left for us."

Replacing the pliers in the kit, Robert closed the seat of his Harley, and went back to the bedroom. He took the hash out of his pocket and stuffed some into the bowl of a brass pipe. Lighting it up, he inhaled as much as he could and then he held his breath. He went through the same action three more times, and the rebellious eye muscles miraculously relaxed. Taking off his leather jacket, he tossed it on the bed and then he peeled off his sweaty T-shirt. He replaced it with a clean turtleneck he got out of his backpack. A folded black corduroy vest and matching pants were folded on the bottom of the pack and he took them out and shook the wrinkles out. It was the best he could come up with to look presentable at the party and he wasn't that worried about it. Buttoning the vest, Robert went downstairs to have Thanksgiving with his family.

Samuel stretched. The clock on the side of the bed told him it was 3:45. He'd gotten over his nerves and he was looking forwards to more impersonation of Latham Donnelly. He got out of bed and stepped into Donnelly's walk-in closet to pick out some dinner clothes. Racks and racks of elegant suits hung there and he browsed through them. When he saw a replica of the same comfortable looking linen suit Latham had been wearing in Las Vegas, he smiled. If that suit was appropriate for recreational attire then it should be fine for a family affair. He took it off the hanger. During the frantic hustle he'd gone through in the suite the day before, he'd packed *everything* in the two bags, and that had included a pack of un-opened cards and a sleeve of red and black chips wrapped in plastic. A CEO wouldn't have things like that with him on a business trip. The casino must have put them in his room as another free amenity. Staring at them, he got an idea. He could use the cards and chips as tools to introduce himself to the family. The new and improved Latham Donnelly. He dropped them into the side pockets of the off-white suit. Opening the door of Latham's suite, he strolled down the hall to enjoy someone else's Thanksgiving dinner with someone else's family.

3:50PM Thursday November 24, 2005 Bass River, Massachusetts

"You all know where the bar is. I've got to run to the kitchen and get the hors d'oeuvres," April said. Slipping out of her coat, she left it on the edge of the couch in her haste to get to the platters of food and she bumped into Robert hard while she was rushed through the door. She was thrown backwards, finding her balance just in time. "Bertie! I'm so sorry. I didn't see you . . . are you alright?"

"Relax Mom, I'm fine. I feel no pain. You shouldn't run around like that. It's a holiday. We can relax and kick back." He grinned and hugged her.

"You're right, of course. I need to slow down. I need to relax. Oh, by the way, you look quite nice."

April's renewed trip began as a normal walk, but it didn't hold on. When she reached the dining room, she was almost jogging into the kitchen. Getting into the walk-in cooler, she took out two trays holding shrimp puffs, cucumber sandwiches, and black caviar on water crackers . . . there was even a *third* one, but she had to leave it behind. She'd take that one out later on.

Robert, Holly, David, and Justin were sitting around the coffee table in the center of the room, when April re-appeared with the food.

"Move everything off the table, please," April said, and everyone did as they were told. She put the trays down, and glanced over at the clock on the mantle above the fireplace. It was time. "Look kids, I basted the turkey at three and Vince wants us to baste it once an hour. Since it's almost four, one of you has to take that chore off my back. Would you do it Justin?"

His mouth was filled with caviar and cracker, and the only thing response she could hear at first was crunching and gargling. Then he came out with, "Noprrobblemm!" And crumbs sprayed out of his mouth. He finally gulped it down and stood up, while everyone laughed at him. Walking away, he nervously giggled along with the crowd.

When he got to the closet in the hallway, he stopped for a second to remove the black case out of his coat, and then he ducked into the bathroom only a few feet away. He locked the door behind him. Raising the case to the overhead lights, he found the tiny lever on the side and he pushed it. The box opened. Resting it on the back of the toilet, he took out the bottle of tetrodotoxin and the syringe out of their cut-outs in the grey foam. He'd gone through these final actions a thousand times in his head and it should work out without a hitch. He punctured the foil top on the tiny bottle with the needle, filling the syringe to the top. Taking the needle out, he put toilet paper around the point to absorb the last drop and he tossed the used tissue into the bowl. He used more tissue from the dispenser on the sink to build a nest for the loaded syringe in the right pocket of his jacket. Replacing the empty bottle into the case, he closed it and put it in his other pocket. He flushed the toilet, left the bathroom and walked through the swinging doors into the kitchen.

The smell was mouthwatering as he rested the sizzling pan on the center island. He basted the bird. Placing the brush on a plate near the sink, Justin made sure no one was coming by standing motionless next to the door to listen. Only silence, and that's great. Painstakingly removing the syringe out of his pocket, he tossed the extra tissue into the garbage.

He plunged the needle into the oyster stuffing and he pushed the plunger down. In his mind, the deed was already done. Getting the black case out of his pocket, he returned the needle to its place in the foam and he dropped the box in his pocket. Putting the oven mitts back on again, he gently slid the turkey back into the oven and closed the door. He briskly stepped out of the kitchen on his way to the library, pausing for a second to drop the case back into the pocket of his winter coat.

When his family starts to feel the effects, he'd call for official help. In that small envelope of time, between the call and the arrival of a response team, he'd throw the box into the creek. No one would see him. No one would ever know. For the first time in a long he slowed down, actually sauntering into the library to count the eggs before they were laid, a wonderful high of premature satisfaction.

"Was there a problem, Justin? It took you forever and a day," April said.

"No, no problem. The turkey smelled as good as it looked! I just had a pit stop." Grinning, he slid a glass from the upper rack over the bar, and then he tossed the glass in the air. It somersaulted and he snatched it, to pour himself a victory drink. Vodka, triple sec, cranberry juice, and orange juice, of course the main ingredient was Grey Goose vodka. Leaning against the bar, he realized Dad was still missing. Justin's sudden impatience vanished a minute later when Samuel walked into the library. He thought the drunken vows they'd made the year before had been upheld and he believed this reunion would be their last.

"Happy Thanksgiving, everyone! Sorry I'm late, but the meeting in Vegas was a drag and it wasn't easy to get home. Everybody was in my way and everyone wanted to fly." Samuel walked over to April and kissed her on the cheek, placing his arm around her waist. The rest of the family was gracious in their hellos, but Latham's affection towards his wife mystified them. Samuel didn't know he was cracking April's shell and the thin crack was widening fast. His sudden fondness was turning her well-crafted beauty into a rictus, and April was frozen in place; a display of female horror in a wax museum. Holly saw her mother's imminent collapse, and she sailed in like the cavalry, turning Samuel's attentions away from April with buckling speed.

"I compliment you, Dad. You appear well rested, considering all the miles under your belt. I'm impressed with your stamina. How 'bout I make you a drink?" Holly exuded her own hypnotic version of affection, and she gave him a warm hug. Samuel returned her embrace with enthusiasm, happily peeling away from her mother. He followed her over to the bar. April lurched to the couch and sat down next to Robert to find her bearings.

"What would you like, Dad?" Holly asked.

"Gin and tonic, please."

Holly glanced over at the group and one was watching, so she had enough leeway to play with Samuel's head for a minute or two. The sapphire jewel twinkling at her throat, she made his drink with frightening velocity, like a bolt of blue lightening. Sam sat at the bar and watched her, and that's exactly what she'd wanted. He'd never seen anyone mix a drink that fast in his life. It hadn't looked human. When her super-sonic shake, rattle and roll was over, a perfectly balanced gin and tonic glided across the bar, stopping in front of his right hand. He picked up his drink, and swallowed most of it, trying to find his tongue. Holly was smirking like a teenager.

"It tastes great, thanks Holly. Your technique is out of this world . . . you're faster than a . . . I don't even know what. You had to have gone to school to tend bar at some point in your life."

"Now, now, *Dad*. You've been on the road way too much. You've forgotten what I've been doing and it wasn't tending bar." Holly started giggling.

"It was only a compliment, is all. You must have been born with a knack for it, anyway," Samuel said, afraid he'd stumbled. Maybe she suspected him. Looking at his reflection in the large mirror on the wall across from him, there was a professional portrait of Latham Donnelly nearby and his concern evaporated. Feeling much better, he raised his voice to get everyone's attention.

"There was no time for me to gamble in Vegas, but they did leave these things in my room as a consolation prize." And he lifted the cards and the package of chips in the air. "Why don't we play a game of cards? The chips could be markers as hundred dollars bills. It might be a hoot. However the cookie crumbles, everyone would certainly have fun, with no harm done. Well, maybe a little bit of pain, easily forgotten when we dig into the food. What do you think?" An extended silence ensued. Samuel was getting nervous again, until Justin chimed in.

"Sounds great, Dad. What game did you have in mind?" He stood up and walked over to his father and Holly at the bar.

"Poker, five card draw, my gents and ladies. Tried and true. A classic, and nothing is wild," Samuel said, and he winked. "At least nothing will be wild in the beginning of the game. Is everyone okay with hundred dollar chips?" Samuel had started to smile ear to ear.

Everyone accepted the terms, except Robert. He didn't like the game idea at all, and he continued to stare into a large glass of brandy as he swirled the golden liquid around until he frowned and stood up. He walked off to the unlit section of the library to sulk. The rest of the family re-arranged the furniture and removed the glasses and plates off the coffee table. Samuel sat in one of the armchairs, shuffling the cards and Justin parked himself in a chair to his left. Done with the shuffle, Jay cut the deck. David was sitting across the table from Sam, on the edge of the divan, and April stayed where she was on the couch. Holly took Robert's place, on Samuel's right.

The game began, but something was wrong. Samuel and Holly won every pot. Seeing general frustration, Holly decided to do something about it when the deal came around to her again.

"Can you see that?" Holly said, as she pointed at the garden window.

It was almost dark outside, and two things happened at the same time. A big white bird, it could have been a swan, flapped up against the glass, and Holly lowered the playing cards under the table. Her fingertips lit up for a few seconds and after that the bird fluttered off. Wondering where on earth the bird could have come from, their attention returned to the table. Holly was holding the pack out to Samuel to cut, but he only tapped the pack with two fingers. *He . . . he just didn't feel like cutting the deck,* possibly because Holly was staring into his eyes with paralytic frost and from that point on, Holly and Samuel didn't win every game. Justin and April, respectively, won the next two hands.

"Deal me out for a couple of minutes, okay? I've to take care of a personal matter," David said. Leaning forwards, he got out of the deep armchair and walked a couple of feet away. He paused, and looked back. Robert was still hiding around the corner, but the rest of the family was engrossed by the game. It was a good time for him to check the warming trays; see what Vince had rustled up for their dinner. Entering the dining room, he lifted up the covers on the containers lined up on the steam table. Yams, chestnuts, petite fresh peas . . . homemade cranberry sauce. He left that cover to the side.

Dressed in a suit made out of grey gabardine with thin orange stripes, David was debonair as his hand moved across the peach colored silk lining of his jacket to remove the bag of yew berries and plastic gloves out of the inner pocket. He put the gloves on, and then he squeezed the berries into the tray. The color of the wild invaders was very similar to cranberry red and he was pleased. Picking up the ladle in the tray, he mixed the toxic slush into the sauce and then he replaced the cover. The murderous deed was done.

Spending months obsessing about the perfect life he was going to have, he stared down at the plastic bag in his gloved hand and he found himself dead in the water. *The gloves and the plastic bag.* He couldn't flush them down the toilet. It might clog the system. In all that time, he hadn't figured out a way to dispose of them, but he was boosted on adrenaline, and he quickly came up with a plan. He cracked open the door leading to the hallway. No one was there, and he ran the length of it into the great room. He sprinted around the koi pond to get to the fire.

He didn't remember anything about toxic fumes coming from burning the yew, and he didn't know if there would there be any. At this juncture, he didn't have any time to worry about it. Carefully taking off the gloves, he stuffed them inside the bag, and he threw the entire noxious ball into the fire. He pushed the curling lump of plastic deeper into the flames with the poker. Dropping the heavy tool on the hearthstones, the resulting ring of metal bouncing off stone had turned into a starter pistol for him. He raced away from the fire. Standing next to the library door, he had to wait for his breathing to normalize before he walked in. After minute or two, he thought he was fine, and he opened the door and moseyed over to the bar to pick up his drink. From there, he went back to his chair and sat down.

"Deal me back in, okay?" David was going through the motions of his plan in his head, and it seems he'd done it flawlessly . . . well, almost flawlessly, and he was content. The most difficult part of the evening was taken care of.

"You really do want to play this game, don't you son? Sounds like you ran straight here from the bathroom," Samuel said, smiling, and he included him in the next deal.

4:56PM Thursday November 24, 2005 Bass River, Massachusetts

"It's almost five o'clock. One of you has to take the turkey out and baste it," April said, staring down at the cluster of diamonds on her wrist. She started to blink way too fast until she snapped out of it. She went back to sipping at her grapefruit juice and vodka with a vapid expression on her face. Samuel had found one of Latham's illegal Cuban cigars in a humidor on the desk, and he lit it. A cloud of smoke floated towards the ceiling. Historically, Latham would do almost the same thing at the same time, and April would say, "*Not when we have guests*". This time she didn't say a thing.

"Maybe it's time for an intermission," Holly said. "Justin or David could take the turkey out of the oven and Mom and I can relax. We could play cards again in about fifteen minutes, just for a few more rounds before dinner. What do you think?" Everyone nodded, and Holly strolled to the bar with uncanny ease. Her joints must have been filled with oil, not tendon or bone. Perching on one of the bar stools, she'd hooked one of the two very long blue heels of her shoe on one of the supports, and it shone like a spindle of blown glass. She poured herself another drink and looked out the window. Leaves were dancing across the backyard, while the powerful wind caressed the roofline of the mansion, but only Holly could hear its lonely northern song. Robert had gone upstairs to refresh himself in his own way, and Samuel sat down next to her.

April had followed Justin and David into the kitchen. With his elbows on the counter, David watched his brother-in-law take the turkey out one more time, and the lady of the house fluttered around the kitchen like she was on speed. Opening cupboards and peering into storage trays, she pushed into David on her second trip to the walk-in cooler. He tried to help her.

"Where did Vince put my parmesan cheese? He always leaves it in the left drawer in the cooler or on the counter before dinner. It's always there. How can I eat dinner without my parmesan cheese?" April was talking to herself. David backed out of the way of the swinging metal door of the cooler. It was important to him to relax her. He needed her to enjoy her Thanksgiving dinner, and she was getting more and more upset.

"Mom, you've got to calm down, I mean, sprinkling cheese over your food is almost the same as putting salt on it . . . Mom . . . April."

She wasn't listening, too focused on her task. Her cell phone was in her silk clutch on the table in the hall and she rushed out to get it. She called up Vince and then Mirabelle. Neither call was answered and she was running out of options. Otto's Delicatessen was seven miles away, and April thought it might be open. To her relief a girl picked up the phone, telling her they'd be open for another twenty-five minutes. Closing her cell phone with a snap, she snatched up her evening bag and bolted out of the kitchen. She dashed through the great room and into the entry hall without breaking stride. Latham's car keys were on the end table near the front door. Her car was still inside the garage, and since the Mercedes was already parked outside, using his car might shave off a minute or two. Picking up Latham's car keys, she opened the front door with the strength of the damned and April left the house on the hill, never to return.

It was 37 degrees outside and the north wind made it feel much colder. She hadn't put on a coat, but she was so distracted, the bite in the air didn't bother her. In the very near future, she would sell her soul to the devil if he told her he could transport her back in time to that chilly moment in the auto park; if he'd allow her to go back inside the house and put the car keys back where she'd found them and have dinner with her family without the adored cheese. Of course, a supernatural rescue like that wouldn't have made any difference. If the horned one had actually shown up, the new contract he'd make with her would bowl him over with laughter.

5:05PM Thursday November 24, 2005 Bass River, Massachusetts

David's valiant attempts to assuage April's need for cheese hadn't worked, and he watched her tear out of the kitchen on an on-stoppable quest. Justin was basting the turkey for the last time, leaving the bird on the counter to cool down before Latham carved it up.

"She's flipped out! Have you ever seen her that crazy before, Jay?"

"Nope, not really. Something else is bothering her besides Parmesan. Don't worry about it, I mean, women in general are all nuts. The two females at the reunion tonight, Holly and Mom, should really sum it all up for you. Mom will be back in twenty minutes holding the sacred grail, and she'll be fine. Looking forwards to losing another round of poker to me, hmm?"

They walked back to the library together, and David looked over at his brother-in-law and narrowed his eyes.

"Should I be concerned about the food tonight, bro? Last I heard, you didn't even want to show up, yet lo and behold here you are. Maybe you've found a different reason to be here, besides the power of love?" And he sniggered.

"Actually, I was really considering sending you all to the grave, but my customers took up all my time this year and I couldn't get it together," Justin said. He shrugged. "Next year . . . wait a minute, maybe *I* should be worried about the food? What have you been up to, day after day in that house in New Bedford?"

"Squat. I get soused and I go to the golf club and play golf and then I eat the fattening club food." His tone became serious. "What was the real point behind our conversation in Boston, anyway? I went down in flames in court and I think we both needed an excuse to blow off some steam. It was a very depressing part of my life. We had a lot of fun dreaming up things that only happen in the movies, didn't we? Things have turned around for me now. Holly's going to buy us a new boat and we'll sail off together into the sunset. I think she wants to start things up between us again."

Justin laughed, "You can't be serious. You're talking about the devil in a blue dress in the library with Dad right now. The same one you went down the aisle with? Nope, it can't be. You've lost it completely or she's hypnotized you."

David had to act the part all the way to the end and he threw his hands out to appease Justin's barb. "Actually, being a house husband as turned out to be a lot less stressful than saving lives with a scalpel. The idea of lying in the sun on a boat next to Holly without looking over my shoulder at a defibrillator is looking better and better everyday!" And he started to laugh. Justin couldn't discern the lunacy in the high notes of David's ongoing cackle.

Justin wasn't worried about David poisoning *anyone*, and David felt the same way about him. Sitting down at the bar with Holly and Samuel, they refreshed their drinks. Coincidently, they both felt regret about what was about to happen. Robert sidled into the room to fill his glass with Jim Beam, and then he retreated to the darkened bookshelves in the rear of the room.

"Where's April? I thought we were all going to play cards a little longer," Samuel said, looking around.

"She'll be back in about twenty minutes. She drove to Otto's to buy some more parmesan cheese, after she couldn't find it anywhere. I can't believe the deli was actually open!" Justin said.

"She took her car, right? She took the Fiat?" Robert's voice quivered out to them from the shadows.

"The deli wasn't going to stay open for long. She got up and ran, probably took Dad's car since it wasn't in the garage. That would have sped her up," Justin said. He tried to make his younger brother out in the unlit part of the library, when he streaked past him like a road runner on speed. The rest of the family didn't notice his abnormally hasty departure.

Robert streaked through the great room, and erupting out of the front door. Digging into his pants pocket for his motorcycle keys and the cell phone, it was probably too late to save her . . . *but he had to try.* Without any leather on, the wind raised goose bumps all over his scrawny frame, but his mother's imminent death trumped everything. Just like April, he didn't feel the cold. Racing towards his bike, he hit speed dial on his phone, but he got nothing but voice mail and he shoved the phone back in his pocket. He was pushing his body as hard as he could, and he had started to wheeze when he jumped on the bike. Pulling the clutch in, his foot shifted the bike into neutral. Backing up 1200cc's of hog as fast as he could was making his leg muscles shake.

He started the engine, toeing down into first gear. Twisting the throttle, he kicked the shift pedal up with ferocity, sending the transmission into second gear . . . third gear, and then fourth. He was gunning down the driveway too fast. The mix of cocaine, alcohol, helplessness and frustration drastically diminished his abilities as a rider, and as he negotiated the ninety-degree turn onto Bass River Road, he was already traveling 45 miles an hour. It wasn't going to work. At the end of the driveway, he leaned into the curve too far, and he lost traction. The motorcycle started to skip sideways across the pavement until he hit the curb on the other side of the road. A thousand pounds of metal hopped into flight . . . quickly grounded by an oak tree. The Harley was twisted beyond repair, but Robert had been thrown in the opposite direction and even though he looked bloody awful, he wasn't badly hurt. He found himself lying in the middle of the road. It was pitch black and the wind had revved up into a gale. Slowly standing up, he painfully swallowed his accountability in his mother's death like a capsule of strychnine. Robert looked up at the brightly lit mansion apparently suspended just above the never-ending front lawn, and what was left of his sanity slipped away. The graceful arches he saw in the distance were replaced with a vision of his father's body falling into an open grave.

April had to get to the Deli before they closed. Driving fast, she was heedless of tree branches sweeping out like clawed hands to scratch the side of the car and oblivious to swirling leaves in front of the wheels. Her husband's latest actions occluded her attention to the road.

Rolling into a tight turn, she hit the brakes. The power left in the system was gone, so pressing the pedal down didn't help. The Mercedes sped up and her heart muscle contracted with a new rhythm. April had never felt that beat before and her dreams of dancing the nights away on a tropical island with Peter were instantly replaced with the confining interior of Latham's car. Claustrophobia changed her panic into white noise, knowing the final conflict she was hurtling towards would arrive very soon. She'd turn off like an old TV. The picture would suck into a tiny intense dot of light, winking out with an electrical crackle. Her pulse was pounding like a drum and rivulets of sweat ran into her eyes, blurring her vision. Icy fingers clutched at the wheel, and April was hanging onto the road by a hair. She would try to make it to the bridge, but the turns rose up at her, faster and faster. Glancing at the speedometer with horror, she saw the awful truth. *66, 67, 67, 68*, and it continued to climb. Under the grinding pressure of dread, the power of self preservation imagined a happy ending for her. She'd live through the ride after all. She would make it to the bridge, and Bass River

Bridge is straight, and the road on the other side is straight and all she had to do was ride out the extra speed and roll to a stop.

Circling over the Donnelly's property, Slethim knew something was about to happen at the river. It broke away from the repetitive circling to fly closer to the action. The wind was gusting to forty-five, but it maneuvered through the air with the greatest of ease. A very tall black pine overlooked the Bass River Bridge, and it found a tree branch on that tree, thick enough to support its weight. It landed for a perfect view.

The Mercedes was too close to the edge of the road. A branch crashed through the passenger window, but it didn't trigger the air bags, instead whipping into April's head with dizzying speed. The concussive force left her dazed with a head wound bleeding profusely. It looked as if an Indian had partially scalped her. Imminent death switched every synapse in her brain on, and she was snapping and crackling like an electrical circuit board on overload. Time slowed to a crawl. Staring down at her lap, April was startled by the sudden introduction of red circles in the pattern of her white skirt . . . she didn't remember them in the design before. Confusion over her skirt dissolved into memories of her life shuffling by like a pack of old Polaroid's, but she wasn't connecting to the images. The wheels of her husband's car slipped across on the pavement, and the river was going to be an accomplice in Robert's matricide. The Mercedes broke through the guardrail on the right side of the bridge, and the air bags exploded at that point. April was swaddled as the car sailed thirty-five feet out in space. Hitting the water, the car's forward flight stopped and it began to sink.

On the passenger seat inside her purse, squished under the other air bag, her cell phone was playing a song from Rod Stewart, called *Forever Young*. April wasn't listening to the optimistic ring, and she couldn't have answered it, anyway. A picture of her daughter had staunched the flood of memories, and when the vision of Holly faded away, there was nothing left. No pain. No fear . . . no nothing. Very deep inside, she surrendered, welcoming the culmination in, while a point of extraordinary conception beckoned to her in the distance. Hovering in nullity with no light or dark, she drifted and didn't drift in a void. And then it was replaced with space. A velvety black poured in, filling the emptiness like coffee in a cup.

A huge eye blinked into existence, followed by another one, and they floated in front of what was left of her consciousness, supported by nothing. Alien colors slipped across the irises like oil on water, creating ribbons of unfamiliar rainbows. April felt relaxed and content, as if she remembered those inhuman eyes, perhaps remembering them from many years ago before her third child's birth.

Traveling through the river water, the steel roof of the Mercedes, the air bags, and the skull of the drowning woman, a layered voice began to communicate to April. The last flicker of her life was sputtering out in the salty water, and something or someone needed her to hear their indebted appreciation while she still could.

"*Thank you, April. I will always remember you.*"

It was 5:30PM. Slethim's interest in the river and the bridge was gone. It leaned forwards, dropping its head in a rolling motion, simultaneously hunching its shoulders. The creature dropped off the branch and opened its wings in one stroke to catch the air. It rose 75 feet up with only four powerful beats. Already far above the tree line, it kept ascending. A mile above the earth, Slethim resumed its languid orbit above the estate, like a vulture waiting for something to die . . . or perhaps to be re-born.

5:30PM Thursday November 24, 2005 Bass River, Massachusetts

After a long and painful walk, Robert opened the front door. He paused in the entry hall, momentarily confused. He couldn't quite remember what he was supposed to do. Unfortunately, it all came back. Lurching up the main stairs, he went to his room and he opened his backpack. Getting out his stash of coke, he used a razor blade to build a phalanx of white lines on the polished top of the end table next to the bed. He put the glass tube in one nostril and then the other while he snorted it all up. The drug hadn't been stepped on very hard, and what he'd just ingested was very close to an overdose. Avoiding a fatal heart attack, he did have a seizure, but after that crippling response abated, he was left surprisingly alive. He'd gotten deep scratches from the accident, and he went into the bathroom to get the blood off his hands and face. He'd get way too much attention if he didn't clean it off. Grabbing his motorcycle jacket out of the closet, he put it on, and then he went back to the library.

What was left of his family was still playing poker, and they didn't notice his return, anymore than his previous exit. He picked up a bottle of Jim Beam at the bar, and stuffed it under his arm. Walking to the door in the back corner of the library, he put his hand on the knob and turned around. He glared at Samuel Eveland. The loathing he felt towards his father was exceptional. His eyes were molten, but no one saw that either. He opened the door and left the house.

Still ridiculously high, Robert stepped onto the patio flagstones as he raised the whiskey bottle to his lips to fuel his intemperate fury. Wandering into the backyard, he planted himself on a filigreed iron bench facing a woodshed only sixty feet away. There were no lights illuminating the bench, and his black clothes erased him, a turbulent shadow inside a shadow. Robert was calming down the best he could.

Stretching his legs out, he dug his booted heels into the sod, and the whiskey bottle hung loosely in his hand.

Oxygenated air and the secretly filtered orange\pink lights in the library left everyone feeling healthy and wise. Samuel was relishing Latham's cigar, and Holly had no intention of saying anything as she was enjoying Eveland's deception to the hilt.

"It's almost six o'clock, and I'm getting hungry. I mean, Mom hasn't shown up yet, but by the time we carve up the turkey, she'll certainly be back," Justin said. He stood up and leaned back, hands flat on his lower back to stretch out his chest and shoulder muscles.

"Why don't you carve up the ham you sent, and I'll operate on the bird," David said, with a soft laugh. "Unless you'd rather take care of it, Latham?"

"Oh, no. This year I'm more than happy to have you do the work," Samuel said.

"When we're done slicing and dicing in the kitchen, we'll bring it all out on the side table and let you guys know it's there."

Justin and David left, leaving Samuel alone with Holly at the bar.

"I've never seen you quite so dexterous with cards before this afternoon, Dad. What really happened to you in Las Vegas? It was supposed to be business meeting for Heinem, not a gambling tutorial." Holly was grinning and Samuel cringed. Pouring herself a dollop of Bailey's in a shot glass, she patiently waited for an explanation, and Samuel faltered into a half-baked answer.

"I've been using cards as a kind of meditation to control my nerves. When I'm on the phone or waiting for something to happen in a deal, I shuffle them or play solitaire or something. I guess I just got good at it . . . the more you do, the better you get," and he shrugged. He wondered what Latham would have really said, not realizing the breadth of the real divide between them. Holly would have never asked her father anything like that and if she had, Latham's answer would have been nothing but a shriveling stare.

"I wish it *had* been a gambling event. I would have had a lot more fun." Samuel furtively glimpsed over at her. Under the gun for so long, he was afraid his cover might be blown . . . with Holly anyway. *He couldn't be sure.* Looking around, he saw the fireplace in the back wall, unlit. He decided to put some distance between himself and Latham's daughter.

"With that wind howling outside, maybe I should set up a fire. Yeah, so after dinner we could all come back here, and it'll be burning nicely by then."

When the sun was up, he remembered seeing a woodshed not too far from house, and he didn't think he needed a coat. Samuel gulped the rest of his drink and left it on the bar. He went through the glass door, and stepped outside to bring back some wood to arrange the fire and take his mind off Holly.

5:47PM Thursday November 24, 2005 Bass River, Massachusetts

Edgar was a good driver and the low slung rental was close to new and it didn't take them long to get there. Flying over Bass River Bridge, Latham felt a jolt; a bump that hadn't been there before, and he peered through the back window. A part of the guardrail was missing, but he didn't trust his eyesight. Moving off the bridge and around the corner in a fast clip, it was easier to control the weight of the Lincoln driving *up* the grade, and Edgar's speed stayed constant as he hugged the curves. They got to Donnelly's driveway in minutes.

"What kind of holiday is your family actually having, Samuel? There's a motorcycle demolished in the trees over there." Lazzo powered the electric window down and pointed. Edgar slowed the car down until he saw the crash, and then he hit the brakes and stopped to smirk.

"If you weren't doing well in Vegas, it looks like you aren't having much of a hold on the home-front either . . . at least from what I can make out. Those skid marks are coming from your own driveway," Edgar said.

"I don't have to explain my son's drug problems to you. Most of the time, he's never here and this is why," Latham said. It was possible that Robert might be bleeding to death in the woods, but he could care less. He had to placate Edgar and Lazzo and get his own life back on track before anything else.

Edgar drove the Lincoln up the driveway, and he parked haphazardly in the center of the auto-court. Everyone got out. Latham faced the dangerous men with new resolve. He was going to take control over the next few minutes of his life, if he possibly could.

"Nobody wants to frighten anybody in the house, if we don't have to. Listen, I'll go inside, get the money and bring it out to you. It's on the second floor in a safe, so you'll have to give me enough time to get to it. Please, just wait here."

"Why should we believe you, Sam? You could close the front door and call the cops and drag your family into a panic room," Edgar said.

"But I won't call the cops! I told you, I have to get to Russia tomorrow. Calling the cops would screw me up for weeks. If you want the money, we can get through this snafu without derailing. I'm advising you to wait here for ten or twenty minutes. If I don't show up with your cash, you can come inside and get me. We don't have a panic room, and there's no way the cops can get here that fast anyway. Just look around."

"You're pretty convincing Samuel," Lazzo said. He turned to his partner. "I'd give him the time and see what happens."

"It does sound pretty logical. There is no one close enough to save him, that's for sure. Alright . . . okay, I'm looking at my watch right now. It's five after six. If you're not back in twenty minutes, we're coming in. You should think about your family's safety and show up on time," and Edgar waved his hand towards the front door. "Go ahead, Sam. We'll wait for you and your mythical million." A devilish grin had spread across his face.

Looking at his own watch, Latham quickly calculated out how much time he'd need to get to the safe and return to the parking lot. He needed a little bit of wiggle room. The front door was unlocked and he jogged inside. If Samuel Eveland was actually inside his house, all his problems with the lunkheads would be over, and he had just enough time to check that possibility out.

The second Latham disappeared into the house, Edgar gave Lazzo new orders.

"I don't know what he's really going to do, so you better jog around the house and keep an eye on the back. We can't let him bolt into the woods and get away, and we don't even know if he really owns this place. There's a flashlight in the travel bag on the front seat, so grab it and go!"

Lazzo trotted over to the Lincoln to get the flashlight and he did what he was told, picking up speed with every stride. Going around the corner of the house, the north wind plowed into him, powerful enough to slow most people down. At 250 pounds, Lazzo was a storm-front on his own and the wind didn't interrupt his progress at all. Avoiding the yard lights, he climbed a raised berm running all the way to the tributary behind the house. 15 feet away from a woodshed, he stopped on the embankment. He was only three hundred feet from the back of the house, a reasonable place to keep his eyes on the prize. There was one door exiting onto a walkway around the pool, and the other one opened on a patio, even closer to his position. Lazzo didn't have enough time to catch his breath, when he saw Samuel appeared on the patio. The man walked farther into back yard, and Lazzo put his hand under his jacket to unsnap the leather band holding his gun in the shoulder holster, yet it didn't look like Samuel was running away. Taking the Glock out of the holster, he flicked the safety off just in case. He even took the silencer out his pants pocket, screwing it onto the muzzle of his gun. Better to be safe than sorry. The intractable gambler strolled calmly over to the woodshed, unaware of Lazzo staring down at him. Samuel began to pick through the pile of wood, and in Lazzo's mind, he was searching for a hidden panel; the safe had to be hidden in the shed. Maybe they'd get even more money out of him; maybe they could take *all* the cash!

Robert took another pull on the whiskey bottle. It felt good swallowing liquid fire. He watched Samuel come out of the house in that ivory suit. It was actually glowing in the manmade lights and he couldn't get his eyes off him. Walking up to the woodshed, he stopped right in front of him, apparently selecting pieces of wood to bring back to the library and Robert straightened up. He put the liquor bottle down on the grass very quietly, and then he slowly stood up. There was a splitting maul leaning against the shed door and Robert silently crept closer to Samuel. He was thinking that his father would probably appreciate his help in re-splitting some of the wood.

Neither one of the two men had noticed Robert's dangerous approach. Lazzo's attention was zeroed in on Samuel, and Samuel was distracted by his wood gathering. Suddenly, Robert turned into a blur, crossing the remaining space between himself and his father like lightning. At that point, Samuel was holding as much wood as he could in his arms, and Lazzo stood above him, utterly perplexed . . . but not for long. Part of Lazzo's confusion evaporated by the incomprehensible surprise of a monster in black rising up in front of him. The creature had come out of nowhere . . . and it was holding a long handled axe. The blade was poised three and half feet above Samuel's head. Robert Donnelly's face had convulsed into a rage so intense he looked deformed and he swung the maul down in an accurate stroke. Lazzo raised his gun and screamed,

"NOOOOOOOOO!" against the upcoming mutilation. The ruffian's frustrated howl sailed away in the wind as Robert planted the axe deep into the top of Samuel's head. Sounding like a ripe melon opening with a thunk, a restrained spray of blood splattered Samuel's back, Robert's front, and a few pieces of wood. A drop or two made it to Lazzo's shoes. As far as Robert knew, he'd just split his father's head almost in two and he felt deflated. Samuel Eveland's body had crumpled to the ground. The wood he'd held was scattered on the grass around him. The small spray of blood was over and a black-red pool was slowly leaking out of Sam's head and Lazzo stared down at Robert with indignation. Whether he was an alien, or an interloper from hell, he'd just taken the fortune they were about to have away! He'd already aimed his gun to stop the attack; two seconds too late and Lazzo's finger trembled on the trigger. He held back long enough for Robert to look up and enjoy the sight of a massive figure looming over him on the berm pointing a gun at his head. He had no time to figure it out, and a bullet burrowed into his forehead like a whisper. The silencer muffled the explosion, and no one in the house heard a thing.

Edgar was leaning against the Lincoln. His arms were crossed against his chest, while he patiently waited. Hearing Lazzo's scream riding towards him on a gust of wind, he instantly followed his partner's trail as quickly as he could. With only a small penlight to navigate through the darkness, he was panting when he reached Lazzo's side. The larger man was motionless. He was staring down at the woodshed. Edgar followed his gaze to the ghastly scene below him, and the first question he was going to ask Lazzo died on his lips. Samuel Eveland was on his belly with an axe coming out of his head, and the handle stood straight up in the air. And there was another body down there. Robert had been thrown backwards by the force of the bullet, and he was on his back with a frozen smile glued on his face. Edgar was stunned.

"Oh shit, what the fuck happened, Laz?" Edgar breathed out the question with a hint of awe.

"I don't know. I really don't know what happened. Why Sammy would come out here to get firewood is just as confusing as a stranger coming out of nowhere to kill him. I tried to stop him, but, he . . . ah, damn it, I tried as hard as I could. It was too dark, and I didn't see him coming. I really thought Samuel was out here to get the money, but now we'll never know. I'm sorry, I couldn't help it. I had to even out the score."

Edgar's mind reverted to '*escape clause*', eclipsing his curiosity. He didn't want anyone in the house to notice anything at all until they were long gone.

"There's no way we can figure this out right now, but we gotta get a picture of this mess to give to Cindy. After that, we'll haul them both to that creek and throw them in. We've got to roll out of here fast. Let's hope the rest of the family doesn't come out here to find them."

Edgar went back to the car as fast as he could to get the camera. When he got back, he told Lazzo to stand right behind him as a light barrier, thinking it would be harder to see the flash from the house. He snapped only one picture, and he put the camera in his pocket. With a curt nod to Lazzo, he let him know it was time to move the bodies.

Samuel's body was a lot heavier than Robert's, so Lazzo picked up his heels and Edgar was relegated to the scrawnier one. Shoulder to shoulder, they dragged the dead to the water. The gentle slope was helpful and the low cut grass, slightly slippery, gave them a wonderful surface for pulling. The axe had persistently remained stuck in the back of Samuel's head and the long handle swayed back and forth with every step Lazzo took; at least for part of the short trip. What was left of Sam's face bounced in and out of an unusual furrow left in the grass by the wheel of an oversized lawnmower, and that lurch finally dislodged the maul. It fell out with a squishy plop and the deadly duo left it behind. The bloody implement would remain invisible in the grass until dawn. At the edge of the creek, they dropped the bodies on the shore.

"We're going to have to swing them out, one at a time, to avoid getting our feet wet. I'm pretty sure we can toss them far enough out there, especially if the bottom drops off fast. With any luck they'll disappear for quite a while in the deeper water," Edgar said.

"Yeah, that sounds fine. Let's go for it."

Lazzo picked up Robert's wrists and Edgar grabbed his ankles. Swinging back and forth, they started to count. *"One . . . two . . . three!"* At the highest point in the third arc, they both let go simultaneously, and the body soared almost fourteen feet out before it splashed into the water and sank. Under the circumstances, it was the best scheme they could have come up with, and they went through the same thing with Samuel's body. They had to work a bit harder, doubling the amount of time they spent swinging the body back and forth to build up more momentum to get to the same high point they'd achieved with Robert's, but it that had worked perfectly. Turning away from the second splash with a feeling of accomplishment, the persistent north wind was at their backs as Edgar and Lazzo walked briskly towards the house on the last leg of their escape.

6:05PM Thursday November 24, 2005 Bass River, Massachusetts

Exhausted, beat up and stressed out, Latham shivered in the entry hall. He was listening. He wanted to make sure Samuel wasn't in his house living out a nasty masquerade, and he needed to know about it *before* he gets the money. Silence sent him through the great room and into the long hallway. He dragged up the last of his reserves of energy to find his doppelganger and throw him into the snapping jaws of the jackals waiting for him in the driveway. He heard a conversation going on in the kitchen, and he sped up and walked in on David and Justin. David dropped the carving knife, and Justin walked towards his father.

"Are you alright Dad? What happened to you? Did you fall down the stairs outside or something?" Justin asked. Doctor Dave rushed over to hold his father-in-law's elbow, trying to guide him to one of the kitchen stools.

"Tell me what hurts. I'll get you some water, and . . ." Latham interrupted David's ministrations, and he shook his hand off his elbow at the same time.

"Where was the last place you saw me?" Latham was probing into his son-in-law's eyes with intensity. He hoped that would sway the man into giving him a straight answer to a ridiculous question. It worked.

"Ten minutes ago you were in the library with Holly. Look, it's obvious. If you're not sure where you were, you must have fallen on your head," David said.

Latham turned away and trotted out of the kitchen as if David and Justin had just blinked out of existence.

"He didn't seem quite himself, did he?" David said.

"Nope, and he also looked very upset. He was fine, when we left him in the library with Holly. Something must have happened, I mean, you saw the suit. It was wrecked. It looked like he hasn't slept in days. It's weird," Justin said.

"Maybe my wife told him something very bad or he had an arm wrestling match with her." They both started laughing. David went back to arranging the white and dark turkey meat on the platter.

Latham hurried through the dining room and into hallway, bursting with anticipation. He opened the library door . . . and no one was there. Deflated, the bone-deep weariness squashed his intelligence for the moment, and paranoia took over. Samuel might have opened his safe, and stolen all the cash, disappearing into the woods. That impossible vision drove him to the elevator with another jolt of adrenalin. Justin and David were taking the ham and turkey into the dining room and he dashed past them as if they weren't even there.

"You okay, Dad? Where are you going? Can we help you? Dad . . ." Justin pleaded. David chimed in, "I'd like to check your vitals. It'd only take a second."

Latham disappeared through the swinging doors, crossing the kitchen and into the service hallway. He took the elevator to the second floor. Striding along the corridor to his suite, he imagined Samuel cowering on the floor when he opened the door to his suite. *Again, no such luck.*

He stepped into his walk-in closet, and he pushed his suits out of the way to reveal nothing but a white wall, but he kicked a smudge on the lower molding with sincerity. A section of the wall above the dirt mark rose behind the sheet rock above it and there it was. His safe. Three feet in diameter, it was welded to a solid steel pillar. Whirling in the combination, the metal door swung open and the imprisoned air puffed into his face. Of course the cash was there. Why had he flipped about it in the first place? Reality landed back in his head, and he realized the time limit Edgar had given him to return to the car with the money had elapsed five minutes ago. He couldn't hear anything going on downstairs. Certainly not the ruckus he would have expected. Something else must have gone wrong, or maybe they were giving him a few more minutes. Either way, he wasn't bringing them any money, and he re-locked the safe. The man they were looking for was on this property. He was going to find the imposter and put things right!

Taking the elevator back downstairs, he found Justin, David, and Holly in the library waiting for the rest of the family to show up for dinner. They'd opened a new bottle of vodka, and a herd of wild horses galloping by wouldn't disturb them in the least. It was obvious that Lazzo and Edgar were not in the house. Maybe they'd already found him? Even more unsteady on his feet, he must stop the confusion fast before he loses it completely. He loudly interrupted the revelers.

"Holly, I know you were talking to me here in the library, but where did I go? I know it sounds crazy, but I need the answer right away!"

Smiling up at him from her barstool, Holly wasn't bothered by his disheveled appearance or the odd request, and David and Justin were resigned to it.

"The last time I saw you, you went out the side door to get some wood from the shed. You wanted to start a fire here in the library."

Latham propelled himself across the room, and the north wind thumped the door closed behind him. Justin and David turned back to the bar, irritated. He was gone again. The *whole family* needs to be there. Both of them were absorbed with their dinner plans, and they didn't notice the change in Holly's appearance. The azure light in the sapphire around her neck intensified while she began to radiate an unworldly incandescence. Holly looked like a subject a famous portrait painting, a living breathing icon. It was no trick of the light. Her fleeting metamorphosis was a harbinger of things to come; good or evil and it quickly faded away. Holly hadn't felt a thing. Apparently, the odd presentation hadn't been acknowledged.

Outside, Latham walked off the patio and onto the lawn. Was it possible Samuel had swum across the brook, escaping into the undeveloped acres on the other side? Or maybe he was hiding somewhere on the estate? Latham squatted and he peered into the shadows under the nearest bush. He stood up. It was starting to turn into a joke. Staring out at the tributary, he saw Lazzo and Edgar walking away from the edge of the water. They were moving straight towards him.

6:31PM Thursday November 24, 2005 Bass River, Massachusetts

Trudging up to the house, Lazzo removed a cigarette from his case. He slid the gold container back in his pocket, and he used his jacket as a windbreak to light up his smoke. Edgar had the courtesy to wait for him. He passed the time by looking up at the mansion in the distance. Nudging Lazzo in the shoulder with his fist, he pointed towards the house with his other hand.

"Look, damn it, look! It's Samuel's ghost up there. It's floating near the house. *Oh!* Can't you see it drifting towards the woodpile? Laz, do you see it? Do you?"

Edgar was whispering. He was afraid something sinister might hear what he was saying. Lazzo ignored the jabbing punch in his shoulder muscle. He was too busy trying to light his cigarette. He'd labored through a disappointing job, and he believed smoking one cigarette was a piddling reward for the hard work he'd done. Finally igniting his prize, he inhaled as much smoke as he could, and then he followed Edgar's pointing finger up the slope. His mouth opened and the cigarette fell out and rolled away on the grass.

"I see . . . I see it! But . . . but it can't be a ghost, it has to be Donnelly or Samuel," Lazzo said. Whatever it was drifted back and forth in the distance and they walked towards it. Suddenly, the mysterious figure started to travel rapidly down the gentle slope towards them.

Latham was smiling. "You saw him, didn't you? You believe me now. I'm not Samuel. I'm Latham. I am *Latham Donnelly.*"

"How could we have known, sir? We feel really awful about the misunderstanding." Lazzo knew Latham's statement was true, and he did felt guilty for the bruise he'd slapped over his eye in Las Vegas. "I'm really sorry, Mr. Donnelly. I hope you understand why this mistake happened?

You know it tricked us. You both look exactly the same." During his apology, he didn't want to tower over the Latham and he'd spread his feet apart to lower his height. Edgar felt miserable too. Jobs were supposed to be under his control, and this one had blown up into a boondoggle. His expression was pinched in displeasure.

"What happened to Samuel? Where is he? I thought you wanted to get a lot of money out of him?" Latham said.

Lazzo and Edgar looked at each other uneasily. They didn't have enough time to make up a feasible story so one of them was about to trip over their own feet.

"Um . . . we watched him run out of the house and we ran after him . . . and . . . ah . . . and he dove in the creek and swam across, and we didn't want to get wet. You know how damned cold that water is! We'll just drive around and flush him out on the other side." Edgar knew it sounded ultra-lame, but to their relief, Mr. Donnelly accepted this fairytale equably enough. The difficulties he was having with them were over, and his plan was reinstated. He didn't have a care in the word. During their short conversation, they'd retreated back to the house. They were standing in the biting wind on the patio, and a picture of the turkey and ham on the side table in the dining room materialized in full color in Latham's head. He was famished, and a Thanksgiving dinner was waiting for him inside. Looking through one of the library windows, he imagined the convoluted story he was about to tell his family over dinner. Holly, David, and Justin were still huddled around the bar waiting for the rest of the family to arrive. Shouldn't he use Lazzo and Edgar as living props to shore up this extraordinary tale?

"Listen boys, I know this may seem strange, but you have a long trip in front of you and I have a Thanksgiving dinner to partake in *right now*. Samuel has duped my family and I'm here to replace my replacement with the real me." Latham chuckled. "I have no interest in calling anyone about anything you've done to me, or anything else you two may have done without my knowledge," and he stopped for a moment, narrowing his eyes. "Anyway, you should slow down long enough to have dinner with us. We'll bury the hatchet and break bread." Lazzo recoiled and Edgar sniggered.

"From what I can make out, my kids are soused, and you don't have to worry about them. They won't interfere." Latham was swaying in the wind, waiting for their answer.

"You're inviting us to *your* table for dinner . . . *really?*" Edgar was puzzled. "Well . . ." He considered the depth of the water in the creek and what was floating there, against how hungry they were. How much time would it take them to eat and run?

"Yeah, okay, I guess. It's generous of you, but shouldn't we walk in the front door . . . or . . . or maybe you should walk in first and explain things to them?"

"At this point, our reunion has rolled completely off the rails, and I'm not worried about you guys just walking straight in. I told you, my son and my son-in-law are liquored up, and my so-called daughter has never been afraid of anything in her life. Let's get out of this hellish wind and get some hot food in our bellies. Tag along behind me, and we'll deal with introductions at the table." Latham opened the door and entered the library with an announcement.

"Thanksgiving dinner is served. I don't care where April and Robert are. My acquaintances and I are going to sit down and eat. If you're puzzled about my actions today, I'll explain it all during dinner."

Like ducklings, the outlaws followed him through the door, obediently following him into the hallway. David and Justin got up in surprise; however they too fell into line, like oversized ducklings themselves. Watching the parade with amusement, Holly stayed at the bar for five more minutes. Eventually, she strolled into the dining room to enjoy the last Thanksgiving dinner with what was left of the Donnellys and their new found guests.

Putting turkey and oyster stuffing on his plate, David no longer knew what the length of his mother-in-law and Robert's life spans would be, and that bothered him. He no longer knew what their roles in his future would be. Lazzo's hulking presence towering over him, didn't bother him at all. These peculiar guests would support his innocence in the upcoming investigation. Whatever had brought them to the table would certainly muddy the water. Robert's survival wouldn't make much of a difference; however the possibility of April being around could really shrink his winnings . . . ah, well. Holly has a lot of money of her own and he was the only beneficiary in her will. Even if Robert and April don't eat the delicious meal, he would still be a fairly rich free bird. Who knows, he might make a bundle if he wrote a book about what was about to happen; the only eyewitness account of a dreadful experience.

Justin piled ham on his plate, surrounding it with peas, yams, and lots of homemade cranberry sauce. Looking forwards to hearing at least part of his father's story before the poison took hold, those enigmatic visitors would support his innocence. Their clothes reeked of a casino in Las Vegas, and their ominous aura made him feel even better. Mom hadn't shown up yet, but he wasn't that worried. He would guide her through the deposition of the will easily enough, and Robert was already tied up in a trust he had complete control over. Justin was optimistic. It hadn't worked out as perfectly as he would have liked, but the end results would shake-out alright. He wasn't going to hide his sexuality anymore and he could retain his inheritance. Considering the length of time that had passed since she drove off to the store, Mom probably had an accident. Depending on the severity of the crash, his plans may still come out perfectly.

Latham sat at the head of the table and Holly faced him. Justin was on his father's right and David on the left. Lazzo and Edgar bracketed Holly.

Four exquisitely sculpted candles circled a white vase. The vase held noble fir branches, blooms of a white hydrangea and bright orange mums. Arranged in the center of the table, it was pleasing enough, but it didn't match the horn of plenty April had made the year before.

After everyone was seated, the poisoners checked their dinner plates. No one had been shy with stuffing *or* homemade jelly, and the dangerous happenstance of their thoughts merged David and Justin's emotions into drunken conviviality. Eyes locking across the table, it seemed their brainwaves had linked as well, dovetailing into one. The short psychic connection between them was enhanced by the thick nihilism eddying through the atmosphere in the dining room. Singing in silent harmony, '*The key to happiness is tremendous wealth at any cost*', they both felt a punch behind the phrase and they didn't have the faintest idea where that sudden power had come from. *Too bad.*

Impressed by the luxurious presentation and heavenly aromas wafting towards him, Lazzo's religiosity took control. It wasn't right to partake in so much food without a blessing, a prayer of *thanks* on *Thanks*giving Day. Before Latham could start describing the bolloxed up gaffe they'd dragged him into, he politely asked for a moment of prayer.

"Look, I don't know how you each see the world, but my family always said grace before every meal. This is a holiday, so maybe you guys wouldn't mind if I recite a short prayer." The request was followed by silence. Latham looked at Lazzo with a half smile and Edgar snickered again.

"I see no reason why . . ." Holly turned to Lazzo, "what's your name, sir?"

"Mr. Tony Malazzo," he said. He proffered his hand to her and Holly shook it gently. She didn't want to frighten the man.

"I see no reason why Mr. Malazzo couldn't give us a prayer. Perhaps it could ring some imaginary bell to call Mom and Robert to the dinner table with us." Holly's shoulders rose in uncertainty, and there was a consensus of nods around the table.

"Go ahead, sir."

Lazzo stood up, and he somehow seemed to absorb most of the light in the dining room just with his height. Over 6'4", his tan leather jacket stretched across his torso and shoulders and the color magnified his bulk. His normal speaking voice broadened out with power, and everyone at the table listened to him with their own degree of abhorrence. Only Holly embraced his entreaty with aplomb.

> *"Merciful God and Father, we pray. Let our hearts not be weighted down by the cares of this life, nor become too deeply attached to earthly and perishable things. May we be nourished to everlasting life from the eternal food of your word. Please bless the meal we are about to share together today and we invite you into our hearts and your love in our lives. Amen."*

After Holly spoke out her lonely 'Amen', Lazzo inhaled loudly and sat down. Just three seconds went by before Justin and David started to pester Latham with questions. Standing outside the Donnelly's dining room, the sounds of conversation, classical music and the off beat muted rhythm of clattering silverware painted a vignette of a happy family enjoying the holiday together. At least for another twenty minutes.

6:07AM Friday November 25, 2005 Bass River, Massachusetts

Cleaning up the reunion would be harder for her this year. Mirabelle was exhausted. Chauffeuring her family around town the day before, she still intended on arriving at work on time. White shirt pressed and tucked neatly into her black skirt, her thick black stockings disappeared into some clunky looking work shoes. The first stop on her commute was the deli. A steel bowl filled with small plastic containers of 'Stok' was sitting on the counter, and she poured two of them into her coffee cup. She had just added 80 milligrams of caffeine on top of what was already in her cup. She shouldn't have done that. Soon, Mirabelle's eyes opened wide, and her hands began to shake.

It was dark when she drove over Bass River Bridge. She gazed to the right towards the ocean. The wind had died, and the trees along the shoreline looked like stage props. The rushing river water under the bridge was molten glass. *Had she seen a break in the guardrail?* Mirabelle tossed the fuzzy image out of her head, yet the wrongness picked at her like a gnat.

Moving through the dips and turns of the road, she started to feel queasy. She chalked it up to the coffee in her belly. She turned into the driveway. Robert's motorcycle was wrecked in the woods on the other side of the road, and she assumed he'd be sleeping it off somewhere. Parking in the employee lot on the side of the house, Mirabelle walked briskly over to the service door. There were a lot of cars parked outside and she stopped and looked around. It was strange. Everybody had decided to spend the night? Beyond that, there was a car she'd never seen before sitting haphazardly in the center of the auto court. It was in the way of all the other cars.

The sun was rising. The increasing daylight reassured her a bit. The day was going to be clear as a bell and invigorating . . . but . . . but it was dead quiet. The squirrels and rabbits weren't scurrying around. Even the birds weren't chirping and Mirabelle remained anxious. Using her key at the service door, she let herself in, and hung her coat in the workroom. She'd start her cleaning with the library, bringing the glasses and food trays back to the kitchen. Music was coming from the dining room, and she frowned. She went over to the stereo console in the kitchen, and she switched it off. That was weird. Usually they would shut the music off on their way to bed. Moving through the dining room and into the hallway, the steam table was on her left and the oval table was on her right. She walked through the one of the open double doors leading into the library. Mr. Donnelly had fallen asleep on the couch. She knew he'd feel more comfortable in his own bed, and she began to softly nudge him awake. It was more difficult than it should have been, until she reached a point in which she was pushing way too hard on his shoulder. Noticing the grayish sheen to his skin, her attention traveled across the room and she stopped moving. Edgar's right upper arm had been pierced on a long shard of thick glass coming from the wood panel of the door leading out to the patio. His torso was also impaled on another one of those scarlet icicles. The two glass panels of the door had been built with traditional craftsmanship, and the contractor had used one piece of heavy glass in each section, not the double-sealed safety stuff. A convulsion brought on by Edgar's ingestion of taxane and tetrodotoxin had thrown him through the door, producing a horrifying tableau. The rest of his upper body had drooped over the high wooden frame, and his head and shoulders were out of Mirabelle's line of sight. She didn't think she'd ever get out the large black stain in the carpet around the bottom of the door. As an appalling certainty entered her personal world, Mirabelle's day-to-day reality was departing. Snapping back into her paralyzed body, she understood she was holding the shoulder of a corpse and that knowledge transported her into a living nightmare. She started to gasp in tiny rapid puffs accented with high-pitched peeps like a terrified wild bird. Mirabelle's hand spastically let go of the Latham's body, and she got out of the library expeditiously. She'd never moved that fast before in her life, but her frantic escape was about to end abruptly. Not taking the same path she'd used through the dining room on her way to the library, she went on the other side of the table. Two bodies were tangled together there, and one of her feet hooked under Lazzo's leg. Momentum gave her wings. Soaring eight feet into the wall, she'd knocked herself out. Four and half minutes later her eyes opened, and she was greeted with an atrocious sight only twenty-four inches away from her nose. Lazzo and David's bodies had intertwined while they died, as if they'd been in a convoluted wrestling match. Fate had been generous to Mirabelle. She hadn't broken any of her weight bearing bones in her collision with the wall, so terror revived her and put her back on her feet in seconds. Streaking around the corner into the kitchen, she was already trying to rub out everything she'd seen, erasing it out of her head forever. She sprinted around the center island and into the workroom, grabbing her coat off the hook. Her car keys were in the coat pocket. She barreled out of the service door, leaving it wide open as she ran to her car. Getting inside, she started the engine and put it into drive. Her cell phone was inside her purse, and her purse was on the back seat. Mirabelle couldn't slow down to get to the phone to call anyone . . . not yet. Putting the gas pedal to the floor, the back wheels of the Taurus couldn't find traction at first. Clouds of steam rose up into the chilly morning air until the car finally leapt forwards, leaving short skid marks on the tiles.

She didn't want to know what had happened to the rest of the people inside Latham's dream castle. She didn't want to think about it. Driving way too fast around the curves, she made it over the bridge. When the road straightened out, she sped up. Mirabelle needed help, and she took one hand off the wheel to reach behind her. She hauled her purse over the head rest and into the passenger seat, blindly digging through the bag to find her phone and her eyes were like saucers when she pressed 911 on the keypad.

Justin's body was face up in the narrow hallway near the elevator and Holly lay on her belly in the center of the great room, left hand floating in the koi pond. An orange fish with a white splotch around its face was affectionately nibbling at her cold fingers, and that was the extent of the missing information Mirabelle didn't have about the rest of the Donnelly family.

9:12AM Friday November 25, 2005 Cedarville, Massachusetts

Vomit green paint was flaking off its walls and a lot of roof shingles had been blown off. Five miles south of the New Hampshire state line, the farm house was disintegrated in the center of a forty acre apple orchard. The property had gone into foreclosure three years ago and the penniless owners had packed up and moved out of state. The ultimate outcome for the property had stalled in court, and the worm-riddled apple trees had been left alone to die.

That day was deceiving. A searing blue sky above and a gentle breeze below, Mother Nature had a thin cloak of early spring around her shoulders. The air felt warm, but it was nothing but a masquerade. Standing on the sagging porch to gaze out at the orderly lines of apple trees, the shriveled buds on the ends of the gnarled branches in the distance looked as if they'd flower. Nevertheless, the hidden bite in the air would return at sunset, and the cold coil of the darker months of dead winter was circling in like a snake.

Ryan Porretta parked his white station wagon on the dead grass on the side of the rutted driveway leading up to the farmhouse. Getting out, he buttoned his trench coat and stamped over to the steel doors leading down to the basement. It had been a long drive and his feet were numb and that was responsible for a preposterous hop in his walk. He was trying to bring back the circulation. At 53, his hair was almost completely grey, with only a recollection of blond. A sturdy man, he stood at 5'10". His family had emigrated from northern Italy, explaining his light complexion and grey-blue eyes. Ryan was 35 pounds overweight, but it was distributed evenly over his body. He looked more solid, than fat. Lifting one of the two doors, he climbed the filthy concrete steps into the cellar.

A thick concrete pillar stood in the center of the basement, a part of the building's foundation. The body of an eight-year old girl was tied to it with packing twine. Trussed to the column while she was alive, the correct placement of the twine allowed her body to remain upright after death. Ryan kneeled down, and leaned forward, inches away from her face. Her mother had dressed her in formal clothes a few days ago. Claire was still wearing her baby blue dress adorned with a white pinafore, and the extravagant ruffles of the apron had miraculously remained virgin white. Reaching into the pocket of his trench coat, he removed a pair of latex gloves and he put them on. Gently examining her hands, he softly squeezed her fingers. He was unconcerned that dirt was grinding into the knees of his black woolen pants, until he finally moved back on his heels. Looking over at the bright yellow tool-box right next the body, he reached over and slowly opened it. There were pliers, a chisel, and a power drill left inside, and Ryan didn't budge for a long time. He was considering all the uses inherent in the different tools. Startled by footsteps pounding down the wooden stairs from the first floor, he closed the tool-box and looked up.

"Inspector . . . Inspector Porretta, there's a helicopter coming for you right now!"

Rushing down the stairs, a young detective called Cassidy was shouting until he saw the Inspector crouching on the cellar floor, and then he dropped the volume.

"Detective Andes will have to unscramble this case without you, Porretta. There's a red ball on Cape Cod and the chief wants you to catch it. Wants, forget wants, he's ordering you over there, ASAP."

A red ball was a slang expression in the department acknowledging the media frenzy and public scrutiny attached to certain homicide cases. And those cases were divvied out only to individuals able solve the crimes with inhuman speed as they face turbulent crowds and famous news anchors holding microphones. There aren't many investigators able to deflect a barrage of questions without losing their nerve or their concentration.

Ryan stood up and slapped at the dirt on his knees, and then he peeled off the gloves he'd just put on.

"Okay, okay. You're telling me it's a migraine. Why would Coleman get me out of a case I've finally got a handle on . . . and what is wrong with Ferguson? He just closed the Daisy Chain Case last week. I know he's free."

"I don't know, sir, but the Chief won't accept any changes in his orders. It has to be you and no one else. It's on the Donnelly estate. So far they've found six bodies. The CEO of the Hienem Pharmaceutical Corporation owns the property, and no one knows if he was in the list of victims yet, but either way, this is big. Even if you think Ferguson should be on it, Coleman thinks this is too much for him, and I agree with him."

They climbed the unstable stairs to the first floor. The two men avoided the rotten parts of the wooden boards under their feet to avoid going back to the cellar in a painful descent. Loud creaks followed them to the front door but the sound was masked by the engine noise rumbled through the thin walls of the farmhouse. A police helicopter had landed in the yard outside, and Porretta couldn't hear what the other detective was saying either. An officer just outside the front door gestured towards him, and Porretta crouched over and ran under the rotating blades. Getting in the copter, he closed the clear plastic hatch. The pilot had been explicitly told not to turn his engines off, vehemently ordered to: *"Land the thing, pick up Porretta, and fly him directly to Bass River!"*

In thirty minutes of flight they were over the river. Looking down through the bulging windshield extending under his feet, the generous assortment of vehicles surrounding the derelict farmhouse in Cedarville, paled in comparison. Five hundred feet before the Bass River Bridge, the town road was closed. State Police cruisers were parked nose-to-nose to stop any through traffic. A tow truck was angled on the bridge itself, next to the gap in the guardrail. He saw scuba divers flip their way into the water from the bank of the river. In seconds, the helicopter hovered above the estate, and they were dropping altitude fast. The official presence was extensive, and to Porretta, it looked overblown. He whistled through his teeth. A white colored 75 foot wide tent was set up behind the house as a central hub for evidence collection. Nine police cars lined up along the driveway, as well as six ambulances, and three ATVs. A forty foot long RV was parked on the grass near the mansion, and every single one of those vehicles had their lights on. After sun set, the locals might think a carnival had pitched their tents above the river . . . if the grapevine doesn't tell them otherwise.

Landing on the front lawn, Porretta bent over again for the first twenty feet, and then he straightened up and trotted over to the house. He walked through the open front door to find the entry hall deserted, but that would change dramatically in about fifteen feet. Stepping into the great room, he was swept up into a crisscrossing current of uniformed people going in every direction as officers and medical teams tagged, prodded and labeled evidence.

The long-term pressure had finally snapped the lock and blown off the cover, and the Donnelly's palace turned into Pandora's Box over-night. Inspector Porretta was astonished by the potency of what had been left behind and that material detritus was as unsettling as seeing graffiti sprayed all over those beautiful walls. Casually weaving through the room, he was on his way to the tent outside, when a patrolwoman sidled up to him and handed him a two-way radio. He flipped it open.

"I assume Detective Ciacia has been overseeing things?" Porretta asked.

"Yes sir," she said, and the Inspector got Ciacia on the radio. He instructed him to meet him outside under the tent, and two minutes later, he sprinted around the corner of the house. The detective was holding a clipboard and a flashlight and he didn't have a single hair out of place.

"Good morning, Inspector . . . well, I don't know if 'good' is the right word for it, but it's still good to see *you*." Porretta acknowledged the other man with a distracted nod, already gnawing on the puzzle around him.

"From the helicopter I made out a blob of white floating in the middle of the small tributary at the edge of the property."

"That sounds suspicious, sir," Ciacia said. He gave the Inspector the clipboard he was holding. Porretta was scanning the first page and giving orders to the other officer at the same time.

"Everyone is beating the bushes and weeding the flowerbeds, because a splitting maul is lying in the middle of the yard with a lot of blood on it. We haven't found a body with injuries to match what that implement must have done. Please divert one of those divers at the river to the creek, *right now*."

Porretta got on the radio to talk the police at the bridge and those at the motorcycle crash site at the end of the driveway. He examined the bodies inside the house, as well as the two bodies they dragged out of the creek. The amount of contradictory clues got bigger. Then it became a mountain. The intense complication in the case would encumber almost anyone, but the Chief had singled out the best man for the case. He knew Ryan Porretta thrived on complexity, and deciphering evidentiary minutiae like an android was one of his many gifts. Sifting out the pertinent information out of an avalanche of debris, he could answer the equation and pinpoint the guilty. The upcoming wave of media fascination would be a blitzkrieg, and most people on that teetering stage would at least feel uneasy. Not Porretta. He embraces the spotlight with calculation. If it gets even brighter and hotter in a red ball like this one, he simply gets colder . . . a lot colder.

The State Police found Mirabelle parked six miles past the Bass River Bridge. The only witness they had, her breakdown didn't stop them from questioning her relentlessly . . . in the beginning, anyway. They wouldn't let her to go to the hospital for treatment, and they hid her in the RV next to the main house, plying her with hot soup and a lot of diazepam. She *would not* go back inside the mansion for hell or high water, and they couldn't get a straight answer out of her. Detective Ciacia was linked to the medical staff in the large vehicle, and he was waiting for a break. The second she was stable enough to give them anything, he'd call the Inspector.

Asking Vince for information had been a washout. He'd been with his family in Providence, and every question they'd thrown at him had been met with blank expressions, underlined with 'I don't know'. The neighbors were just as bad. The Quintins next door, seven and half acres away, had actually been at home during the commission of the crime, but all they gave the detectives was nothing but politesse. Swimming in their new indoor pool for the entire evening, the only thing they remembered was who brought the fresh lime in from the main kitchen to the pool bar, and even that was in contention.

The Inspector was going through the contents of a small garbage pail he'd spilled out on one of the folding tables under the tent. A young lab assistant burst out of the large door facing the pool as if the house was on fire, and he ran directly to Porretta.

"Inspector . . . Inspector! Joel told me one of their hands moved and . . . and . . . dead bodies can't move at all, and he called over one of the medics. They found a pulse! They put it on a stretcher and right into the ambulance." Telling Porretta these things as fast as he could, the ululating howl of a siren started up from the other side of the building.

The Inspector was as incredulous as the young assistant who'd brought him the news. As the ambulance raced off to the closest emergency room, in his mind he was troubled. What was going on shouldn't be happening. He'd gone through the first floor of the house three times, and all the victims were extremely departed to him. By every measure he had, the Donnellys and their guests had been killed by someone with a cruel hand. Nevertheless, if someone had actually lived through this massacre, he'd have a great source of information, but . . . but . . . *how could anyone still be alive*?

"Which one of the victims was it? Were they conscious?" Porretta asked.

"I'm not s . . . s . . . sure, sir, he didn't tell me. I'll . . . I'll go ask him, hold on," the assistant was stammering and he started to run back to the house.

Porretta raised his voice and stopped him, "It's alright, son, we'll sort it out. Thank-you for the heads-up."

He answered the Inspector with a relieved 'you're welcome', and the young man went back to his regular duties. Detective Ciacia walked up to the Inspector.

"Someone in the ambulance is on the line," the detective whispered in Porretta's ear. He gave the Inspector the mobile phone he had in his hand.

"This is Inspector Porretta. Tell me all about your new charge," and he listened to what the medical team was telling him. "Alright. Ah huh, and that's everything you know right now? Thirty minutes or thirty days . . . . okay, thanks." Ending the call, he gave the phone back to Ciacia.

"Right now, I can't ask our new witness any questions at all. The victim is comatose and they don't know for how long." He shook his head with frustration, and he returned to examining the garbage. Trying to connect the men from Nevada to the Donnellys, he knew they'd rented the Lincoln Town Car parked in front of the house in Logan Airport just hours before the murders. Why were they there? Their driving licenses had Las Vegas addresses, and they both had handguns. One of them had a digital camera in his pocket and Porretta was hoping the images in it would be informative. Divers had retrieved the two bodies from the creek, and Latham Donnelly's wallet was in the pants pocket of one of them. Over twenty hours under salt water and the grievance injury to the head had left the face of the corpse unrecognizable, so they couldn't use the sodden driver's license as identification. The other body they'd dragged out belonged to an emaciated young man called Robert Donnelly, and the bullet wound in his forehead looked like a professional hit. An execution.

An hour later, Ryan walked into the library holding Latham's dried out license in his hands. He stared at the body on the couch. The identification in his pocket indicated he was Samuel Eveland from Las Vegas, the same place the gun-wielding men hailed from. One of the bodies they'd found in the water was wearing the same suit Samuel Eveland had on. Porretta was intrigued by the remarkable similarity of their faces on the two licenses, and he was piecing together part of the twisted story. The officials at the bridge radioed they'd just winched the Mercedes out of the river, and according to what they found in an evening bag on a floor mat, it was likely to be Mrs. Donnelly's body at the wheel. Ryan Porretta sighed. That was a dismal culmination of an atrocious list, delineating the possible extinction of an entire family.

2:32PM Saturday November 26, 2005 Finalhaven, Maine

Attison Korybante sat at his mahogany desk in a great room bigger than the Donnelly's. Flames crackled in an oversized fireplace behind him. Sculpted pieces of different marble had been seamlessly joined together for the mantel and the chimney, ranging from twelve inches to over six feet. The artist had followed classic realism during the Hellenistic period in Greek history, and every chunk of that stone mimicked a part of the human form. The composition was exquisite on its own, but he'd also ingeniously arranged the different marble pieces by their diverse levels of refraction. Light and dark moved like a wave along the surface of the naked marble bodies all the way up the chimney to the ceiling; an entrancing illusion in an erotic display.

One hundred and fifty-five feet in front of him, a wall of glass afforded him a bird's eye view of the Atlantic Ocean, but Attison wasn't enjoying the view. He was too busy realigning the worldwide Hienem network, as well as drafting a slew of papers to legalize the status of the new owner of the company.

His bags had been shipped to a palatial home he'd rented in Yarmouth. The heat and lights in that sprawling place were already on. It wasn't far from the Donnelly estate. Attison hadn't needed to look at a television or read a paper to know what had happened on Cape Cod. An official from the police department was about to call him up in the next ten minutes, and he knew that too. Leaning back in his oversized office chair, he relaxed his neck muscles and closed his eyes. He began to line up his responsibilities by their level of priority, speculating on how much of his own interference would be necessary to direct the outcome of the case. Sitting up straight, he moved his computer to the side of the desk, putting a crystal tumbler in its place. Pouring seltzer into the glass from a bottle he'd taken off a wheeled refreshment bar next to the desk, he picked up half a lemon off a small silver plate and he squeezed the piece of fruit flat. Every molecule of liquid inside the lemon dripped . . . no, more like poured into the bubbling water. This off-handed act was a three second testament to his outrageous physical strength.

The phone rang. It kept on ringing. Without looking, he tossed the desiccated lemon rind over his shoulder and into the fire behind him. Drying his hands with a linen cloth, he listened to Inspector Porretta record a message for him.

". . . and it's extremely important you contact us at once. My personal cell phone number is 505 85 . . ." but Attison broke in and picked up the phone.

"Good afternoon, Inspector. I'm Mr. Korybante, the family attorney and the executor of Latham's will, of all the last wills within the family, actually. I'm devastated. Who or what is behind this tragedy? Did you just mention someone was still hanging on?"

"Ah, there you are! Hello, Mr. Korybante. It seems you're already up to par and I don't have to explain the gravity of this crime to you. The only survivor was transported to a hospital in New Bedford yesterday, but because of the gravity of their condition, they were airlifted to the Boston University Medical Center a few hours ago."

"I have medical guardianship, so I'll make appointments with all the doctors involved. I'll be at the hospital on Monday, and I shall be at your disposal to answer any pertinent questions you may have about the family history." Attison sipped at his very lemony seltzer.

"Thank you, Mr. Korybante. This on-going inquiry has clearly gotten too complex for a telephone conversation, and I agree. It's important we get together at the hospital on Monday."

"What about a meeting at 2:30 in the afternoon?"

"Sounds fine. I'll wait for you at the nurse's station on the sixth floor."

"See you there, Inspector."

As soon as he got off the phone, Attison called his pilot instructing him to pick him up at nine thirty that night on the helicopter pad on his roof. He'd be in the hospital in Boston a day and a half before he has to talk to anyone about anything.

1:45PM Monday November 28, 2005 Boston, Massachusetts

Doctor Thomas Berman was pudgy at 43. Until a couple of days ago, he was relaxed and content at his job. However what had been going on in a room on the sixth floor of the hospital over the past few days had him so nervous he was afraid his wavy auburn hair would turn white and fall out. Sitting in his office on the second floor of the Boston University Medical Center, the late lunch he'd eaten in the cafeteria was burning a hole in his belly and he peeled off two more antacid tablets from the roll he had in his pocket and he popped them in his mouth. The patient from New Bedford had been admitted on Saturday afternoon, and the digestive acid in his belly was changing into formaldehyde while his knowledge of the facts of the case expanded. Reading the lab reports one more time, he remained baffled. The living victim out of the massacre in Bass River had a stable pulse, even with toxin in their blood high enough to kill a moose. The esteemed toxicologist in Massachusetts had been dealing with a flurry of questions concerning the survivor's condition, and he'd been ducking and jiving, using similar cases as a barrier. It was a very tenuous escape, as there really weren't any cases like this one. The flurry was about to turn into a snowstorm, and he turned his computer back on to delve into more medical history. Berman was trying to hunt down anything relevant, even though it was turning into a pointless endeavor. Before he pulled up another file, he started staring at the colorful screen saver. He escaped for a moment into a school of tropical fish languidly swimming in a digital sea.

The knock on his office door was a steel barb, like a hook and he was pinioned back to disbelief. Through the glass panel of his office door, he saw a gold badge clipped on the man's belt, and Berman waved him in. *More questions.* He crunched another antacid between his teeth before he stood up and shook Porretta's hand.

"Good afternoon Doctor. I'm Inspector Porretta in charge of the Donnelly case. I'm hoping you can give me some information about the fatal dinner and how the patient is doing. Is there anyway I can I ask her some questions?"

"Hello, Inspector. I'm sorry to tell you that Ms. Donnelly is still in a coma, and I'm not sure I can help you anymore than she can right now. The blood tests indicate she's filtering the poisons straight out of her system. Somehow, her liver is washing them all out. Both toxins should be gone within the next ten hours. I'm not sure if the influx of contaminants in her system on Thursday night will permanently injure her brain or not. Only time can tell," Doctor Berman said. Sitting down behind his desk, he invited the Inspector to sit in the chair across his desk, and Porretta gratefully accepted.

"I need to know why everyone else at the dinner party died and Holly Donnelly didn't. Did she unknowingly eat some kind of antidote before dinner? Does she have a rare chromosome or an unusual blood type to give her support against the poisons?" The Inspector asked.

"I would feel much better if any of those options were true, but no, there are no antidotes for taxane or tetrodotoxin. I won't waste your time with statistics, but some of the food on the dinner table was so virulent it could have killed a lot more people. Why the murderer decided to use two agents, when one would have done the trick, only invites the world of socio-psychosis through the door, and in that realm we can't always explain the inexplicable."

The doctor leaned back and dropped his hands in his lap. He was going to tell the Inspector what was plaguing him, something he hadn't told anyone else. It was getting scary and he didn't want to be left alone with an equation that pushed logic off the board. Besides, Porretta was an outsider. He assumed he had no medical degrees, and that was reassuring to him.

"As I've already said, there are no antidotes, and there aren't any blood types or organic molecules that we know of that could forestall what these two poisons do to living cells, and I've been dealing with a conundrum. From her respiratory system to her renal function, Holly is perfectly normal. I can't find a single thing that would support her longevity under these conditions. **Nothing**. Besides her lethargic brain waves, she comes out on all the tests like an Olympic athlete . . . and even that isn't normal." A layer of perspiration appeared on his face, and he looked flushed. Porretta knew it was tearing him up.

"Thank you Doctor, thank you very much," Inspector Porretta said, as he intertwined his fingers and pressed his thumbs together. "I have a good idea where you are right now, and it's not a happy place. In my own life, I've come across cases that have confounded me too, and when I can't find an answer in these unyielding riddles, I turn to my colleagues. It has saved my sanity and my soul. They'd give me an angle I hadn't seen or a plausible theory anyway and if nothing works, their camaraderie was a wonderful salve for the enigmatic."

Porretta was lying. His job was to unravel puzzles, and most of the time he relied on his inherent gift for deduction. Not finding the answer, he accepted it as a standing mystery and he believed that even the fictional Sherlock Holmes couldn't have figured it out. It was different for the doctor. Berman was in pain and the Inspector wanted to give him a hand up out of his quandary, or at least accept it.

"You're right, sir. I can see I've got to let go of it. I've got to relax. I'll just call up Carter in Providence and throw these facts on *his* desk. I'm not personally responsible for these findings and I have to acknowledge that. As soon as I have him believe the evidence and talk him out of calling the men in white coats to drag me away, I can't wait to see how he'll feel about it. I don't think he can come up with anything to figure it out!" Taking a deep breath, he slowly exhaled and a lot of his tension let go. Replacing his self-imposed isolation with commiseration, he could stop solving this twisted Rubik's cube. The squares would never ever line up. The paradox of Holly's improving health had been hooked off the main-stage of his concentration like a bad act. Porretta had punctured the man's over-inflated detachment and confusion with a tiny white lie.

"Only one more question, Doctor. I understand how he could have gotten taxane, but how did he find the concentration of tetrodotoxin? Was it in the oysters?" The Inspector already knew the gentle bi-valve had nothing to do it, but he really didn't know how the murderer could have found it. His latest deceit was only a way to get Berman to leak out more information about had taken the Donnelly family's breath away.

2:15PM Monday November 28, 2005 Boston, Massachusetts

With no light or current under the surface of the water, she did feel the rough texture of the leaves rubbing against her scaled flank, and she swam deeper into the pond. She stopped against the man-made wall. She felt tired and hungry. Looking out at the other fish, a large white koi with an orange spot over one eye bobbled over and kissed her. Without any normal eyelids, it was hard for her close or open her mind. She had to fly away from a dangerous boredom as she floated endlessly in a koi pool. It was a claustrophobic situation. Using her psyche in a new way, she imagined a country field with a thin covering of snow, and she made the top of it frozen. It wasn't long until the vision became real for her, and she was walking across the crunchy surface towards an ocean beach in the distance. Halting a thousand feet away, she was close enough to watch the powerful waves crash on the shore. The turbulent ocean she'd imagined soothed her as she kept on fluttering her fins in the same place against the wall of the pond.

Attison Korybante sat in an uncomfortable plastic chair right next to Holly's head. Previously pale, she was now a block of alabaster. Attison had listened to the doctor's gloomy predictions, but he knew better. Holly would soon wake up, more adept and more attuned than she'd ever been before. His heavy mane of hair was long enough to slip across his shirt collar and he had to shake his head to sweep his bangs away from his eyes to see the display on his wristwatch. 2:27PM. Standing up, he straightened the papers he'd been working on into a neat pile. He put them into his briefcase. Leaving his long leather coat on a chair in the corner of the room, he wasn't worried. For some reason, no one ever touches his possessions when he wasn't around. He left the room, and walked down the corridor to meet Porretta at the nurse's station and he saw Attison waiting for him with a gold shield and a gun at his hip.

"Hello Inspector Porretta," Attison said. He shook the officer's hand with an expression of solemn gravity on his face.

"Mr. Korybante." The Inspector nodded as he looked up into the taller man's eyes.

"Perhaps we should adjourn to the cafeteria and sit down. I need a cup of coffee and something to eat. What do you think?" Attison asked.

"Good idea, but I'd like to see Ms. Donnelly first."

"You know she's unconscious, right? The doctors aren't even sure if she'll ever wake up . . . but of course, Inspector. We'll stop at her room on our way to the cafeteria and you can observe her for a long as you wish," Attison's voice was soft and melodic.

Porretta was stunned when he entered the hospital room. Doctor Berman had described the flawless topography of her internal organs, but he hadn't mentioned to him that her external ones were just as miraculous. Holly's transcendental grace broke his day-to-day inertia like a double rainbow after a rain storm, and that was linked in his mind with her cryptic survival. She had utterly captivated Ryan Porretta. Yet he couldn't waver from his duties in handling the red ball he was on, and it didn't matter how badly he wanted to uncover her secrets. His curiosity had to be left on a back burner.

In the elevator ride to the first floor, Attison glimpsed into the Inspector's mind. He wanted to make sure the officer would stay on the straight and narrow. As the only survivor, Holly could easily be used as a scapegoat, but after his quick look, it was clear he didn't have to do anything at all. At least not yet. Porretta's intelligence was going to lead him only to the truth, and the threads he was pulling at would untangle most of the knot. None of it would touch Holly. She made up a few stories, but she certainly wasn't a murderess.

On his trip from the sixth floor to the concourse, Inspector Porretta wished he could look inside Attison's head as well. Using the only tool he had, he'd poured over anything he could find about the man the day before on his computer. The man had gone through an exemplary education, and law school awarded him all the diplomas he needed to get his license and start his career. He had a worldwide reputation in commercial law, but Ryan found huge gaps. Digging into a global data base, (including a few federal sites), he couldn't find a single nugget of information about what Korybante might have been doing before college and any of his social connections weren't available. He didn't know how anybody could hide anything from the technological eye of Mordor, but he'd done a phenomenal of job of it. Attison's invisible cloak was holding like tungsten steel. According to the file he was 50 years old. Standing right next to him, the Inspector was impressed by his vibrancy and his intense physicality blatantly refuting the fact. Ah, the details in the Donnelly case became more cumbersome by the hour.

Placing cups of coffee and sandwiches on their trays, they sat at one of the booths. Attison politely waited for the Inspector's first question.

"How much do you know about the dynamics in the Donnelly family, Mr. Korybante? Was there a rivalry or a lifelong hatred?" Porretta asked, and then he started to eat his BLT.

"I tried to give the Donnelly's their privacy over the years, so I can't help you with their dirty laundry. I can give you Latham's current business contacts and you're cordially invited to call me for any questions in that regard. I may be able to help you in any other area in the case, possibly becoming a sounding board for you. I'm staying in Falmouth right now and you can stop by anytime and bounce ideas around if you feel like it."

"Thank you Mr. Korybante. I just may take you up on that. Right now, I'm turning over every single rock I can find letting me put the whole thing in rewind. I know you worked with Mr. Donnelly for years, so you must have gone to the estate once or twice. You had to have grown some kind of fondness for the family and I ask you to reconsider, *please*. You have to have some personally knowledge about them, because anything you can come up with, whatever you might know, even something inconsequential to you, could be of great worth to me."

"Alright sir, I'll go over my recollections and tell you what comes to mind." Attison gave the Inspector a fleeting half-smile.

"Do you know what the reason behind the convention Mr. Donnelly attended in Las Vegas right before Thanksgiving was? Three of the victims hailed from Las Vegas. It's possible the business conference is connected with the murders."

"Well, I know it wasn't a convention in the normal sense. Latham was about to spearhead a project in Russia. Hienem is going to invade the pharmaceutical market over there in the next couple of years, and he about to introduce his American replacement to all the section chiefs."

"Was there someone out there wanting his job and they were furious that they'd been overlooked? Could jealousy be a motive?" Porretta picked up a napkin and blotted at his mouth. His expression brightened with the possibility.

"Nobody knew who was going to replace him besides myself, Latham and Jeremy Berlin, the executive we'd picked out for the position. Besides, even if there had been a leak, the long term preparation and the deviousness behind the slaughter can't support a theory like this."

Ryan knew he was right, and he sighed. Pushing his sandwich plate away, he mimicked a buxom model's extravagant wave, jokingly introducing Attison to a nonexistent crowd as he'd turned into a brand new automobile, "Then I guess you have to be behind the whole thing!"

Attison's brown eyes deepened into black, and he flashed his very white teeth at the Inspector's extravagant humor.

Their conversation continued for another fifteen minutes, and at the end of the meeting, Attison graciously underlined his invitation to the Inspector to call or stop by anytime. Parting ways at the cafeteria entrance, Attison walked back to the elevators and the Inspector left the hospital. Porretta had never met anyone like the Donnelly's lawyer before in his life and he could not stop thinking about him. Absolutely stoic to the core, he had to believe the chill in his bones was there only by the cold wind whistling down the streets of Boston.

3:14 AM Wednesday November 30, 2005 Boston, Massachusetts

In his office on Tuesday afternoon, Doctor Berman told Attison that Holly Donnelly's blood was normal. All the poison was gone. Pessimistic about a full recovery, he didn't think she'd ever wake up. Attison had nodded grimly and thanked him for his expertise and any help he may still give them in the future, but he was grinning with anticipation as he walked back to Holly's room.

He sat back on the uncomfortable plastic chair next to her head, and he began to meditate. Staying by her side until the afternoon darkened into night, he only left the room once to get more coffee and another sandwich. Tuesday turned into Wednesday at midnight, and at three in the morning, Attison went out to the nurse's station to have a conversation with the young man at the desk.

"Good evening, Mark. It's extremely important that Holly Donnelly in room 329 has complete privacy for one hour. We need your vigilance to sustain it." At that point, Attison's eyes weren't brown or black. They'd turned bright blue . . . and they were pulsing with a subdued and gentle light. "No one can enter Donnelly's room. No medical staff. No hospital employees; not even the janitor, okay?"

Mark nodded and grinned, "Alright, Mr. Korybante. I'll take care of that for you." His voice sounded friendly and normal as he talked to thin air. Attison had instantly whirled away from the desk, the second he was done talking to nurse, intent on getting back to the room in short order. He knew the young man at the desk would do exactly what he had been told to do, having cemented his odd orders into his mind like concrete. Mark would keep on trying to do them even if the ceiling fell on his head. Attison had even inserted one of his own gifts inside the man. The night-nurse could use a certain vibration in his voice to stop any visitors in their tracks and turn them away, if he had to. Of course, after the select hour ticks away, he won't remember the orders, or the grafted power, and that too would shrivel away with the recollection.

Re-entering her hospital room, Attison softly pushed her hair away from her forehead and then he held her hand. A hint of color had flowered in her cheeks that morning, removing the pallor that had been holding her in its grip. He knew it was time. Gently removing the different plastic tubes they'd inserted into her veins, he lifted her off the bed. He stripped the backless hospital robe off of her as the cloth would have impeded the progression. The green fabric fell to the floor. Holly had to be naked. Arranging her on top of the blankets on the bed, he sat back in the plastic chair again, and he closed his eyes. Relaxing his body, he connected his consciousness with hers, and he used his own form of astral projection to leave his body. Free from the weight of it, he had nothing to anchor his awareness down. With no material boundaries, his search could go *anywhere*, and he was on a hunt for something important. Trillions of miles away, he found the stellar cluster he was looking for. He tightened his hold on Holly's hand, while flashes of blinding light, like tiny nuclear outbursts, vented out her other palm and the bottoms of her feet. Anyone staring them without protection would burn their retinas, leaving permanent injuries.

The ceiling lights flickered out and the atomic bursts of blinding brilliance abruptly ended as well. The room was wrapped in black velvet until Holly's body started to shimmer. A layer of radiant frost glazed every inch of her skin, but it was only the foundation and icy blue fire erupted along the entire length of her body. The cold flames blazed up to three feet in height, and she began to rise off the bed. Attison could not hold on to her hand anymore. Ascending, she stopped close to the ceiling, and she stayed there. Hundreds of luminous spheres materialized around her. Miniscule meteors, they orbited her body, building a cocoon of iridescent light. They were infusing every single one of the molecules of her body with a concentration of stellar magnetism.

Soon, the transformation and the ritual were over. As the visual effects faded away, the fluorescent lights in the ceiling tremulously struggled to come back on. Gravity reasserted itself on Holly's body, and Attison watched her descend to the bed. He checked the time on his watch. No longer comatose, she was peacefully asleep. Taking the hospital gown off the floor, he put it back on her body, and he reinserting the tubes into her veins without waking her up. Then he rearranged the blankets, and he tucked them in.

Having orchestrated the final phase of Holly's re-birth, Attison was filled with the warmth of accomplishment and adoration for her. Without a trace of smugness or vanity in his heart, he also had no pride and that was miraculous.

. . . .

Mesmerized by the hurricane surf, Holly gazed out at the ocean and her sense of time was gone. Kneeling on the frozen sand, she was oblivious to the cold. The wind ruffled her hair, and she looked up. Small cumulous clouds raced over her head and in the distance pinkish-orange thunderheads were glued on the horizon line. Suddenly, her attention was powerfully directed to a pointless spot at land's end and she was stuck there, hypnotized. Light dwindled away and she remained mesmerized, staring out at the nothing in the dark until two alien-looking eyes, the size of headlights, popped into existence. Hovering only six feet away from her, a voice began talking inside her head.

"*Hello Holly, can you see? Can you feel? There are more things inside you now, and I will guide you home . . . you need to come home.* ***It's time***," and it sounded as if three different female voices were talking to her as one. A blended chorus.

The surface of the irises in the oversized eyes was reminiscent of spilled oil on wet pavement. Dazed by those shifting alien colors, Holly easily surrendered to the melodic directions, and the eyes blinked out and the voice went silent. The susurrus of the ocean's lullaby song she'd conjured up was quickly replaced by the sound of bubbles rising along the inside wall of the fishpond in her parents house. And even that was receding and harder to hear. The time in which her essence had to be inside the body of a koi fish was over. The awful hum of the fluorescent bulbs in the hospital room's ceiling easily overpowered the noise of the Donnelly's air compressor chugging along over one hundred miles away, and the boring sight of the walls of the koi pond dissolved. Holly opened her eyes to see a light brown metal door and a table standing next to it across a room she'd never seen before. Looking up, she saw an IV bag hanging from a metal pole above her head and a plastic tube was taped into a vein in her arm. Then she felt the warmth of a very large hand with dusky colored skin holding hers and it was wearing a 24 karat gold onyx ring.

"Good morning, Holly," Attison Korybante said.

Epilogue

10:56 AM Friday December 16, 2005 Bass River, Massachusetts

Attison enjoyed the view from Latham's former desk on the second floor of Holly's palatial home. A snowstorm the night before had turned the lawn into a piece of sparkling white paper as if the young heiress could now write out her own version of the Donnelly legacy.

A week ago, Inspector Porretta had stopped by at Attison's rental property in Yarmouth. He wanted to explain his partial resolution of the case, and Attison was pleased. Porretta had clearly deduced that Samuel and Latham were visually identical, and coincidence had joined them together forever. Justin or David, or possibly both of them were involved in changing the holiday meal into a decisive one. David had died by tetrodotoxin and Justin's sayonara was heralded only by taxane, and the Inspector wasn't sure if their respective avoidance of the other poison was serendipitous or not. Parts of the case remained unsolved and Attison was actually rooting for Ryan to unearth the whole thing, knowing that none of the evidence would incriminate Holly. Even if Porretta somehow knew what she'd said to them all, she'd only be culpable of fabrication. Holly's guilt comes from metaphorically rolling out a strip of spikes on a road no one should have driven down alone.

In her only interview with the Inspector, she had been gracious and polite, and she hadn't given him squat, explaining her busy work schedule at the hospital had blinded her to the dangerous pressure building in her family. The intrepid officer had not accepted that excuse at first, but Attison gently *'explained'* to him that Holly was blameless and she needed solitude to heal from the tragedy. The worldly lawyer's potent dominion over her was unbreakable, and the highly driven Inspector had no way to get onto that island. Forced to leave Holly alone, in their last meeting in Yarmouth, Porretta had asked Attison how Ms. Donnelly was doing physically as he hadn't seen her since the interview in the hospital. The man was powerfully drawn to the impossible mystery of her survival, and Attison saw that captivation in his eyes. He may need to use a smidgeon more of his unusual ministrations at a later date, since he could clearly foresee a future entanglement in which they're both supported by the other.

At his death, Latham's holdings reverted to Hienem and there was no divvying of the estate between members of the family. Latham hadn't know that his lawyer and personal confidante had owned over fifty percent of the company as Attison had cleverly masked that dangerous knowledge in a string a dummy corporations. After the CEO's death, Attison then owned 98 percent of the swelling giant. If Mr. Donnelly's ghost knew that his last selfish act would end up rewarding the daughter he so reviled with every penny he had, he'd twirl in his grave faster than the blade in a Cuisinart.

On November 25th, Attison transferred his ownership of the Hienem Pharmaceutical Corporation to Holly Donnelly, so ipso facto; the breathing lump of flesh in the hospital bed in Boston became disgustingly rich. The day after she woke up, Attison had her sign her name on a pile of contracts and legal documents on the plastic table next to her bed.

Attison had been on the phone for most of the morning to the president of the Goddard Bank in Toronto. He was shifting and molding Holly's financial power into an indestructible megalith she would overlord for the foreseeable future. Continuing to advise her about different financial opportunities, he would also help her as a counselor on her own projects.

Closing the office door behind him, Attison went out to find his fledgling. Her recovery was taking time. She hadn't bounced back one hundred percent quite yet. Whether she was grieving over the erasure of most of her family or not, he knew she was confused about her own rebirth. Like a baby learning to walk, Holly was flexing her new mental muscles tentatively and he wanted to give her a pep talk; maybe even an inspirational display to underline what he knew she could do.

Holly's old house in New Bedford was on the market, and the estate in Bass River had become her home . . . *as it should be.* She didn't want to stay in either one of her parent's suites, so for the time being she slept in the most extravagant of the guest quarters. Waking up at 9AM, she'd rushed down the stairs to the dining room, and Vince had cooked eggs benedict for her. The chef had been devastated by the calamitous use of his Thanksgiving dinner, but after a three week hiatus, he went back to work. Holly was relieved he'd weathered through.

Mirabelle was in therapy. She would be therapy for a long time. Stirred by the blameless housekeeper's wretchedness, Attison set up a ten million dollar trust fund for her and a bank check of $12,000 was automatically deposited in her bank account every month like clock work. It would continue for the rest of her life. A thoroughly vetted new housekeeper, Cecilia McLain had taken her place.

Opening the swinging doors with her butt, Cecilia backed into the dining room holding a tray with the mistress's breakfast on it. Short salt and pepper hair and a muscular physique, her bright green eyes always danced with her love of life.

When Holly was done with breakfast, she wandered into the great room feeling lackadaisical. Curling up in front of the fire with her PC, she worked on one of her projects for a few minutes, but she was too restless to stay in one place.

Don Cooper had worked for the Donnelly's as a landscaper for years. After the tragedy, Attison's assistant had called him to see if he was still interested in working on the estate, and he'd sweetened the deal by offering him a hefty bonus. Cooper stayed on, so of course he had watched the storm pile up a lot of snow the night before. At the crack of dawn, he arrived at the estate. He plowed the driveway and the auto park, but he wasn't done yet, and he cleared every walking path on the property. That included the garden maze and the sitting area around the central fountain.

Cecilia had been told not to touch any of Holly's possessions and her winter cloak was crumpled on an armchair near the fire where she'd tossed it. Closing the computer, she decided to go out for a walk over the new fallen snow and she grabbed the black velvet cloak. With purple satin lining, it had a gothic style high collar that worked perfectly as a wind barrier. Leaving the mansion through the repaired library door, she followed the plowed path into the garden. A figure in black on a field of white, Attison watched her walk into the maze from a window on the second floor of the house.

Snow was crackling under her boots with every step, and she could hear it precisely. After living through a near-death experience, all of Holly's normal senses had become acute, while her more unusual abilities had followed suit. Stopping at the fountain in the center of the maze, she closed her eyes and centered her thoughts. She slowly inhaled the cold air deep into her lungs. Forgetting her gloves, her hands had been in her pockets during the walk, but she raised her arms in a V. She opened her hands in supplication and the cold didn't matter. Her red fingernails were vibrant exclamation points against the radiant blue sky as the white snow reflected and amplified the sunlight to brighten this transitory stage.

"Hello, Holly." Only three feet away from her, Attison startled her badly with his voice. He must have walked over the same crackling ice formed over the packed snow, but somehow she hadn't heard a thing, and she remembered what she'd done to David in the auto-court a year ago, surprising him that way. It seemed that what goes around does come around once in a while.

"Hello, Attison." Holly put her hands back in her pockets.

"Thought you'd like to know I've finalized your holdings this morning. The empire has the financial stability of a tectonic plate."

"That's wonderful, thank you." She looked up at him and smiled. When she came out of the coma, she had quickly accepted him with trust and affection . . . as if there had always been a link between them.

"Your life has been nothing but a prelude until now. You have the world at your fingertips and no one can make it better than you. So many changes have all just begun and we can reap what I have sown," Attison said. Stepping over to a snow drift near the fountain, he scooped up a handful of snow and he molded it into a *very* hard snow ball. "The western world has lost social cohesion in the millennium, and I know we can slip into the chaotic fabric of things without a hitch. We don't have to hide anything anymore . . . no, we won't have to hide at all," and Holly could feel a melody hidden behind in his words.

"Anybody would gravitate to astonishing things or anything that drips with sexuality; or I can give people monetary profit from a new outlet, and from there it could go viral," she said.

"Bedazzled, spellbound and overwhelmed, they'll put palm fronds on the ground in front of you," Attison said, laughing. Wearing black leather gloves, he pressed the snowball into granite and then he threw it past the fountain with a lot of power. It exploded on the trunk of a silver birch seventy feet away. He bent over to scoop up more snow to make another one.

"I don't think you realize the magnitude of your powers, my dear. You have the key within yourself, but you haven't accepted it fully. The extraneous world is still diverting you from your course, but those days should be gone. You don't need anymore camouflage to link you to the past. Now that you're free from normal constraints, you can sculpt the environment to fit your needs."

Attison's dark eyes changed into an ultramarine blue as he effortlessly tossed his second snowball four hundred feet straight up above the silent and drained fountain . . . and it hung there, immune to gravity. It twinkled in the sun. And then it turned into a dove, wings flapping, energetically alive. The bird fluttered down to land on the highest tier of the fountain and it began to croon, but Attison's short presentation for Holly wasn't over yet. The dove shattered into a mist of ice particles drifting slowly to the ground, and a wellspring of liquid rainbows bloomed out of the top of the fountain. Clouds of steam roiled off them as they cascaded into the lower basins. The blue in Attison's eyes faded, along with the dreamlike tableau he'd built. He put his hand protectively on his charge's shoulder, whispering his urgent request in her ear.

"Wake up, Holly . . . . wake up and fly!"

A Prequel: Introducing Kieth Fischer

11:35AM Tuesday May 13, 1986 Ricker Basin, Vermont

Spraying another layer of white latex paint on the side of his church, he tossed his plaid shirt over a broken fence post, happy he could get away with working in only his cotton undershirt. Even after the accident, Billy was a pretty good carpenter, and the town was almost done. After three years, he'd put up five houses and a general store and they were lined up along a flattened dirt track. And of course, there was the church on the ninety-degree turn on the unpaved trail. He'd built them all on ancient foundations he'd found out there in the woods, the only clue he had to resurrect the tiny town. Turning right 90 degrees at the church, the dirt trail rose on a gentle grade for another thousand feet. It ended at the door of the house that overlooked the town.

Ricker Basin came into existence in 1783, as settlers had picked the site between two streams. They called them Cotton Brook and Stevenson Brook, and they built three grist mills. The rushing power of the water ground their grain into flour for forty-four years until a deluge of biblical proportions left the town in shambles in 1927. All of the mills were destroyed. The intrepid colonizers had been tricked by the slight elevation of the land between the streams and the previously content had to emigrate out. Just as well. Nine years later, a second flood washed more of the town away. What was left disintegrated in the wild woods of Vermont, and Ricker Basin turned into a ghost town.

The state of Vermont erected the Waterbury Reservoir inside the Little River State Park. Ricker Basin was only 12 miles away, so the government decided to absorb the empty town with eminent domain. State workers were sent to dismantle the dregs of the Basin in 1960, with a single exception. Some of the older residents in Waterbury remembered the last years of Ricker Basin, and the bureaucrats told the workers to let Goodall's house stand. Almeron Goodall's house sat higher than the rest of the town, so it weathered through the two floods pretty well. The word on high, to spare it as a sentimental monument was a trite excuse. They just didn't want to pay the extra money involved in dragging the fool thing down. The fleeting presence of human beings stamping around again in Ricker Basin ended as soon as the construction of the reservoir was over, and the return to desolate abandonment turned into months and then years. No one ever went there. No one could remember where it was, and the years yawned into decades. The bricks from the fallen mills eroded in the streams like bones and the invading tentacles of the living forest crept over the stone foundations to devour the corpse of the town. The forsaken home of the hill stood sentinel over nothing.

Billy put the paint gun down, and he limped over to his truck. Scrabbling through the boxes and bags in the back, he found a beat up pack of menthol cigarettes wedged under the corner of his toolbox. He lit one up. Leaning against the side of the 350, he started puffing out smoke rings, and they disintegrated fast in the slight breeze. Thinking over what he'd achieved so far and what was left to be done, his body had responded valiantly to his obsession. At 42, his dark hair and goatee displayed only thin streaks of grey.

Billy Lieden had been incarcerated in a federal prison in Danbury, Connecticut between 1972 and 1978. Released three days after his 30th birthday, he continued his career in the construction trade. In 1981, he was working on a project in upstate New York when he tumbled twenty-eight feet off a ladder. He'd shattered his left hip and cracked his skull, leaving him comatose. After a month he woke up, to the insurance company's dismay, and the circling lawyers instantly landed at his hospital room like vultures on a new carcass. Finding something wrong with the ladder, the company responsible for its construction and the developers settled out of court, paying him 13 million dollars in reparations. A year after the devastating fall, Billy had six and half million dollars in his bank account. The carrion eaters had taken the rest.

After he left the hospital and the following rehabilitation, he was directionless. That was about to change. In 1983, in the month of October, Billy was driving his brand new 350 Ford truck north on 95. He was on his way to see his friend, Butch Dawes. Butch lived alone in a ramshackle farmhouse in Waterbury, Vermont, and after they hugged in his driveway, they started to drink six-packs of beer and watch sport games on TV. The next day they tramped into the woods to hunt deer. Billy was separated from his friend for quite a while as he'd followed some hoof prints down a different trail. Walking out from under a screen of dense foliage into a sunlit clearing, the Goodall house surprised him. It was standing smack-dab in front of him. Its coincidental precipitousness burned into his heart with unnatural significance, and the dilapidated old wreck had become an inviting dream of some kind instead. Whether it was the classic carpentry or the thick aura of separation swirling around the grey shadow, the building had drawn him in like a wraith. And from there, he was fascinated by the rest of the ghost town. Hobbling around, he looked down at the old foundations, and something definitive clicked into place inside Billy Lieden's mind. When he limped into the cemetery, he relaxed on a fallen gravestone. Suddenly transfixed by another revelation, he decided he would raise the dead by raising the fallen town. It would become a stairway to heaven of his own device, a wonderful conduit to get to the other side.

Meeting up with his friend an hour later, he told him he hadn't see anything. To Butch, Billy looked punch drunk; like he'd fallen down and bonked his head on a rock or something.

Since Ricker Basin meant nothing to anyone, the state employees in Montpelier accepted his generous bid to buy it. They quickly inserted a clause in the transfer papers permanently releasing them from any liability from anything Mr. Lieden or anyone else does or doesn't do on the lot of land proposed in the contract. Three weeks later, he returned to the state capitol with a bank check of $100,000 dollars, paid out to the State of Vermont. After his check was deposited later on that day, Billy Lieden became the proud owner of thirty-seven acres of land encompassing Ricker Basin. It was difficult to get to, and the place had no electric lines and no public water system, but he was ecstatic. He had more than enough money in the bank to make his dream come true.

After a three day marathon with a chainsaw, he'd cut away enough of the overgrowth on the trail off Little River Road to squeeze a flat bed truck through it. He hauled two gas driven generators and a John Deere tractor with a back hoe up to the desolate remembrance of what had once been a thriving town. Since he was staying in the Goodall house, the first thing he did was replace the floors, the interior walls and the weight bearing beams of the building. He hadn't had enough time to flatten the godforsaken six miles of trail leading to the site, so he couldn't plow it. In December, January and February he lived in a rooming house in Montpelier. Stuck there, he poured over the blueprints he'd made for more construction in the spring. Twice a week he'd go over to Butch's house, and they'd get drunk and play cards. Making it up to the derelict town in March, he still had to wait for the ground to unfreeze before he could finally grade the trail, but he had no intention of having the same thing happen to him next winter. By the end of the summer, the trail was groomed and ready to be dug out of any succession of terrible blizzards that may arrive. Installing a well point next to the Almeron Goodall house was one of the first renovations in a list of things he was about to do to up-grade the primitive conditions in the structure. He changed that swaybacked ruin into a comfortable place to live in, with two working bathrooms, a full kitchen, electric lights, a fireplace, and propane heat.

He had never been an architect. And he wasn't the *best* carpenter either. Without a single word of advice or counsel, the entire resurrection of Ricker Basin hadn't come out quite right, but to Billy it was perfect. The town was magnificent. Exceptional. If a roof line was slightly tilted, or a windowsill a smidgeon off true, there was no one there to pester him about it.

He'd painted two of the houses light blue, another one was a pale yellow. The rest of the buildings were white, and all the shingles on the roofs were dark grey. Every window had blinds and curtains and the glass was shiny clean. The general store even had signs out front telling the non-existent public there was a sale on sprinklers and millet seed. Half of the churches windows were done in stained glass. All the front door knobs were made from brass, and they gleamed in the sunlight like gold. The public well in the middle of the main track was brand new and it worked perfectly.

A stranger backpacking into the lost village would probably think that things were fine . . . at first anyway. Billy had screwed numbers into the front doors of the houses, starting the numerical series with 29. As a one man band, finishing up was slow going. A vine had grown over the roof and onto the front porch of the first house he completed over a year ago.

It had even spread inside the second floor, and he hadn't found the time to get rid of it. Across the dirt road, in number 30, things had gotten even worse. A slender tree branch had broken through one of the side windows on the first floor, *from the inside out*. When he'd first started construction on it, he'd cut down an oak in the middle of the foundations. New growth had grown out of the stump, breaking through the thin plywood flooring. Since the second house was only a shell, there were no interior walls to stop the new stalk from reaching the lower windows. Besides Goodall's place, number 29 was the only other building in Ricker Basin with a second floor, and that one was very rough. The framing inside all the other structures were only there to support the outside walls.

The forest was slowly creeping back into the Basin, and Billy was only fighting it back haphazardly. Too preoccupied, he was busy connecting the final pieces of his puzzle. He was oblivious to the crumbling edges of his twilight town. A white birch tree grew right in front of the entrance of the church, and so far he hadn't taken out the rest of the tree stumps in the middle of the road he called Main Street. *It didn't matter*. It was almost done. He was about to use his town for the purpose he'd built it for, and a few weeds couldn't slow him down.

3:27PM Saturday May 17, 1986 Waterbury, Vermont

Lackadaisically winding north to Mad River Glen, Route 100 dangerously crossed the Winooski River in the center of Waterbury. Folded into a hairpin curve right before the bridge, it was very tricky when things iced up. Half-a-mile away from the bridge, the owner of the local hardware store closed the register drawer so he could to ring up the next customer. His son Clarence was stocking shelves in the back of the room. The screen door closed behind Billy Lieden with a slap as he left the store holding a bag of hinges. Clarence trotted up to the front, untying his work apron at the same time. He tossed it over his head. Hanging the apron on the corner of a cardboard display for windshield washer fluid, he sprinted out the door and down the five steps to the sidewalk as his father's baleful stare bored into his back.

"I know you're building something out there in the woods and I want to know what it is . . . hello . . . *HELLO!*" Clarence yelled this out to Billy, and Billy ignored him.

His pickup truck was parked on the other side of the empty street, and he got in the cab. During nonstop construction, he'd beaten and abused the 350 and its maroon paint was coated in dirt. He was mulling over the idea of buying another new truck when he heard the same voice he'd disregarded punching into his personal world again.

"I've seen you in the store before, but you never hang out in town. You're never anywhere. I watched you haul a John Deere around that damned corner a while ago, and I still don't know how you managed it. I tried to follow you on my dirt bike, but you were long gone."

"Go away," Billy said. He started the engine.

"Hunters were in the store yesterday and they told my father they saw something through the trees . . . told him they saw construction at Ricker Basin."

The filthy vehicle slowly rolled out of the parking space as Billy hit a button to close the driver's window. Clarence was jogging along with the truck, yelling through the glass.

"You might not know it, but there are ghosts in the Goodall house and all around the Basin. I've heard the stories. You should be really careful if that's where you're going!"

When Billy heard the word '*ghost*' in the teenager's ranting, he stopped the truck on a dime. He lowered the window he'd just raised.

"What are you talking about? You don't know shit about that place. *I* know what's really up there." Billy was angry.

Clarence's guess was right. He'd slammed the nail home and he wanted to smile, but he restrained himself. Reaching the truck, he brushed his dark hair out of his eyes.

"You *are* working in Ricker Basin, aren't you?" His voice had dropped into an easy northern drawl, and Billy stared at him. Most of the time, Lieden pushed everybody away, yet he was strangely torn between curiosity and disdain. The kid didn't look like a country boy. He was almost six feet tall, and his fingernails were painted black, blue jeans ripped to shreds. Alice Cooper could have looked a lot like this kid when he was 17. Another minute went by.

"Why do you want to tell me ghost stories about Ricker Basin?" Billy asked.

"I could tell you every single one of the stupid legends linked to the Basin. Most of them are crap, and I don't really want to tell you anything. Listen man, I'm bored with life as I know it and I can tell whatever you're doing up there might be a good outlet for one of my projects. Hell, I could even give you free labor for the opportunity."

Clarence looked over his shoulder. Dad was standing on the stoop of the hardware store, yelling and gesturing for him to come back to work. The teenager was unmoved. He waved nonchalantly in his direction, instantly returning his attention to Mr. Billy Lieden.

Billy started laughing. Curiosity won the war. Besides, there seemed to be a strange magnetism pulling him towards the wild looking boy. Maybe he'd found a kindred spirit to help him connect the last dots? He wanted to populate his ghost town somehow, and the kid could possibly give him some new ideas.

"What's your name?"

"Clarence Hanson. What do they call you?"

"It's Billy," and he opened the driver side door of the truck so they could shake hands. "There aren't any ghosts in Ricker Basin. The only thing I hear at night is bears going through my garbage. I've been living in the Goodall house for three years, *so I know*. Oh, by the way, it's my town now. I *own* Ricker Basin. I could change the name to Lieden Basin if I wanted to. Right now I'm almost done with the first phase of my plan, so if you're really interested, I wouldn't mind your advice on the next step."

12:14PM Sunday May 18, 1986 Ricker Basin, Vermont

The birds had returned right on time, and their songs blended in with the loud and boisterous ballads coming out of the Cotton and Stevenson brooks as they swelled in the spring thaw. Out of hibernation, plant life painted a patina of light green like fairy dust across the forest floor and the imprisoned tree branches broke out in a rapture of buds. What was thin would now become fat.

If Billy Lieden hadn't stumbled onto it like a stoked up faith healer, Ricker Basin would have vanished under the blanket of exuberant life. Nailing young flesh on its old bones, Clarence was the first person to be introduced to the Basin its new form and the enclave of buildings was truly surreal. After telling him to meet him in the playground in half-an-hour to have lunch, Billy gave him freedom to look anywhere. Clarence started his tour by raced inside all the buildings as fast as he could.

Billy had hoped a playground would work as a magnet for the spirits of dead children. He bought one; a steel swing set, a slide, a jungle gym, and a runabout. Two years ago he'd cleared land next to the cemetery to set-up the equipment, but there had been no response. He hadn't seen anything. No floating orb of light, no twig sculptures left for him to find. Nothing.

Instrumental in creating a new ghost in 1971, he remembered the conversation he'd had with it right after the violent and bloody transformation. The knowledge he believed he'd learned from the supernatural chat was part of what had inveigled him into the construction of the town. To Billy, the recreation of Ricker Basin was a clarion call to invite the deceased population out of their graves to inhabit his town in a mass haunting. So far, that it hadn't worked either. He was stymied. In his mind, the return of the departed would be his salvation; the ultimate stability he craved . . . *and there had to be a way to get them there!*

Clarence and Billy were sitting on the swings eating the ham and cheese sandwiches they'd bought along from the luncheonette in Waterbury. Jawing over the history of the Basin, they'd both heard the same story about the trapper's disappearance in 1940. He'd been camping next to Stevenson Brook when he was tossed into the water and drowned by the angry spirit of one of the first settlers. Clarence told him another muddled tale about a jealous husband, a dead hound dog, and a drunken hunter, but none of these silly stories would solve his problem. As their conversation evolved, Billy decided to invite the boy into his secretive dementia.

"So you've built your own ghost town in the woods and you haven't had a nibble? Do you have any ideas on how to fix that?" Clarence said.

"I have no idea how to bring them here or how to wake them up, anymore. No clue . . . well, I do know of an easy way to do it, but it's not something I should really talk to you about right now."

It didn't take Clarence long to realize that Lieden was deeply psychotic. With this new understanding, he seamlessly adapted to the length and breadth of the man's insane debauchery for his own devilish reasons. He knew that Ricker Basin would be *perfect*. The two of them could invest their time and efforts to increase the invisible inhabitants of the town for a long, long time, and it would remain their little secret.

"I know exactly what you're worried about Bill, considering the money and time you've already put into this place. Exasperation is glued onto you like a third arm. Since you've found the initiative to go ahead and asked me for advice, I'm going to tell you what I think. It's a travesty to build a container like this and leave it empty. Don't you think the atmosphere in this town would be heavenly if the new found spirits came from innocent young females?" With an easy rhythm in his words, Clarence sounded erudite and mature.

Billy's eyebrows raised in surprise. Was it possible? Did Clarence have the same exact dream in his head too? He wondered if the boy had any idea how difficult it would be to bring that vision to life . . . *or death.*

"Of course, it'd be phenomenal if I can come up with a way to transport spirits like that here! Right now, I don't know how to invite specific ones floating out in the ethereal world to . . ." Clarence interrupted him.

"I'm going back to school tomorrow and I'll put my plan into play. The local stories will give your ghost town a lot of appeal, and all I have to do is print out a few invitations to a haunted weekend retreat to a few select candidates. After I give them the historical foundation of Ricker Basin, they'll be revved up about meeting the ghosts that aren't really here. Don't worry about it anymore, Billy. I'll entice those succulent visitors into your welcoming arms in just a week or two."

They went on hashing out the nefarious scheme to bring in candidates to become newly minted ghosts in Ricker Basin by hook or by crook . . . more likely by hook and crook, plus the highly possible coincidence that there would be even more unspecified weapons besides.

11:48AM Monday May 19, 1986 Harwood High School South Duxbury, Vermont

Only 18, Kevin Fielding would remain skeletal until he packed on more muscle in the upcoming years. It was his last year in high school and he still hadn't made his mind up about his career. His unwanted gifts drew him to a place he wasn't very happy about. At 6'2", his blonde head was stuck in the sky for a lot of reasons.

Some people are born with talents so impressive they climb new pinnacles in human endeavor. Idolizing them, we certainly aren't afraid of them, but then there are other remarkable individuals who haunt the outer limits of our purview, and we do not acknowledge them. Kevin's blue eyes were twenty-twenty, but he could also discern the uncanny and most of us with normal sight are blind to that strange range. While everyone else curls up asleep in a comfortable silence, he can hear otherworldly voices. Heavily linked to that conduit, he can touch and sometimes sculpt unimaginable things without using his hands.

Kevin tossed his books in his locker. He padlocked it and walked down the hallway to the cafeteria. Clarence and a couple of girls were talking in an empty classroom and when he passed them he got a funny feeling in his gut. Something wasn't right. Months ago, he'd noticed an emptiness in the guy, possibly a menacing one, but the feeling hadn't been powerful enough to evoke a response. Kevin's previous assessment had changed, but there was nothing he could do about anything for the moment. If there was smoke, there'd be fire and the tinge he'd felt in the hallway might indicate the likelihood of an inferno.

Mindlessly inhaling fish sticks and carrots off his plate, Kevin was miles away. Other students at his table were comparing notes and laughing and gossiping, and he just sat there like a stone. He had watched Clarence walk in the cafeteria with the girls and he'd parked four tables away. Kevin stood up and went by them again. They weren't talking, they were whispering and that secretiveness increased Kevin's interest. Some of his acquaintances were sitting at a table right next to them, and he sat down to talk to his friends as a subterfuge. He was close enough to tune in on the murmurings going on between Clarence and the girls.

"A haunted weekend at Ricker Basin just for you," Clarence whispered, "including a confrontation with an angry spirit! You guys will know the real truth behind all the stories of the abandoned town. Hell, I can escort you through this invisible maze, and if you don't run away, the International Ghost Hunters Association will issue a certificate of courage for both of you. Remember, this is on the QT. We don't want a lot of people to know about this place. It would weaken the aura. Right now, nobody knows about the importance of the secrets we'll learn next weekend, so whatever you do, don't tell your family or your friends. You're going to have to make something up about where you guys are going on Saturday."

"That won't be a problem! We always go to Daryl's house on Saturday to work on our science project in the garage. We'll just tell her we aren't coming and tell everybody else we are. It's more than worth the lie. I mean, we've tried to communicate with the dead for a long time, and the Ouija Board and our séances haven't gotten us anywhere," Rebecca said, and Nancy nodded in agreement. They'd fallen for Clarence's artfully composed spiel, hook, line, and sinker, and the young Svengali was reeling them in like fat juicy trout.

Kevin's precognition gets stronger when he gets closer to the people and places involved in the event, and his understanding of it expands as the time before it happens, shrinks. So far, he knew an older man was part of it . . . part of something unspeakable, and as he strolled towards his Biology class at 12:45, Kevin realized he had a problem on his hands. He couldn't figure out what to do about it yet. He had to go to Ricker Basin and scope things out.

6:55PM Wednesday May 21, 1986 Colbyville, Vermont

Kevin was living with his grandparents in Colbyville, seven miles north of Waterbury. He was lying on the bed, arms crossed behind his head as he gazed up at the ceiling. Right before dinner, he'd asked his grandfather about Ricker Basin and how to get there. Lenny Fielding used to assist the local fire department and the police with any electrical breakdowns in their equipment, so it wasn't a surprise that he'd given him a detailed answer. He told Kevin that he'd been drinking coffee with one of the volunteers in the firehouse years ago, and they'd been talking over local history. The man disappeared into a back office to return with a very old map and he gave it to Lenny, and then Lenny had scrounged it up a few hours ago to give to his grandson. It clearly delineated where the old town had been, as well as marking the path off Little River Road that led up to it. Kevin didn't want to announce himself to anyone up there, so he scoured over the old map to find another way in. A dotted line with *Harrier's Loop* printed underneath it looked extremely promising as it petered out in the woods on the other side of Ricker Basin; the opposing direction from the main trail. Lenny told him it was an old trail made by trappers, and hunters still occasionally use it. Knowing he could get to it from the Interstate, made up his mind and he got off the bed. His quad needed to be in good working order to handle the upcoming trip through some very wild woods, and he went to the garage to work on it.

To get to the Basin and back home before dark, he skipped out of school early. He loaded the ATV in the back of his pick-up and then he high-tailed it onto Interstate 89. Glancing over at the old map he'd left open on the passenger seat, he started to count the mile markers. He saw a small dent in the solid line of trees at the edge of the highway, and he slowed down and parked on the shoulder. Getting out, he jogged over to check it out. It was obviously the start of Harrier's Loop. He dropped the tailgate and locked the aluminum ramps onto the bed of the truck, and then he rolled the quad onto the grass. Putting his helmet on, he started the engine and hit the gas. Like threading a needle, he expertly squeezed the four-wheeler between two oak trees. Small branches snapped off, and whipped into his face as he jolted onto the underused trail. Fighting through a tangle of vines and shrubbery, it was slow going. Seven rough miles later, the track abruptly ended. After hiding the quad under a pile of brush, he was still two miles away from the abandoned town. The untamed forest became an uncomfortable obstacle course, but he'd seen that coming. Kevin had put on leather pants and a corduroy shirt as armor against the sharp thorns imbedded in the walls of entangling thicket. Needing to stay on a northwest line, he continuously checked his compass.

By the time he got the first glimpse of the Goodall house between the trees, he'd sustained only one deep gouge on the back of his hand. Moving quietly towards the building, his perception of the upcoming tragedy sharpened and he knew the builder of this stage set wasn't around . . . he was in Waterbury. He'd be there for a while. Kevin could investigate things without interruption.

Sprinting around the house to the front door, it was unlocked and he walked into the foyer and then the living room. There was an oval table on an oriental rug in the center of the room, and high backed chairs were tucked in around it. Tall brass lamps stood in three of the corners, and there were heavy olive colored drapes with gold tassels hanging funereally at all the windows. At the far end of the room was a fireplace. The whole thing looked staged, as if it was set up for a psychic reading or a séance, and Kevin realized the dreadful main event was going to unfold inside this house on the hill on Saturday night.

He scouted out the rest of the house, and ended his lickety-split tour by bounding down the wooden stairs into the basement. Standing on the cellar floor, he stared up at the rickety steps. It was getting late, and he raced back up the stairs and left the house through the back door. Trotting into the woods, he gathered a collection of small logs and branches, and he secreted them under the back steps. After that, he retraced his thorny trip back to civilization.

On Thursday and Friday, Kevin drove straight back to his grandfather's workroom in the basement as soon as he got out of school. He was assembling the necessary electronic devices he'd need during the implementation of his scheme to stop the murderous attacks over the weekend, and he didn't have a lot of time to do it.

10:15AM Saturday May 24, 1986 Ricker Basin, Vermont

Sitting on a bench in front of the un-blessed and empty shell of a church, Billy and Clarence were both excited about the evening get-together they'd arranged.

"What time are you supposed to meet them?" Billy asked.

"6:30. I told them the séance starts at eight."

"You know we have to go to Montpelier to get the incense, the candles, and the white wine, and we *can't* forget the tablecloth. It'll be more inspiring to escort them into their new state if we make the perfect atmosphere to do it in."

A chuckle burped out of Clarence, "Escort, my ass. We'll amuse ourselves like cats playing with mice."

The sugar-sweet stream of platitudes he'd endlessly supported Billy Lieden's psychosis with had faltered for a second, and Billy frowned. Limping over to the 350, his shoulders were wrenched up with irritation and he got in and started the engine. The dirty pick-up truck began to slowly roll forwards, and Clarence had to get off the bench and run. He opened the passenger door, and jumped in at the last possible second. They drove to town in silence.

11:11AM Saturday May 24, 1986 Colbyville, Vermont

A long time ago, Kevin's grandparents had given up asking him about his *'projects'.* That morning they watched him pack his truck, praying he'd come back to them in one piece. He'd bungee corded a large metal suitcase securely on an aluminum rack he'd installed on the back of the ATV, and the four wheeler had already been rolled into the bed of his truck. Two sandwiches, two bottles of water, a fleece jacket, (*and an illegal handgun that no one knew about*) were stuffed in his backpack, and he'd tossed that in the cab.

After another trip in the gnarly woods, he hid the quad and went on to struggle through the remaining two miles. This time was harder as Kevin had to haul the suitcase through the underbrush. It was cumbersome, and the backpack wasn't helping. Eventually, he made it to the house with every tool he'd need to win the day, *or the night.* He knew they wouldn't be around for hours and he intended to use that time for the preparations. It turned out the backdoor was unlocked too, as he dragged the suitcase through the kitchen and the dining room. Leaving it in the living room, he went back outside to retrieve his cache of wood under the back stairs. He strategically positioned the pieces on the grate in the fireplace. Removing a magnesium charge out of the suitcase, he inserted the charge in the center of his pyramid of logs and branches. Kevin took out a small container of starter fluid from the side pocket of his backpack, and he drenched four or five of the smallest twigs near the explosive charge. He knew that most of the liquid would evaporate, but some of it would soak into the core of the dry wood, and the drenched twigs would remain flammable for hours. Kevin wasn't worried about Billy or Clarence noticing the wood in the fireplace, correctly predicting they'd assume the other was responsible for it. Caught up in their party plans, it was a lot more likely they wouldn't see it at all. Taking out the rest of the magnesium charges, he put one under one of the tall standing lamps, another under a reading lamp on a small table near the windows. He used two under the heavier brass clock on the mantle to send it flying later on. Turning his attention to the audio transducers, he mounted three of them; one on the stairs leading up to the second floor, another on a ceiling beam, (he had to bring a stepladder up from the basement to get *that* job done) and the final one he taped under the mantle piece. At exactly the right time during the upcoming festivities, he'd turn the wireless microphone he'd have in his hands and distort his voice through an audio processor. He'd blanket the entire room with eerie noises and ghostly pronouncements, complementing the audio effects with smoke and fire . . . plus things falling over and moving around by themselves.

Teetering on his toes on the back rest of the antique sofa, he hid a remote video camera about the size of a double A battery into one of the dusty wooden scrolls adorning the upper corners of the living room windows. The camera would transmit a view of the entire room and part of the stairs going up to the second floor to the black and white monitor he would be staring at in the cellar. Jumping off the sofa, Kevin went over the list of everything that had to be done in his mind and he smiled. Everything was copasetic, and he snapped the suitcase closed. One strap of his backpack hanging off his left shoulder, he grabbed the metal case and pounded down the stairs to the basement.

Forty-five minutes later, Clarence and Billy got back from town, and they didn't notice the pile of wood behind the screen in the fireplace. Kevin had done his job perfectly and the rest of the living room looked untouched.

6:43PM Saturday May 24, 1986 Ricker Basin, Vermont

Rebecca was driving her older brother's four-wheel drive Jeep to the séance. Clarence was waiting for them on Little River Road, and when the girls saw the headlight of his dirt bike, they slowed down. He waved and turned the bike around and Rebecca followed him onto the trail. Bouncing along behind him, they were tossed around in their seats, but they didn't want to slow down. They were too excited.

Rebecca and Nancy wanted to look 'psychic'. They'd draped yards of gauzy material printed with multi-colored flowers around their bodies, and they applied sparkling eye shadow and purple-red lipstick with lip-liner. Their lips seemed bigger, wetter and more sexually inviting. Attempting to blend-in with the evening's festivities, they ended up looking like underage performers on a cheap X-rated film and that wasn't exactly what they were hoping for. At least they'd held on to enough common sense by leaving their blue jeans and their sneakers on beneath the yards of silliness.

Parking next to Almeron Goodall's house, Rebecca and Nancy stared out of the jeep windows to behold the new face of Ricker Basin and they were astonished. Lamps glowed in all the windows of the shell houses on Main Street, and candles happily twinkled in the cathedral windows of the church at the end of the road. They didn't know those cheerful spots of brilliance below them were battery driven, and the exhilarated seekers also didn't realize the electricity in the house they were about to enter was only there because two large generators fifteen feet away were chugging along in a waterproof shed.

Clarence got off the bike and walked over to the girls, helping them out of the jeep. He suavely herded them through the front door. The first floor of the house was bathed in real candlelight, and a silver candelabrum was blazing in the center of the oval table. More candles burned on the mantelpiece over the fireplace, and on the two tables under the windows. The thick embroidered tablecloth Billy had found in a thrift store in Montpelier earlier that day covered the large table in the center of the room, and it had been a perfect choice. Stepping out of the small alcove surrounding the front door, they entered the living room, and Billy was waiting for them there. He was wearing a dark suit and he'd trimmed his goatee and mustache. Hitching towards the girls he looked a bit devilish, however that beckoning image would soon be replaced by a force akin to suppuration. Billy would give that chaotic power ecstatic control over his actions in the next few hours, sending the fallen angel himself back to heaven to avoid his own erasure.

"Good evening, ladies. My name is Mr. Lieden," Billy said. He shook their hands with a tender touch. "I'm the new owner of Ricker Basin and it's a delight to meet you. Clarence advises me you're interested in finding out more about the other side. I believe I can easily open a channel for your questions to be answered."

Rebecca and Nancy looked up at him with nervous smiles, while Billy glanced over at the fireplace. He was impressed that Clarence had decided to set it up and he thought about starting a fire. Ah well . . . maybe not. Things were rolling along too perfectly and he didn't want to interrupt that easy pace. Clarence took the girls off for a tour of the house. The moment they went up the stairs, Billy picked up the candelabrum and put it on the top of a bureau in the corner of the room, and then he opened the top drawer. Removing a crystal ball out of some sheepskin, he placed it on a plastic cradle in the center of the table.

Clarence had the girls in tow as he climbed the stairs to the second floor. Rambling on about the sordid history of the Almeron Goodall family and the disastrous end of the town over a hundred years ago, he was spinning most of the stories straight out of his head. A gifted conversationalist and deceiver, Rebecca and Nancy hung on his every word anyway. In the final part of the tour, they tramped down the back stairs until they all stood in front of the door opening onto the cellar stairs. Clarence's hand was on the knob, but he didn't turn it, and Nancy bumped into him. His head was muddled for a minute or two, and he'd changed his mind about taking the girls down there.

"Um . . . I think . . . it's getting late. We should go back to the living room and begin the séance," Clarence said, and he turned away from the cellar door. Stepping through the short hallway leading into the living room, the odd mental hick-up disappeared and he continued with his discourse as if nothing had happened.

"The spirits are gathering around us now, I can feel it. They know we're here. The departed are breathlessly waiting for us to build the bridge they've been hoping for during those many years in which they were left forgotten in the woods. We're about to stretch a living hand out to them and I know they want to hold it," he said.

"Is there anything we can do to help open the pathways?" Nancy said.

"You must clear your minds from material thoughts and allow yourselves to guide your feelings to your third eye." Back to having a lot of fun ladling out gobbledygook like it was heaven sent, the girls followed him into the living room, still entranced.

Billy had given the crystal ball center stage. Reflecting the candlelight, it drew everyone in the room closer to get lost in its airy depths. He'd covered the cheap plastic holder with a piece of purple velvet, and it elevated the orb four inches above the surface of the table. He'd bought the crystal ball in a yard sale the summer before for only fifteen dollars, and it turned out to have been a steal. The piece of glass was obviously deepening the layer of mystery in their careful deception, and the teenagers were goggle-eyed. Billy ostentatiously pulled out chairs for them to sit down at the table.

"There are powerful waves in the air tonight. We're going to have an exceptional connection. You ladies, Rebecca . . . Nancy", and he acknowledged them both with a small bow, "are the perfect yin to my yang."

In his room the night before, Billy had been sharpening the knife in his pocket for hours. When it couldn't get any sharper, he kept on with the repetitive sweeping stroke, skimming the steel blade up and down the strap; a counter-point to the growing anticipation in his heart.

For the first time in their short visit, Nancy and Rebecca were physical close to Billy, inching their anxiety into low-grade fear. Knowing and not knowing was a tricky thing. Not knowing their host for the evening had a ten-inch long switch blade in his jacket pocket, a primal intuition was still ringing a warning bell in their heads. Disregarding their own intense uneasiness, ignoring the alarm, they kept on trying to enjoy the evening of enlightenment without distraction. To incite the commercialized vision of the unknown in, they negated the powerful push from their own sixth sense.

It was time for everyone to hold hands. Clarence started an incantation to awaken the sleeping spirits, to bring them to the séance. He'd found it in a book in the public library in Waterbury and he'd memorized this plausible gem.

When he heard Clarence on the other side of basement door, Kevin dissuaded him from coming down the stairs by setting up a mental barricade and it had worked like a charm. He was able to continue sitting on a milk crate and stare at the monitor he'd precariously put on a three-legged stool he'd found in the corner of the basement. The remote control and the microphone were in easy reach on a stair tread. It would take him half a second to snatch them up when the time came. Positioning his different tricks in the living room, he'd bumped into some fishing line tied to the legs of two the six chairs at the table, and he also saw a wooden gavel hidden beneath the tabletop. He chuckled at those slapstick attempts, knowing his tricks would utterly eclipse them. Watching what was going on upstairs, he waited until it was time to start his own production.

There's always a chance something could go wrong and ruin his plans, and the final straw, in the form of a hand gun, lay in the bottom of his backpack on the dirt floor. He does have another talent, and it would be extremely unfortunate for Billy and Clarence, if he had to use it to save the girls. Kevin always brings along deadly insurance on every one of his projects. ***Just in case.***

Billy was surprised by the authenticity in Clarence's overture to the spirits, and for a second he thought it was going to work. The optimism quickly vanished as he knew from experience that *nothing* would populate his ghost town without the necessary life and death blood offerings. His ruminations were interrupted when Clarence ended his sing-song entreaty. He was supposed to take over the show.

"Everyone unclasp your hands and look into the bottomless sphere . . . that's right, look deep inside," Billy said. "Almeron Goodall, are you there? Olivia where are you? Evelyn, Johnny . . . you've got to stop playing and come down here and talk to us right now!"

Clarence had told him he'd looked up the real names of the rest of the Goodall family in an old registry in town hall in Waterbury. Billy thought he was using even more veracity in his simulation, but his partner in crime hadn't really looked up anything. Almeron could have been a bachelor, for all he knew, and he made up every moniker in his head.

"Put your fingertips on the globe, that's right . . . just leave them there. We'll cross a conduit that's magnetized now and the space between the two worlds is shrinking. The dimensions are getting nearer to each other, and soon they will become one. Aaah! I can feel them connected together," and Billy's voice got louder. "*You must appear and speak to us . . . tell us what you want and how we can appease you.*" Besides a gentle wind sighing through the trees outside, only silence answered his request. He hadn't given up yet.

"Honoring your memory and what you lived and died through, we await your presence."

Two powerful knocks rocked the table. Billy's eyes remained closed as he swayed back and forth in his chair.

"One knock will tell us you are Almeron, two, Olivia, three Evelyn, and four means you are Johnny," and two more knocks loudly answered him. Rebecca and Nancy were even more frightened, but they wanted the fictitious certificates of courage *and* the difficult secrets the spirits were about to impart to them, so they dutifully stayed at the table with trembling fingertips on the crystal ball.

"Ah, so it's the good lady of the house. Please, couldn't you get a bit closer to us?" Billy said. The empty chair between Nancy and Clarence jumped backwards and fell over, and then another one skittered backwards only to slide back to the edge of the table.

Clarence whispered to the girls, "Don't be alarmed. Olivia will tell us what happened to her children, and we are . . ." but he was abruptly silenced by a loud distorted hum in very low register. The monotonous droning was having no effect on Billy, assuming that Clarence was responsible for the unusual sound. Eyes closed, he was content to communicate with the other world. An explosion ignited a crackling fire in the fireplace, and the girls looked over at the flames with widening eyes and mouths agape. The vibrating bass note suddenly stopped, and Billy opened his eyes in time to watch a lamp in the corner of the room fall over with a crash. Nancy and Rebecca were coasting into a full blown panic attack, and Billy glared at Clarence with disapproval. New noises, higher in pitch and volume screeched into the living room, until a terrifying wail apparently dove down the stairs from the second floor. It bounced to the fireplace to rebound back up the stairs.

"AAAAAAAAGH . . . . OOOOOUUUEEE." It sounded like a woman was being tortured alive, and it seemed that a crack had really ripped opened between the worlds. The heavy brass clock left the mantel and crashed to the floor in the middle of the room, and another standing light fell over near the front door. The bulb popped like a firework and then the terrible howls formed into words.

"No . . . ah . . . noooooo . . . aagh . . . mm . . . IT'S TOO LAAATE FOR ME. THEY WON'T p . . . p . . . PUUULLLLL MEEE OUT OF THE WELL . . . AAAAGH!"

With the soul searing power of a screech owl, the tortured entity had true pathos in her garbled message. She would either break hearts or stop them in terror, as her appalling cries and pleading went on for another three more minutes. Slowly dropping into quieter gasps and wheezes, they finally faded away.

The first reaction to Kevin's auditory attack had instantly turned Rebecca and Nancy's fear into horror and that feeling swiftly condensed into lumps of dread in their bellies. Pushing away from the table, they leapt to their feet, expeditiously. No platform shoes or five-inch heels to impede their flight, the rubber soled sneakers gave them wonderful traction in a race for their lives. As terror the instant sponsor, adrenaline propelled them across the room like balls of female lightening and Clarence's diligent attempt to snag Rebecca's ponytail left his hands pawing at thin air. Nancy opened the front door so hard the knob dug into the sheetrock of the wall with a muffled thud and they bounded into the night like gazelles.

Billy had to believe that Clarence was responsible for these over-the-top theatrics, but he was becoming apprehensive nonetheless. He started yelling at him anyway.

"Well, go ahead and bring them back here before they drive away, you lunkhead. Go on! You gotta go *right now!"* While Clarence ran towards the open door, Billy's attention was completely diverted. Someone had just slammed the back door of his house open and closed as loud as possible, and then he heard the interloper trudge up the back stairs to the second floor. His left hip wasn't dragging on him very much in his energetic and angry trip to the back of his house to confront the trespasser. Grumbling about what he was going to do to anyone interfering with his plans, he didn't look over his shoulder to consider the odd dilemma between the front door and Clarence.

The terrified escapees had left the knob planted in the sheetrock like an anchor; however, the door had freed itself and re-closed on its own. When Clarence reached for the knob, the door opened again with ferocious speed, knocking him off his feet. He was tossed backwards, landing on the floor, arms and legs akimbo. He hadn't had enough time to get back on his feet to go through the re-opened door before the damned thing swept closed again with a conclusive click. Clarence believed that Billy had frightened the girls off and he was livid. Why hadn't he told him about the extra stuff he'd added? That got him even madder. And he orders him to race out there and corral the bitches, only to throw him on the floor in his efforts to do so! It was the last straw! Billy was going to have to hunt them down himself. He stood up with the intention of walking out of the entire thing . . . but he couldn't. The door was stuck. *Seriously stuck.* Clarence's attempts became more violent until he was pulling and pushing on that door like a maniac. It didn't matter. The infernal plank of wood would . . . . not . . . . budge. It wouldn't budge an inch, but he wasn't going to give up. ***He was going to . . . get . . . get . . . get that . . . door to open one way or another!***

Peering up the back stairs, Billy saw a strange looking man disappear around the corner that led into the second floor hallway. He climbed the stairs as fast as he could to reach the landing, only to watch the oversized man disappear into his own bedroom. The trespasser had even closed the door behind him! He was furious as he seesawed down the hall. Pushing into his bedroom aggressively, he found himself face to face with an enormous guy wearing a camouflage jacket and a hunting cap, and he was holding an ancient looking rifle in one hand.

"Who the hell are you and why are you in my house?" Billy shouted. He actually didn't care whether he got an answer or not. Ignoring the switchblade in his jacket pocket, he reached around to the small of his back. A handgun was squeezed hard against the waistband of his pants and that weapon appeared in his right hand so fast it was almost magical. The safety was already off and Billy pointed the gun straight at the stranger's left eye.

"I have a house warming present for you. I guess we'll just have to figure out the mystery without you. I'll let you unwrap it right now," he snarled.

Looking down at Billy, the hulking man's face was red as a turnip and badly swollen, and his reaction to Lieden's aggression was a burst of speed of his own. He slapped the gun out of his hand, and then he leaned *all* his weight into his shoulder, turning Billy into a human pancake as he ground him into the wall for a half-a-minute. After that he sedately walked out of the bedroom. The door swung closed behind him. Badly shaken and completely out of breath, Billy quickly bent over to pick up his gun anyway, driven by his fury. He shot three times through the door, expecting to hear a thud. The intruder should have fallen to the floor on the other side of the door, yet he didn't hear a thing. He was dumbfounded as he could not have missed!

Hearing the gunfire from the second floor, Clarence went over to the coat closet. *At least he was able open that door!* He took out the rifle hidden there. Turning around, he saw a stranger wearing hunting clothes climbing down the front stairs. As soon as he saw Clarence looking up at him, he stopped and aimed his gun at the teenager. Clarence wasn't worried. The rifle stock was already nestled into his shoulder, and he aimed at the man's heart. Firing three times, he knew his target hadn't had enough time to shoot back.

By then, Billy had left the bedroom, and unbeknownst to Clarence, he was standing behind and above the man on the staircase. Neither one of them realized where the other one was. Angling his shots downwards, Billy thought he was sending three more bullets into the hunter, *again*, as his partner below him fired his gun at the exact same time. For an instant they were content they'd shot the man, waiting for him to fall over and die.

In any other scenario, the trespasser would certainly have bled to death on the stairs, but inside the Almeron Goodall house something extraordinary had taken place. Whatever the thing on the stairs had been, it hadn't been solid enough and Billy and Clarence's friendly cross-fire pinioned them. Billy fell on the stairs, dead in sixty seconds and Clarence was thrown onto the living room floor again. This time he was losing a lot of blood and hanging on by a thread. The insubstantial hunter lowered his rifle and climbed down the remaining three treads, walking gingerly around the boy. During the remaining seconds of blazing life left to him, Clarence blurrily watched the impervious creature float *through* the door he hadn't been able to open.

Kevin had blown up all his special effects with panache, transforming his voice into a frightening force with nothing but a slap dash technological ploy. He'd seen the girls run for the hills and out of harm's way. The end result was achieved. He hadn't figured out what he was going to do about stopping Billy and Clarence from doing the same thing all over again, but that problem had just been solved without any of his intervention. Astonished by the evening's performance, it was clear the paranormal play had ended as all the actors were off stage or dead. Unplugging the monitor, the first step in packing up and leaving, he couldn't help but mull over what on earth had happened.

Clarence could have brought in a Trojan horse and the innocuous incantation from the library might have had some power . . . or perhaps the forces in the area had been dormant until Billy Lieden and Clarence had showed up to stamp on their ectoplasmic heads. Or maybe there was something lonely out here in the woods, and it didn't want innocent girls for company, craving barbarous souls like Billy and Clarence for eternal rapport. Did their fiendish future plans to murder more naive girls in Ricker Basin infuriate the restful dead into action? He had no answer.

There would never be a resolution. Falling back into its desolate slumber, the ghost town would dissolve in the tangled cover of the forest.

Kevin made sure the girls had actually driven away. The Jeep was gone, and whoever had been at the wheel had put the pedal to the metal, leaving very deep ruts in the dirt of the track.

When the cops do find the bodies, he didn't want them to know he'd ever been there, and he trotted back to the house. Kevin packed everything he'd brought with him and when he left the house, he made sure he hadn't left anything behind . . . like fingerprints, or hairs, or small personal items. ***Nothing!***

Struggling back through the woods, he reached the vehicle and he pulled off the camouflaging branches. Bungee-cording his suitcase and backpack down, he started the engine and rode away.

The Ultimate Transformation: Escape And Return

Kevin never had a choice. The inevitable fell on his shoulders like a royal mantle. In his eccentric career, he advised people to avoid self-serving motivations, attempting to guide them towards the uplifting. Using tarot cards to bridge the difficult gap, **'FIELDING'S FINDINGS'** grew into a nationwide enterprise and he became rich. And then he got richer.

The prejudice against his gift within the police department and the FBI diminished as he always gave them results. Finally, they would routinely ask him for help, and he was beset with an unending list of unsolved murders. Painfully clinging to the frozen touch of intensely evil people, he was linked to the bottom of the human barrel and beyond. Beyond into an alien fringe, individuals or entities that have no designation and only he can sense their presence behind certain crimes. The whole thing was weakening his stamina.

No children were produced in his short-lived marriage, and he was single again in 2000. The romantic heart break he'd gone through had fortified a new personal resolve to avoid anymore future entanglements with women. At the age of 31, he found himself standing at the crossroads, broken and drained. He limped away from the battle lines to heal in peace.

Kevin Fielding became Keith Fischer. Working alone in a new trade that gave him a lot less mental static, he found tranquility. Garnering a serious reputation, it raced through the grapevine like quicksilver. Extremely adept, the fisherman at the commercial docks called him MacGyver, a character from a TV show from the eighties able to stave off armies of technologically-advanced adversaries with only a Swiss Army Knife, a paperclip, and some duct tape. Concealing his abilities from the world, he certainly couldn't negate them and his speed and ingenuity at his new career was breaking records. The fame he'd left behind followed him in another form, as some of his sudden stop-gap saves from apparent ruin looked miraculous. Keith turned out to be the best marine technician on the east coast; perhaps even leading the pack nationwide. The new guy on the dock could take care of any electrical problem on anything that floats . . . with one hand behind his back.

Living alone in a six-bedroom house on Shannon Road, he was surrounded by 17 acres. His closest neighbor? A graveyard, and that was just fine. His cellphone *and* the landline in the house rang nonstop. Everybody wanted him.

11:35PM Sunday November 27, 2005 Portsmouth, Rhode Island

The Mary-Louise was a commercial dragger and she was docked in Portsmouth. Her radar display no longer displayed, and Keith was there to fix it. Normally he worked at night if he could, because that meant no one was around. He had the radar functioning perfectly in only three hours and he left the wheelhouse with the handle of his oversized metal toolbox in his hand. He crossed the foredeck and hopped onto the dock and from there into his van. It was 4:45 in the morning when he got home. Parking the van in the garage, he stumbled out of the vehicle and straight to bed.

And he slept like the dead. He stayed dead until almost noon. Sitting on the edge of his bed, he didn't care if it was still Monday morning or not. He wanted to go to the local deli. They had fresh ground coffee and the daily paper so he put on his leather pants, a cotton undershirt, and a thick sweatshirt, adding socks and his motorcycle boots as an afterthought. Walking out of his bedroom, he went to the coat closet in the hall. Wearing his motorcycle jacket and a down vest over that, he opened the metal door that led into the garage. This time of year, he'd usually take the work van, but the roads were clear and there was no wind, and he decided to go for it. Putting on his helmet, he got on his Kawasaki 750 and he turned the ignition key. The engine roared into life. He pushed a button on the wall and the garage doors clattered open over his head. Squeezing the clutch, he dropped the transmission into first gear as he rolled out onto his long driveway. He stayed at 20 miles an hour until he turned onto Shannon Road. Gazing out at that long empty stretch of pavement, he opened the throttle and raced into his two-wheeled dash to Exeter.

Right after Thanksgiving, Keith knew something somewhere out there was going to get apocalyptically bad. It was a pretty powerful feeling, and he studiously ignored it. He'd built a nice wide moat around himself. He didn't want to go back. He didn't want to cross that bridge of sighs again. At 37, he was fairly stable, accepting his reclusiveness with calm resignation.

Parking the bike in front of the Owl's Roost, he took off his helmet. He locked it on a hook on the side of the bike, and then he brushed his fingers through his hair, attempting to undo what the helmet had done. Inhaling the crisp air, he stepped briskly towards the entrance of the deli, optimistic that the horrible feeling of *wrongness* was going to fade away. The door closed behind him, and a tiny bell screwed next to corner hinge rang as the smell of freshly baked donuts and coffee brought a smile to his face. The headlines on a newspaper across the room instantly flipped his smile into a scowl.

THANKSGIVING DAY MASSACRE

Nine Bodies Found at Estate on Bass River

His hands were trembling when he picked up the paper. The nastiness at Bass River instantly crushed into his faint hope of escape from the forecast he'd been negating like a sledgehammer on good china. Filling the thermos, he picked two blueberry muffins out of the wicker basket on the counter. He paid for everything at the register and he rode home, crestfallen. Parking the Kawasaki, he closed the garage doors and sluggishly climbed the four steps back into the house.

Imprisoning his old self over the past few years, the combination on the lock of the cell door was clicking into place while the accompanying files, buried deep in his subconscious were rising up and sliding forwards. His heart recoiled from the unwanted transformation and Keith's spirit balked like a wild stallion backing away from its new handlers. He walked through the dining room and into the kitchen, tossing his backpack on the elevated and intensely polished thick slice of mahogany wood he'd made into his kitchen table.

The entire southern wall of the room was glass, and he looked at the blue sky outside and shook his head. A sea change was coming. Clumsily removing the thermos, the muffins, and the newspaper out of the backpack, he sat down at the table very slowly, moving like an old man.

Pouring the coffee from the thermos into a large mug already set out on the table, he read the article about the murders on Cape Cod. The headlines had fudged the real number of victims found dead at the scene, but since Holly Donnelly's medical status had her comatose and probably brain dead, most readers would let that embellishment stand. Her chances of recovery were slim to none, and someone on the medical staff had hinted to the reporter that Ms. Donnelly would be dead in a day or two.

Keith put the newspaper down. Biting into one of the generously buttered blueberry muffins, he swallowed the first installment of his very late breakfast, and then he re-read the article. Something unusual had happened in Massachusetts, and it wasn't over yet. He knew the medical reports about the young heiress were wrong. She wouldn't die; she'd flourish, stronger than she'd ever been before.

Page A32 in the second half of the New Hampshire Globe sat in front of him on the table displaying a lot of photographs of the Donnelly's estate, but he wasn't looking at them anymore. He was staring out into space instead. His layers of camouflage were about to evaporate as mercurially as a beautiful summer day, and Keith Fischer's self-imposed reincarnation as a repairman was almost over. He would have to contend with an adversary with enough power to eclipse his own and he wasn't very happy about it. Like a paper-boat in the outer currents of a massive whirlpool, the suction of his own conscience was dragging him in and he couldn't hide in somebody else's wheelhouse anymore.

Was he hearing only thunder in the distant or were they booming footsteps of titans marching closer? A warrior finally healed, he must still drink deep from a wellspring of faith to thicken his threadbare armor or he could be a lamb to slaughter, lifeblood pulsing into a carved out stone track on a nameless altar in the unknown.

Nine acres comprised the Veterans Memorial Cemetery on South County Road and it bordered his land to the west. On a clear day, he could make out the closest monuments and tombs. Leaning his wooden chair backwards on two legs, he rested his motorcycle boots on the mahogany table and he crossed his long arms behind his head. For the thousandth time, he stared out at the graves in the distance, but the restful scene distorted for a second and he saw aberrant looking things squirm in the shadows behind the headstones. Disappearing with the same abruptness in their materialization, the peaceful tableau returned as if nothing had happened and he had to believe it had been nothing but a trick of the light. But he didn't like it. He didn't like it at all, and a harrowing chill ran down his back.

NOEL is the name of next book in this *Holiday Series,* and you don't need to wait for it long. A maritime adventure, it includes the shattering and deadly relationship between a husband and wife, evolving in the middle of an environmental melt-down. Punctuated with an explosion, Keith will finally meet Holly and their provocative introduction won't be an easy one. Ryan Porretta and Attison Korybante will have their own roles in the upcoming fight against a riddle of an enemy.

The first scene of *NOEL* is attached to pique your curiosity. I pray you have enjoyed the ride thus far.

4:22AM Monday **February 11th 2004**
The Ocean Swan **6 degrees North of Kiritimati**

Walter Pratt had signed on to work in the galley of The Ocean Swan, and for the past six months he'd been a competent ship's cook, however making breakfast for the crew of seven that morning was turning into a difficult prospect. They were on a trek across the Pacific to drop off their cargo at Mutsa Ogasana on the coast of Japan, but the captain had turned south to avoid the bad storms tracking straight into their previous path. The strategy hadn't worked. The angle of the galley floor had just tilted dangerously to the left and Wally was holding onto the top of the anchored work table while the container of salt in his other hand flew towards the ceiling. He wasn't even sure if the meal was going to happen at all.

Over the low and insistent pounding of the huge diesel engines and the howl of the gale screeching passed the porthole, he heard the sound of gunfire. Wally took off his apron and lurched to the other side of the room and he hung it on its metal hook. The pantry, at six by eight, was filled with produce and grain. He opened the door and stepped inside. Covering himself with piles of bags of potatoes and onions, he prayed that everybody would forget all about him.

It had been an upsetting voyage from the beginning, and they were already running a day late from a paperwork snafu in France. That stall slowed down the process of lifting the three nine ton casks off the dock and into the hold of the ship. Eventually, everything was straightened out and diligently held in place and they started the trip. They'd decided to go through the Panama Canal to shave a little bit of time off the voyage and that had been a disaster. Members of an environmental group called Green Peace illegally boarded the Swan during the slow ride through the canal, and it was a mad house on shore. News vans and trucks, and hundreds of protesters, (possibly thousands of them) lined the edge of the road that followed the narrow waterway. In retrospect, they should have gone around the horn instead. Way too much flack using the shortcut.

The Ocean Swan was docked at Puerto de Balboa for two days. They had to refuel and load in more supplies before crossing another ocean. On their second night there, they heard noises around one in the morning, but they never found an explanation for them. While Walter realigned the bags of onions above his head, the answer to that puzzle came to him. *It had been stowaways getting on board . . . dangerous ones.*

Three days ago, at 12:55am, when the freighter was roped to a commercial dock in Balboa, five young 'eco-terrorists' dressed in black with duffle bags strapped to their backs, snuck on board. Invisible on the moonless night, they opened a hatch on the front deck, and like drops of stygian mist, they disappeared into the body of the Swan. They ended up in the chain locker at the bow of the ship, where a hundred feet of anchor chain was stored. Entering the small enclosure, they closed the metal door behind them. With rations, guns and plastic bottles they'd use to pee in, they'd curl up and hide there for at least twenty-four hours while the boat was under power. The freighter would be way out there by then.

The crew wouldn't have anything to rely on but the depth of the Pacific rolling beneath them.

After waiting through the hours, they emerged from their hiding place. Since they were about to take control of the transport ship, the five madmen stood up and stretched to get the kinks out of their muscles. Moving silently down the short gangway into the narrow passages under the foredeck, they stopped near the door of the bunk room; what the crew called a 'fo'c'sle'. Their leader gestured to two of them to take care of the crew asleep in their cots. The others would hunt down the man on watch and they trotted off on the unstable corridors to get to their prize. Harris, the mastermind, had left the final job of subduing the captain in the wheelhouse for himself.

The attack on the dozing crew took place without a hitch. Opening the bunk room door, the heavily armed invaders flicked the ceiling lights on, surprising the crewmen into submission with the frightening sight of two automatic rifles pointed at them. They herded the men up the stairs to the mess hall. One of the masked men ordered them to sit down on the long bench against the wall, and one of his fingers was only a hairbreadth away from the trigger of his gun when he said it. His partner tied them up. Pinioned in the beckoning eye of a muzzle of an AK47, none of the crewman, tough as they may have been, fought back. Having secured them all, they radioed to the others to check of their progress.

Mackie was on watch that morning. He saw two men he'd never seen before run towards him on the transom. They looked like rejects from a bad Zorro flick, but they were heavily armed and therefore dangerous. He tried to get back inside to get to the wheel house and radio the authorities in Panama, and he was almost through the hatch when a bullet burrowed into his left leg. The shot knocked him off his feet. Dealing with unsteady footing on a wet and heaving deck, a strong wind, rain and darkness, one of those attackers must have been a very good shot. One guy pinned Mackie down, and the other one closed the swinging door. Hauling him to the mess hall, they pushed the limping man into the main room. One of his captors staggered off balance by another surge from a bigger wave going under the boat, and his crony grabbed his elbow to support him before he turned back and closed the door against the howling wind. A slick of blood followed Mackie's shuffling progress to the communal bench.

"Mack, are you alright? What did those sons-of-bitches do to you? Hey, let me loose! I have a first aid kit under the counter right over there." The crewman couldn't point as his hands were tied, but at least he could nod in the right direction. "I can help him. Come on, damn it!"

Assuming he was the medic or something, one of the pirates stared down at the good intentioned man with contempt. In his world view, everyone on that freighter was partially responsible for destroying the world by transporting highly radioactive casks in the hold of their ship. Right or wrong, his idea of fix it was so badly warped it may become catastrophic.

"Why don't we let him bandage it, Vic?" the other man said.

"If *you* want him to do that, you better ask Harris first. He's probably done with the captain by now. I'm surprised we haven't heard from him yet."

Captain Zack was brooding over a glowing screen displaying the current radar. Irritated that his jog south hadn't done the trick, the damned squall had followed them towards the equator like a lap dog. He was listening to the radio exchanges going on between the nearest boats out there on a speaker over his head and he certainly hadn't heard any gunfire . . . hadn't heard the wheel house door open either. Harris struck him on the head with the grip of his gun and the captain slid from his cushioned command chair like human pudding. Unconscious on the floor, Harris bound Zack's hands in front of him using the plastic restraints he had in his pocket. The leader of the eco-terrorists had learned enough to navigate the freighter himself without any help from the captain, and he opened the navigational charts on the counter to his left to find his bearings. He had no intention of going to Japan, but they couldn't get anything done until they're out of the storm. Glancing over at the radar, he figured out the fastest track out of this nasty spit. He turned back to the navigational charts again. All he had to do was go straight north, and it shouldn't take them more than 12 hours to escape the worst of it. He deftly nudged the two long levers next to the captain's chair to increase the speed of the ship, while he inserted the new coordinates into the auto-pilot. The Ocean Swan would continue on its new track without anymore attention. Bending down, he checked Zack's pulse. The man's eyelids were fluttering slightly, and Harris saw that he still had good color in his face. The captain would wake up soon. His latest task over with, he answered the buzzing coming out of the radio on his belt.

"I have the wheel house under control. How are you guys doing?"

"Great. That means the boat is ours. The rest of the crew is tied up in the mess hall," Vic said.

"*Hey, what about letting me see to Mackie's leg, you assholes!*" Harris heard the crewman yelling in the background.

"It's only a flesh wound. I had to stop him from getting to you and the captain, and I just nicked him. No worries." Not caring about any of the men in his charge, his leader had a bit more compassion in his heart.

"Victor, I want you to let the medic take care of that man's injury. Think about it for a minute. They'll be more compliant and less aggressive, if you give them some leeway. Start acting like you care, OK."

And Harris cut off the connection. He sat down in the captain's chair to stare out into the turbulent darkness.

The Ocean Swan bucked in the pounding waves on her journey north out of the worst of the storm, and it had taken her almost 24 hours to find calm enough waters to let the mad men go on with their plan. Eating up a day and most of the next night to get there, Harris dropped the freighter's speed to only five knots and he left it there. Three hours away from dawn, he didn't want to use hydraulics in the dark and he also didn't want to use up any more fuel than they have to. He just needed the ship to remain stable and ride straight into the waves as they were still dealing with an eight to ten foot sea. He'd told his men to move the captain to his private quarters while he was still knocked-out. They left him chained to his bunk with just enough play in the chain to allow Zack to reach the metal pot on the floor if he needed it.

The captain woke up five hours later, and it took him a few minutes to orient himself. He was in his own cot, and his wrists were tied with a plastic restraint. The cheesy handcuffs were attached to a chain locked around the leg of the bunk. He couldn't figure out why anybody would want the poisonous garbage he was hauling around, but what's happening is happening and he was going to do something about it. Afraid for his life and those of his crew, he also wanted his boat back and he thought over his options. Staying tied up was not an optimistic one. He mulled over ways to get free from his cut-rate cuffs. They were only plastic after all. The terrorist that had left him bound in his cabin had been too busy or too stupid to realize he had an expensive lighter in the back pocket of his jeans. He got off the cot on his knees. Rubbing his back pocket against the wood under the mattress behind him, the golden lighter squeezed up and out of his pocket. It sat on the edge of the bunk and he turned around and grabbed it. It fired up with a flick of his thumb. Angling it the best he could on one part of the plastic, he understood it would be a painful extrication. Zack couldn't get his wrists far enough away from the heat, but his need for freedom was powerful. He endured second degree burns on his left wrist and the pad of his right thumb. It took him three hellish hours to melt one section of the plastic to stretch it out and loosen it to get free.

On a high shelf in the locker in the corner of the room, packed between different sizes of bandages was the EPIRB. Short for *Emergency Position-indicating Radio Beacon*, it was mandatory for any commercial craft to have one on board. The size of a paper back book, there was nothing on it but a red button and a small light. Zack took it off the shelf. Praying with every ounce of faith he had in his soul, he punched the button. The red light came alive as an emergency signal was transmitted up to an orbiting satellite. From there, it bounced down to all the coast guard stations and military bases around the world. Any hail coming in from an EPIRB bobbing out there in the wild and salty would have the station commanders give those coordinates to every vessel in the area to rescue the ship in distress. There was an official alert in their communiqué, and it was a lot more like an order. Zack hit that button, he knew the cavalry would certainly arrive, but his prayers continued. He didn't know how far away the closest ship could be, and he curled up on his cot to begin a nerve wracking wait. As the hours crawled by, he hoped the rescuers would show up sooner than later, pleading to God it wouldn't be too late.

When Harris saw the fragment of the lip of the sun on the horizon, he radioed the whole crew. It was time. Wilson, one of the men on his team, had experience with on-board hydraulics, and Harris looked through the large window in the wheel house to watch him open the oversized hatch doors in the center of the main deck. From there, he sat down in the working chair right in front of the hydraulic controls and the engine responsible for pushing the hydraulic fluid around started up. The rest of his men were in the hold, quickly setting up a web of steel around the first of the three casks. They'd unload all three of the containers into the Pacific and then they'd escape. They thought this dangerous action was going to shock the world into stopping the practice of shipping radioactive waste across the Atlantic and the Pacific and then back again. In their disjointed reality they weren't going to hurt anything in this enterprise. The lead on the casks was so thick it was impervious to degradation and the containers could sit on the sand forever without any damage. In their surreal, impossible and paranoid vision, '*real*' terrorists would commandeer a freighter just like they had, but they'd open the casks and use the rods to pollute a heavily populated city center with deadly radiation.

After dropping the iron kegs into the water, they'd escape in a dingy to meet up with an escape boat waiting for them a couple of miles away. Harris had called the captain of that boat on the sideband at midnight the night before, and they were following a simple equation to guesstimate the general location of the Ocean Swan when the sun comes up. The getaway boat should be near enough to hear their personal beacon after they all get in the dingy.

Zack looked out of the porthole of his cabin. It was getting light outside, and he could see the main hatch doors were open. He couldn't figure out why on earth those guys wanted the casks. Whatever it was wouldn't be good, but so far he hadn't come up with any ideas to stop them. He had no handgun and he didn't believe that anyone in his crew had one either. The man who'd knocked him had to have some armament and at least four or five men with him. The sun rose higher, and he was horrified to see the hydraulic winch had rotated over the open hold. One of them had to be attaching the metal clamps on one of the casks in the hold and his fists were clenched with frustration. Besides the mortal danger they were all in, he wasn't going to be paid for the transport if those bastards steal it. He really needed the money. Zack hadn't even wanted to move that awful stuff, but he was about to go belly up financially and the power plants were paying him through the nose. The situation was disintegrating by the second, until he saw a bump on the horizon. A tiny spot. It might be exactly what he was waiting for! He stepped over his locker to grab his binoculars. Focusing the glasses, he could make out it was a military frigate . . . couldn't read the name on the bow yet, but he guessed it was probably American or British. Armed rescuers were on their way towards the Swan, and he found the courage he needed to act on his own. The bandits were in the process of unloading the first of the casks. To hold on to his boat, he had to have the money promised to him after the offload in Japan, and he slipped out of his cabin to do what he could to hold on to his radioactive gold.

Harris's attention was on the action going on in the middle of the deck below, and he didn't notice the blip on the radar screen behind him. He also didn't look out towards the horizon. The USS Nicholas, an American frigate, was bearing down on the Ocean Swan at thirty-seven knots. It wasn't the fastest the frigate could have done, but it was adequate. The eco-terrorists only had 45 minutes before their piracy would be addressed by an immutable force; capture or death. Their leader was still in the wheel house talking to Wilson on the radio. The other men were helping to direct them in their efforts. Fifteen minutes passed and the 9 ton cask, wrapped in its steel cradle hung twenty-five feet in the air by the thick cable coming off the winch. Harris was making extra sure the Ocean Swan would stay straight on into the waves, as they were right in the middle of a very precarious part of the transfer. Even though the ship was still running on auto pilot, he kept one hand on the jog lever to make sure he'd have the ability to change course by a few degrees if there's a shift in the wind direction or by the sudden intensity of a rogue wave.

Captain Zack slowly opened the door the wheel house as silently as he could, and Harris didn't hear his approach. The captain would return the favor the man had done to him by knocking the asshole out with a twenty pound book about piloting, but the madman turned around too early and he ducked and punched Zack in the midriff. Harris was twenty years younger than the Captain, and that fact made him faster and stronger, yet the older man was much bigger with a lot more experience, so it worked out as an even match. Wrestling back and forth across the small chamber, their respective punches had little effect. They were too close to each other. Harris pushed Zack up against the closed door and he'd leaned back to raise his right arm for a powerful blow into his opponent's thorax. Giving himself that extra distance he'd used a miniscule splinter of time, but that had created a chink in the armor of his attack and the Captain pushed him backwards like a piston. Harris was already off balance when Zack aimed a punch at the bridge of his nose. The freighter lurched over a ten foot wave, and he missed, hitting Harris hard in the throat and then he was thrown into the jog lever.

The accidentally shove against the lever turned the rudder hard twenty degrees to the left, while Harris's head crashed into one of the shelves behind him with ferocity and he fell to the floor like a bag of bricks. He was out for the count. Harris's idea of making the Swan stable during the relocation of the heavy casks was utterly gone, and the big boat plunged sideways. Another ten footer plunged into her hard, broadside. The deck slanted at a dangerous pitch and the heavy cable holding the cask couldn't withstand the strain of being pulled into a tight angle. The cable snapped, lashing across the deck as if it was alive. The huge container bounced off the starboard rail and into the water. The Ocean Swan was swiftly moving sideways across the surface of the water and in the first instant of the cask's rapid descent, the freighter moved right over it. Unbeknownst to anyone, a razor-sharp blade of the swirling prop sliced into the lead covering the cask. It was a small intrusion, but the cut was deep enough to matter. The blade had even nicked the skin of one of the twenty-eight metal rods inside. The radioactive glass covered rods tightly installed forever in that metal barrel slowly tumbled end over end to its final resting place on the bottom of the Pacific, but after that injurious scratch they might as well have been shaken free like oversized toothpicks.

The Captain used the jog lever to face the Swan back into the waves again. Checking on Harris, he could tell he was going to be out of it for quite a long time. He made sure the autopilot was re-set correctly, and then Zack left the wheel house. He'd certainly screwed things up for the pirates, and he was relieved he'd stayed in one piece. Deciding to hide until the frigate arrived, he squeezed into a crawl space off the short corridor leading out of the wheel house.

Two of the outlaws were left standing on the deck and one was crouched in the hold. All of them were slack jawed with shock as they stared up at the frayed steel threads curling out of the end of the snapped cable as it swept wildly in the wind above their heads. The immediate disorientation passed away, and Victor attempted to reach Harris on the radio, getting no response at all. Wilson had been knocked out of the controlling chair where he'd been directing the winch and he was painfully standing up when he saw it. The USS Nicholas was only five miles away and it was closing in fast. Wilson knew the frigate would to reach them in only ten minutes. He whistled loudly to his cronies, and he pointed to the northeast. When everyone else on the deck saw the military ship barreling towards them like the grim reaper, it was time to pickup their skirts and run . . . and they better run fast. It may already be too late. Looking down into the hold, Vic threw orders at the man positioned down there.

"Billy, get to the chain locker right now and get our wet suits. We'll meet you at the stern. Something went wrong in the wheel house, and I'm going up there to check on Harris."

Wilson and the other man, Dean, in tow, followed Victor up to the wheel house. Bursting into the room, they found Harris on the floor unconscious and Victor kneeled down and checked his pulse. He tried to wake him up with a brisk slap. Nothing. Dead to the world at the moment. Vic looked up at the others and mournfully shook his head. There was no time to revive him and they couldn't bring him along as dead weight. Leaving him behind on the floor of the wheelhouse, they raced off to meet Billy at the stern of the boat. He was supposed to be waiting for them there with wetsuits, the un-inflated dingy and a personal beacon so they could radio the other boat.

"Sir, we haven't gotten a chirp from them on the radio." An officer wearing head-phones had turned to relay the news to his Captain who was standing behind him.

Looking through the observation window in the bridge, another crewman was scanning the length of the Ocean Swan with the help of an extremely precise pair of binoculars.

"I can't see anyone on any of the decks and no one appears to be in the wheel house either. The freighter appears to be running about five knots into the waves. It must be under autopilot. What are your orders, sir?"

"Rustle up one of the copters, and drop six men on the main deck in battle gear. After that we'll know exactly what's going on over there."

The ship had three SH-60 Seahawk helicopters on board. It only took them nine minutes before heavily armed young men were sliding down three ropes hanging from the belly of one the whirly-birds. Remaining in place over a flat surface on the main deck of the transport ship, whatever control the terrorists still had over the boat was gone.

Some of the soldiers untied the crew in the mess hall and others burst into the wheel house to find an unconscious man dressed in black on the floor. Zack quickly reappeared and as soon as the soldier's understood who he was, they let him go. Assuring the soldiers the man on the floor was the leader of the pirates who'd taken over his ship, the captain of the Swan had no idea where the rest of them had gone. The Navy men radioed to their ship to tell their superiors what they'd found. The helicopter pilot was ordered to go aloft and search for the hooligans in the water, while the men on board swept the freighter from top to bottom to flush out anyone who might still be hiding there. The pilot quickly saw the men floating in the water only seven hundred feet away from the Ocean Swan. One of them pulled the cord to inflate their raft, even if they knew it was way too late. They all got into the dingy, and they kept on paddling away. A motorized launch, holding more armed men emerged from the USS Nicholas to collect them. Every single one of the eco-terrorists wanted to live; consequently none of them picked a gun or raised a hand in protest, knowing what the instant reaction would be from the Navy if they did. The entire group, including Harris, was abruptly thrown into the brig.

Having bounced, (or more precisely thudded) off the rail of the Swan and into the ocean, the grievously damaged cask tumbled downwards for three miles, landing on the edge of a volcanic rift. The hole was over twenty-five feet wide and the fissure was two and half miles deep, ultimately ending above a pocket of magma. The iron container sat on the fine sand for about six hours, but the problem was the ground wasn't flat. It sloped. Nine tons of abhorrent poison began to slide into the rift itself.

Captain Peterson of the USS Nicholas quickly learned about the awful fate of one third of the shipment stored in the Ocean Swan. He deployed an unmanned submarine to search for the lost container. A camera on the exploratory sub relayed information to a computer screen on the frigate via a digital signal, and wherever they sent the sub, someone on the bridge was watching the ongoing feed. It was a grainy picture, but they could certainly make out what they were looking for. The whirring motor of the underwater vehicle propelled it above the bottom for hours before it found its injurious quarry. The cask was resting on the damaged side, completely hidden from the camera, and they assumed the rest of it was just as unblemished. Why shouldn't it be? Nevertheless, the man in charge was still not happy. He could see it was sitting on a volcanic rift, and the blurry image didn't express the real gravity of the situation. The lines on their sonar display did. The captain wanted to retrieve it right away. He wanted to put it back into the hold of the Ocean Swan and send the boat back on its merry way to Japan. He considered his options. When the EPIRB had gone off on the Swan, all the ships close enough had turned towards the coordinates. A research ship called Equinox had been on route to the Ocean Swan, yet he'd turned them away. Captain Peterson really thought they could handle the emergency without any help, and ninety-nine times out of a hundred that would be true. As it turned out, this was the long shot. The USS Nicholas didn't have the equipment to raise anything, and the cask was almost three miles down. The Equinox did. Peterson radioed back to her, and asked for their help and it took three more hours for the research ship to get there.

The first thing the science team on the Equinox did was to send one of their more advanced drones down there, and it wasn't long until they called the USS Nicholas with a terrible question. Had they given them right logistics? There was nothing down there but a hollow in the sand. It had fallen into the rift, and everyone on the Equinox and the USS

Nicholas knew there was no way to retrieve the container at that point. It had tumbled completely out of reach.

A high level of radiation was generously leaking out of the damaged cask, as it rebounded from one side of the narrow chasm to the other. Two stony outcroppings were jutting out right before the bottom, and it easily wedged itself tight between them; 8 feet over a hot flume of sea water gushing out of a crack in the floor of the fissure. The spent fuel rods could hang forever in those lightless depths as scalding hot water rushed over the punctured container. It was disbursing radiation throughout the water column above it, including limitless miles of the Pacific. The apparently accidental conditions were so disastrous, it looked a lot more like it was meant to be.

On the surface, Captain Peterson had work to do. He called up an Admiral for guidance and he gave him a quick response. He was ordered to tell the crew of the Ocean Swan that they would be paid for three casks when they arrive at the nuclear plant on the coast of Japan. The American government would support the discrepancy behind the scenes. The Japanese authorities and the owners of the power plant don't care what happened to the missing cask, and they certainly won't mention it's disappearance to anyone. They would remain silent as a tomb, and the crew and the captain of the Ocean Swan would be just as reticent. If people knew about this monster of a screw-up, all ocean shipping of nuclear waste could stop in its tracks. The officials in the highest levels of our military-industrial complex would skew a few particulars in the story and change history. They'd erase the problem, and what had gone badly wrong would suddenly go right. Right as rain, or at least they thought so.

Wally's hiding place had worked well. The terrorists had never asked the crew if they'd gotten everyone on the ship in captivity, and the men tied up in the mess hall weren't talkative at all. Of course, the pirates had checked the food pantry, but the cook's vegetable camouflage had done its job well. Passing the hours peacefully enough, he'd nibble on some of the provisions around him. Once in a great while, he'd slip out of the pantry and into the head on the other side of the galley. When he heard a helicopter engine floating over the main deck, he was almost positive they were going to be saved. When the door of the pantry slammed opened a few minutes later, he peeked out behind a bag of potatoes. The man towering over him was wearing a Navy uniform, and Wally emerged from his hiding place with his hands up and a smile on his face.

After a day and a half of interviews and the ongoing scouring of every inch of the ship to find any last piece of evidence, the USS Nickolas vanished over the horizon. They'd given The Ocean Swan freedom to go on with her trip to the coast of Japan.

On the second morning of their resumed trip, Wally leaned against the door jamb of the mess hall, drying off his hands with a work towel. He had just served a relatively sedate meal, and he was enjoying the warmth of the rays of sunlight beaming down on him. He looked up. Nothing up there but blue sky and a couple of cumulous clouds. The upcoming weather system was supposed to be a calm one, and it would stay with them all the way to the coast. Overhearing the crew talk about it over breakfast, their voices were almost giddy. Wally didn't feel the same way. The events during the entire voyage hadn't seemed to fit together correctly. Worse than that, he had a premonition. Something was coming, and things were about to go badly wrong. A bad moon was rising and good weather had nothing to do with it.

As if the devil had just thrown his last dart to win a global game, The Ocean Swan had been at 145` West longitude and 37` North latitude when the cable supporting the radiated cask had snapped. The container slowly sank through miles of seawater, only to end up clamped between two stony outcroppings right over the current center of the Northern Pacific Gyre during its sedate migration north.